CHRIST

NEW YC
JOSE

REAPER'S GAME

REAPER'S WORLD: BOOK ONE

G ad would have been hard pressed to find an open eatery after ten on a weeknight in any other city, but Vegas needs its pleasure-seekers up all night, ready for the next opportunity to lose cash and all track of time. Pinky's walk-up window stayed open 24/7 and the hot dogs were a foot-long for just a couple bucks and change.

The cheap white tabletops around him were empty save for plastic salt and pepper shakers, crumbs, and sticky condiment droppings. The nearly starless sky stretched out over the desert; dark, still and windless.

Gad chewed silently, gazing at inky shadows through the dark hair that flopped just barely over his eyes. Being away from his ambulance radio made him uneasy.

"Hey. Hey you. Drippin' red off your fingers."

Gad stared hard at the rest of his hot dog, poised with both hands inches from his mouth. He stopped chewing, his jaw tight. He would not look at the guy, would not even flinch.

"Yoo hoo, Mr. Manny Man. You an' I both know I'm here, but you're pretendin' I ain't." A balding man in khaki shorts and a loud Hawaiian shirt snapped his grubby fingers several times a little too close to Gad's nose.

Gad grit his teeth, focusing on the translucent green globs of relish dribbled across chopped onion on his hot dog. This guy was clearly set on interrupting his once-a-week indulgence, one of the few he could afford in both time and cash. He leaned in to take another bite.

"Hey, asshole!"

Gad's dinner flew out of his hands and rolled under the plastic table. He sprang up to his full height, his hand tingling from the slap. His fingers hovered near his thigh over the iron shears protruding from his tactical gear pocket.

The man's eyes widened, apparently surprised to find a stranger react to his rudeness. He thrust his palms out toward Gad in supplication. "Sorry, buddy, sorry, didn't mean to ruin your meal there. My name's Frank. I just wanted you to acknowledge me. I need help, y'know."

"That's for sure," Gad said, bitter. He wiped his fingers clean of ketchup and crumpled the empty hot dog wrapper and napkin into the trash.

"I'm real sorry, it's just I have to...It's my wife, y'see," Frank continued unabated. "I gotta' meet her here and I've been lookin' all around. Can you help me find her?"

And there it was, the inevitable ask. Gad sighed and crossed his arms over his chest. "Okay, Frank, think for a minute. When was the last time you saw your wife? Five minutes ago? Five hours? Five days?"

The man's pale portly face fell. "Oh, that don't exactly mat-"

"How long you been here?"

"In Vegas, y'mean?"

"No, in front of this place. In front of Pinky's."

Frank blinked behind thick glasses that only comically

enlarged his eyes. His mouth opened and closed like a fish out of water.

"Seems like you've been here quite a while," Gad said.

Frank's generic tourist outfit could've been from just about any decade, but the Polaroid camera slung over his shoulder, his bushy ginger mustache, and his giant, square glasses smacked of the early 80s.

Frank's face went red. "Nah, that's crazy talk. That can't be right." He shook his head with confidence, but his voice faltered.

The fine hairs on the back of Gad's neck lifted. Goosebumps prickled along his forearms. He didn't want to say the words he knew he had to. "Frank, I've had this same conversation with people like you about a thousand times."

"Lost people?" Frank's face was the picture of mistrust. He blinked repeatedly.

Gad steeled himself. "Look, I hate to be the one to tell you this, but your wife is long gone. Hell, it's been so long, there's a good chance she's waiting for you on the other side. You need to move on, too."

Frank moved from denial to panic. He took an unsteady step back. "What're you sayin'?"

"It's time for you to find a reaper and move on, Frank. You don't want to spend all of eternity at a hot dog stand, do you?"

Gad strove to push past the sudden sinking feeling in the pit of his stomach. Spirit empathy was one of several effects of communicating with the dead, and he could sense Frank's suspicion that Gad was right about his existential existence. And Gad, having gone through this same conversation about a thousand times with all sorts of spirits, knew what was coming next.

The ghost wavered and contorted, his facial features unnaturally shifting color and shape. Frank's skin darkened to scarlet and sagged, his glasses slipping from his face without support. His blue eyes filled with black.

Frank was beginning to remember he was dead.

"So what...you sayin' you can't help me?" His voice was no longer human, more like a recording being played at half-speed, guttural and slow. "Or won't?" The ghost loomed over Gad, unnaturally contorted with ever-growing anger.

"Hey, back off." Gad snatched up a white plastic salt shaker from the table and held it toward the ghost whose size and shape were steadily increasing. He gave the container a few good shakes, but it was empty. He tossed it aside.

Frank's black eyes bulged, death wounds bloomed all over his rising body. A gash ripped across his forehead and poured blood. His neck bone snapped in half, leaving his head to hang at an impossible angle. His right arm cracked and bent into three distinct breaks. Frank lifted it.

"Don't!" Gad tried to step backward, but Frank's unnaturally long and broken arm swung forward and his hand fell upon Gad's shoulder, solid and warm.

Gad gripped the table, suddenly nauseous. A vision swam before his eyes, overtaking everything.

His wife, an overly tanned woman with bubblegum-pink lipstick, a floppy hat and a sundress, waved him over to the pizza-by-the-slice stand. She grinned at him from across the street and his heart skipped a beat. He held her insulin pen in his grip; silly thing forgot it on the hotel nightstand. Time to eat! He stepped off the curb, seeing only her, and-

Screeching tires. WHAM! He flew through the air and skidded across hot pavement, flesh tearing, unimaginable agony in every...something hot and wet dribbling across his face...coppery smell...A scream. Everything going black...

Struggling through the pain, Gad fought to touch the closest iron object he could reach, his shears. His head exploded with torturous anguish, like a metal rod boring into his temple. His right arm had gone numb.

And finally, there it was, the cool metal at his fingertips. Like lightning on cursed earth, the touch of iron cleansed all spirit influence from Gad. The vision and the pain instantly vanished, his head clear once more.

"Back off, I said!" Gad whipped the iron weapon from his pocket and leveled the shears at the ghost.

"Can't leave. Sandi." The spirit's bloated, bleeding lips didn't move with the words that filled Gad's head. Arms extended, stretched, fingers elongating to grasp Gad.

"She's gone, Frank." Gad said, unmoving. "I'm sorry, but she's not coming back." He always wanted them to listen, to leave their pain behind and move on. They hardly ever did.

Frank's elongated fingers brushed Gad's neck on both sides, his black eyes wide in a face growing ever-closer to Gad's.

Gad thrust the shears through the ghost's torso. They cut a clear path through the spirit's chest. The spirit's blood-curdling screech rent the night, and his body dispersed into the air like dust on the breeze.

The electricity in the air instantly dissipated. The hair on the back of Gad's neck relaxed. He fell to the plastic bench to rest.

Iron didn't destroy or banish ghosts, but it hurt them enough to keep them from reappearing for a few weeks typically. That wasn't the case here in Vegas, though, where ghosts had plenty of neon, lights, and machinery from which to draw energy at all hours, all year. It would probably take Frank a week or so to gather enough energy to manifest again.

The flash of a shutting curtain in a window stories above caught Gad's eye. If that person had been watching Gad out of the hotel window, he probably looked like a crazy man fighting invisible monsters. Not that it would be terribly out of place here to be high out of your gourd and battling unseen forces with scissors at the hot dog joint. Come to think of it, that curtain probably wouldn't get a second swish.

Gad picked up the wasted hot dog from under the table and chucked it in the trash, a pang of guilt pressing another sigh from him. He was so angry, but at what? Ghosts couldn't help their bad behavior. Something about passing over unprepared left souls stuck in their final emotion, which nine times out of ten, was guilt or anger. And because spirits are pure emotion, they get stuck there, like a record skipping for all eternity.

He hadn't always been insensitive to ghosts and their needs. Before becoming an EMT, there had been a year-long phase where he had tried to help every lost spirit he encountered. He had kept a journal with him at all times, collecting names, facts, death dates and asks. But as time wore on, Gad found that, although the dead claimed they wanted help, they rarely really did. They seemed to prefer the comfort of remaining in known despair rather than face the unknown of What Comes Next. That's when Gad concluded that he had a better chance at helping the living just before they die, especially after he found the pocket watch.

A glance at the walk-up window told him the pair working the Pinky's graveyard shift hadn't seen a thing. They were probably smoking in the back or some such. That also meant, he realized ruefully, he couldn't order a replacement wiener before his break was over. He leaned on the wall, willing himself to blend right into it.

G ad leaned on the wall, mulling over his exchange with Frank. Why didn't the ghosts in Vegas just suck up all the energy in the city? They were so troublesome and so many here, feeding off the never-ending power source that is a 24-7 city. Why weren't there any massive marshmallow creatures stomping down the strip to bring about Armageddon? Pulled abruptly from his musings, Gad turned toward the sudden sounds of an angry thug.

"And don't show your face around here no more!" A white-haired older guy, arms pinned high behind his back, came spilling out the door ahead of a massive casino thug's shove. The evicted man's nice suit crumpled, his shiny shoes scuffing as he stumbled to keep up. With another hard shove, the man pitched forward onto the sidewalk.

Gad winced. The guy never had time to get his arms up, landing flat on his chest to skid face first across the cement. Gad stepped further back into the shadows, waiting for the goon to leave so he could check the injured man over.

This scene was not unusual at air-conditioned casino entrances, with only age and gender varying for the unfortunate getting kicked to the curb. What was strange about this scene was the unfortunate himself.

The guy propped himself up against a fake-marble column with a shadowbox advertisement. His tailored suit had to be from The Forum Shops at Caesars, the kind where the shop attendants stood around sneaking bored glances at their phones because hardly anyone could afford to shop there. His shiny shoes alone were worth more than several months of EMT pay. His golden tan implied frequent visits to exotic places Gad could only imagine. The hand he held to his bleeding, puffy nose was perfectly manicured. Altogether, this was not the usual casino deadbeat being tossed out on his ear.

"Aw c'mon Red, this is bullshit. You all know I'm good for it!" The injured man grimaced, crimson smears bright across his perfectly bleached teeth. He pinched the bridge of his nose and tipped his head back, coughing on blood trickling down the back of his throat.

"I know you think you are, Tom. But you've got debt on the ledger."

"We're square on cash and you all know it!" Tom said with emphasis on the word "cash".

Gad studied the thug's reflection in a shadowboxed advertisement of the casino's nightly magic show. A sinister curve of the bully's lips raised gooseflesh on Gad's arms.

"Sure. But we're not square just yet. You gotta' pay to stay. Looks like you don't got enough." The thug, Red, turned to go back in through the gilded gold casino doors.

"I'm never coming back to this shithole, y'hear me?" Tom's voice sounded pinched behind his injured nose.

Gad watched the shadowbox glass above Tom's head. The top half of Red's reflection paused, his hand on a golden door. "So that's it, huh?"

"Yeah, that's it. I'm not doing it. You guys went too far this time. Just too god damned far!" Spittle droplets flew from Tom's mouth and peppered the sidewalk pink.

"And you didn't go far enough. Too bad, huh? See ya some other time, Tom." In the framed glass over Tom, Red pulled something from his jacket. "Here, stop bleedin' on my sidewalk."

A shiny black handkerchief hit Tom in the chest and fell rumpled in his lap. Red's reflection disappeared through the gold doors.

If Gad had been drinking something, he would've done a spit-take when Red said the bit about "You don't got enough to stay". Holy hell, what kind of minimums did they require that this guy couldn't pay? What was this place?

Gad stepped away from the wall to read the elegant white script on the golden door: "Inferno".

"Hey buddy, you been there the whole time?" Tom's muffled voice cut through the silk handkerchief he held to his bleeding nose. He cradled his other arm like a broken wing against his stomach.

"Uh, mostly, yeah. I was just finishing my break and about to head out when you, uh, landed. Can I help you up?"

"Yeah, please." He extended a hand to Gad. "There's no telling what he'll do if I bleed on *his* sidewalk." His tone was rueful as he moved to get his feet under him.

"Absolutely." Gad sprang into action, hooking his hands underneath Tom's arms to lift him gently upward.

Tom's sharp intake of breath clarified that there was more damage than Gad initially thought. "Hey, your arm. Let me look."

"No, I'll be fine." Tom tried to turn, but Gad was already at eye-level with Tom's wrist. It was swelling, hanging limp, and his little finger hung crooked.

"Betting that's a sprain, maybe even a fracture. Can I give you a ride to the ER?"

"The hospital?"

"Yeah. Unless you think you can drive yourself there with your knees?" Gad gestured from Tom's left gimpy wrist to his right hand, holding the bloody handkerchief to his nose.

"Oh. Yeah." Tom pulled the wet cloth away from his face to assess his wrist. "I guess the arm wouldn't hurt so much with drugs, right?"

"Yeah, that and immobilizing it with a brace or a cast. Wait here, I'll get my bus."

Tom's gaze flicked briefly to the immense golden casino doors. "If it's all the same to you, I'll just wait across the street over there."

Now that he stood directly in front of the gold doors instead of their partially blocked reflection, Gad realized this casino entrance was unusual. Most casinos had transparent glass doors or no doors at all, tantalizing guests with the visual possibilities of all that could be experienced inside. Inferno's doors were solid and obscured whatever was on the other side, as though going through them meant never coming back out. Maybe that was part of his nagging need to get away from the place.

Gad pulled his white ambulance up to the curb, where Tom waited across the street at a safe distance from the lavish casino. With two years of self-taught experience, he threw open the back doors and unlocked his portable gurney.

Tom scanned Gad's ambulance. "Mercy, huh? That the name of the hospital you're bringing me to?"

"Nope, it's the name of my business. Mercy Emergency Transport Services." Gad nodded to the green stripe across the white ambulance proclaiming "MERCY" in bold blue lettering.

"Ah, got it. Mercy Emergency Transport Services. I wasn't a fan of the Mets before, but I am now." Tom finally pulled the handkerchief from his face and smiled for the first time.

"Always been an Angels fan, myself," Gad said as he dropped the ambulance ramp to the street with a clank.

"No accounting for taste then. Say, how does a beanpole like you manage to get tubbos like me up into that thing all by yourself?"

"First, you're not a tubbo." Gad guided the gurney in its wheelchair configuration down the ramp. "Second, I'm five foot eleven, thank you very much."

"Like I said, beanpole. How'd you end up in the ambulance business?"

"I inherited the business from someone who retired a few years ago. Bought the bus, poured over the procedure manual, got the recommendation from the medical director at Saint Lucy's, and...here we are." Gad held the gurney-wheelchair in place for Tom.

"Hey, my legs aren't broken. It's my arm and my face. What's with the wheels?"

"C'mon, sit down, it's the rules. Besides, after what you just went through, just get on and relax."

"Fine." Tom eased onto the seat and let Gad buckle him in and wheel him up the ramp to lock it in place. "So did you have to get a nursing degree, too?"

"I'm not a nurse. I'm an ACLS EMT." Gad pulled the ramp up and set it with a slam.

"I don't speak acronyms, kid."

Gad laughed. "Advanced Cardiovascular Life Support Emergency Medical Technician."

"Huh. On second thought, stick with the acronyms. That's a mouthful."

Gad got into the driver's seat and started Mercy. As always, the engine turned over with precision and was loud enough to drown out conversation with anyone inside its walls. Gad checked his mirrors and pulled out onto the road.

Mercy sped down the road, lights flashing and sirens blaring. Gad's mind whirled, searching for the best way to ask Tom about the earlier events.

"So, uh, you want to tell me what happened back there?" Gad fished, his voice cracking with the effort of volume. Having spent his formative years cooped up in a mountainside cabin with only his dad, social etiquette was not his strong suit.

After a moment, Tom responded. "Nope."

Gad frowned, twisting the wheel to turn Mercy down a different street. Time to play the bureaucracy card.

"Gotta give me something. I have to file a report with the ER staff and we're almost there." Gad held his breath. Aggressive was not his cup of tea.

"Ok, sure. Tell them 'The goons at Inferno suggested I vacate their premises and I tripped on the way out.'"

Gad took a deep breath and pushed onward. "Sorry, Tom. I was there long enough to see that you didn't trip. What really happened with that guy Red?"

"Nothing." Tom's tone was getting testy.

"But Tom-"

"Listen, E-M-T, A-L-F-whatever kid. You've been great. Really. I appreciate you getting me to the hospital and all, but I can take care of myself. Capiche?"

Gad had seen enough mafia movies to know that 'capiche' was a conversation ender. Anything after that usually ended with somebody cut down in a hail of bullets and blood dripping down the walls.

Gad shut off the lights, parked at the red curb, and transported the now stoic man to the admittance nurse. Tom sat thin-lipped in the gurney-wheelchair, his arm held tightly against his stomach and blood dried in crimson streaks on his chin.

"Well, well, well, if it isn't the Great Gadsby?" A young woman with tawny skin smiled, dimples accentuating her full, pink lips.

"Hi Lorraine." Gad felt his face warm as though suddenly lit by a hot spotlight. He leaned on the glass separating her from the patient. "Got a broken nose and possible ulna fracture for you."

"Does ulna fracture have a name?"

"Yeah. Thomas 'Ulna Fracture' Johnson. My parents were funny like that."

"Nothin' but the best from you, Gideon." She winked. "You new here, Tom?"

"First time," Tom nodded. "And hopefully the last."

"Okay. I'll just need your driver's license and then you'll sign a few forms."

With great effort, Tom used his good hand to pull his card from his wallet and slide it through the open tray to Lorraine.

"Thanks. Let me get this scanned and print the forms. Be right back."

"You're in good hands, Tom. I'll finish up the report with her in a few." With the satisfaction of a mission accomplished and mild regret that he hadn't sprung for a soda at Pinky's, Gad turned toward the soda machine.

"Wait, kid. What's your name?"

"It's Gideon. Gideon Goodwin."

The corner of Tom's lip curled upward. "Surely Goodwin and Mercy shall follow me all the days of my life."

"Oh." Gideon winced, and then grinned at the pun's mixture of corniness and brilliance.

"Had to be said, buddy. Hey, listen." Tom's jovial expression melted away. He leaned over, his voice low so Gad had to bend down to hear him. "You're a good guy, Gideon. I didn't mean to be a jerk or anything. I just can't, well...I'm not allowed to, talk about-" He leaned back and shook his head. "That place. It's not like the other places with, just gambling, y'know? I've been in and out of casinos like that for years, gets boring doing the same old, same old. So, the place you found me at. They're into more, shall I say, real stakes. Not just money. Life changing risks. Red threw me out because I finally told them no."

"Told them no? No to what?"

"Just listen. Stay away from..." He glanced over his shoulder and scanned the room before continuing. "From Inferno."

"Why? What happened? What did they do?" Gad asked, lowering his voice.

The white-haired man gazed at the floor, seeing something unpleasant replay in his mind's eye.

"Tom?"

The ER glass doors slid open and two EMTs from a competitor company, Trauma Response 1, pushed a gurney with a yellow body bag belted to it. "Hey G, what up?" The larger of the two, Carlos, jerked his chin up to Gad in greeting as they rolled the gurney in. The other EMT saw Gad and let his head drop. His blond, lanky hair fell over his eyes.

Las Vegas proper had about twenty-eight ambulance businesses in service, and any of those services could have from one to ten ambulances on call at a time. Some supported patients with basic Emergency Medical Transport, while others used intermediate ACLS EMT's like Gad. TR1 used all employed levels, including fully educated Paramedics like Carlos. With two years of schooling and a bunch of required testing, a Paramedic was the next best thing to a nurse or doctor if you had to get to the hospital in one piece.

"Hey Carlos," Gad called out. Carlos's teammate, Jesse, never acknowledged Gad's existence, so Gad reciprocated by ignoring him.

Trauma Response 1 was Gad's stiffest competition for work with over a dozen busses ready to respond on life-threatening calls. Therefore, Gad ran into Carlos, Jesse, and the TR1 guys more often than others. Carlos was a good guy in Gad's book as one of the few people that would deign to talk to Gad. He supposed this was because the other bus techs couldn't explain why Gad was typically first to arrive at the direst scenes. And lesser EMTs like Jesse spread rumors about Gad, questioning how Gad could get to a call where someone is at death's door before the call even went out on the radio. They all talked behind his back, calling him the Angel of Death. Gad had attained the level of Feared Spook in his own line of work thanks to assholes like Jesse.

"Whatcha' got there?" Gad said with a nod to the body bag on their gurney.

"Overdosed Jane Doe, D.O.A, no identification. Someone found the body and called it in. Is Jody back there?"

"It's Lorraine tonight, she'll be right back."

"Okay. We got a few minutes to wait, I guess." Carlos ran his hand through his tall dark hair, lifting his near-pompadour even higher. "Someone found Jane here in the bushes behind Bellagio. Tracks up both arms. Transient, by the looks of her."

"Bellagio? That's not a typical hangout for the homeless." Gad crossed to the gurney. "You sure?"

"Yeah bro, check it." Carlos unzipped the bag. It was a woman in her fifties, her auburn-dyed hair stringy and matted with dead leaves. Carlos was right. Her clothes were layers of mismatched shirts, a torn sweater, and jeans. Her front teeth were missing, likely casualties of heroin addiction. Her lips and skin had gone grayish blue. She looked like she'd died within the last few hours, but that was for the coroner to determine.

"Hey, you mind watching the stiff while we grab a coffee from the machine?" Carlos asked, under his breath.

"Sure. I'll let Lorraine know you have a report and then you can get Jane downstairs."

"You're the best, G," Carlos slapped Gad unceremoniously on the back. Jesse was already ambling through the doors toward the vending machines.

Gad leaned against the wall next to Tom. "Sorry, we're not alone anymore, I guess."

Tom studied the dead woman, her cold eyes open and staring at the ceiling.

"It's not like she'll interrupt, though," Gad added.

Gad's joke went by unacknowledged. Tom had locked a horrified gaze on the corpse's face, his jaw slack.

"Tom? Do you know her or something?" Gad wasn't sure if there was more to his reaction outside of the shock of seeing a dead body.

His lips shut with a twist and he shook his head, wide-eyed. The hand not pinned to his chest began to tremble. He suddenly turned to Gad, snapping out of his stupor as though remembering something important. "I don't think Red saw you, Gideon. So, just stay away from there. Don't go near that place. It's bad news."

So, what were you doing there tonight? Gad wanted to ask, but bit his lip knowing what Tom's reaction would likely be.

"It's all fun and games, at first. They have perks for joining the club, like anywhere else. But it's not just points or discounts at the spa. The more time you spend there, the more you're willing to do...And then things happen."

Gad searched his face carefully for signs that Tom had hit his head too hard on the sidewalk. "What do you mean?"

"I mean, things happen. Life-changing." He gingerly lifted his gimp arm to show Gad his wrist with a gold Rolex watch. On his pinky finger was a white gold ring encrusted with sparkling diamond chips. "This ring alone could buy my first house in North Vegas. My wife and I scrimped and saved for years for that down payment."

Gad blinked. "What, the casino gave you that ring?"

"No, no, no. I sell insurance, kid. And I was horrible at it for years. My wife left me, she took the kids." Tom's slightly puffy eyes turned a deeper shade of red. "I literally took my last hundred bucks to Inferno meaning to drink and gamble it away. Red was there, he opened the door for me. It was like he knew I was coming or something. Ushered me right over to the roulette table. They brought me my favorite whiskey like they'd known me for years. And wouldn't you know, I was hot! Couldn't lose. I walked out of there several grand up plus a free surf 'n turf dinner with champagne. I bought a new suit. They asked if I would join the club. I said 'yeah, sure, whatever' and thought they wanted my e-mail. But then, and here's the really weird part, they said their membership is more exclusive than that. They had me sign this fancy stack of paper. I still don't know what it said because, I mean, who wants to read pages of legal terms? I was high on bubbly and didn't give a crap. But once I signed that paper, things changed."

"You're just lucky, Tom. You were due for an uptick. Things

started falling into place." Gad shrugged, baffled that anyone would put credence to a casino having anything to do with life taking a good turn.

"No, I swear to you, it wasn't just luck." Tom's brows furrowed, forming a crease in his well-tanned forehead. "The more weeknights I spent there, the more calls and business came on weekdays. They'd offer perks for me and my clients, so I'd bring them there for drinks. The more clients I brought, the better things we got. Those clients became members, too. Then you get higher in their circle. I got to Level Four. You see?"

"What, do you have to pay fees at different levels, like a pyramid scheme?" Gad didn't see at all. By Vegas standards, it sounded above the board.

"No. It's not about money. It's about people. And...they ask you to...do things." Tom suddenly went silent. His eyes strayed back to the body. "I'm not supposed to talk about Inferno. To any-"

Tom recoiled, his face etched with fear. He pointed with a trembling finger to the body. "What the fuck?!"

Gad spun about. The woman's head had turned toward Tom, her gray lifeless eyes staring at him. She brought her arm, covered in black and purple track marks, out of the bag and put a bloated purple finger to her dead, smiling lips.

Gad's heart pumped and he shot to his feet as the body collapsed back into immobility. Could Tom see ghosts, too? he wondered. He stepped closer to the gurney with one hand on his iron shears, ready to act in case the ghost wasn't done messing with them yet. Thankfully, the body didn't move as he drew closer, and Gad hurriedly used his other hand to stuff the woman's arm back into the bag and zip it shut.

"Sorry, Tom, that was so bad of me. Shouldn't have left that thing open," Gad began, turning to Tom with apologies on his lips but stopped when he saw the other man's face etched with terror.

His eyes were round, the whites so exposed his irises looked like pinpoints. He trembled uncontrollably, his gaze locked on the window. Gad shot around to see what Tom saw.

Something watched from the shadows outside the window. It stood in the dark, unmoving, a silhouette facing Tom. Gad couldn't tell if it was a man or a woman or a ghost. It was as if it were made of shadow, and it was unlike anything Gad had ever seen before.

At that moment Lorraine reappeared with a thick clipboard in hand. She plunked down into her chair, eyes on her paperwork, oblivious to what was going on. "All right, Mr. Ulna Fracture, I will ask you a few questions. Then I just need a few things from Mr. Goodwin so we can get you into a room. Sound good?" She finally looked up.

Tom cried out, clutching his good hand to his chest. His eyes squeezed shut.

"Tom? What's going on?" Gad spun around to put his hands on Tom's shoulders and gasped. Touching Tom sent hot searing pain shooting through his fingers and up his arms.

"Chest...can't...breathe..." Tom forced the words out between gritted teeth, his face turning red. He gulped for air, his eyes bulging within a face rapidly turning from pink to blue.

Lightning bolts of agony fired through Gad's arms and shoulders, and into to his own chest, squeezing his lungs and heart in an ever-tightening vice. He fought to force his fingers open, releasing contact from Tom.

Tom collapsed in the gurney-wheelchair, clutching his chest.

Having felt what Tom felt, Gad knew the other man was in full cardiac arrest. "Code Blue, code blue! We need a defib and a doc!" Gad called out weakly, his heart fighting to pump blood again. His panic overwhelmed him. Some external force was causing this. He did not understand how to stop it or how to help Tom without the ability to touch him.

Lorraine leapt out of her seat as two ER doctors threw open the door, the smaller doctor rushing to the other side of the gurney to assist. "Lay him back, help me triage," she instructed.

Jumping into action with something he could do, Gad released the wheelchair back and carefully lowered the gurney until it was flat. Within seconds, they wheeled Tom through the swinging doors into triage.

"Was he in for chest pain, Gideon?"

The smaller female doctor on call, Dr. Wilson, grabbed the defibrillator while Lorraine flattened the gurney and ripped Tom's shirt open.

"No, he had a bad fall," Gad said, pushing through his own alarm.

"No pulse," Dr. Wilson confirmed, with her fingers over Tom's carotid artery. Dr. Pullman, the taller male ER doctor, stood behind Lorraine and prepped his stethoscope to listen to Tom's heartbeat.

"He got into a fight earlier. I brought him in with abrasions and a fracture. But at the front desk, well, he just grabbed his chest," Gad fumbled to form the words as quickly as possible, his own chest tight.

Something buzzed and tingled in Gad's shirt pocket. His stomach dropped.

Dr. Wilson tipped Tom's head back and began CPR. Gelled pads were applied to Tom's chest and side. Someone pulled Gad out of the way. Everything was happening in slow motion.

Without looking, Gad knew the thing that was buzzing was his pocket watch.

Tom was about to die.

4

"Stand clear!" Dr. Wilson announced with a sweeping motion of her arm.

Tom's ripped silk shirt hung open, exposing tanned skin. Silver hairs curled around the yellow AED pad over his heart. The red pad on his side measured his heart rate. 300 joules of electrical energy shot through Tom; his chest jumped. Dr. Wilson began the next round of CPR while the defibrillator analyzed whether to prep another big shock or several rhythmic minor shocks to establish cadence.

Next to Gad, the gurney's shadow moved and shifted. The air took on a distinct chill.

The frantically buzzing pocket watch was growing uncomfortably hot in his shirt pocket. He retrieved it and popped open the silver cover.

The shadows merged and rolled. Like oil, they ran together and snaked across the floor to the area behind Gad.

He wouldn't look.

He couldn't.

The watch read 10:23 pm. The intricate silver big hands on the obsidian watch face ticked toward this inevitable time past crimson roman numerals, the tick mark that glowed bright on the bezel just seconds ahead now. To Gad's growing despair, the only hand on the watch face's smallest silver dial pointed straight down. The doctors needed to save Tom, and they needed to do it now. The chill of the room seemed to seep through Gad's skin and into his blood, turning liquid to ice in his veins. Even the pocket watch's heat could not help quell the panic Gad fought to hide.

"We need to ready a drip and epinephrine," Dr. Pullman said.

"No pulse." Dr. Wilson continued rhythmic pressing on Tom's chest.

Gad fixated on Tom, willing the doctors to make his heart beat before the shadows, black as pitch, could draw together completely. He wouldn't turn to look at what he knew was forming behind him. It was worse than any ghost he had ever seen. And it was coming for Tom.

The long hand ticked over to 10:23 p.m. The watch vibrated impossibly in his hand, almost too hot to hold. His heart banged against his chest as he slid the watch back into the silicone pouch in his pocket. He couldn't draw breath; his chest was too tight. He willed the defibrillator to work with every ounce of his being.

C'mon, c'mon Tom!

Dr. Wilson stepped back with a wave of her hand again, and the defibrillator's robotic voice advised all. "Stand clear."

The long beep sounded, and Tom's chest bounced slightly with the shock.

Behind Gad, the shape of a looming presence obscured light. Gad did not want to turn and acknowledge it.

A reaper was here for Tom.

The smell of it permeated Gad's sinuses, an indescribable funk of sickness, sickly sweet and nauseating. Death.

Gad's hands trembled. His knees locked, rooting his feet to the floor.

The shadow of a massive scythe stretched grotesquely across the floor, raising higher until the shadow hovered on the wall above Tom's prone body.

The air around Gad's ankles was frigid, swirling gusts visible only to Gad. The cold crawled up his legs with a sensation of pulling, sucking him through the floor. He needed to run, to flee, but terror rooted him to the spot.

SWISH.

Gad squeezed his eyes shut, his hair ruffling in the icy breeze that passed just before him and through the body.

He couldn't watch. Tom had been such a nice man. What had he done? The sounds of concrete cracking and crumbling came from beneath Tom's gurney.

The maw to the void opened in the floor. Gad forced himself to open his eyes but kept his head turned away. Around his feet, a black smoky vapor circled toward the void beneath the gurney like water around a drain. And the proverbial drain, it hissed. It giggled. Unintelligible voices wailed, chattered and moaned.

"Patient is non-responsive. I think we need to call it."

Gad looked to Dr. Wilson, who visibly sagged with defeat. She drew her white sleeve across her sweat-shined forehead, oblivious to the sounds of a soul being devoured by hell. Concrete crumbled again, the sound of stones grinding back together. The voices of purgatory softened. It would close now, if Gad dared to look. He couldn't.

Dr. Pullman exhaled, his shoulders hunched. He glanced to the clock high on the wall. "Time of death is 10:23 p.m."

"Time of death, 10:23 p.m.," Dr. Wilson echoed.

Gad looked to his feet where a wisp of black swept past and disappeared. It seemed like it was over, but he pulled his pocket watch back out to be sure. It had fallen quiet again and showed the next death at the same time it had always had: 11:59 p.m., October 31. Gad brought his fingers together across his eyelids, pinching out the pooling moisture.

"I'm sorry, Gad. That was unexpected." Lorraine touched his shoulder lightly, her face the picture of empathy.

"You win some, you lose some." Gad faltered, not sure how one should respond to losing a patient. In his case, most of the time, he won. Yet this time, inexplicably, something had interfered. Something he'd never encountered before. Something bad.

"My shift is over in an hour. Did you want to grab a drink?"

"With you?" Gad shifted his gaze from the lifeless body on the gurney to Lorraine's hopeful amber eyes.

"Yeah," she chuckled. "With me."

Gad felt his cheeks warm with embarrassment. What slipped out as genuine astonishment had come across badly. Gad had a sinking feeling that whatever had just happened with Tom was only the beginning of a much bigger trouble brewing.

"Thanks, Lorraine. But I don't know if you saw, but Carlos brought in a Jane Doe that needs to be booked."

"Ah, okay," Lorraine replied, with a sigh of resignation.

"I should head home, anyway. I'm worn out tonight, I think." "Worn out" couldn't even begin to describe the level of awful he was feeling, with a queasy stomach and legs of rubber.

She patted his arm. "Maybe some other time then. I'll finish up in here and tackle the morgue report. You write your report for this man and head home, okay?"

Gad tried to smile through the feeling that he had taken the one thing that could've made the night a little better and crushed it like a cockroach. Yet he hadn't lied. As the adrenaline faded from his system, the sheer exhaustion of the evening hit him with all the subtlety of a semi-truck.

To his great relief, Lorraine left him to his form-filling as he tried to quash the feeling of failure weighing him down. Thankfully, Carlos had retrieved Jane Doe's gurney and wheeled it away to the morgue. With the way the night had gone, he was certain that body stood a good chance of unzipping its bag and beginning some unholy act by grinning at him, too. He pushed through the forms, filling out all the pertinent details for Tom's pick-up and delivery.

He dotted the last "i" and crossed the last "t". It was long past the time to head home.

GAD WAS grateful that his drive remained uneventful. In Vegas, it was not unusual for his self-imposed ten-hour shift to end and, on the slog home, feel his pocket watch go nuts with another nearby emergency.

Drake, his roommate and fellow night-shifter, would likely be in their kitchen by now reheating whatever leftovers were available at\ the end of the night. He parked Mercy on the street adjacent to their apartment, a humble two-bedroom on Queen Victoria Street. Just about twenty minutes from the strip, it was far enough away that he could get to it quickly without being trapped in the insanity itself.

"Hey, I traded Matt at Shake Shack for a gallon of cheese fries. Want some?" Drake's baritone voice came from the kitchen.

The scent of twice fried spuds swimming in cheddar and American cheese made Gad's stomach growl fiercely. "Hell yes." He threw his keys down and nearly vaulted into the kitchen. "What'd you trade with?"

Tall and brawny, Drake reclined against the counter, one dress shoe crossed over the other. He still wore a white dress shirt and black slacks, the mandatory dress code at the five-star

1920s-themed club he worked for. He smoothed down his spiky auburn hair and crossed his arms across his broad chest. "We had some leftover poached sea bass and a little caviar about to go belly up. Says his girlfriend will do anything for caviar."

"Since when are cheese fries the trading equivalent of sea bass with caviar?"

"You know, that is a valid point." Drake stabbed the air with a drippy fry.

"Yeah, he gets laid and we get...reheated fries." Gad shrugged at the microwave.

"And chocolate concretes." Drake slid a solid paper cup across the counter to Gad with the dexterity of a frosted beer mug on a polished oak bar.

Gad scooped up the cup, its white-frosted surface sparkling with tiny ice crystals under the fluorescent kitchen light. After a moment of digging to loosen the solid chocolate ice cream with a plastic spoon, he dropped a piece onto his tongue. "This makes it a little better."

Drake scanned him with a smile, his green eyes narrowing. "Rough night?"

Gad nodded. "Found a guy near Pinky's getting worked over by casino security. He seemed okay at first, but then he went into cardiac arrest."

"Did he make it?"

"Nope. Not even the ER doc could help."

"Oh man, that sucks." Drake scowled. "OD or alcohol poisoning?"

"Neither that I know of. I mean, I suppose there could have been something in his system before I picked him up, but he was lucid on the bus."

Drake shrugged. "Sorry to hear it. But hey, you of all people know this, Gad. Sometimes, no matter what you do, it's just someone's time, you know?" The microwave beeped. Drake used an oven mitt to pull out the grease-stained cardboard carton. It overflowed with gooey cheese fries, steam shooting from the bubbles that rose and burst rapidly across its surface.

"Yeah, I know." Gad stabbed at the chocolate concrete's center rapidly with his plastic spoon, only to have it snap in half as it hit the unyielding surface.

"Dude. Here," Drake handed him a metal spoon from a kitchen drawer.

"Thanks." Gad's voice had the lack of enthusiasm normally attributed to a dentist visit. He slammed the tip of the metal spoon deep into the center of the frozen milkshake, this time prying a significant chunk up and out. "Sounds like you had a good night, though?"

"Cheesy fries was my only win. Rest of the day, total crap. Had to pull a double when Justin called in sick, and since Wednesdays are slow anyway, it was twice the hours at a third of the tips. Plus, the new manager is a royal douche." He swept a soggy fry up into his mouth and, after a moment, frantically fanned his open mouth, eyes bugging. "Shit, shit, shit, shit!"

"So, what'd he do?" Gad heaped a stringy pile of fries onto a saucer with his spoon.

"Ass-hat measured my socks." Drake took a tentative bite out of the end of a fry.

Gad blinked. "Sorry, don't think I heard you right. He 'measured your socks'? I hope that's a euphemism."

"No, it's not. And anyway, he's not my type. It's straight up what I just said. He. Measured. My. Socks. So that happened."

"How does one measure socks?" Gad laughed.

"With a ruler, dude. And while he held that ruler to my shoe, he told me that, by health code requirements, the height of my sock needed to be at least one point five inches above my ankles."

"So, do tell. Were your socks health code compliant?"

Gad shoved a small stack of fries in his mouth.

"Yes, apparently. But bubble dancer got sent home to upgrade his."

"Bubble dancer? He a stripper?"

"Food service lingo, bubble dancer's the dishwasher. Anyway, here's the best part. I tried to find the sock rule online and guess what? There's not one word in the Nevada Food Safety and Sanitation Code Standards about socks."

"Serious?"

"Deadly. I found rules about fingernails, hair, hand and arms, even runny noses and all of that. But not a word about stuff below the belt. I'm pretty sure Ass-hat's just a straight-up psycho."

"What're you going to do, Drake?"

"Not work for psycho, that's for sure." He shoved a pile of fries into his mouth and chewed slowly.

"I can ask around, see which places have full-time bartender slots open."

"Sure, yeah. But it sucks to leave, you know? That place pays better than most. Bartenders get around fifteen an hour plus tips, and that chain of hotels pay more. Plus, the tips at a five-star restaurant are over the top on good nights. One bachelorette party on a Friday night and I'm set."

"I know. It's why you have the master bedroom and I'm in the kiddie quarters." Gad snorted.

"No Gad, its cause you've got a good heart and you have a job with morals and shit. You gotta be like me and take the jobs where cash and respect flow."

Gad nodded. "Where socks must be taller than ankles."

"At the bare minimum," Drake agreed with a smirk. "Hey, did you do like we planned yet?"

Gad looked at Drake, lost. "Win the lotto, you mean?"

"Your girl, Lorraine. Did you ask her out yet?"

Gad shoved another pile of fries in his mouth and shook his head, letting his gaze drift away to avoid encouraging the impending tirade.

"Serious? Gad, you are killing me, man! We just talked about this. You would be all confident and be like, 'Hey girl, let's grab a coffee.' What happened?"

"I know. I just wasn't feeling it tonight. Lost that patient and all."

The frustration disappeared from Drake's face. "Okay, I get it. But don't keep putting it off. She's hot, you two have a lot in common and-"

"She asked me out for drinks," Gad said, shrugging sheepishly.

"Wait, *she* asked *you* out? Dude!"

"Yeah, but like I said, it wasn't a good time to do it. I would've been a downer."

"But she's into you. That's great! There's hope for you yet, Goodwin." Drake slapped his shoulder.

"So you'd like to think. But this is the part where I thank you for saving the day with grub. I'm so wiped, I was just going to go to bed hungry. Think I need to pass out now."

"Cool. I'm gonna' make a drink and kick back. Catch ya' on the flip side."

Gad moved to the stairs, his feet somehow carrying the rest of him to his smaller room on the second floor. He didn't even bother switching the light on, letting a patch of moonlight through the curtains guide him to bed. He unbuttoned his uniform, letting everything fall to the floor with a clank, pockets full and then collapsed onto the bed. The cool sheets and the soft pillow never felt so good.

5

The Wednesday night shift began right around five p.m., per routine. Gad climbed into the driver's seat and wondered again if he should switch to a day shift for a little while. After all, he'd get more sleep and, on a schedule with the rest of humanity, he'd have a better shot at an actual love life. But each time he thought it through, he came to the same conclusion he did now; there's more work at night. The need for on-call paramedics in Vegas rose drastically after sunset. Gad's thoughts drifted to the empty seat to his right. Drake had asked him on more than one occasion why he didn't hire a ride-along EMT. Don't you guys always work in pairs? That was before Drake really got to know him and how he felt about playing well with others. It's not that he couldn't work with a partner, he just didn't need one. On his own, he set his preferred hours. He was his own boss, and he never had to worry about being disappointed by anyone. Between his paramedic work and help from the billing service that handles the insurance paperwork, he was quite satisfied to work alone. Autonomy was the only way he could freely use his pocket watch and truly help those in need.

Gad pulled Mercy out of his complex and out onto the street's cracked cement where rays of light stretched bright from one sidewalk to the other. He flicked the scanner on to familiar sounds. "37417, have a good evening," a male voice said, followed by static.

"61347, I have a 10-6 when you're ready." Static.

"Still waiting for police 434325, we're close to the silver Mazda." Static.

"Copy."

"10-24 Mary Adam. Switching to Channel 2." Static.

"...with a white box trailer. Northbound on the offramp. Going all over the place, left and right. Driver is screaming out the window."

Gad snorted and turned down a residential street.

"10-6 when you're ready." Static.

The cool heavy hunk of metal in Gad's shirt pocket suddenly vibrated. Gad instinctively cupped his hand over it and pulled over, putting the bus in park but leaving the engine still running.

The silver watch buzzed frantically, making Gad pull it from his pocket and grasp it tight. He popped the lid open. The glowing point of light on the bezel edge pointed northeast, straight toward the ramshackle house with blistering paint he had just parked in front of. The time of death showed he was about eight minutes away. The little hand of the small watch face pointed down.

"Ruh-roh, Shaggy," he muttered and jumped out of Mercy. He strode across the lawn, adjusting course as the dot of glowing light on the bezel adjusted to point the way to the body about to give up their ghost. He leapt up three cement steps to a small covered porch and tried the door by jiggling the door handle. It was locked.

"Get away!" a woman cried from within.

Gad hustled off the porch and jumped the short chain link

gate into the side yard. He ran along the side of the house, which was covered with dying ivy. Pulling back brittle vines, he uncovered a basement window and kicked it in, shattering it. Gad reached carefully through, twisted the lock, and flipped the window open to reveal a washer and dryer sitting in a musty cement basement with wooden steps leading up to the level above. Without hesitation, he slid down in through the window, feet first.

The setting sun sent rays of light shining across the basement. Gad followed them to the floor where a small puddle of blood pooled next to a bloody hacksaw. From the puddle, a stream of red lined the staircase wall in even arcs all the way to the open door at the top. The sound of drawers opening and slamming closed drowned out the creaks of steps. Someone in the room above was pacing rapidly back and forth.

"God damn it, where is it?" The same woman's voice broke with pure anguish.

SLAM.

Gad crept up the staircase, placing one foot gingerly over the other. He pulled a small taser from his pants pocket and pushed the readying pin in, holding it out with his right hand as he slowly pushed the door open with his left.

The owner of the voice was a woman in a sheer ivory nightdress. She looked to be in her late sixties. Occasional blue-green spider veins marked her spotted, wrinkled skin. Her pale frizzy hair stood on end as, barefoot, she rushed from drawer to drawer in her kitchen, frantically rummaging through each one. Big red droplets gathered at her right elbow to drip, drip, drip from a ragged, gaping cut on her inner wrist. Crimson spattered and smeared the yellow vinyl floor's cheerful daisy pattern.

Gad swallowed hard, his stomach tightening. This, this was why he regretted not having a partner. This woman needed help, and if she was on (or off) meds of any sort, attempting to restrain her on his own was risky business for the both of them. Gad pushed his trepidation to the back of his mind and moved cautiously into the kitchen. He lifted his flashlight taser up and pointed toward her center of mass. As he put weight on his foot, the floor creaked.

The woman whirled toward him, her eyes wild and a small paring knife in her hand. She held it pointed toward him. "What do you want?"

"I'm not gonna' hurt you. I'm here to help you," Gad said in an even tone. "And we don't have much time."

"I'm the one who doesn't have much time, son. Something awful is coming for me. I've got one chance to end it or else what's coming is a whole lot worse."

"Worse than death?"

Gad's heart raced. The possibilities of what the woman might do with her paring knife mingled with the thought of having to see a reaper right now. It was a one-two punch of his desperation to stop her and his rising fear.

She raised the paring knife to her still uncut left wrist.

"I'd already be gone if the damned hacksaw wasn't so blunt. But this'll do the trick."

She pressed the blade into her flesh.

"No, no, no, no, no!" Gad stepped toward her. Immediately, the paring knife was back to pointing at him.

The pocket watch buzzed with urgency over and over in his front pocket. The air had taken on a brisk chill.

"Hey, we got off on the wrong foot. What's your name, ma'am? Mine is Gad." He held his hands out in front of him, imploring, as he took a cautious step toward her.

Her eyes narrowed. She didn't flinch. "Harriet. And you can stop right there, Gad."

Gideon froze.

Shadows behind her began to move.

"Harriet, listen to me. I don't know what you think is coming, but I have an ambulance right outside. There's no place safer than the hospital."

"Ha!" Harriet's nasal retort was not jovial. "That's the first place it would find me. No hospitals." She pressed the knife hard into the flesh again, this time splitting it. The small knife sank in and she cried out, squeezing her eyes shut.

"Harriet, stop!" His watch was uncomfortably hot in his front pocket. That meant it was just seconds from her time of death.

Behind Harriet, the shadows had gathered to shape the inevitable looming void of light behind her.

Her reaper had arrived.

Gad had no choice but to look at it if he was going to save Harriet, who unknowingly stood between them both. He didn't want to look up, but he would have to. He hated and feared them more than anything. They were purely horrendous in every form they took, making his skin crawl and his bowels weak. Contrary to pop culture's idea of a bad-ass grinning skeleton in a flowing black cowl, reapers each had their own unique blend of horrific features and sickening details. This was because, when a reaper takes a soul, it takes on a gruesome aspect of the way the person died, wearing it forevermore like a scar. If a reaper takes someone who died from an under-chin gunshot, expect the top of the reaper's cranium to have a gaping hole leaking viscera into the air around it. Likewise, if the same reaper had taken a motorcyclist with road rash and crushed torso, the reaper might also have decimated skin or a misshapen torso. Only three aspects remained consistent from reaper to reaper. They were huge, often standing anywhere from twelve to sixteen feet tall. They all carried the tool of their trade, a scythe used to pull souls from bodies. Last, while their chests appeared to be skin over ribs, they were actually a series of bone-sized arms and hands that unfolded, blossoming into an unholy maw that reached out to pull souls through to the Onward. Reapers were not only death incarnate, but also the doorways to whatever was next.

Gad looked up.

The reaper stood the full height of the room, the top of its hairless head brushing the popcorn ceiling. Its eyes were black pits with the appearance of having been pushed inward, and its neck had a distinct gaping line that trickled reddish black vapor out and up into the air around it. Its wrists bore similar suicidal damage.

Gad swallowed his rising gorge.

With a jaundiced hand, it made a motion as though holding an invisible staff in its fist. Twice, it banged the invisible weapon against the floor, and instantly, a scythe manifested in its hand. It stood the full height of the room with a shining arced blade above Harriet.

The floor was quickly growing cold. Sounds of hissing and distant screaming issued from the place the reaper stood. It raised the scythe up and back as Harriet raised the paring knife for a final cut. This was it, now or never.

"Goodnight, Harriet!" Gad charged at Harriet, taser-forward.

All in one moment, the taser connected with Harriet's side and all of her muscles, including her arm, went rigid. The paring knife remained frozen in her tightened fist without the ability to let go. Harriet groaned with the shocking pain coursing throughout her entire body, her face tight and red as her muscles remained locked. Behind her, the scythe lowered.

After four seconds of electric agony, Gad released the button and Harriet collapsed into his waiting arms, her paring knife clattering to the floor. He didn't waste a moment. He scooped her up onto his shoulder, leaving the reaper waiting, and moved as fast as he dared out to Mercy holding Harriet in a fireman's carry.

"YOU LET me out of this thing, you son of a bitch!"

Gideon grimaced into the rearview mirror at Harriet, the suicide patient that he had, for her own safety, restrained to the gurney.

"Can't do that. You're in a dangerous state of mind."

"Oh, that's an understatement. Where're you taking me?"

"The hospital."

"Look, I told you before. You take me there and my goose is cooked. Just let me just end it my way, on my terms."

He caught her movement in his wide rear-view mirror. Her balled fists shook and pulled the blue rubber restraint cuffs over her duct-taped wrists. "Ow, goddamn it!"

The slotted cuffs, meant for violent emergency patients, kept her hands bound to the gurney in an upright position to slow blood loss. Each time she pulled against the restraints, they pressed into the thick tape on her wrists. It had been a good thing her literal hacksaw-job on her right wrist had been shallow and ragged. It was the small but piercing slit in her left wrist that worried Gad. That was why he had skipped the sutures and grabbed the duct-tape, which never failed to surprise patients like Harriet in the ways it could hold the world and life-threatening cuts together.

"Harriet, you've got to get those gashes sutured," Gad called over his shoulder as they sped down the road. "I'm not going to let death win. My job is to save people. I have to get you to a doctor."

Harriet snorted. "I keep telling you, and you aren't listening. Something is coming for me. Tonight. And when it does, you and me both will wish I had kicked off instead."

"What do you think is coming for you, Harriet?"

He had scanned her pupils for abnormal dilation in case

drugs had taken her over, but her eyes had gazed steely back into his.

"You wouldn't believe me if I told you. Just let me go."

"You'd be surprised at what I'd believe," he countered.

Harriet laughed ruefully, shrugging. "Fine. I don't have much longer, anyway. Do you believe in God and his angels?"

"Yep. Raised Catholic, ma'am."

"Then you also believe in the Devil and his demons."

"Well, I guess, in theory."

He slowed at a busy intersection, gaze darting left and right as they passed through the red light.

"In theory, huh? What if I told you that demons surround us here, every day?"

"Here, like on planet Earth?" Gad glanced into the mirror, second-guessing his no-drugs assessment.

"Here, like Vegas. Sin City. Taking advantage of mortals and their every desire, every wish, every selfish need."

He could see the age lines in her forehead deepen as she spoke. Gad squinted. He had, in fact, a lot of insight into the darkness in this town, thanks to his father and Pete. He knew the depths people would sink to in order to exact revenge or to get ahead. But anything more powerful than spirits or reapers was a whole other matter, well above and beyond anything Pete or his dad had ever broached.

"You can't see them because they stay behind the scenes here, working deals, influencing us all to do their dirty work. Well, I stepped in it royal with one. Real nasty. And he's not sending humans after me."

"Well, then what, Harriet?" They had come to a solid wall of cars, each honking and waving to the idiot car still needing to pull over for Mercy. Gad looked into his mirror's reflection of Harriet's pale face.

Her eyes widened. "He's ordered an alastor to get me tonight.

I'm fucked." She glanced to the windows in the rear doors. "Sun's just about down."

Through the tinted glass, the last third of the sun shone golden over a stretching horizon of pink and orange.

"What's an alastor?"

"Look, you got pills or a shot of something? Anything quick?" She gazed out the window. She was transitioning from panic to acceptance as the sun sank slowly lower.

"Harriet, answer me. What is an alastor?"

"A demon. A lesser demon, but it's all about exacting revenge. And I don't mean the 'coming to kill me' sort of revenge, this isn't some Count of Monte Cristo shit. I mean, alastors are specialists in torture. It'll keep me alive as long as possible. And it'll keep hurting me and hurting me as long as I keep breathing."

"But Harriet, if you kill yourself, the Catholic church says you'll go to hell. Suicide is the unforgivable sin."

The corner of her reflection's mouth curled up. "Oh hon, I'm going down no matter what. I took out the bastard that got my husband, so I'm a murderer. But if I kill myself now, my alastor is shit out of a job tonight."

Gideon pushed down on the gas pedal.

"You're not taking me to the damned hospital, are you? I told you, it'll find me there."

"Nope, Harriet, not to the hospital. I'm taking you to church."

6

The last rays of soft purple stretched across the twilight sky as Gad keyed in the code to the chapel's back door. He held it open for Harriet to slip silently inside, careful to shut the door softly behind him. He set the next two deadbolts and dropped the wooden brace across the steel door.

The strains of "Can't Help Falling in Love" warbled through the tinny speaker in the back office. Another *Love Me Tender* ceremony had just begun. He offered Harriet the black leather office chair. She plunked into it and swiveled toward the monitors, confusion clear in her expression.

A happy couple held hands at the chapel pulpit as a six-foot-three pant-suited Elvis crooned, occasionally turning to grin into the video camera mounted in the corner. With a press of a button hidden on his giant gold belt buckle, a flash popped, and the video camera paused filming to snap a picture of the bride and groom next to Elvis at the altar. The bride swayed to the music in her short white T-shirt dress and the groom, holding her hand tight, smiled through his own gold Elvis sunglasses at his beautiful bride.

"C'mon, everybody, sing!" Elvis said into his microphone between lyrics.

All three sang the song's chorus, the bride and groom looking dreamily into each other's eyes. The pews behind them in the small hall were empty, as was the norm. Couples didn't come to The Chapel of the King for the dream wedding their families had always envisioned. These wedding and vow renewals were purely for the joy of starting their new life together in the fashion that the couple wanted. For some, a marriage bound by the King was the perfect start.

Harriet swiveled her chair around, one eyebrow raised. "Thought you said you were taking me to a church?"

"This is a church, Harriet, have no doubts. The land beneath us is blessed by a priest. He consecrated the building, too. Even the water that flows through these faucets is holier than thou. You're safe here."

"So, this is where it all ends for me, between these bright Pepto-pink walls?" She took in her cluttered office surroundings with an air of resignation.

"Oh, this is just the back office. The chapel is more of a warm Creamy Cocoa. I know because I helped paint the place. It took nine cans to finish it."

"You mean beige."

"It's Creamy Cocoa, Harriet."

"So, you know Elvis?" She pointed at the pant-suited man in the monitor gyrating his rhinestone glittering hips to "All Shook Up" alongside the happy couple.

"Better than anyone. He's my godfather. He's taken care of me since Dad passed."

"Wow." Harriet nodded her approval. "Pretty neat godfather."

"I think so. C'mon, you need to lie down and let me suture

your wounds. I'll show you where you're staying tonight." He pulled open the door to a darkened hallway.

Harriet sighed and shook her head. "What's your name again? Glad?"

"Gad. Gad Goodwin."

"I'm not making any promises, Gad. You're a sweet kid, really. But you seem to think you know best. Truth is, you haven't got a clue about what I'm telling you is out there. If that thing gets in here-"

"It won't." Gad cut her off.

"Listen to me, Goodwin-"

"I can see death, Harriet. It was standing behind you in your house, ready to take you, and I stopped it. I can see spirits, and I see things that most people wouldn't believe. And," he put his hands on her shoulders. "I believe you think you're in trouble with something unholy. That's why I brought you here. Nothing unholy can cross the threshold into this place. Nothing."

"I don't *want* to die, Gad. But I'm old, I'm tired, and I'm staring down the maw of the most awful way to die imaginable. So, I'm more scared than I've ever been. And you sitting here talking at me is wasting what little time and courage I have left to get it done."

"What if Pete knows how to call off the alastor? Or better yet, vanquish it?"

Harriet smirked. "Elvis the Pelvis is going to 'vanquish' my torture demon?"

"Can I make you a deal? Give me one hour. If I'm wrong and it gets in here, I promise I'll kill you myself."

"Still damned to hell."

"Not necessarily. You confess to Pete and ask God for forgiveness on that revenge murder deal. Then, I kill you, that's not suicide. You might be headed to the pearly gates."

Harriet blinked, considering his words. "Mr. Sparklepants is the priest you've been talking about. Uncle Pete."

"Pete is a bona fide priest," Gad insisted. "I know he doesn't exactly look it, but he is, trust me. He's helped perform exorcisms for the Catholic Church in Rome. I'm sure he'll know what to do to help you out of your mess."

"Fine, whatever. Here's the part that matters. In one hour, you promise to kill me?"

"Cross my heart, hope you don't die."

Her lips twisted. "I will trust you, Goodwin. This wouldn't be the first time I've made a poor choice, and it will probably be my last. But my gut's telling me I should trust you, even if your logic is half-assed."

"Half-assed, maybe. It's still better than your idea."

After another moment's consideration, she stood and gestured to the open door. "Okay then. Lead the way."

"Keep your arms elevated. Follow me."

Fear was creeping back into his stomach as Harriet's lack of faith radiated from her being. She glanced to the small rectangular window above the office's steel door. It was dark.

Nighttime was here.

GAD FLICKED the switch at the top of the wooden stairs. Pools of light illuminated the path down into a sprawling basement.

"There's a bed, a stocked fridge, and a toilet and a shower," Gad said, naming an amenity with each step down. "It's insulated with heating and air conditioning from upstairs, so...Harriet?" He looked over his shoulder to the woman frozen in the doorway.

"I'm not going down there."

"Harriet, I wouldn't save your life just to murder you in a basement."

"There's that half-assed logic again. It's about being trapped, son."

"Demons can't enter a church, Harriet. This whole building is a church."

"There any windows or escape routes down there?"

"Uh, no. But-"

"Nope."

"But Harriet-"

"Tick-Tock, young man."

He sighed and trudged back up the steps. "Okay, this way then." He flicked the light off.

"Congrats again! Go start that honeymoon, uh-huh." Pete executed a flawless double finger point, hip swivel maneuver toward the happy couple waving from the decorated "just married" stretch limo. With one last wave, Pete stepped backward into the foyer to let the compression latch door shut slowly of its own accord. It clicked shut with a soft hiss.

"Uncle Pete," Gad began from the chapel door.

"Ho-lee!" Pete jumped and spun, thudding to a ready stance halt.

"Sorry, I let myself in through the back."

"You can't do that to me, Gad. At least hit the doorbell twice so I know it's you." He snatched his over-sized rhinestone sunglasses from his face and pulled Gad into a bear hug. "What brings you over on a Wednesday evening? Tell you what, I'll close up shop at eight, we can crunch-burger, my treat."

"Actually, I kind of need you to close up shop now," Gad said, shuffling awkwardly.

"What, why? My best business is the seven o'clock walk-in couples. All tipsy and joyful..."

"You have a visitor in the chapel and she really needs your help."

"Is it a depressed damsel in distress? She need a quick 'Love Me Tender' pick-me-up?"

"No. This is a white-collar situation. It's serious."

Pete's fingers reached up instinctively to touch the ridiculously high collar of his jumpsuit. "Give me a few to get out of this get-up then."

Gad grabbed Pete's arm. "There's no time. She says there's a lesser-demon coming for her tonight."

Instead of the slew of normal-people questions that should have followed, like "what is a lesser-demon" or "did she just escape the institution", Pete's old blue eyes narrowed.

"She say its name?" His black-dyed eyebrows furrowed.

"It's an alastor," Harriet replied. She stood behind Gad, her small frame silhouetted against the chapel's bright stage lights. Her gray hair stood on end, and the sunken patches under her eyes were dark. She leaned against the open chapel door-frame, her bandages growing redder at the wrist.

"Harriet, I told you to stay put. Lift your hands over your heart." Gideon guided her to the back pew nearest the foyer, across from the front desk. He put her feet up on the pew.

Pete said, "Nice to meet you, Harriet," then pulled a gaudy black velvet Elvis pillow from the display case and handed it to Gad, who tucked it behind Harriet's back.

Harriet held her red-gauze wrists upright over her chest as she leaned against the wall. "You must be Pete. And as Gad here tells it, you're the priest that can save me."

"An alastor?" Pete's face scrunched up, his gaze drifting up to the right in thought. "That the revenge demon?" He pulled his wireless microphone out from the v-neck of his jumpsuit.

"On the nose."

"So let me explain-" Gad began.

"You hush, Goodwin, I don't have time." She turned herself toward Pete. "So, here's the count. I was trying to kill myself before your godson here broke into my house, tazed me, and kidnapped me to your Elvis chapel. There's a lesser-demon created specifically to torture me to death, meaning literally, until pain and torture puts me to death. I'm scared shitless and Gad has promised me the alastor can't get in this Elvis chapel because it's supposedly holy ground."

"Damned straight, it is." Pete affirmed, unbuckling his sparkling bedazzled belt. "Even the water you brush your teeth with here is holy; water heater's blessed and has a crucifix."

"Whatever you say," she said with a wave of her hand. "Last part is, you as an ordained priest will hear my confession over the asshole I murdered what murdered my husband, name of Gary."

"Gary your husband or Gary the asshole?" Pete folded the belt onto the glass counter of the front desk.

"Gary's my husband. Bob's the asshole. Anyway, then Gad here has minutes left to kill me so I can go with Jesus."

"Well, this is quite the Wednesday." Pete flipped the switch on his OPEN sign to off. "Gideon, I need my cassock, my collar and my crucifix, stat. Harriet, get ready to repent."

7

"Harriet Conover, when was your last confession?"

Pete had donned his black priest garb inside of two minutes to Gad's great relief. Hopefully, no one had caught any eyefuls through the wide foyer window with its blinds pulled open.

Harriet crossed herself. "In the name of the Father, and of the Son, and of the Holy Spirit. My last confession was probably more than, uh, twenty-something years ago? There's probably a lot to confess since that last one."

"Well, for every sin, are you repentant?"

"Oh, absolutely."

"Then to get straight to the heart of the matter, what is it you'd like to focus on in tonight's confession?"

Gad sat on the stool behind the front desk to give them the impression of privacy, even though he couldn't be over five feet from the chapel entrance.

"I'm repentant for the life that I took. Even though that life robbed me of my husband."

"Now Harriet, you actually need to repent or this is all for naught," Pete chided.

"He took my husband, Pete." Her voice caught, and her lower-lip trembled. "We were married forty-six years. We were having trouble making ends meet, so he took a new job. They called it an 'opportunity'. And he said yes when he should have said-"

A high-pitched screeching sound stopped Harriet's inevitable retort. It was like a speeding locomotive's brakes grinding metal on metal before a head-on crash. The horrific sound sent Gad flailing backward on his stool, his hands pressed to his ears. It drove straight into his brain, as though long sharp claws drew tiny, silvered curls from metal walls. The extended screech continued along the front of the chapel.

Harriet's eyes went round, the blood draining from her already pale face.

"It's here," she gasped. Her body shook.

The screech stopped just at the door handle. After a moment's silence, the long handle moved and clicked.

Pete stood, his Bible in hand. "It's hell-born. It can't get in."

The door-handle jiggling stopped.

Beads of sweat lined Pete's forehead. He began a Latin prayer under his breath, his eyes trained on the door.

The screech resumed, from the front door and along the chapel's welcome sign on the outer wall. A dark form passed in front of the window through the slats of the closed shade. It moved as though hunched over, almost crawling past. The screeching sound doubled in pitch as the material changed from wood to glass.

Gad got up from his stool and backed away from the window as the sound turned the corner toward them. The open window shades left the window uncovered.

"Father, I regret that I took Robert's life. He was Gary's boss."

The screeching came closer to the window, painfully slow and unrelenting, like nails along a rusty metal pipe.

"Gary was a chemist. Robert wanted Gary to make synthetic heroin. The day Gary said 'no' was the day he was murdered." Tears spilled uncontrollably down Harriet's face. "Robert came to tell me the same would happen to me if I said anything. So, I followed Robert into a dark club and gave him a huge dose of his own product. And Father, I am sorry to my core I killed that man. May God forgive m-"

Black horns, twisting skyward, filled the five-by-five pane of glass behind the desk. Gad and Pete backed up against the wall.

Red eyes with black slits reflected light like a cat's, set within ghastly alabaster skin slick in the chapel light. In place of a nose were red lips set in an unnaturally wide grin that stretched from one side to the other, showcasing row upon row of needle-like teeth. Gad, Pete and Harriet flattened themselves against the wall. The demon ignored the men, its gaze sweeping past them to lock on Harriet. Its grin stretched even farther, and its teeth parted. A long red tongue unrolled impossibly far, crimson and wet as if it had already dined on flesh before its arrival.

Its lolling tongue looked to be two feet long or more, ending in a forked point. The demon licked the window at an achingly slow pace as though anticipating her exquisite flavor. Its red eyes wide and large like its smile. It lifted its hand to the glass, a foot-long skeletal set of skinless, pointed phalanges, and it tapped its sharp bone forefinger on the window at her.

The smell of hot urine filled Gad's nose. It was Harriet. She cowered, whimpering, her nose running.

Pete gripped his bible, his face red. "Yes, that's an alastor. But first, let's finish the confession." He strode to the pew and knelt next to Harriet. "Harriet Conover, do you repent the taking of Robert's life as having offended God and, in doing so, detest all your sins, because you dread the loss of heaven and the pains of hell?"

"I-I do," she cried.

"Then give thanks to the Lord for He is good. For His mercy endures forever."

"P-praise God in the h-highest."

"Amen." Pete stood, a vein popping out from his temple.

"A-amen," Harriet repeated and crossed herself, never letting her eyes break from the demon's taunting stare.

"Good. Now let's deal with this son-of-a-bitch," Pete said, marching over to the window and putting his hand on the lock.

"What're you doing?" Harriet cried.

"Pete," Gad warned.

"Watch and learn." With the flick of his hand, he unsnapped the window lock and slid the window wide open.

Harriet's piercing scream filled the chapel.

The enormous demonic head rolled forward, tongue lashing in at its first chance to enter. The forked tip stopped at the window's edge, smoke rising from its dripping red tip. Blood-red drips spattered the window pane just outside the window's rail.

"See?"

The demon's chortling gurgle filled the room.

"Haaarrrrriiiiieettttttt..." Its pointed bone claw held fast toward her. "Miiiiinnnne."

Pete snatched up a large glass vase filled with a beautiful fresh flower arrangement. He pulled the flowers out and laid them on the glass desk.

"Harriet, listen to me. Lesson number one, I consecrated the grounds. Robert here can never come in. Long after bombs have vaporized Vegas from the planet, demons will still be prevented from crossing onto this land. Lesson number two. As I mentioned previously, all the water in this chapel is holy water, thanks to Blessed Bertha, our water heater. So, this is how we deal with Robert until I find a better answer."

He pitched the full vase of holy water into the demon's giant, grinning face.

The walls shook as black smoke rose from the demon's face and an unearthly howl rent the air. The alastor fell back from the window, its white skin and red lips bubbling away to reveal bone beneath. The stench permeating the room was somewhere between rotting death and burnt pork.

Gad wretched.

Pete tossed the flowers one by one in the demon's bubbling face, each landing with a sizzle followed by a growl or a screech.

"Now fuck off, Bob!" Pete slammed the window shut, twisted the lock, and dropped the shade.

8

"So why did you name it 'Bob'?"

Gad lifted a slat on the vinyl blinds and scanned the front porch for signs of the beast. The narrow tip of its spiny tail uncurled over the rain gutter and down into view, the afternoon sun glistening on its bony gray-puce skin. When he had driven into the parking lot, the demon was perched gargoyle-like on the roof peak.

"It's an alastor, a revenge demon created by whoever Gary worked for from the remains of the aggrieved. The aggrieved body was Robert. Hence, 'Bob'."

"So, if Robert was the aggrieved, how'd the demon get made? Bastard died. How does that work?" Harriet sat in the same back pew again, which she had insisted on scrubbing clean against Pete's nagging that she needed to rest. The pew emanated a lemon polish scent mixed with the overpowering floral smell of the clean-scrubbed rug below.

Pete chuckled, turning another gold-leaf page of the leather-bound book laying open across the glass desk. "Who did Robert work for? They can only make this demon from the body of an aggrieved death. Someone else had to know Robert's grievance and then act on it. They had to perform the rite over the fresh body, and..." Pete turned another page and pointed to an illumination. "They transform the body into a vengeful hate machine that won't quit until it gets the person it wants."

Gad stared down at a detailed painting of a monstrosity surrounded by hellfire, screaming humans gripped in each clawed hand. It held one down in a boiling pot while holding the other head-first above its gaping maw. "So that alastor asshole might be after more than Harriet?"

"Doubt it," she said and shifted into a more comfortable position against the wall. "I'm the only one that went after Robert. And I made sure those bastards knew it was me and only me."

"What bastards? Who made Bob?" Gad finally turned from the window.

"Inferno. They ruined Gary's life and mine. I wanted them to know it was me and why. So, they made Bob to come get revenge on me. Brought it on myself." Harriet rested with her head against the wall, her eyes closed. After what she had been through the night before and knowing what waited for her just outside the door, she had weariness etched into every line and shadow of her face.

"Did Gary work for Inferno, too?" Pete glanced up from the horrific illumination.

"No." Harriet's eyes popped open wide and fierce. "Gary would never join, no matter how Robert pressured him. He only agreed to manufacture the product. He refused to get any more involved than that. And Lord in heaven, if I knew then what I know now, he never would've even talked to Robert. Gary'd still be alive if he had just stayed away. Too late for us now." She turned her face away from them, suddenly silent.

"Well, again, the good news is that we can come and go as we please. Bob here doesn't give two squirts of piss about anyone else. So we got you covered, little lady. Least until I figure out how to send this thing back to wherever it came from." Pete shut the book with a whump.

"Yeah, whatever you need, we're on it. Clothes, groceries, movies, booze, whatever." Gad crossed the entryway and sat next to Harriet on the pew.

She wiped at her eyes and managed a smile. "Well, I'm no charity case, boys. I earn my keep. I'll clean this place up and do what needs done to help."

Pete blinked. "You know how to work a computer?"

Gad laughed. His godfather, bless his heart, had always had to ask Gad for help in that area. Computers were the bane of his existence. Even the chapel's website remained stuck in 1996 until Gad asked for the help of web-savvy friends. They were happy to update the webpage of the King.

"I run a mean Excel spreadsheet. Beyond that, I might figure some things out with time."

"Done deal. But for now, why don't you go rest for a bit? I need to prep for a commitment ceremony at five."

"And I need to grab food before my shift. What can I pick up for you while I'm out, Harriet?"

"Uh, some unmentionables, so to speak. I've only got what I was brought here in. I'm an extra-large and 42 Double-D." Harriet's cheeks flushed.

"Lady, don't worry about it. I'm an EMT in Vegas. Asking for underwear would be like the least embarrassing ask I've ever gotten."

Gad moved to the window and knocked on it. In a flash, the giant head dropped into the windowpane, upside down. Its glowing red eyes scanned for Harriett through the gaps in the blinds.

Harriet startled, her hands shook.

"Stop it," Pete admonished. "Don't test it." He turned to

Harriet and placed his hand firmly on her ankle. "Remember who it really is and what he did to you. Don't let it win by getting to you."

Harriet swallowed, staring at the beast. Its gaze found her, and it let her know by slapping a long forked red tongue against the glass. The long rows of needle teeth appeared in the gaps between the blinds.

Harriet brought herself up straight and squared her shoulders. "That's right. It's your fault we're in this mess together, Bob." Her lower lip trembled, but her jaw thrust forth. She extended her middle finger to it.

"That-a-girl." Pete grinned and snapped the vinyl blinds closed.

OVER THE NEXT FEW DAYS, Gad didn't have a lot of time to check on Harriet. She couldn't leave sacred ground, so Gad made sure to drop off supplies whenever he could.

"Hey Bob," he'd nod at the gray-green terror perched the roof peak. Thankfully, Pete was right. It would not acknowledge him. To the alastor, Gad didn't exist. Yet it didn't make passing through the chapel's threshold beneath the looming hell-spawn any less disconcerting. Its massive face hovered over the composite wood roof tiles, listening intently for sounds of its victim within, like a cat poised over prey hidden in a hole.

Gad dropped off bags in the chapel lobby with a various colors and styles of "I HEART Vegas" and cheetah-print lounge wear along with her requested unmentionables. It wasn't the classiest wardrobe around, but it would have to do. Going back to Harriet's house to retrieve anything would first require a few blessings and wards that they didn't have time to take on just yet and this was the best way he could think of to stretch the few dollars they'd managed to scrape together for Harriet's clothing fund.

Gad found the most recent post-it penned in neat red ink at the front desk in the scheduling book and stuck to two hundred-dollar bills. *I can only wear this shit ironically. Please find something nice to wear at front desk.*

He swept up both hundred-dollar bills, scrawled a reply post-it and pressed it to the glass countertop. *Fine. No accounting for taste.* He grabbed the cash and left, ready to start his shift.

The sun dipped low in the desert sky and disappeared behind twinkling hotels and towering neon signs. Gad sat behind Mercy's wheel in a massive casino parking lot on the strip, listening to his scanners.

The sidewalk bustled with packs of people, young and old, happy and sad, sober and drunk. A bachelorette party clicked down the sidewalk in colorful stiletto heels, all the shapely women pouring out of their tight sparkling cocktail dresses and stumbling to hold one another and their glowing plastic cocktails upright. They could not see the deceased, once-handsome man that pushed between them wearing a finely tailored suit. His sickly pallor, bulging eyes, and neck held at an impossible angle told Gad he had hung himself. The spirit shuffled awkwardly between them, searching each woman's eyes for any sign of recognition. The ghost stopped his ambling suddenly and swung around to face Gad.

"Aw shit." Gad dropped his gaze to his lap and fiddled with a gum wrapper on his dashboard. "Don't come over here."

Most people can't see ghosts. Ghosts can't see one another. To be seen, to be heard, these are gifts that could bring a ghost out of its hellish existence in a world devoid of social interaction. If a spirit could feel being seen by someone like Gad, someone with The Sight, that spirit more often than not became a relentless haunt.

Gad kept his face down but looked up through lidded eyes toward the broken neck ghost. It stood rooted to the spot, staring wildly toward his windshield and swaying side to side.

"One...two...three..." Gad counted aloud, deliberate, and slow. He focused on the gum wrapper and its shiny metallic surface. "Four...five...six..." White paper on one side, silver on the other. Focus on anything else. "Seven...eight...nine..."

Gad looked up again, careful to not raise his head. Broken neck had returned to shuffling awkwardly away between the masses.

"10-52, 3700 West Flamingo Road," a somewhat distorted female voice announced on his second scanner. Gad twisted the volume up. "10-50," she added. Dispatch had sent out an ambulance request for an emergency at the Rio.

He snatched up the radio microphone. "102372, 10-76," he replied to dispatch with his ambulance number and the code for "en route".

"10-4, 102372," the dispatcher acknowledged Mercy as the responder.

Gad hit the lights and the road.

9

Police lights splashed the massive hotel walls in alternating reds and blues. Gad pulled Mercy up to the back entrance of the Rio and jumped out just as a firetruck pulled in behind him. He grabbed his ALS carry bag full of its array of medications, airway management and IV equipment, and strode to the scene by the door.

The hotel floor manager and a waitress, biting at her nails, stood behind a balding man lying prone on the sidewalk. A cop knelt at his side, speaking with words too soft to hear. From the man's business casual sweater vest and nice pants to his stylish sports shoes, he looked every bit a well-to-do tourist ready to hit the links.

"Name's Gad. What happened?" Gad knelt at the patient's opposite side.

"Hey, I'm Ray. Guests pulled the Rio floor manager over when this man fell from his bar stool. His speech is slurred but I don't smell any alcohol."

People talked behind hands to one another along the walls and sidewalk, unable to get any closer with several of the Rio's managers and staff forming a large circle around the emergency scene.

Gad pulled his pen flashlight from his shoulder sleeve. "Sir, can you tell me your name?"

"Uhhhnn," was the man's response before his head lolled to the side. His ashen skin glistened with a fine sheen of sweat. Gad pushed each drooping eyelid fully open and shined his light in both eyes; the man's pupils had contracted to pinpoints.

Ray pulled the man's wallet from his pants pocket and flipped it open. "Name's Douglas Aiken, 57 years old."

"No medic alerts anywhere on him?" Gad asked, checking Doug's pulse at his wrist. "Heartbeat's erratic." He noted that, instead of a healthy pink, Doug's fingernails were blue. "He's not getting enough oxygen."

"Heart attack?"

"How'd he get outside, Ray?"

Ray scowled. "Witnesses all say he stumbled outside, put his hand on the wall, then he collapsed."

"Check his pockets." Gad monitored Doug's breaths in and out, which were shallow. In touching his clammy skin, Gad was getting a strong feeling in his gut that the man had taken too much of a bad thing. "I think-" A sudden vibration against his chest disrupted his thought, the sensation like a buzzing bee trapped in his shirt pocket.

"Ah, here you go." Ray fished a rattling brown pill bottle from one of Doug's pants pockets and held it label-out for Gad to see.

"Shit. Oxycodone. Bet he took a dose, forgot, and took another. He needs a stomach pump. We got to get him on my gurney and fly him to the ER."

"I'll help you load up. Go get your cart. I got him." Ray slipped his arm behind Doug's back to lift him gently up from the pavement.

"Is he gonna' be ok?" The waitress behind them called out, one foot curled anxiously around her other ankle.

Gad had to move fast. The pocket watch was tolling for Doug.

He had scarcely jumped into Mercy to pop the gurney out before telltale gooseflesh rose across his arms. An icy breath passed over the back of his neck. "Nuh-uh, not yet, you asshole." Gad gave his gurney a mighty shove and stood on its back bar to ride it down the ramp at the void of shadows taking shape over Doug. The watch buzzed furiously in his pocket, growing warmer with each passing second.

"He's seizing!" Ray carefully laid Doug's convulsing body flat.

"Shit, shit, shit." Gideon quickly aligned the gurney parallel to Doug and did his best to not see the hazy and shifting darkness that had taken diaphanous shape behind them. The familiar presence of death brought with it the overwhelming sense of dread. It permeated his core, twisting his stomach. "Help me get him on the cart!" The fine hairs on the back of his neck stood rigid.

"But he's seizing," objected one fireman who had gathered around them.

"We're not supposed to move him," objected another. "It's dangerous to move him when he's seizing!"

"Screw that, he's dying," said another.

"Help me, I'm losing him," Gad yelled and grabbed Doug's shaking ankles.

Ray and the firemen heaved Doug onto the gurney where Gad buckled him in. Doug stopped moving, his eyes wide. Over his shoulder, the pointed arc of a scythe reflected the flash of the police light.

"Nope, not yet!" Gad heaved at his end of the gurney. A scythe blade whooshed downward past Gad's foot as he rolled the gurney at top speed up Mercy's ramp. Without a backward glance, he locked the wheels in place while the firemen retracted the ramp and shut the doors. With a double-knock on the window from Ray, Gad was good to go. He didn't even bother buckling, instead putting Mercy into gear with the siren wailing and lights spinning.

Cars pulled to the side. Gad rocketed over speed bumps with no forgiveness for his suspension.

The pocket watch was now so hot, he was certain it would burn a hole through his uniform and into his flesh beneath. He reached into the front pocket and scooped it out, dropping it into his cup holder. It vibrated in its circular jail like a nest of angry hornets.

Cars and taxis would crowd the strip at this hour, so he cranked Mercy's wheel hard right to get to the overpass and onto the freeway. Gad glanced into his rearview at the patient. Doug's head bounced a bit with the movement of the ambulance but otherwise was still. He had likely slipped into unconsciousness. Then Gad made the mistake of looking into his side mirror.

Just behind the ambulance was the somewhat transparent and pallid form floating just behind them like an otherworldly flame, towering above all. It drifted toward them with frightening speed, its shining blade high and wide to reap the soul it had come for. Even though Gad stared hard forward, that one glance at the reaper was enough to burn into his mind's eye. Jaundiced, sickly, it was split from forehead to pelvis, half biped and half dark vapor. It's mouth, parted down the center, was open wide with rows of broken teeth, one side of its jaw hanging lower than the other. Its legs bent backwards, sprinting awkwardly through the air after them.

Gad swore under his breath, a bead of cold sweat trickling down his temple. This had literally become a race for this man's life.

He turned the wheel and guided the ambulance around the

freeway on-ramp as fast as he dared. The reaper existed outside the rules of the road and drifted straight across the landscaping to meet Mercy at the bottom. The reaper, vast and terrifying to behold, towered over the front of the vehicle and swung its arched blade through the ambulance. Gad swerved, ducking to miss the vast blade. It passed inches above Doug's nose.

Stomping on the gas, Gad gunned it for the hospital. SUVs pulled to the side and, as was typical, some cars took their sweet time in moving over. A giant tour bus in the fast lane was being denied room to move over.

"Fuck it," he grumbled and sped onto the freeway's inner shoulder. "Hang on Doug, it's gonna get bumpy."

"Who am I," came a weak and nonsensical reply.

"Oh good, you're awake! Stay with me, Doug, we're almost there."

Mercy bounced over all manner of debris and gravel. Gad radioed in the information for his incoming patient. "10-17, 102372 inbound to St. Lucy's, coming in hot, Code Blue."

"10-4 102372," dispatch replied. "Trauma team will be ready at the door."

Gad saw his opening and pulled across four lanes, off the ramp and down the street to the hospital. One glance into his side mirror and he bit his lip, drawing blood. Death followed just behind. This was too close. He swung Mercy into the driveway. The tires squealed and bounced over the speed bumps to the open side door where the triage nurses and an orderly stood ready.

"Okay Doug, lets g-"

In his rear mirror view of the patient on the gurney, the tip of the scythe swept through the back of the ambulance and caught on Doug's solid torso. Gad shrank back against the wheel, the hairs of his arms standing on end. The black void filled the back of his ambulance, so big that the reaper's shoulders must've floated above Mercy's roof.

Gad's heart banged against his chest. He sat frozen, his back against his wheel as the scythe tugged once, twice, and finally wrenched the black vaporous soul of Douglas Aiken from his body. Light reflected in the mirror sharply in Gad's eyes. He knocked the mirror away from his eyes, anger and adrenaline causing his hands to tremble. The maddening buzzing in the cup holder stopped.

Gad slammed his fist against the dash, the sudden shock of pain raced up the side of his hand to his elbow. He slumped in his seat and expelled all the air that he had been holding in his chest. "Fuck it all anyway." His chin fell to his chest.

The back doors of his ambulance swung open.

"Code Blue?" The doctor looked in expectantly with the orderly over her shoulder.

Gad sighed. "Not anymore. Overdose."

The doctor climbed up into the ambulance bay and quietly pressed her stethoscope to Doug's still heart. After a moment, she nodded. "We'll call it and take it from here. I'm sorry." She turned to the orderly and added a "10-79".

That was the code for the coroner.

10

N ight had fallen by the time Gad gave his report to the doctor and to the coroner at the hospital. Douglas had been on vacation with his wife and sixteen-year-old daughter, who were shopping at The Forum and tragically unaware of his medical emergency. When they arrived, Gad escorted them into a private office with the doctor to help convey the news. As often as such heartbreaking news needed giving in his line of business, it never got easier.

A common saying among EMTs is that death is a dance partner. In that daily dance, sometimes the EMT leads and sometimes death leads. Yet Gad had the special gift to beat death at its own game by having the foreknowledge of its approach. Nine times out of ten, Gad not only helped that patient escape their reaper, but for some, also gave them that all-important glimpse into the horrors of hell that awaited. With a second chance at life, that saved patient had the chance to turn their fate around. Yet despite his gift, he had lost not one, but two patients to the reapers inside of a month.

Gad drove Mercy through the crowded streets with his mind on autopilot. He couldn't stop seeing Douglas's daughter.

Rebecca was her name. In his mind's eye, he kept replaying the way she broke down at the news of her father's passing. The way her face contorted and her tears spilled straight down her deep red cheeks. Her mother's cry of anguish, followed by coughing and then heaving. The emotional weight of what had happened that day was like a cement truck. Gad's self-imposed shift was only a little over halfway over, but he knew he would be no good to anyone for the rest of the night.

He tuned back in to the scene before his eyes to find he had pulled into the casino where Drake worked and had shut off the engine. Apparently, it was such a bad day, his "no drinks on a weeknight" rule was out the window. He would have to have a drink to calm his nerves to have any chance at sleep. The one time he tried sleeping pills, they had worked a little too well, and he slept through the pocket watch's death alert, missing the chance to save a neighbor being hit by a car on their street.

Numb, he locked Mercy up and made his way through the casino's bustling first-floor gamblers, up the escalators, and across the quiet third floor. The swanky restaurant was hidden at the far end of a wide hall and around the corner, sensibly tucked away from the dinging and chatter of gaming two floors below.

The walnut door's brass handle reflected the soft light of Tiffany lamps. Beneath his steel-toed black boots, a rich red runner carpet led the way to the host's stand.

"Hey G, how you doin' tonight?" Carl greeted him with a warm smile that instantly melted. "You okay, man?"

Gad took in a deep breath to consider the answer. "Hm. No, it was a hard night. I was hoping I could catch Drake. He makes that, uh, the thing I like with the big ice cube." Somewhere in his head was the name of the drink, but he lost it in the wave of emotion that was drowning simple thought.

"Yeah. You go right on ahead, take a load off," Carl said with a sweep of his arm.

The high-end eatery was a perfect replica of a 1920s speakeasy. Low-lit and punctuated by splashes of color from stained glass, red leather couches and high-backed green dining chairs, it gave a sense of timeless cool and mystery. Gad slipped along the wall of the packed dining room and crossed the polished wooden floor to the bar in the back.

Drake blended in perfectly to his surroundings with a white dress shirt, rolled sleeves and black pants with suspenders. He looked up from the leaves of mint he muddled with the twist of his wrist, surprised. "Gad, what're you doing here so early?"

"I'm done for today." He slid onto the red stool and cradled his head on the bar. "I need one of those giant ice cube drinks."

"Old fashioned. You got it, just gimme a minute."

Drake moved with the complexity and speed of a juggler. Somehow, he completed three different cocktails and loaded them onto a tray for a server while getting the order of a couple to Gad's right. Before he knew it, his old-fashioned with the prerequisite giant ice cube clinked onto the bar in front of him moments after the couple to his right received long island iced teas.

He wasted no time in bringing the short glass of liquor to his lips. Whiskey burned its way down the back of his throat, making his eyes water. The pleasant flavors of citrus and bitters mingled on his tongue. In just a few minutes, heat would travel along his neck and shoulders to loosen tightly corded muscles and carry his hurt away, at least for a little while.

"Another one of those, please." A heavyset man with thinning hair caught Drake's eye and gestured to the drink in Gad's hand.

"Comin' up," Drake flipped a cocktail glass from one hand to the next. He had a goofy expression as he poured liquor over another giant ice cube, somewhere between a knowing smile and wide-eyed excitement.

The man leaned on the bar next to Gad and smoothed down his remaining silver hair. "Hey," he lifted his chin to Drake. "Anyone come in here asking for me?"

"No sir, not yet anyway," Drake slid the old-fashioned across the bar into the man's waiting hand. "If they do, you want me to bring them over?"

"No," he replied firmly and threw back a swig of whiskey. "I want to be left alone to enjoy a quiet meal. You got a place I can do that?"

The man's arm brushed Gad's, and Gad was suddenly awash in anxiety. He glanced over and caught the look in the man's pale gray eyes. He was giving off the illusion of cool and collected while inwardly nearing panic.

"Absolutely, sir. We'll get you a VIP table in the nook back there."

Gad followed Drake's glance to a set of curtained inlets, each with a private table. Most likely set up for recognizable people, it offered anonymity in the shadows.

The man nodded and slid poker chips with green ticking across the bar to Drake. "Anyone comes asking for me, I'm not here."

"You got it." Drake said with a solemn nod. The chips disappeared under his hand with the dexterity of a magician. "Carl, table for one by the piano."

"Of course. Right this way, sir." Carl, who had apparently been hovering feet away with a menu in hand, snapped to action and led the man to a private table in the furthest inlet. He drew red velvet theater curtains closed save for a small gap in the center to peek through, leaving the man in seclusion.

"Holy shitballs, dude." Drake grabbed the edge of the counter. "Do you know who that was?"

"Some famous rich guy?" Gad swallowed another mouthful of whiskey. The feeling of liquid fire down his throat lessened with each subsequent sip.

"Are you kidding? That was Vincenzo Luciano. He runs a whole chain of casinos here and-"

"And the mafia?" Gad finished the sentence with a mocking snort and tipped his drink into his mouth. He was feeling a lot looser now.

Drake raised an eyebrow.

Gad swallowed. "Really?"

Drake circled his face with a pointed finger. "This is my serious face. And get this. I'm pretty sure he just slipped me half the rent for next month."

"Drake." Carl motioned Drake to the far end of the bar.

Gad's pocket vibrated. His mind worked slower than usual in realizing it was his watch coming to life. He fished it out and flipped it open. The time showed impending death was less than three minutes from now. The small hand spun up, around, and then stuck pointing down. Gad frowned. Whoever it marked for death and the highway to hell had to be in this room. If he acted fast enough, he might turn this horrible day around.

The soft point of light on the bezel stopped in the upper-left. He squinted in the dim light, turning left on his stool. The light adjusted to the top of the bezel, and the vibrations became stronger. The once cool silver metal warmed quickly in his hand.

Gad stood, slowly, and walked in the direction his pocket watch led him with its tiny light. He seemed headed straight for the curtained inlet.

A wave of cold washed over Gad's neck and down his back. He gasped and turned, half-expecting to see someone with an empty water pitcher over his head. A figure stood in the doorway near Carl's host stand. He blocked the light. Or, rather, light could not escape his presence. He stood tall and silent, his suit finely tailored and all black. This was the man he had glimpsed outside the hospital window the night his patient Tom had abruptly died. And still he could not make out the man's face. It was as though the man were in an out-of-focus picture.

The sound of curtains being slid back made Gad turn. The red velvet curtains were, in fact, slid aside and now breaking from their rod ring by ring. Vinny Luciano hung onto the curtain gripped in one hand as though for dear life, his other hand on his throat. His eyes and the veins in his neck and temples bulged through purple skin.

Gad pocketed the watch and got to Vinny just as Vinny's eyes rolled back into his head. He fell to the floor like a bag of wet cement.

The air around Vinny stilled, frigid and stale. Shadows ran together, oil across the floor joining bit by bit to form something larger and darker.

Gad breathed in and slowly exhaled, pushing out with it the intense fear trying to scramble his thoughts. Skin is warm and moist yet purple. Dark eyes. He held fingers under Vinny's nose. No breath, he couldn't breathe. He looked to the table for any clues. No pill bottles. Spilled drink.

The death rattle of air drawn over papery vocal chords confirmed the feeling of a looming darkness hunched over him. That insufferable stench...a reaper had arrived for Vinny. The feeling of ice crawled across Gad's feet and hands.

On the table, a small loaf of bread had a large moon-shaped bite taken out of an end.

As fast as he could manage, Gad shoved his hands under Vinny's armpits. He strained to pull him into a sitting position.

"What's going on?" Drake appeared in a panic next to Gad, fully unaware of the scythe blade wheeling back above his head. Gad had seconds before it would cut Vinny down.

"Choking!" Gad groaned, pulling Vinny upward. He dropped him several inches to the floor. The blockage did not dislodge. "Hold him," Gad ordered.

Drake held Vinny's shoulders firm. Vinny's chin rolled against his chest while Gad got his arms around and under Vinny's ribs. He formed a ball with his fists and, with one mighty pull upward, popped a wadded ball of wet doughy bread to the front of Vinny's mouth. Drake, his face etched with fright, hooked a finger into his mouth and pulled the doughy ball out.

WHOOSH.

Vinny breathed in with a great sucking rasp. The tip of the hooked blade held still against Vinny's heart. Gad held his breath, his heart pounding.

"Help me," Vinny rasped. He pointed to the wall with a shaking finger.

Gad stumbled backward. He could see what Vinny was seeing. A pair of leathery hands, black as pitch, with impossibly elongated fingers like claws protruded from a black void in the blossoming chest of a reaper. The reaper's chest was fully open with its myriad of small boney arms and hands outstretched, fingers reaching and grasping to pull Vinny inside, all surrounding two large and long black leathery arms reaching for Vinny's face. The fingers themselves stretched, their sharp black tips drawing deep along his cheek.

"You're ok, sir. We got it out. Just breathe," Drake told him.

Vinny's body trembled in Gad's arms. Black twisted horns emerged from the void, followed by a face and yellow cat eyes. They crinkled at the edges. The thing was smiling from within the hole in the reaper. Whispers upon whispers filled their ears.

"In Christ's name, in Christ's name." Vinny genuflected, unable to pull his eyes from the horror threatening to pull him in.

The fingers withdrew from his cheek instantly; the creature

reviled by the power of the name Vinny repeated. The blade retracted from Vinny's chest. Gad couldn't help himself this time. He turned to look up into the reaper's face looming over his them.

Gad's heart banged in his chest.

This reaper's visage was skinless and skeletal. It seemed to grin at him. A fingertip only half-covered by flesh tapped Gad's chest and trailed down, down, down to his pocket watch on the floor at his side.

"Soon..." the whisper floated to him on a supernatural wind.

Before Gad could flinch, the reaper drifted backward through the solid wall. He shivered, his blood running cold. He didn't know reapers could speak.

"Mr. Luciano?" Drake asked with a mixture of panic and puzzlement. "You okay?"

Vinny grasped at his heart, leaning on one hand and praying in a litany of Italian. He reached into every pocket in his jacket, pulling out every poker chip he could find. They fell to the floor one by one, all marked with green, orange or black with red hatching. They bounced and rolled here and there as he repeated his mantra. "No more. I'm out. No more."

Gad scooped up his watch, still in a daze. He offered his hand to Vinny. "Let's get you to the ER. You just had a brush with death."

Vinny grasped his hand so hard, Gad froze. His gray eyes were wild. "Thank you. Grazie mille, thank you. I owe you everything. I-I..." He glanced about, lost for a moment. Then, conviction gripped him. "We'll take your ambulance, but not to the hospital."

"But," Drake began.

Vinny shook his head.

Gad frowned. "Where?"

"Take me to the police."

Drake shrugged. "All right then. You two go, I can clean this up."

Gad helped Vinny to his feet, causing one last chip to fall to the floor. Drake swept it up and held it to the dim light.

"What, that place again?" Gad turned and followed in Vinny's rapid footsteps to the exit, bothered why that place seemed to become more than mere coincidence. He left Drake kneeling in the inlet, staring at the casino's elegant golden name in the center of the black chip with red ticking.

INFERNO.

"Inferno? This again?" Gad muttered, as they prepared to leave.

GAD WAS nothing more than a bundle of numb nerves. He was not a drinker, but he didn't have the courage to get into bed and close his eyes.

Drake understood Gad's pain. Gad didn't know where Drake had driven them to, it was some dive bar with a quiet dark corner.

Drake listened to Gad, and how Gad had lost Douglass Aiken, and how Gad had saved a notorious crime lord from death. He had saved someone, yes, but he was a crime lord. In saving Vinny, had Gad doomed countless others?

Drake would never know Gad's true fears. He let Gad sit silently to stare at the liquor bottle before him. Gad silently worked through the trauma of having seen two reapers in one day. And Drake would never know the full truth of how Gad had saved a notorious crime lord from hell's grasp. It was rare for Gad to drink to the bottom of a bottle.

At the end of the night, Drake had driven Mercy and then walked Gad upstairs, made him drink enough water to be safe, and helped him fall into the comfort of his bed. Without a shit-ton of drinks, he would have been curled up in the corner, his knees to his chest with just one image swimming in the dark before him...in front of Vinny, in front of the reaper and its gaping portal to hell...and reaching out its claws from hell to snatch up its prize, the horned beast...those eyes...those yellow eyes...

11

D rake reached for the golden door handle, his fingertips stopping against the cool metal surface. He couldn't bring himself to push it open. Something pulled at him, urging him to turn around.

Just walk away now and nothing bad happens.

He stared at the back of his hand, his fingertips slipping over the handle. *It's just a casino.*

Not just any casino. This one belongs to Vinny Luciano. He pulled his hand back from the door and turned away. That felt better.

Drake opened his other hand, palm up, and stared at the black poker chip with red ticking. *But this one chip could be worth five grand.*

Or it could be worth one hundred. And it's mafia money.

But you didn't have to kill or sell anyone for it. And free money is free money.

Walk away.

Walk the line.

The devil and the angel on his shoulders were about to go all fight club on each other. "Life is short," Drake muttered. He strode back to the golden door and gave it a mighty shove. It swung wide open.

Drake's jaw dropped. This casino made the five-star place he worked at look old and tired.

Opulence stretched out before him with clear glass paths hugging merlot leather couches in booths with polished walnut flooring. Rich rose gold curtains complimented copper railings surrounding all. Each side of the ramp displayed half of a Hieronymus Bosch artwork painted on glass and lit from within to enhance the colors of his *Garden of Earthly Delights*. Before Drake, the glass ramp stretched out and over a round diamond blue pool to another landing with a white Greek atrium and the main gaming hall. Above his head, a placard welcoming visitors into the vast casino proclaimed in large lettering, "The Vestibule". Beneath that in smaller lettering, it added, "Surrender your desires within."

Despite it being well into the post-midnight hours, a time when casinos typically saw a dip in their attendance numbers, this place was still full of people. The long curving couches along the water's edge seated well-dressed men and women gathered around small tables with countless empty drink glasses.

Oddly, the vibe was off-putting. Drake's club radiated laughter and loud music. While this place had just as many guests, they were indifferent to their opulent surroundings, their faces expressionless. Everything here was so posh. Could be that the clientele at this casino were too baller even for the likes of him. Drake shifted uneasily. He did a quick shoe-check to see if they were dressy enough. The frosted and elegant script on the glass beneath his feet labeled the water flowing beneath "Acheron". He jingled the poker chips around in his pants pocket as he weighed whether to acknowledge the powerful tug of his proverbial angel urging him to leave.

"Hello!"

Drake nearly jumped into the water feature. The voice belonged to a hostess in themed uniform, a black leather corset with peekaboo red push-up bra and two draping metal chains across her midriff. Her black and red skirt covered down to her thighs, but just barely. Her black name tag spelled out "Caron" in gold.

"Welcome to Inferno. Is there anything you desire?"

Having worked at a casino longer than any person probably should, he knew what was being implied. "Anything he desired" was not actually on the menu, but if an open-ended entendre from a scantily clad woman made him feel welcome enough to open his wallet, it was the perfect greeting.

Walk away. The little voice nagged. He jingled the chips in his pocket again. "Uh, yeah. Can you please point me to the cashier's booth, um, is it pronounced 'Karen'?"

"Yes, that's right." She smiled with full candy-red lips and led the way over the glass ramp. "Come with me." Her black heels clicked along the arching glass. "Just a common name spelled uncommonly, I guess. My father was a lot more creative with my brothers' names."

"Oh, yeah?" Drake asked absently, his attention suddenly lost in the pure ice blue water below the rust-colored railing. It was strange to not see the bottom. But hotels were all about illusion, so this had to be the latest and greatest in casino effects. Draw them in with fake lavishness, keep them in by catering to egos.

Caron smiled again. "This way." She hadn't answered his question, which meant the answer was personal and therefore fell outside the bounds of acceptable hostess banter.

They crossed the water to the other side, where the area opened to the main gaming floor surrounded by three rooms. Depending on the mood of the moment, this casino had it all.

The darkened blue-gray room on the left stretched further back than Drake could see. Filled with gyrating bodies, a thumping rhythm pulsed in time with blue lasers. A DJ, also in gray and blue, manned a half-moon stage and pumped his fist to the driving bass. The people danced in time to the beat, but it was not with the high-energy of other dance clubs. This was almost trancelike with swaying and slow head-bobbing. Maybe it was the late hour, and the DJ was prepping to close his set.

In the middle, a tastefully decorated red-lit lounge with white matte round settees offered furry matching throws and red accent pillows to lean on. He couldn't see the entire place in the dimness, but it was likely a bar or lounge. Unlike the rest of the club, nothing in that room was shiny or gleaming. The guests dressed tastefully, but only just so. And apparently, the rules for public affection were lax. There was a person, or multiple persons, for everyone there to be intimate with. Couples and groups sat in one another's arms kissing, chatting quietly, or making out.

"Just over this way," Caron motioned him to follow along the path past the white and red lounge. Along the wall and between the engaged romantics was a marble throne and a king with a serpent wrapped around his torso. A young man, tanned, muscular and shirtless, ran his hands over his male lover amid their lip-locked embrace. He looked to Drake with only his eyes and winked. Drake quickly turned his attention toward the enticing scent of food.

The partially walled off third area had see-through slats to herd customers one-way to the cashier's stands. This was a typical Vegas buffet. As they passed by, it surprised Drake to see people in line. "Don't you guys clear down by midnight?"

"Oh no, the buffet is always open," Caron gestured to the dining area where, like everywhere else in the casino, patrons filled the room. The winding buffet bar stretched impossibly far.

Signs over aromatic dishes described each represented continent's food in an enticing display. Steamed red lobsters, pink shrimp and fresh gray-white oysters chilled on beds of sparkling ice with bright yellow lemon wedges. Braised BBQ meats and golden chickens dripped fat on spits over flickering flames. Rich soups steamed, crispy salads audibly crunched. As with the rest of the casino, there was something here for everyone, sweet and pungent Asian cuisine, spicy Indian dishes, garlicky Italian pasta, and thick juicy steaks with loaded baked potatoes. Even the rectangular dessert bar gleamed with glittering sugared confections, decadent dark chocolate cakes, gelatos, pastries, and creme brulees. He hadn't walked in hungry, but Drake's mouth watered.

Through vertical curtained beads, they passed a large couple seated at a table with short stacks of dirty bowls and dishes. The couple had reached a corpulent size in the hundreds of pounds. They gnawed the gristle from rib bones and used pudgy fingers shiny with butter to crack open crab claws. The sounds were worst of all, almost like pigs grunting at a trough. Drake turned away, the growling in his stomach instantly ceased.

The main area contained every opportunity to gamble away money, from cards and dice to roulette and slot machines. The artwork, statues and advertisements all depicted the same idea: spend your money here to win piles more. Sequined beauties posed happily on piles of cash. Roman statues posed upon hills of treasure like ecstatic hoarders.

"There you are," Caron gestured to the cashier's booth, discreetly behind the gaming area in a subdued corner. "If you need further guidance, you know where to find me."

"I'll definitely holler," Drake replied with a grin.

The cashier's booth, although smaller than expected, was no less intimidating. Thick gold bars vertically lined the windows before black paneled keeping stacks of plastic and real cash safely separated from the public. The hulking banker with the close-cropped hair perched stiffly on a stool behind the bars at the only open window was no less imposing. His black jacket barely buttoned across his chest and his biceps threatened to bust the seams they strained under.

"Cashing out?" His deep voice was every bit as terrifying as his size.

"Uh, yeah. Just a sec." Drake fished the green and white chips from Vinny out of his pocket first, sliding them through the small window at the bottom of the bars. Inside of thirty seconds, the banker had his tallied total.

"That it?" His look was cold and hard.

"Um, no. Hang on." Drake dug into his other pocket and tentatively slid the black chip with red ticking through the window. This was the chip Vinny had practically thrown when emptying his pockets and life of this casino.

The banker's expression changed to mild surprise. "Where did you get this?"

Drake's heart rate picked up pace. "I'm a bartender. Someone generous tipped me with this. Guess he really liked the old-fashioned?"

"Old fashioned, huh?" The banker swiveled on his seat and picked up the phone, speaking quietly into it.

Exit stage left or see where this goes? Just when he needed them, his moral compass assistants were silent.

A single but equally large member of casino security appeared at Drake's side.

"You need to come with me."

12

"Hey, Ugly," Gad muttered to the pasty green horror as it glued its massive face to the entryway window of Pete's chapel. The front door stood open, and the breeze greeted Gad with the sinus-burning aroma of vinegar water. Pete stood on the porch with his squirt bottle and squeegee at the window.

"You know, at least I shaved this morning," Pete said, completely aware that Gad had addressed the green hell-beast.

"And a fat lot of good it did you," Gad replied, without missing a beat. Their back-and-forth patter had become a well-oiled, sardonic machine with years of practice. He stepped into the entryway. "Harriet! I've got your sneakers."

"Great!" Harriet stomped up the cellar steps. Panting from the top step, she added, "Did you remember the pickled herring?"

"In cream sauce and in mustard." Gad pulled the cold jars from the grocery bag with only minor disdain. "You didn't say what kind, so I got both."

"And the dark rye?" She reached his side and grasped his arm, her face full of hope.

"And the dark rye. I know a guy."

"You are just the bees' knees," Harriet said, hugging him with glee.

"The bees' knees? Is that a good thing?" Gad asked, with a skeptical eyebrow raised.

Pete shook his head. "Bee knees are tiny and, as far as I can tell, not very useful."

"Oh, what do you know?" Harriet tipped her head back, laughing.

Gad admired the new rosy flush in her cheeks. She had really turned a corner, smiling and making jokes of her own. It tempted him to say she was more like her old self, except he had no idea what she was like before the incident. She was a better version of Harriet than anyone had seen so far.

SLAM!

Harriet gasped and keeled back against the wall, her fingers splayed over her heart.

The alastor's huge palm stuck flat against the entryway window and an eye peeked playfully through its fingers at her.

"You royal pain in my ass." Pete scowled and strode toward the window.

"No, let me." Harriet swallowed hard and yanked her shirt down with determination. She swiped the spray bottle from his hand, slid the window wide open and stared into the alastor's grotesque, grinning face.

"Go away!" Without crossing the window's barrier, she gave the alastor's massive green-gold eye a long squirt of holy vinegar water. The roar of pain and keening wail that followed blew Harriet's hair straight back. The alastor's eye squeezed shut as it bubbled and blistered.

The alastor scrambled out of her reach, thumping and banging up the side of the chapel and onto the roof.

Gad burst out laughing. "Way to go, Harriet!"

"Good girl," Pete said. "Now give me back my spray bottle."

Harriet handed it over somewhat reluctantly. "You got any leads yet on how to make that thing vamoose?"

"What, you gettin' tired of my company already?" Pete sprayed the inside of the window and squeakily squeegeed it clean.

"No. I find you to be delightful outside of being an Elvis impersonator. That aside, I'd just like my freedom back."

"Well, it just so happens, that's why Gad's here on our mutual day off. We're headed just outside of town to visit my longtime friend, Dahlia."

"That is great news. Can't wait to hear what you find. Oh, I almost forgot! Did you hear the news about the head of Inferno?"

"Ah yes, saw it in the paper this morning. Ol' Vinny Luciano is turning state's evidence."

Gad's eyes popped open. 'Ol Vinny Luciano, the guy he'd just saved at Drake's bar. Gad had done as asked and called Vinny a cop car escort to bring him to the police station. The request was a much bigger deal than he initially realized. Seeing the maw of hell shut moments before grabbing you probably would make you turn over a new leaf. Suddenly, Gad felt even better about intervening in a reaper's work. A crime syndicate might be brought down by the soul he helped give a second chance. Things were looking up.

"Yeah," she breathed. "This could mean Inferno gets shut down soon."

"And that would apparently be the bees' knees," Pete added.

Harriet had pep in her step as she returned to the cellar stairs with her pickled herring, rye bread, and brand-new sneakers in hand.

Inferno being shut down would be a fantastic thing, Gad knew. They were into drugs and extortion, ruining lives, and sending demon spawn after their targets. He shuddered to think what else they might be up to.

"So, this Dahlia we're visiting. She a demonologist or something?" Gad fell into the armchair by the front door and watched the bony green tail swishing back and forth from the overhang.

"Or something like that." Pete dropped the bottle and squeegee into a box and walked toward the back. "Hey, wait a minute. Did she just say 'outside of being an Elvis impersonator'?"

"I think she did."

"The Monkeys were far better!" Harriet's voice rose from the basement.

Pete's face turned beet red, his lips shrunken into a mere dot under his nose. "She didn't just say..."

"Ooo. I think I left something in the car. See you there in a minute!" Gad shot to his feet and stepped out onto the porch.

A few minutes later, Pete slid into the driver's seat of his old mint green Cadillac.

"You know she was just yanking your chain."

"I know," Pete said, with a smirk. "I've been to the rodeo a few times."

13

D rake's muscles tensed; he was ready for anything as he walked between the security guards. He had no clue where they were taking him. The most he could get out of the burly man leading the way was, "Boss wants to see you." Never mind that Drake wasn't sure he wanted to see the boss; he clearly had no choice in the matter. On the bright side, they didn't have him by the arms or anything. Yet.

The larger of the two over-sized men escorting him held open a glass door. A wall of sound poured through with the promise of good times ahead. The mixture of club music, laughter, and hooting surrounded them beneath laser lights that swung and jumped across dark walls. Billowing fog rolled across the floor in front of the biggest, shiniest bar he had ever laid eyes on.

"Follow me," the other guard said. He stepped through the dual glass doors and straightened his black jacket.

Normally, Drake would have had to make his way through the congregating club-goers, but the security team's sheer mass and intimidation factor easily cut a swath to the back of the room.

In the center of the farthest wall, draping sheer black fabric and strings of sparkling black crystals obscured a booth on a raised dais. The security guard led Drake up the steps onto the dais and held the curtain back for Drake, who followed him in with a modicum of reluctance. The little voice in his head was back, and it was screaming now. *Run, run, run, run!*

In the center of the booth, sprawled causally atop velvet crimson cushions, a dark-haired man in a tailored, pinstripe suit reclined with his arms about the admirers to either side of him.

With his hands folded before his massive frame, the biggest guard leaned down to speak into the ear of the man in the booth. The guard's head blocked any way to see what they might be saying. He spoke at a volume that Drake would never be able to hear over the din. Drake glanced over his shoulder to a door marked "EXIT" across the room.

The guard nodded and straightened up, holding his hand out politely to the pretty men and women to either side of the man in the suit, who ran his hand over slicked back black hair, wavy to perfection, and made apologetic gestures to his follow-ers. Each returned his motions with gracious smiles and nods, grasping his hands and blowing kisses. His gaze fell to the round ass of a lady barely in white; he bit his lip and grabbed a handful playfully. She squealed and he mouthed clearly, "my place in an hour." She nodded, pink lips spread into a grin.

The man's gaze, still pleasant, still smiling, fell upon Drake.

Despite the smile, Drake's pulse picked up significantly. His palms prickled with sweat.

"Come, sit," the man said, nodding to the recently vacated booth space around him. Annoyingly, the security guard remained positioned next to the booth in hulking, intimidation mode. The rest of team remained at the bottom of the steps. That exit door was a million miles away.

Drake slid into the booth, eying the man and the area

around him for weapons. He didn't see any, but that didn't mean they weren't there.

"Hi," Drake said.

"Hello, my name is Xavier Ecko. And you are?" He held out his hand cordially.

"Drake." He gave Xavier one firm pump in the handshake and retracted his hand. He wasn't going to be anything more than civil unless someone gave him a reasonable explanation for detaining him like this.

"Drake, is it? Just the one name, like Madonna? Or Cher?" Xavier's lips curled up on one side, revealing a dimple. "Well, you must be an important person, then."

"I don't know about that," he said, but his tone said otherwise.

"Well, Drake, I can see you are polished with classic style. You hold yourself with confidence and poise. You must be a man of higher purpose. Tell me, are you a vice president, perhaps? A CEO?"

His words both flattered and surprised Drake. A CEO?

"Not yet, but I have aspirations, of course."

"Oh, but you are a leader, surely. That much is plain. You have the presence of a decision-maker. You must be a business owner then. Is it here, in Las Vegas?"

Drake held his breath and waited for him to laugh, the joke having gone far enough. But he didn't. Xavier's dark eyes looked into his expectantly.

"No. But I do work around here."

Xavier gestured to the crowd and, instantly, a server appeared at his side. "My friend's hand is empty, please get him a...?" Xavier looked to Drake for an answer to the question.

"Snakebite." He didn't want a thing, but a game was being played. He politely accepted the offer and chose something small and easily finished.

"Snakebite. Perfect." Xavier said to the server with a nod. The server touched the microphone of her headset and spoke into it as she turned to walk away.

"I'm not. I work not too far from here for a Michelin star restaurant." He felt a twinge of shame. This man genuinely believed he was someone important.

Xavier's expression transformed to pure surprise. "Doing what, pray tell? Do stop keeping me in suspense. Which hotel chain do you manage?"

"I'm at an upscale restaurant."

"Restaurateur, then. What is your eatery's signature dish? And who is your chef de cuisine?"

Drake grimaced. "Mr. Ecko, why am I here?"

Xavier smiled again and reached into his jacket.

Drake tensed, watching his hand like a hawk.

"Straight to it, then." His hand withdrew and placed something on the table, then pushed it toward Drake with his finger. It small enough in the darkened club that it took Drake a moment to recognize it.

"It was brought to my attention that you wanted the payout on this."

The red and black poker chip's gold writing shone in the swinging lights of the club.

Drake wouldn't give anything up. "And?"

Xavier's dark eyes glittered. "And a cash out of this value requires approval. I assumed it was a request from one of our shareholders, because, as you are most certainly aware, these chips are only given to our shareholders."

Drake's mind raced. "I earned it as thanks. A very high-profile player came in one night and I made sure he was well taken care of. This is what he dropped to me as heartfelt thanks." It wasn't a lie.

"And who was that?" Xavier said, eyebrows high.

Drake smiled his most winning smile. "I'm sorry, Mr. Ecko, I can't tell you that. What happens in Sin City stays in Sin City."

Impossibly fast, the server reappeared with a cocktail napkin and his shot of lime juice and bourbon. He picked it up and downed the shot, then held the empty shot-glass in his palm. "I'm a man whose tastes have always exceeded his means. So, I do what I can to be around the very best until the day it's finally mine."

"Do tell." Xavier leaned forward.

"I may not be a shareholder now, but I will be one day."

"Indeed. So what stage of your plan are you at right now?"

"I'm a purveyor of elixirs," Drake said, holding the empty shot-glass aloft. "But I'm always looking to find something a little more suited to my skills. I work my ass off and I work my way up. I don't waste a single opportunity."

"I see." Xavier sat back, considering. Mysteriously, the poker chip had disappeared from the table. "Tell me about your skills, Drake."

"Communication," Drake replied, without hesitation. The warmth of the snakebite crept through the tense muscles in his neck and shoulders and released his anxiety. His confidence was rising. "Having spent so much time listening to people and being there when they need to talk, I'm pretty damned perceptive. I've talked to so many types of people, I just know what they need and what they need to hear."

Xavier's focus on him intensified. He held up a finger to the server for another drink, and then leaned toward Drake. "So, you have people skills."

"Oh, it's way beyond that, Mr. Ecko."

"Call me Xavier."

"Sure, Xavier. So, a lot of folks come to the bar because they need something. They need a drink, sure. But they're down on their luck. You listen, you learn, you say what they need to hear and you brighten their prospects. They leave a little more hopeful. I think if you can take anyone in a certain mindset and you can get them to follow a different path, you're a born leader. I think my communication skills will lead to a floor management position in a VIP area someday, which is right up my alley. I can cater to those with finer tastes."

Xavier leaned in, very close. He tapped Drake's arm as he spoke. "Drake, I've found in such a role that those with finer tastes, those who really 'who have it all' quite often do not know what they really truly want."

Another snakebite appeared on the table on a fresh napkin, but Drake barely noticed the flash of the server's hand and flounce of the retreating skirt. He was focused on Xavier's next words.

"They have it all, you know. Are you up for playing a little game?"

Again, the little voice on Drake's shoulder yelled at him. But his mind was fuzzy and the adrenaline pumping through his veins made the voice hard to hear. "What kind of game?"

"A test of skills, you might say." He slid another small thing across the table. Two small things. It was a clear packet with four blue pills and another with two orange pills.

"Is that?" Drake began to say "drugs" but didn't want to say the word out loud.

"Oh, they're very minor mood enhancers, Drake. Nothing to worry yourself over, quite common in this club, really. But here's the deal. Do you see that table over there with the couple and a gentleman dressed in blue, all sitting together?" Xavier pulled back the dark curtains.

Drake stared through the dark and moving lights to a table on the opposite wall. "I see them."

"Convince them they need to take these pills. And here are the rules. One, you cannot lie about the pills and what they do.

Two, you may not take any yourself. Three, each person at the table must take at least one dose of either set of pills. Four, you must come back empty-handed."

"All of them?" Drake counted the pills in the bags again. He looked at Xavier, his heartbeat picking up pace. "It won't hurt anyone, right?"

"Oh, no," Xavier shook his head and patted Drake's hand. "As I mentioned, these are very mild. Now, the blue is a hallucinogenic and the orange is a form of ecstasy. Remember, if they ask, you must tell the truth."

Drake stared at the small, round pills and nodded slowly. The plan was already forming. He looked up suddenly. "Do I get anything if I win?"

"The Floor Manager position here at Inferno." Xavier replied. "If you lose, you leave Inferno, nothing gained."

Drake swallowed. For a moment, he was frozen in Xavier's gaze, unable to move or believe the offer at hand. This was his chance.

The corner of Xavier's mouth curled up. "Do you want to play?"

Drake grabbed the second shot, downed it, and slammed the empty glass on the table. "You're on." He swept both baggies into his pocket.

"I'll be watching, Drake," Xavier warned. "Remember the rules."

"Then watch this." Invigorated, Drake shot up from his seat and pushed through the warm bodies crowded around the bar. A server pushed past with a tray full of drinks. Drake deftly swiped one and made his way to the designated booth.

The couple were in the middle of a kiss when Drake slid into the booth next to the one in blue. "Dave, holy shit! I haven't seen you since, oh who knows, how long has it been?"

The boyfriend in the couple stared hard at Drake, his mouth

hanging open with a half-smile. "I'm sorry, I uh," he shook his head and shrugged. His girlfriend looked from her boyfriend to Drake and back, as though spectating a tennis match.

"It's Drake! Oh, come on, you remember." Drake scanned him. Tall, caramel skin, basketball jersey, goatee, shaved head. "From college, I came to all the games. You were, um, oh...what's the word..."

"Played center, yeah," the guy's eyes flickered at the connection. "Name's Logan, though. Dave was point guard."

"Dude, that's totally right, I'm sorry!" He lifted his hand up and held it out, and like clockwork, Logan grasped it and pulled it in for a bro-hug. "How you been? And who is this lovely lady?"

Before long, Drake knew every name, their favorite drinks, the concert they were in town for, where they were staying, and the wedding date Logan and Celeste were planning for. He steered the conversation to partying, and from partying, flawlessly spun the conversation back to Dave.

"You know what was great about Dave? He was the life of the party wherever he went. The guy could turn a wake into a rager, y'know what I mean? He had this knack for knowing who needed what, too. Like, that guy over there. He's having fun, but if had a little X, this would be the beginning of the best night of his life."

The guy in blue, Devin, snorted. "X? Ecstasy? That shit is so weak."

"So, what would you say I need?" Logan said, with one eyebrow raised.

Drake pretended to analyze him. "Religious experience. You look like someone to me who's been clean your whole life, and you've been waiting for the right moment to let your hair down with something not too hard, definitely not addictive, but life-changing." He pulled the orange pills out of his pocket. "Like these."

"What's that?" Celeste leaned over and poked at the baggie.

Drake pushed it closer to them. "Just a light hallucinogenic. Makes the lights prettier, people in pictures on the wall start to dance with you. Why do you think I brought these here? I was gonna' take 'em, but hey, you're the happy couple. You should celebrate! Congrats, they're on me."

"Aw, thanks man." Logan put out his hand and pulled the packet toward him.

Celeste's eyes widened and she shook her head. This was stepping outside the bounds.

"And these, these are X, so they go together." He leaned in and mock-whispered. "Makes sex even better, I swear."

Celeste reached for the other packet, but Devin's hand closed over the packet first. "Me first. I'm headed to the bar. You two do your thing. Catch ya' for lunch tomorrow." Without another word, he downed two pills, grabbed his drink and disappeared into the crowd.

Logan leaned in to hear the frantic whispers from Celeste. There was arguing and quite a bit of shrugging on Logan's part.

Drake could feel Xavier's stare, his chance at the role of a lifetime in this casino slipping away. He studied Logan's facial ticks as Celeste gestured her case, hands in the air. There it was. He didn't like being told what to do.

Drake reached out for the packet. "Oh, I'm sorry guys, I didn't want to cause any trouble in paradise. I mean, happy wife, happy life, am I right?"

Logan's hand slapped down on the packet. "Nah, no worries, bro. We'll both be happy in a few. She's just nervous is what's up, since we've never done this stuff before. But you got us, right?"

"Totally. This is the lowest of the low-end. Damn near legal. Only lasts a couple hours, tops. Just take two each."

Celeste's hardened expression relaxed a little. A minute later, the four orange pills were swallowed. Drake faked getting a call.

"I need to take this, but congrats again, you two!"

They smiled, and Logan reached out for another bro-hug before Drake slipped back into the crowd, his phone to his ear. A momentary pang hit him. Had he done the right thing? What if the drugs did hurt them somehow?

The thought was fleeting as he saw the congratulatory grin on Xavier's face and eased into the booth. The security guard dropped the curtains he had been holding out of the way for Xavier and they settled back in front of the booth.

"Well, Drake, you're going to have to give me your full name now. You're hired."

Drake soared. "It's Reiner, sir."

"Everybody, drinks all around! We're celebrating Mr. Drake Reiner, our new Floor Manager!"

A cheer went up from the crowd around the booth and bottles of champagne came flowing on trays as people he didn't know crowded the small booth. Corks popped. Foam and champagne flowed everywhere.

As Drake put a bottle to his lips and swigged, Xavier leaned in with a wicked grin.

"Tell me, Drake, do you have a girlfriend? Or boyfriend?"

"Not at the moment. Haven't had much time for dating," Drake shrugged, his face suddenly warm.

"Ah, now that's a shame. How about family? Anyone you spend time with not slaving away at work?"

Drake scowled, trying to quash the sudden discomfort intruding on his celebration. "No, they're all in California and Arizona. Does that change my chances with the job?"

"Oh no, not at all. Just getting to know my new head of house, is all." Xavier slid his arm around Drake's shoulders and gave him a playful jostle.

Drake's little voice was a mere echo in the background now

as he downed nearly half the bottle of champagne to the delight of his new friends cheering him on.

Xavier gave him a playful squeeze. "I'm so glad you came to us tonight, Drake. And we want to know all about you, what you like, what you hate. Tell us everything and don't spare a detail."

Drake's mind was suddenly very fuzzy and compliant. His new boss wanted to know all about him. This felt good. Maybe like a new home. "Sure," he blinked, trying to clear the sudden dizziness. "Where do you want me to start?"

Xavier grinned. "How about...what's the worst thing you've ever done?"

DRAKE CRACKED open one blurry eye. Somewhere above him, his reflection peeped back at him through one half-open eye. Weirder yet, a topless dirty blond sprawled across the white pillow to his right. Fragments of the night before swam through his mind, disjointed and hazy. There was a bar, new friends, gambling, too much top-shelf tequila, someone playing guitar...a magician?

"Kaylee? Katie?" he muttered toward the dozing woman. His answer was a snore.

"She's Kalynn. I'm Cameron," a male voice behind him replied.

Drake shot up, wiping his eyes clear. He realized with even more of a start that he was completely naked.

"Relax, Drake. We invited you here. You were too wasted to go home." The blue-eyed man next to him had wavy dark-blond hair, a perfectly trimmed beard, and piercings in both ears.

"Right. Cameron and Kalynn." He remembered winning at the dice table because Kalynn blew on the dice in his hand. She sat in his lap at the bar afterward. Foggy images of the guy next to him ordering another round of shots confirmed that he must have come here willingly at some point.

"What time is it?" Drake rubbed his eyes again.

"Almost noon," Cameron said. Also naked, he slid out of the massive hotel bed and sidled to the bathroom, stretching.

This wasn't a hotel room. This was a suite in Inferno. Drake peered over the edge of what had to be three white king beds side by side on a platform. The walls, the curtains, the carpets, the pillows and the leather armchairs were all crimson.

His left shoulder ached. He slid out of bed and stepped gingerly down three stairs to the window to pull back the blackout curtain. Daylight breeched the dark suite. They were floors above the Strip. All of Vegas stretched out before him for miles under dark clouds.

Why didn't his head feel like a freight train had run through it? He remembered the tequila. A bender like that should have meant a stomach-churning combo of migraine and nausea. If anything, he had a hankering for a sub-sandwich, a gallon of ice water, a shower, and another nap.

It was time to hit the road and go home. His shift would be starting in hours and he needed to eat and get cleaned up. Drake quickly shimmied into his work clothes, sour with tequila sweat and who knew what else.

The shower turned on and steam poured out of the bathroom in a billowing puff toward the bedroom's canned ceiling lights. Cameron stuck his head around the corner. "Join me?"

In that moment, Drake really wanted to remember his stay with Cameron and Kalynn. Katie. Kathie. "I can't, I gotta..." Drake faltered, jerking his thumb to the door. "I need to go get ready for my shift tonight."

Cameron raised an eyebrow. "You mean tomorrow night?"

Drake felt his eyes pop open wide.

"Wow, you really tied one on last night, didn't you? Your

orientation here is tomorrow night, bud. In fact, I'm pretty sure I work under you now. You're Floor Manager, fifth floor."

Drake shut his eyes, desperate to summon more information pertaining to what Cameron had just said. A sharp-dressed man, dark hair slicked back, dark eyes, devilishly handsome. Gray streaks at his temples. Widow's peak. Dramatic name.

He checked his pockets and pulled out what he could find. A business card, his wallet, his keys, some large blue pills, some small orange pills and a pair of silky red panties.

"Oh, those're mine." Cameron sauntered over and retrieved them casually. "See you tomorrow night, bossman," he added with a wave and disappeared into the steamy shower.

Drake inspected the black business card with embossed gold writing.

Xavier Ecko - Casino Property General Manager

He flipped the card over, a hazy memory of this man writing instructions on the back. In gold felt-tip ink, it read:

Congrats, my new Floor Mgr! - X
FLOOR 2, 6pm, Thurs.

He'd impressed this man, this Xavier, when he'd challenged him into talking someone into doing something they didn't want to do apparently. What was it? It was the pills in his pocket. Xavier had given him a small handful from a gold snuffbox and challenged him to talk not one, but several specific people into taking either the blue pills or the orange pills. Xavier had a weird sense of humor, he had to hold his stomach laughing when he watched Drake sweet talk the tall muscular guy into taking two. And Xavier lost the bet when Drake got all three to partake. That was it. That's how he'd won the new job. Oh, and the "-X". His new manager preferred being called "X".

Drake breathed in. Floor Manager. That paid nearly triple

what a bartender could earn in a year, tips included. Time to go give the news to the old place. He felt a twinge of regret as he opened his wallet to check the totals on his winnings. They had given him his break as a dishwasher, then a bar back, and finally made him a full-fledged bartender. He might not have gotten this far if they hadn't taken a chance on moving him up internally instead of hiring more experienced bartenders, which Vegas had aplenty.

Drake pulled out his debit card, which had a receipt wrapped around it. He vaguely remembered saying, "Put it all on my card." With a wince, he pulled the receipt fully open to see how much he had spent gambling from his checking account. The bottom read, "DEPOSIT $16,660.00 - BOLGIA RESORTS ITNL".

His body went rigid with shock. It was a good shock, but too much all at once. The receipt fluttered from his hand to the floor. With a shaking hand, he snatched it back up and whipped out his cell phone, opening his bank account application. And after a grueling forty-two second load-time, his bank account balance confirmed the deposit. He'd had the gambling streak of his life last night!

Drake dashed out the hotel door and strode down the hall, punching in the phone number to his old casino's HR office with a trembling finger. He stepped into the elevator and put his phone to his ear. The hotel's server, delivering a tray of room service grub, gave him an awkward smile.

"No time to quit like the present!" Drake grinned to him as the elevator doors slid closed.

14

The Hoover Dam sits astride the Colorado River in a section known as Black Canyon on the border of Nevada and Arizona. Constructed in the midst of the Great Depression, the dam was 726 feet in height, 1,244 feet in length, and 45 feet across at the top. It was also one of Nevada's biggest tourist attractions, full of people most any time during the day. This meant that Pete would circle the free parking area repeatedly until he could claim a space just to avoid the $10 parking fee that the garage charged, a habit that secretly drove Gad nuts. If that wasn't bad enough, it also meant they would need to cross the length of the bridge to meet with Dahlia.

After parking and getting out of the car, Gad sighed and fell into line behind Pete. He kept his hands stuffed in the front pocket of his sweatshirt, with his hoodie up and his head down.

The wind kicked up and a great gust blew his hoodie back. As he snatched at it, Gad unintentionally lifted his gaze to the road ahead and groaned at the sight before him. The ghosts of those who'd thrown themselves to their deaths from atop the bridge lined the protective wall in front of them, repeating their final act in death as they had in life. He could hear them weeping and crying as they climbed over the barrier and leapt off the other side, their terrified screams echoing and overlapping with one another as they vanished from view. Gad yanked his hoodie back up and held it pinched shut, doing his best to ignore what he was seeing and hearing.

"Why did she want to meet here of all places?" Gad asked, making no effort to disguise his irritation.

Pete shrugged. "She hates Vegas, but she loves this dam. It's a pleasant place."

"Says you."

At his tone, Pete's eyes widened, and he turned abruptly to face Gad.

"Is it bad?" he asked, pushing the hoodie back far enough that he could get a look at Gad's eyes.

"Are you kidding me? Do you know how many people offed themselves here? C'mon, let's get across before they notice me. I don't have very much salt on me," Gad said grudgingly.

"Rum?"

"Nope."

"White sage?"

"Nada."

"We coulda' parked closer," Pete offered, picking up the pace to the Visitor Center.

"Really? Now you say that?"

"There! There she is." Pete pointed to the patinaed statue of a winged figure just across from the visitor center. Beneath the statue stood a strikingly tall person with ear-length platinum blond curls flailing in the wind. Pete had described her as somewhat intimidating in size and Gad could only agree.

She smiled at them and waved as they drew closer.

"Hello, my dear." Pete threw his arms wide and wrapped her in them.

"Pete," she returned the hug with equal fervor.

"This is my best friend's son, Gideon."

Gad stuck his hand out. "Gad for short. Pleased to meet you, Dahlia."

"Pete's told me quite a bit about you, Gad," Dahlia grasped his hand.

Gad felt instantly content. With her fair skin, high-cheekbones, aquiline nose and curls framing her temples, it was like looking into the face of a Michaelangelo sculpture. Her clear blue eyes and peach cheeks complimented perfectly bowed pink lips. No make-up, no fake anything. Just natural beauty.

"Gad?" The corner of her lip curled upward as she politely waited for him to release her hand.

"Oh, sorry," he said, letting go. He felt his cheeks grow warm and bashfully stepped back.

"So, to cut to the chase, I told her about your sight." Pete looked to Gad with reassurance.

"That bridge must be a treat, then?" she said with a frown.

Dahlia spoke with a soft British accent, making her that much more charming. Torn between the shock of his secret out there without his permission and wanting to ask her out for coffee, words failed him. "Can you see them, too?" he managed at last.

"Oh no, not me. I'm what you would call a researcher of the paranormal." Her smile was like warm rays of sunlight on Gad.

"Now don't downplay your own gifts, sweetheart," Pete chided and turned to Gad. "She gets impressions from stuff. Touches a thing and gets its history, so to speak. Between that and knowing way more about everything supernatural than this old dog, and that's why we're here."

. . .

"GAD, seeing what you've seen, I don't envy you one bit. I'm certain you could share ghost stories that could make even the boldest cry." She lifted her eyebrows. "And Pete tells me you can see the death dealers in your daily work."

"Reapers? You know about reapers, too?"

"YES, their lore and what I've gathered from a lot of books. That 'Don't Fear the Reaper' song has it all wrong." She dismissed Blue Oyster Cult with a wave of her hand.

"I hate that song." Gad had never wanted so much to sit with someone and talk. Just talk.

"And its many remakes," she agreed.

"Hey, I like that song," Pete muttered, leaning on the statue's black marble pedestal.

"And to make things worse, one just said something to me this week," Gad scowled.

Dahlia's casual posture straightened. "It spoke to you?"

"Yeah. It pointed at my watch and said 'soon'."

Pete stood up, too. "Your dad's watch?"

"The very same." Gad pulled it from his front pocket, flipped it open and held it out. The time and date, as always when it wasn't alerting him to a nearby death, read October 31, 11:59pm. The hand on the small dial pointed down.

Dahlia's expression was unreadable as she spoke. "This was your father's pocket watch?"

"Yeah, James's," Pete replied, his face now etched with worry.

"And do you know where he got it?"

"No," Gad shook his head. "But this is how I know where a reaper will show up. This watch tells me when and where the nearest death will be. I always have a few minutes to get there before the reaper does."

Pete reached to take the watch from Gad.

"Don't touch it, Pete!" Dahlia said sharply.

Alarmed, Pete withdrew his hand. "And why not?"

Dahlia heaved a sigh, silent for a moment. "If you touch it, you will know when you are going to die."

"What?" The color drained from Pete's face. "What're you saying, Dahlia?"

Gad stared at the watch face, suddenly sick. "This is weeks from now. You're saying-"

"The watch is telling you that the reapers will come to...collect...on the last hour of the last day in October." Dahlia spoke her words carefully.

Gad couldn't stop the quavering of his voice. "And the little hand here, it's pointing..."

"Down."

"Dahlia, I know we came here to talk about that little revenge demon problem, but" Pete leaned on the statue, his face pale.

"This problem overshadows that by far," she finished.

Gad was trying to draw breath, but the more air he took in, the lighter his head got. His heart knocked on his chest as he stared at that little watch hand pointing down. He saw those elongated obsidian claws wrapping around his ankles, the yellow eyes crinkling with ghoulish delight at his own feet.

Tingling or numbness in the hands and fingers. Sense of terror, or impending doom or death. Breathing difficulties.

"Hyperventilation," he wheezed out loud just before his tunnel vision pinpointed completely, and his knees collapsed beneath him.

～

"The reapers rarely say a word, their purpose is fulfilling the completion of life's cycle. But if this one truly spoke to Gad, something is amiss." Dahlia's voice floated on the breeze.

"Well, how do we find out? Only Gad can see them. Can he talk to the damned things?" Pete crossed his arms over his chest.

The surface under Gad felt hard and plastic. They had laid him on a bench. His head pulsed with what had to be the leftover adrenaline in his blood post-panic attack.

"Let me research to see if that's possible. But I will say this. Noble as it may be for Gideon to save lives and turn those from darkness to light, ultimately he is interfering with the universal balance."

"Dahlia, he's pulling souls out of the hellfire and giving them another chance to be lifted to grace!"

"Yes Peter, I agree with you. Of course, I want that as well, or I wouldn't be here right now. What I'm saying is that reapers are indifferent to the struggle between light and dark. Their entire purpose is to maintain universal balance and not take sides. In changing the destinies of these individual souls, he may have pissed them off. Had Gideon ever done anything that you're aware of to draw Hell's attention?"

Pete chuffed. "If he did, he's hidden it from me. Been nothin' but a good kid his whole life. So, unless there's a secret serial killer personality hidden somewhere in his brain, I got no clue why he wouldn't be heaven-bound."

"Wait just a damned minute, people." Gad sat up, his heart pumping fast again, this time with hope. "If I can keep people from dying, why can't we stop *me* from dying? I've stopped death tons of times. We know destinies can be changed, I change them all the time!"

"I'm with ya', Gad. But how do we do that?" Pete said.

"Pete, Gad, let me work on that. Let's meet here tomorrow. I will research the collectors."

"Can we help? Please?" Gad implored.

"Gad." Pete squeezed his shoulder.

"Trust me, Gad. If there's an answer, I'm your best shot," Dahlia's lips curved softly upward.

"So, we meet here tomorrow, first thing, at the pointy statue," Gad stood, his fists balled with determination.

"Yes. And they're called the Winged Figures of the Republic." Dahlia scanned over the thirty-foot tall bronze figure stretching its arms and wings to the sky. "They guard the dam, keeping humanity safe from a force which, if unleashed, would cause the ultimate destruction of countless souls. They're part angel, part strength of man. That's why I like this place. It gives me hope."

Listening to her, Gad forgot his woes and relaxed. There was something about Dahlia he knew he could trust absolutely.

PETE SLAMMED his car door shut and turned to Gad with steely eyes. "Son, if you got something to tell me you haven't already, now's the time."

Gad fought the urge to shrink back against his side of the car. "Pete, I swear to you I have no earthly clue why this watch says I'm doomed to..." he swallowed hard, unable to say the last word. Then it came to him. "Wait. Do you think it was when I opened its box? I...I might've killed dad's soul. I might be a murderer. That's probably why I'm damned."

"You did not kill your father," Pete said through gritted teeth. "We've gone over this a thousand times, Gad."

Gad's face grew warmer as his emotional control dwindled. "But you don't know for sure, Pete. He told me never to open the watch box and I did it anyway, and-"

"And he disappeared, Gad. You dropped a watch and he disa-ppeared," Pete annunciated each syllable, spittle flying from his mouth. "Not murdered. You can't kill a ghost."

Gad bit his lip. "I think you can."

"And I think you can't. If ghosts could be killed, we'd be rich in the ghostbusting business. But no, you can only banish them from returning somewhere, trap them, or help them move on. So again, for the thousandth time, your dad's spirit is out there somewhere."

"I know. You think the watch somehow banished him from the cabin. But I've been through the woods over and over Pete. I've combed every piece of dirt within miles of the cabin and there's no sign of him." Shame and years of pain poured through Gad, tears spattering his jeans. He was a grown-ass man who faced death daily, and here he was, crying like a child.

Strong arms pulled him close. "I know, Gad. I know."

Gad shuddered. This was all too much. He wiped his eyes, seeing over Pete's shoulder the scores of jumpers on the bridge repeating their last actions. The thought to just join them and get it over with briefly flickered in his mind's eye.

"Hey, you up for another road trip?" Pete said with determination.

"What if I say no?"

"You're stuck with me, then." Pete turned the engine over and the car sputtered to life.

"Where are we going?"

Pete put the car into reverse and swung it out onto the road, dropping the gear into drive. "Buckle up, son. We're going to the cabin."

15

"Why the hell are we going to the cabin?" Gad's less than enthusiastic tone bordered dangerously close to whining. He caught the sound of his own voice and cringed.

"That watch. We need to figure out how your dad ended up with it and what it really is."

Dad. So tenacious, he would never let a little thing like death stop him. He had a son to take care of, after all. His wife's spirit had long since moved on, tragically moments after bringing Gideon into the world. The doctor did everything she could, to no avail.

Throughout his childhood, Dad would gaze at him with a soft smile and say, "He had her dimples and bluest-blue eyes". It was she who had named him Gideon after her husband's religious grandfather, but Gad was the nickname Dad gave him. Gad was what he preferred.

When his father suffered a heart attack in the cabin while Gad was out in the forest at the age of fifteen, James didn't go with his reaper to the light. Instead, as his father told the story, he told the reaper to piss off and it did so, leaving ghostly James to raise his son to the age of nineteen. That was when Gad committed what he referred to as the unforgivable act.

The deafening patter of a sudden deluge drowned out the comforting purr of the Cadillac's engine; such was the weather in late summer Nevada. Pete guided the Cadillac up the old road to Gad's Charleston Mountain cabin, the only commodity he had to his name thanks to the inheritance from his father.

"Wait here, I'll turn off the alarm," Gad said.

Pete cut the engine and Gad threw open the car door to the warm pelting rain drops. His boots crunched on wet gravel as he strode up the path and fumbled keys slick with water.

He had grown up here. He should feel at home. Instead, Gad shifted from one foot to the other, his unease growing. He pushed the key into the deadlock slow enough to feel the tick of tumblers falling into line.

His stomach rolled. It wasn't the familiar back-of-the-neck free-falling sensation that always accompanied the presence of something otherworldly. This place was safe from all of that; Dad had taken every precaution. The only place safer was Pete's chapel. No, this feeling was more guilt with a side of sorrow and nuances of fear.

The paint on the door trim made it stick in the humidity. Gad gave it a good heave with his shoulder and the door popped, swinging open. The alarm beeped rapidly and Gad punched in the code on the console just inside the door, setting it to stand-by.

Something moved from the wall in front of him to the shadows. Gad froze, his heart thudding. Achingly slow, he reached for the light switch and flicked it on. The overhead fluorescent overhead flickered once, twice, and blue-white light filled the kitchen and living room.

A small brown thing flitted about in the corner against the ceiling.

"Damn." Gad flexed his fingers, letting the fight or flight tightness drain from his arms and legs. He snatched up the nearest thing he could find to corral his small friend; a dusty but large towel from the kitchen counter.

"Hello, you little myotis septentrionalis."

Gad cautiously approached the small, Long-Ear Bat and, when the moment was right, swept the frightened creature gently into the towel. Before it could react, he wheeled out onto the porch and stood on tiptoe with the towel up toward the bat house on the column under the eaves. Eager to get away, the bat crawled up into the safety of the dark box almost instantly.

Gad had built that bat house with his father and burned the finishing touch of a bat image into the front with a soldering iron. His father had always encouraged Gad to get outside and explore, which led to his love of tracking and observation. How many hours had he spent exploring these woods, climbing trees and sketching the things he found in his leather journal? Birds, bats, foxes, flowers, insects...if it lived anywhere he could get to, he had drawn it in his journal, adding its name, species, and distinguishing characteristics next to the image just as his father had taught him. Every day, he had something new to bring home and look up in the encyclopedias on the shelf.

He stepped in and shut the door, chuckling at the sight of the old dusty volumes still on the bookshelf. They'd had a computer with a 56k modem that they could use to occasionally get online, but Dad didn't like to tie up the only phone line. Same thing for TV and movies; there wasn't any cable company access line out in the middle of Charleston Mountain. His dad had bought a little satellite dish at one point, but after hours on the roof with no viable signal, the dish got left in the shed. Gad's TV time was limited to the few channels the antennae could bring in, like PBS. Otherwise, it was an hour's trip into town to buy a new DVD or see the latest action adventure at the multiplex. Add to that the fact that Dad insisted on homeschooling Gad and, well, it was safe to say that Gad ended up lacking in social skills by the time he had been old enough to go to high school. "Painfully shy" would be the nice way that new teachers described him. Yet it was not descriptive enough for the crippling insecurity that overwhelmed him when he went into town.

The books on the shelf above and below the encyclopedias were all well-worn and loved. His finger drifted up to run the surface of each cracked and timeworn spine. His finger came to rest on the gray spine of To Kill a Mocking Bird, a pang of longing gripped him. This was Dad's favorite book to quote and to teach Gad from.

"You never really understand a person until you consider things from his point of view - until you climb into his skin and walk around in it."

How poignant old Atticus's words had been for young Gideon who, ever since he could remember, had always had others reaching out to him for help. This was why that his father had kept Gideon sequestered in the middle of a forest and away from everything. Their house, built on dirt sown with salt and blessed in the multiple ways of varying religions, contained hexes, charms, talismans, and all manner of hoodoo, all to protect his son. Because Gideon could see the dead, and the dead could see him. Just like his father before him.

"Everything okay in here?" Pete stuck his rain-drenched head through the door.

"Yeah, c'mon in. Just had to set a lost critter free is all."

Pete went straight to the braided rug in the hall and kicked it aside. He lifted the ring in the floor and pulled the trapdoor open, which automatically set the lights in the cellar blinking to life.

Dad had never been a "let's throw the pigskin around" kind of guy. Depending on what his problem of the week was, it was more like "toss me the holy water". This cellar had been his office at a job that no one paid him a steady salary for. Dad and Pete worked together as a team to banish unfriendly spirits and entities for those troubled by their presence. Pete didn't have the sight, but he had the power and knowledge of the Catholic church behind him. With James's guidance, they were a ghost-banishing powerhouse.

Pete stepped down into the cellar that, almost item for item, exactly mirrored his own. Besides the extra bed and fridge, his father designed the basement to house the tools of their trade. Bibles, journals, illuminations and mythos lined the shelves. Intricately carved boxes of rowan and willow housed powerful magical wards and curses. Holy water, holy texts, holy canolies. It was all in this cellar, including a few rare artifacts from both sides of the battle.

Gad stepped over to the tinted mirror hanging on the wall in an old dark frame and stared into it, letting his eyes relax. One by one, people appeared in the frame within casino walls, passing by in their business casual dress code, drinks in hand.

"Why did Dad have this? He would never tell me, always just joked that it was gambling TV."

Pete sighed, joining him to watch the passersby. "The mirror has a twin. It's showing us what's going on where it hangs. We can talk about this later though, it's not why we're here."

"So, you want the watch box."

"I want the watch box. Help me find it."

Gad pressed his lips tightly together. "I know where it is."

Moving over to the workbench in the corner, he bent down and pulled open the doors to the cupboard beneath it. Past the cursed feather pen, behind the cursed Japanese tea set, and next to the cursed amulet was, in Gad's mind, the cursed pocket watch box. It's why he had hidden it in the "Do Not Touch" cupboard. While technically not a cursed object, he didn't want to see it. Gad pulled the dreaded box forth from the back of the cupboard and handed it to Pete.

"Huh." Pete squinted at the wooden casing's rudely carved pictographs and words across every surface. "Sumerian, Egyptian, Hebrew. He's got a little of everything on here."

"Any of it make sense to you?"

"Yes. And no," Pete frowned, examining each side. "The ones I understand basically say 'keep out.' I think your dad wanted the pocket watch hidden from sight."

"Why?"

"That's what we need to figure out."

Gad jumped to his feet and held the watch out at arm's length. "Well, shit. Should we put this back in there, then?"

"Nah." Pete pushed Gad's hand back. "From what I can tell, these workings had a one-time use. Box opens, and that's all she wrote. Like here, lookit this one," he pointed to a symbol that, as far as Gad could tell, was a kind of triangle over a box with a squiggle. "This is druidic, kind of like a low-jack on your important secret. If someone who isn't the spell caster uncovers the secret, it throws out a spiritual alert to the owner."

Gad's slinking feelings of guilt suddenly dissipated with a new realization. He shot to his feet. "Pete, what if one of the spells on there had something to do with dad's spirit disappearing? Is that possible?"

Pete turned the box over in his hand, taking in James' scratchings and carvings. "Sure, you could be onto something. There're more than a few on here I've never seen before. Between the two of us, Jim was the ancient occult expert. I'll need to do some research. Let's check his reference books, see if we can figure out what he was up to. And then hopefully, something he put on here will give us a clue on that pocket watch."

Gad dumped out a nearly empty plastic crate and, paying no heed to the layers of dust and grime he was covering himself in, helped Pete load it with books on magic, rites and arcane knowledge.

The watch's warded box had only appeared shortly after his father's heart attack. Dad had stressed, over and over, that Gad never open the box. Every time Gad had asked why, he got a different inane answer.

"There're pixies in there, you'll set them free to spoil the milk."

"You'll send us back in time to the age of dinosaurs."

"You'll open a portal to Limbo."

It had taken four years for the fit of burning curiosity to overwhelm Gad's common sense. It had been a rough week for them both, one in which Dad had argued for Gad to consider attending the junior college at night, and Gad refusing to leave the cabin. Motivated by both rebellion and the need to know what hid within, he waited for his father to settle into reading for the evening and retrieved the carved box from under his bed. He carefully undid the knotted sisal and lifted the lid to a wadded piece of burlap. He unfurled the cloth to find a shining silver pocket watch on a chain.

"Gideon!" Dad's voice bellowed from the living room and, in a flash, he was at Gad's side. "Close the-"

Confusion and fear flooded his senses. He startled, knocking the box over. The watch tumbled from the box, and a blinding flash of light filled his room. Then, silence. His father was gone.

This was the memory that kept Gad away. Being in the cabin was a reign of guilt. Regret enveloped him now, silencing any further chit chat.

When it was finally time to leave, it hadn't been soon enough for Gad. Pete made his way to the car with a dusty box filled with an array of odd items and old books. Gad switched off the lights, shut the door and set the dead bolt. He left the cabin empty-handed, but the repressed memories that had bubbled to the surface would come home with him, resurfacing in the same nightmare he'd had ever since his father's disappearance.

16

Back in Vegas the next day, Gad's ten-hour shift roaming the streets felt weird. Sure, he answered every call he was near. He got the frail old man in the nursing home to his doctor when the man's walker slipped and left him sprawled on the floor. He got the dangerously dehydrated college kid to the ER after one too many whiskey highballs left him unconscious at Harrah's. And while the late-night escort stabbing at the roulette table had turned out to be less alarming than imagined - she'd exaggerated the wound a lot on the 911 call - it still didn't qualify to Gad as weird. What felt weird was the fact that he let the pocket watch buzz and light up, unheeded. This day was what a normal EMT should experience: get the request for help from dispatch and respond. Not once did he veer off course to follow the watch's blinking death compass. And damned if he didn't have to yank that burning hunk of metal from his front pocket and toss it into his lunch cooler, shutting it away to buzz angrily in its smallish insulated prison.

Each time the guilt of a potential lost soul crept to the forefront of his conscience, he stuffed it back down with an out-loud reassurance to himself that this was the way things were supposed to happen. Naturally. Without his interference. And by the end of his shift and exactly seven ignored reaper alarms later, he knew there was no way he would sleep that night. Gad pulled Mercy into the parking lot of Drake's casino and parked.

"Hey, hey! Well, if it isn't the Angel of Death. What up, Goody Two Shoes?" Fellow EMT Richard Hartley grinned from his bar stool, his beer bottle lifted toward Gad. To his right sat a scruffy guy in a similar EMT uniform who Gad had never seen him before. Sparse but longish dark brown hair hung limply above black glasses. The scruff of his five o'clock shadow clung in patches to pale doughy skin. He raised his beer to Gad with a quizzical yet pleasant smile.

"Hey, Dick," Gad replied with emphasis on the "d".

"D'aw, you still care," Richard announced with a mock sniffle, throwing an arm over Gad's shoulder for an inebriated greeting. "Take a seat, I'll buy."

"You got me last time," Gad slid onto the red bar stool on his left.

"I know. Doesn't matter. Hey," Rich signaled the bartender who, to Gad's surprise, was not Drake. "Whatever my friend here wants."

The black-haired beauty paused her glass cleaning in anticipation of Gad's order.

Without Drake, Gad struggled to recall the name of that thing he liked. "It's a, um. Whiskey, kinda sweet, kinda bitter. Shit." Gad massaged his temples, willing the name to loosen from wherever it stuck in his head.

"Whisky sour?" the bartender asked with a shrug.

Gad shook his head with a scowl.

"Manhattan?" Rich snorted. "What are you, a woman?"

"Hey," the bartender warned with a single eyebrow raised.

"Big, big ice cube." Gad was running out of descriptors.

"Old-fashioned!" Scruffy guy lit up, pointing to Gad with certainty.

"Right! That please."

"I'm Sam, by the way," Scruffy guy stuck his hand out around Rich's back and pumped Gad's offered hand. "Sam Beany. I ride with Rich."

"For First Response West?"

The bartender slid the old-fashioned into Gad's hand. He wasted no time for that first gulp of the amber liquid, enjoying the heavy bittersweet burn down the back of his throat. Sweet emotional detachment was just around the corner.

"Yeah, at least until I've fulfilled my ride-along hours. I'm almost done and then, free-agent."

"He's been couch surfing and riding around with me while Grady's in Hawaii," Rich said and tipped his bottle to his lips. His eyes grew suddenly wide, and he grabbed Gad's wrist. Gad nearly spit a mouthful of whiskey across the bar.

"Gad, you own your own successful little business. Why not expand routes with another driver or two?" Rich turned away from Gad before Gad could protest, the sudden swallowing of too much liquid causing a trail of pain down his esophagus like swallowing a ball bearing.

"This guy is *the best*." Rich continued his adoration of Gad with ever-growing excitement. "For reals. It's why we call him the Angel of Death. I know, I know, it sounds bad." Rich waved his nearly empty beer bottle for emphasis. "But it's because he somehow always gets his ass to wherever we're needed before anyone else. Like, impossibly fast. Like an EMT angel." He turned back to Gad. "Sam here is a really good egg, no joke. I'm sure you could use a couple more wagons, am I right?"

Gad's face was hotter than sin. And the whiskey wasn't helping. "I've been managing okay solo, Rich."

"Yeah, maybe, but what about growing your business? You've

made a dependable name with Mercy being the fastest response in town."

Sam, whose bright red face looked like Gad's felt, sheepishly waved Rich off. "Hey, no pressure. If you ever feel like you need a buddy for a day or another driver, just keep me in mind."

There was something about Sam's demeanor that, in Gad's gut, assured him Sam was genuinely a nice guy.

"Gimme' your number, Sam. Things have been hectic lately, so let me give it a think."

"Oh, I uh. Wait, really?" Sam's expression morphed from embarrassed to confused to hopeful.

"Sure. I can't guarantee anything, but I'll think about it."

"Oh well, cool! Thanks," Sam pulled a pen from his arm pocket and dashed out his info on a cocktail napkin.

Gad tucked it into his back pocket. "Thanks."

"Good deal, Sammy." Rich clinked his bottle to Sam's.

"Y'know, now that we've gotten to know each other, Rich, I feel safe in telling you that only my mom calls me that."

"My little forever virgin?"

Sam rolled his eyes. "When I get my next gig, I'll not miss you so hard."

"Oh, you know that's not true."

While the jibes continued, Gad leaned over the counter to the bartender. "Scuse me, did Drake call in sick tonight?"

"Drake? No, Drake quit a couple days ago."

Confusion flooded Gad's slightly tipsy brain. "Sorry, did you just say that Drake quit?"

The one eyebrow went up again as she masterfully combined the contents of two bottles into a glass with dark cherries. "I did. Drake said he got a new shwank job someplace down the road. No notice or anything."

That made no sense. He stared at his drink. While he would definitely be open to new jobs, Drake was loyal to this place.

How many times had Gad heard the story of how the place brought him up from a dishwasher to the head bartender? But he gave no notice? Maybe Drake was in some kind of trouble?

"Hey guys, I'm sorry but I gotta go."

Both EMTs frowned. "But you just got here," Rich said sulkily.

"You need a ride? I can call a cab?" Sam stood, pulling his cell phone from his pocket.

"There're cabs out front. I'll leave Mercy here and come back tomorrow."

"Oh, right," Sam smiled sheepishly. "I'm new to Vegas, forgot."

"Anyway, it was great meeting you, Sam."

"Right, you too." Sam shook Gad's hand again.

"Thanks for the drink, Dick," Gad slapped Rich's arm.

Instead of the expected return fire, Rich looked to him quizzically. "Everything ok, man?"

"I hope so," Gad said and headed for the door.

THE TIME, according to the microwave, was almost one in the morning as Gad slipped through the front door. To his surprise, every room in the house blazed with light. Even more surprising were the half-filled moving boxes in the kitchen and on the landing.

"Drake?"

The sounds of tape peeling and ripping stopped.

"Up here, G. Don't freak out, I can explain."

Gad was certain that no amount of explaining would calm the sea of roiling acid that was his stomach. He had hardly anything in savings and could barely afford his groceries, gas, and half the rent.

Drake had a small stack of boxes to his left, a disorganized pile of electronics, and dress clothes and valuables on the right.

"I'd normally say 'how are you doing', but I think I should just skip straight to 'what the fuck, Drake'?"

"First off, let me assure you, you'll be just fine, dude. I've already paid my half of rent for this month and then the next two, so you've got the whole place to yourself for the next three months. That should be plenty of time to-"

"Find a new roommate?" The words were like ash in Gad's mouth. They had lived together since Gad had first moved out five or six years ago. Since his father's death. Gad had gone from having no one to having Drake as a friend and a mentor to life's social niceties and pitfalls. And Gad had been there to cheer Drake on whenever Drake felt as though he'd never be worth more than a dishwasher in a so-so casino. Drake wasn't exactly the best friend a guy could have, but he was Gad's best friend. Or at least, he had believed Drake was.

Drake pulled himself to his feet. "Look G, I got a new job. An amazing opportunity. I'm a Floor Manager at this new casino, super high end, we're talking ballers with Lambos and Jags. They're paying me like ten times what I earned as a bartender, plus bonus." He rubbed at his left shoulder.

"That's great, Drake. But they need you to move out, too? I mean, how far away are they?"

Drake grinned. "They have apartments for the management *in* the hotel, G. I have my own suite, rent-free. It has a living room, a kitchenette, and an in-room hot tub with a view of the strip. Massive hi-def TV, the works. You have to come over and hang out. And hey, I'm leaving all of this for you. Take it all." He gestured to the TV, a pile of electronics and clothes. "Live it up, man. I don't need it at the new place. They give you everything, a new cell phone, a new laptop, all high end."

Gad's stomach flopped. Nothing about this story sounded

right. Casinos didn't offer employees high end tech, let alone suites in their hotels. Yet he couldn't find the words to express how abandoned he suddenly felt. Not that it would matter.

"I'd try to get you a job there, too, but you're kind of in a different field, y'know?" Drake grinned again. He seemed to be oblivious to Gad's sense of loss. "It's not like there's a hospital wing or anything."

Gad watched Drake chuck a relatively new wireless speaker on the pile, where it toppled over and rolled into the shadows in the corner to be forgotten.

"So, uh, anything else?"

Gad looked at Drake, dumbfounded. "Anything else?"

"Yeah." Drake's gaze shifted from the boxes and things left to pack back to Gad. "Got a lot to do here, so, uh, yeah."

Gad opened his mouth to speak, then shut it, weighing the severity of the painful retort that waited behind his lips. He swallowed and started again. "Drake, I don't understand. I mean, I get the great new job and everything, but...well, aren't things moving a little fast?"

"Fast? Yeah, so?" Drake put his hands on his hips. The look on his face made Gad feel even more lame.

"Yeah. Fast. I mean, you didn't give the bar any notice, right?"

Drake shrugged. "When someone makes you an offer you can't refuse-"

"You leave them in the weeds? I mean, you worked for them for years. They trained you up."

"Yeah."

Gad's mouth fell open. "Nothing? Seriously?"

"It's bartending, G. Not rocket science. They'll replace me in a heartbeat." Drake turned his back to Gad, gathering the books from his shelf and dumping them unceremoniously in the trashcan.

"Hey, wait, I gave you that." Gad pulled a small photo album from the pile and flipped it open to the first page. It was a snap-shot of Drake leaning on the newly-acquired Mercy, and Gad behind the wheel. It was the first day of Gad's new EMT busi-ness, a triumphant moment for them both.

"Oh geez, would you look at that," Drake slid the album from Gad's hands to peer at the picture. "I couldn't even afford a decent pair of shoes then. Yikes." He snapped the album shut and dropped it into Gad's hands. "You keep it, G. I sure as hell don't want to relive the good old days of living hand to mouth."

That was the last straw. Whoever this was, it wasn't Drake. This doppelganger was cold, heartless. Gad turned and walked silently to his room. He swept up the bottle of bourbon from his nightstand and, twisting the cap off, took a deep swig. The alcohol would soon course though every muscle, hurting a little at first before replacing pain with all-encompassing numbness. Gad dropped the small photo album in the trash and slammed his door soundly shut.

17

T he next morning, sunlight poured in from Gad's bedroom window like a spear through Gad's right eyeball. With effort akin to pulling free of wet cement, Gad forced himself up from the tangle of blankets and cradled his pounding cranium. Somehow, he needed to get himself to aspirin and a few glasses of water.

He tenuously stood and gave his equilibrium time to catch up before he rolled the blinds shut against the sunshine onslaught. He trudged out to the hall and stopped to stare blearily into Drake's vacant bedroom. It took more than a few moments for the reason to return; the emotional baggage carried with it a lingering resentment. Thanks to Drake's sudden and inexplicably cold departure, Gad had less than three months to find a new roommate. This person would have to be a roommate in name only, someone who didn't feel obligated to chit chat or hang out. This person just needed to be trustworthy enough to pay rent on time and not steal anything. The whole "best friend" concept had been total bullshit.

But hang on, did finding a new roommate even matter? According to the time left on his pocket watch of doom, he would roast on a spit in the bowels of hell before the full rent came due.

Gad peered over the railing to the first floor, where the couch and mismatched armchair of ultimate comfort remained. At least he still had that. And Drake's high-def TV. Time to move into the master bedroom and make the best of the time he had left.

The phone charging on his bedroom nightstand crooned a bar of Love Me Tender. Gad shuffled at a snail's pace to the phone and squinted at the green text bubble.

"Get your skinny ass over here. I found something, think I have a theory. Bring the watch."

"Rough night, huh?" The taxi driver's empathetic eyes in the rear-view mirror had likely seen more than his fair share of hangovers.

"I'll be okay," Gad shrugged. "Probably."

He pulled back his zippered sweat-jacket to peer at the IV drip in the inner pocket. The rubber tubing taped to his arm led to the needle held securely in his vein, but the fluid was not warmed to body temperature. The saline solution flowing into his veins felt like ice. He shivered, but it was worth it knowing his killer headache and overall queasy feeling would go away soon enough. He owed thanks to avid wine enthusiast Dr. Pullman for sharing this electrolyte-filled hydration trick.

Within minutes, the taxi brought Gad to where Mercy sat waiting in the casino parking lot. He carefully drove over to Pete's chapel and parked in his designated parking space. Bob the alastor perched gargoyle-like on the dumpster, his gaze fixated on the back door of the chapel like a cat at a mouse hole. His ass and legs barely fit atop the warping dumpster lid.

"You're too big for that thing, asshole." Gad flinched at the puce scales glistening with, what, mucus? Bob's impossibly long tongue lolled over the dumpster and onto the pavement. Some kind of glop dripped from the pointed teeth that were as long as Gad's forearm. Gad knew he could safely walk right through that door unharmed, but he avoided Bob altogether and went around to the front.

Harriet sat behind the desk, the phone receiver to her ear as she settled commitment ceremony details with new clients. "Tomorrow at six p.m. Absolutely. Oh, no dear, that's a Neil Young song. Uh-huh. Elvis only. Um, Blue Hawaii? I can ask, sure."

Gad waggled his fingers to Harriet as he slipped by. She grinned back, pulling a sharpened pencil from behind one ear to scribble on a sticky note and press it to the laptop lid.

Through the chapel's door behind the stage curtain, Gad found Pete in his white and gold rhinestone pantsuit, sparkling under the desk lamp. Gad scowled at the outfit, although it was Pete's favorite. He pulled a blue silk scarf from the office coat rack and draped it around Pete's neck to cover his over-exposed chest region as much as possible.

"What? I manscaped," Pete said, looking up from his computer screen and frowning.

Gad waved his hand dismissively. "No one needs to see all those freckles and moles."

Pete's eyes rolled. "The King does not give two shits about your issues with freckles and moles."

"Turn your mike off, please!" Harriett called from the front.

"Ah, shit." Pete fiddled with the small black microphone wire clipped to his gaudy lapel. "Now listen, did you bring the watch?"

Gad withdrew the silver timepiece from a pocket and held it under the lamplight. Its antique silver surface no longer gleamed, and the etch marks were too faint to reveal what the picture had once been.

"Do you know what that image is?" Pete pulled bifocals from a desk drawer and slipped them over his nose. Without touching the watch itself, he pulled Gad's hand closer.

"Nope. All that's left is a pair of triangles or something." He pointed to the faint markings around the circumference. "These might be tree leaves, maybe?"

"Nope. I think it might be modeled after this one I found this morning in this book." Pete hoisted a large book as thick and weighty as a brick up onto the desk with a slam. The musty smells of old leather and mold wafted upward as Pete flipped through hundreds of yellowed pages to a spot marked with tattered gold ribbon. "This," he stabbed an inked image with his forefinger.

Gad breathed in sharply.

The pocket watch on the page was intricately and painstakingly painted. It was minute but distinguishable; the watch had a Scales of Justice. In the center of the scales, the rod holding them aloft looked like two scythes, back to back.

"Whoever made that watch was a fan of Aesop's Fables. They called this one 'The Old Man and Death'. Fed up with having to carry a bundle of sticks, the old man asked Death to deliver him from his miserable stick-carrying life."

Gad fought the urge to step away from the picture. Death held the watch toward the viewer in his skeletal palm. He hovered vulture-like over a cowering old man and his bundle of sticks.

"When was this picture drawn, Pete?"

"Sixteenth century. But that doesn't mean your watch is that old. Does your watch have any names inscribed anywhere?"

Gad popped it open and examined it closely. "Nope. I think a company name would normally be on the watch face, but there's nothing on this anywhere."

"So, here's the fun thing about mystical artifacts." Pete pulled the bifocals from his nose and tossed them on the desk. "They typically wouldn't have demarcations because they're usually a one-of-a-kind item handmade by ritual, or creatures you'd never want to meet face-to-face can summon them from places you'd never want to go. They're unique objects with a single purpose. And that watch has a very unique purpose, wouldn't you say?"

"Whoever made it wanted it to look like it belonged to Death."

"Or someone fascinated by Death. Someone who wanted a hunk of metal imbued with the power to know when anyone will die. No matter how it happened, that's some powerful juju there. Not something any old witch or dark magician could fabricate. This watch was imbued by some seriously scary shit."

"Which explains why Dad put so many magic low-jacks on it, to keep it locked up and hidden." Gad studied the ancient Greek fable's illustration again. And suddenly, in a moment of both elation and stomach-cramping fear, Gad leapt to his feet. "Death isn't just one entity, Pete." Gad vaulted from the door, watch clasped tightly in his fist. "I gotta' go."

"Wait, where the hell you goin'?" Pete yelled after him.

"Got a date with Death!"

18

"Drake! Bossman X needs you." Kiera, Xavier's executive assistant, motioned for Drake to join her behind the office door.

From her ear-length bobbed platinum hair to her shapely va-va-voom figure, Kiera was exactly Drake's type. Maybe younger than he would normally prefer, but lately he found that the formerly black and white rules in his playbook were getting gray. His eyes slid over her form, admiring the way her tight red shirt stretched the button holes over the front of her black push-up bra peeking out. "What can I do for you?"

"Bring this to room 49237." Kiera flopped a sealed plastic gray bag into his hand. It had a decent weight and an amorphous shape.

"Eighth floor? I don't think the elevator grants me-"

She unceremoniously plopped a belt clip with a black badge in his other hand.

"This key is for getting to his suite, and his suite only. Don't lose it." Her brows knitted above her hard stare, brown eyes glittering with the implication that bad things would happen if this key were somehow fell out of his possession.

"So, bring it back to you after?"

"Nope. Hang onto it. He trusts you now." Kiera turned to step back through the door.

"Kiera, what is this?" Drake held the shapeless gray package out.

Her dark ruby lips curled up. "I've learned not to ask." She stepped halfway through the door. "You better get going. He doesn't like to wait."

With a nod of acknowledgment, Drake pushed through the crowded casino and into the elevator servicing the higher floors. The black doors slid shut. He attached the metal belt clip to his front belt loop and stretched the key card to a small panel. The panel lit up green, allowing Drake to press the button for the forty-ninth floor.

The elevator rocketed upward; Drake had to yawn to pop his plugging ears. To the cameras in the dark bubbles on the ceiling, Drake likely appeared bored, but they couldn't track his rapid heart rate or see the sweat beading along his hairline. He had just become that much more important to the casino with Xavier's key hanging safely from his belt loop.

He studied the package in his hand. It stood out gray as death against the crimson rug at his feet. His reflection in the smoky mirrors surrounding him had a crooked crimson tie; he straightened his, smoothing it flat against his black dress shirt. Every hair on his head was in place, yet he ran his fingers through it one more time.

The elevator's rise slowed to a stop with a soft ding. The doors slid open.

Drake stepped out onto glossy black tile, his dress shoes squeaking loudly against vast silence. Goosebumps rose along his arms with the biting cold penetrating his thin silk shirt. He tucked the package briefly under one elbow to briskly rub his arms.

He stepped away from the elevators and peered down the darkened halls to the left and right. They seemed to stretch endlessly into blackness. Panels of light lining either side of the hall's black marble floor illuminated the gray walls. Door frames, spaced far and few between, shone chrome in the floor's illumination.

"Room 49237." Drake stood in silence and carefully examined the dimly lit walls and door frames. He could not find any markers to point him one way or another.

"Mr. Reiner," Xavier's voice echoed to him from the long hallway on the left. "I'm expecting that package. This way, if you will."

Drake's heart thumped hard. *X doesn't like to wait.*

Drake strode through the darkness toward Xavier's voice as though every wasted second increased Drake's chances of being fired on the spot. Each stride took too long, each clack of his shoe on marble echoed as if to announce his lateness. How far away was this room, anyway?

"Just a bit further." Drake could now see his boss's silhouette before a door on the right. Against his better judgment, he increased his pace to a jog.

"Sorry, Mr. Ecko," he said loudly.

"I gather Kiera didn't prepare you for the journey." Xavier's voice was jovial as he came into view, now familiar in his pinstriped suit of the day, charcoal. "Our hotel houses many souls and therefore requires a bit of time to traverse. Keep that in mind as you need to make your way around."

"Yes sir, absolutely. It won't happen again." Drake did his best to say the words evenly despite his lungs begging for quick bursts of oxygen. He held the gray package out with a slight dip, unsure if bowing to the head of the hotel was appropriate.

Xavier snatched up the package with a charming laugh. "Relax! I may be your superior, but I am not royalty."

"Sorry." Drake straightened and relaxed, relieved.

"Welcome to the Eighth Level. This level is reserved for our most established members, so wandering here is unacceptable."

"Got it. This floor is for the exclusive, so only stick to this door. Um, on that note..." Drake glanced nervously to the door and around the frame for any distinguishing marks.

"Ah." Xavier opened his door and reached behind it. The floor lights immediately to either side of his door turned red. "Apologies. Again, this floor is, as you say, exclusive. This establishment goes to great lengths to assure the privacy of all here. Rest assured, once you've earned the company's trust, your badge will grant access to any room you need to find. Just input the door you need into the system and it will give you the floor, the direction, and then..." He pulled a black card from within his suit and held the key card out before him toward the neighboring door. The lights on the floor to either side turned green, and the door opened with a soft click. "There, you see? I expect you'll rise through the ranks in a blink, and on that day, this will open doors for you." He waggled the card for a moment before tucking it away and shutting the door. The floor lights turned white again.

"Now then. Let's not waste any more time with you, my friend." Xavier addressed the gray package under his arm and pulled out a pocketknife. Its black blade poked crisply through the plastic and sliced away the outer bag, exposing a fat clear package of white powder sealed by crisscrossing packing tape.

Drake fought the urge to step backward. Was this a test? *Be cool,* he told himself. *Wait.* He composed what he hoped would be the best indifferent poker face of his life.

He watched his boss push the tip of the knife through the tape and scoop a small pile of the white powder onto the knife tip. Xavier's eyes met his, black and glittering, like a cobra's. He held the knife out under Drake's nose. "They told me this is the very best available. Very rare, too. Literally, this bag costs an unspeakable amount. Fancy a bump?"

Drake's heart thumped against his ribcage. He had never done drugs and had no desire to start. But this was his boss. And this felt like a test. But was it a test to see if he would do drugs on the job or a test to see if he was cool enough to promote? *Shit, shit, shit.*

"You won't know until you try." Xavier's tone was almost mocking.

Drake forced himself to bend his head to the knife. Pressing one nostril shut like he had seen in countless movies, he inhaled the white powder. An awful chemical taste filled his mouth, and something dripped down the back of his throat. He held his breath.

Xavier's lips curved up widely. "There now. Just keep that up and you're on your way to the top."

Drake let out the breath he had been holding. Okay, so that was a trust test and, apparently, he had passed. He could suddenly feel the blood in every vein and capillary in his head pulsing. Everything was moving faster.

"Now, scoot on back to the third floor. You'll be hearing from me soon."

"Yes sir, Mr. Ecko."

"I appreciate the respect of formality, but please call me Xavier. Or better yet, X. Have a wonderful shift this evening, Drake." He smiled, stepped backward into the darkness of the room beyond and shut his door.

Drake slowly turned and began the long walk back the elevator bay with a flood of emotion and powerful narcotics coursing through him. He couldn't believe what he had just done. As an advocate of being completely in charge of his own good judgment, he had always turned down drugs. And yet, it elated him to have just been initiated into what was probably the norm for executive management. With each step on the cold black marble, the scales of emotion tipped further on the side of elation and power, his confidence expanding like a hot-air balloon.

So what if he had to do a bump of blow? Maybe he had always been wrong about what "good judgment" really was.

By the time Drake reached the elevator, he had settled the matter. If selling a little of his soul was the first step to getting everything he'd ever wanted, he'd made the right choice. He was sure of it as he stepped through the elevator doors.

The black doors slid shut, and Drake's long rapid descent began.

19

G ad was terrified of the reapers. It wasn't just that they seemed so impossibly big or that they seemed to grow more horrific looking with every soul they reaped. It was more the fact that their very presence sent some ancient, deep-seated warning system into overdrive so that every cell in his body seemed to be screaming at him to turn and run as far away as he possibly could. So far he'd managed to hold his ground, but Gad always turned his back to each inevitable, looming presence when they appeared, not wanting the walking incarnations of death to realize that he could see them. He wanted the reapers to think he was nothing more than a life-saving EMT, at the right place and, coincidentally, ahead of the right time. His refusing to look in their direction had absolutely nothing to do with the fact that they scared him worse than any ghost ever had, so badly in fact that he sometimes had to drink himself to sleep at night.

Or so he told himself.

Today would be different though. Today, he had no choice but to face them. He'd realized that the only hope he had for finding out if he could prevent his own quickly approaching date of demise was to communicate with one of the death-bringers.

He didn't have any inkling how they would respond to him. Did they even know how to talk? Would they freak out knowing that someone could see them? And most terrifying of all, would they kill him for seeing them?

He drove the speed limit on the cracked and well-worn roads just outside of central Las Vegas, trolling less populated places with his pocket watch in hand, searching for a nearby impending death. He needed to find a quiet emergency as it would be tough enough just trying to talk to a reaper. Doing so in the presence of a crowd would make it damn near impossible.

From noon and until the last bit of sun disappeared behind the horizon, Gad drove slowly through suburbs, business parks, and stretches of near-empty road. It wasn't until hours later when Mercy pulled around a random corner and rolled along a broken-down apartment building that the pocket watch finally began to blink. And even though this is what he had been waiting for, Gad's heart thudded and his mouth went dry.

Dry brown palm trees rustled in the evening breeze against the night sky. The apartment building sighed with the dirty stucco exterior of a sleezy 70s hotel. All rooms faced a swampy pool from behind peeling banisters coated in decades of paint. Gad pulled Mercy to a hasty stop along the apartment's red-curbed sidewalk, got out, and jogged through the open gates. The pocket watch light blinked to the upper-left and buzzed intermittently. Following its directions, Gad turned left to the cement stairs and vaulted up the steps. The light moved sharply to the left, and so did Gad.

Slim and rusting metal numbers hung on pale yellow doors. Twenty-five, twenty-four, twenty-three...Gad's rapid pace nearly caused him to pass his destination. The light floated up to the top of the watch. He pivoted and, with one big step backward, corrected course. The watch pointed straight ahead to apartment twenty-one.

He listened carefully, or as carefully as he could with the watch buzzing urgently in his hand. Beyond the occasional child laughing or a small dog barking in the complex, it was quiet. Tentatively, he tried the mottled doorknob. It was unlocked.

Gad's body was tense like an over-tightened guitar string as he pushed the door open. The living room was dark and silent. Pungent old beer smell hung in the stagnant air. He stepped quietly inside and let his eyes adjust to the dim room.

CRUNCH.

His foot came down on an aluminum can and crushed it flat. Gad nearly jumped out of his skin.

Light shone like a beacon through an almost-closed door in the hall beyond the living room. Steam poured out through the crack into suddenly frigid air. The pocket watch's buzzing and temperature increased. Gad dropped it into its oven mitt in his pants pocket and strode to the sound of the shower running.

He threw open the door.

An older man with wispy pale blond and gray hair slumped in his tub, the shower spraying hot water across his chest. His head lay at an odd angle over the side of the tub which ran with bright red streams over a dropped beer can that glugged its remaining foamy contents over bathroom tile.

"Sir? Sir, can you hear me?" Gad quickly turned off the water and checked the man's breathing. He wasn't.

Pulling open one eyelid, the man's pupils did not dilate. He reeked of beer. The man was at death's door and there was no way Gad could save him. The gash in his head was deep; he was losing blood too quickly.

The hair on Gad's arms suddenly stood at attention, and the hot moist air grew instantly frigid. An invisible finger drifted along the back of his neck.

The reaper was here. Gad could feel its cold presence just behind him, blocking the only way out.

SHINK.

The unmistakable sound of the scythe's metallic blade issued from somewhere high behind his head.

Gad forced his legs to obey and push him slowly up on his feet, the pocket watch hot against his leg even within the oven mitt. His heart was in his throat. With all the courage he could muster, he turned.

It looked as though someone had taken a sledgehammer to the reaper's cranium. The right side of it face was caved in, black liquid-like tendrils leaking supernaturally upward from the rest of its face. Its head hung at a crooked angle, and it held its gray mottled arms up over its shoulder, the scythe poised to swing. Gad gasped.

The scythe whirled in an arc, disappearing through the bathroom wall to reappear sweeping toward Gad.

This is it! Gad braced for impact.

The scythe lodged with a squelch, yet Gad felt nothing. He looked down, wide-eyed, his body electric with fear.

The scythe remained motionless, the long, crooked staff passing straight through him harmlessly. He followed the weapon to its pointed end, stuck into the torso of the dead man in the tub. With one tug, then another, the blade in the dead man's chest yanked at his core until the resisting luminescent spirit pulled free of his body.

"Say something now," his brain screamed, even as a voice on the other shoulder had him almost convinced he should try again some other time.

Gad turned to speak to the decaying reaper, whose rib cage of reaching arms and splaying fingers opened wide, golden light pouring forth from the reaper's core. Before Gad could pivot, the dead man's spirit floated into the luminescent maw and hundreds of arms embraced the soul, the bony fingers curling over it with a flash of light. By the time Gad had completed his pivot, the reaper had melted into shadows that ran like water into the floor.

His bracing fear ebbed and a wave of relief washed over him, followed immediately by self-resentment and anger for not accomplishing what he came for. Then he realized as he scanned his surroundings, which included a dead body in the tub, that he couldn't exactly just walk away.

"Well, shit."

GAD CALLED in the death and dutifully brought the body to the morgue, reporting that he had been dropping off a package to a friend's doorstep when he heard the man cry out for help. It was too early for Lorraine to be working the graveyard shift, so it forced Gad to endure the skeptical and penetrating stare from the older and...well, older head front office manager, Lucinda.

"Did the man give you explicit permission to enter the apartment?" Lucinda's brown eyes bored holes into Gad over her bifocals.

"I told you he cried out for help before he slipped and hit his head." Gad could feel his patience slipping like a clutch losing grip on its gears, hot and approaching loss of control.

She scratched out something on her intake form with her pen and clucked her tongue for good measure. There it was. Patience gone.

"What, Lucy? You think I murdered him for his stash of cheap-ass beer?"

"It's Lucinda. And no, I don't. But I think you have a nasty habit of ignoring the law and one day, you're gonna get burned."

She stood and, with one last pointed glare, disappeared through the hospital door and left it swinging in her superior wake.

"Oh, you have no idea," he said, rubbing at the pain stabbing his right eye from within. With a grimace, Gad shoved himself upward from the office chair and marched out of the hospital, his pride worse for the wear.

20

T he next night, stars remained hidden above a sky thick with dark clouds. The scent of moisture seeping into the dirty Vegas streets was sickly sweet with the promise of rain.

His ambulance passed nondescript houses as he patrolled outer Vegas with the pocket watch dangling from the rear-view mirror, his miniature navigator. Determined not to chicken out again, Gad knew the worst thing he could do about his quickly approaching death was nothing.

Several wet plops splattered across Mercy's windshield. He flipped the wipers on and they slipped back and forth over the glass to the rhythm of his music. For his own amusement, Gad had a playlist that randomly shuffled through every remake of Blue Oyster Cult's "Don't Fear the reaper". Apparently, many bands had covered it in every conceivable style. A lot. He wasn't sure how much more cowbell he could take.

The road remained nearly empty and the pocket watch silent on his patrol of the outskirts of town. Gad entertained heading back into town where the death alarms were fast and frequent. To drive fruitlessly night after night with no answers in sight was rough; to save his ass sooner than later seemed worth letting people witness a crazy EMT talk to thin air.

The pocket watch buzzed once, the brief vibration leaving it twirling on the end of its metal chain. Gad pulled up to the limit line of the stop sign and swept the watch up into his palm. The light blinked weakly at the bottom of the watch face.

"Okay, something wicked this way comes."

Gad drew a deep breath, the fear of facing death again akin to that debilitating fear from seventh grade recitals and having to walk out onstage in a packed theater. He checked his mirrors for any sign of where to go. It was a block of new town homes and condos in the late evening and nothing unusual stood out. He snatched the watch from the mirror, locked up Mercy, and hit the sidewalk to determine where the watch led him. Cold rain drops penetrated his hair and trickled down his scalp.

He turned left and right, but the light on the watch face continued to drift back and forth at the bottom. With a frown, he turned to the road behind him. The watch vibrated urgently; the metal warmed fast in the cradle of his fingers. Confused, he peered down the road he had just come from.

An engine throttle buzzed in the distance like a wasp. Far down the suburban road, an oncoming shape took form. The spattering rain thickened and began to cascade in curtains, making it more difficult to see ahead. The roar of the motor carried toward him, growing louder by the second.

A flash of white light illuminated the clouds in the distance for a fleeting moment. Gad had to move his non-stop vibrating pocket watch into its oven mitt. Whatever was coming was coming now. And he saw it finally. A black motorcycle tore through sheets of rain like a bat out of hell.

Gad cringed, his heart hammering again. He knew what was coming, and there was no way to stop it. The motorbike was going way too fast on freshly wet roads.

The screeching of brakes carried over the cacophony of pouring rain, followed by metal tearing across the pavement. The bike laid sideways and carried its rider skidding directly into a telephone pole, sending out a shower of sparks and a sickening crunch. The metal pole bent inward, and the light went out.

Gad ran through the pouring rain toward the rider. The motorcycle's front tire continued to spin. The back half of the bike had collapsed into an unrecognizable mass of twisted metal. The rider was nowhere near the wreckage.

Gad spun, putting his hand to his eyes to block the torrent of rain water long enough to find where the rider landed. It didn't take long. Under the next lamppost, the curtains of rain parted over an impossibly tall flowing form. Light fell around it, as though unable to penetrate the darkness beneath.

"Wait!" Gad tore across the pavement toward the reaper.

Something glinted in the lamppost's fluorescent cascade.

His feet slapped the wet pavement and splashed through puddles up his pant legs. He had to get there in time. It was hard to see what was happening through the thick sheets of rain.

Gad stopped just behind the statuesque darkness beneath the lamppost. A cone of light fought to illuminate the surroundings through the volumes of falling raindrops. The rider's body lay mangled, pelvis nearly backward and legs twisted up and over hips.

"But I'm not ready!"

The translucent form of the rider stood before the reaper and Gad, just behind the body. Black-gloved hands came up to the helmet and flipped the tinted visor up. It was a woman, thick stands of red hair swept back from a mascara-stained face.

The reaper, twisted and misshapen, pointed upward with one deformed hand and disturbingly long fingers.

"No, I can't. My wedding is next month. I'm only twenty-two! This can't be it. This isn't fair!"

The reaper's knobby pale fingers pulled aside the tattered dark cloth that hung over its giant frame. Light beamed from the opening hold in its chest, cutting through the surrounding night. It pointed to the light.

"Why? Why now?" she sobbed.

Gad spoke. "Move on. If you stay here, you will be nothing but alone for years, watching the world go by. Trust me, move on to the light."

"But where does the light go?"

Gad shook his head. "You go on. To the next great thing."

"But my parents. My mom will be so-"

The reaper took a step backward, letting the cloth fall back into place over the open gateway in its chest.

"You've got to go now," Gad insisted, raising his voice over the patter of the rain. He pointed to the fading light. "This is your chance, don't blow it."

With reticence, she tossed her helmet aside and stepped forward. With each step she took toward the light, it grew. The reaper again held the cloth aside, waiting. The tiny arms that made up its ribs stretched wide open.

The girl peered into the light, the pain and sorrow in her expression melting away, replaced by wonder. "Grandma?" The steps that had been slow and unsure became solid and swift. "Grandma," she cried, lighting up. Her soul's form fell away from a discernable body and into a swirling vapor that stretched toward the reaper's light.

The light swallowed her in a blink. The small gray welcoming hands and fingers curled closed, the arms folded and knit neatly back together until the reaper stood facing Gad. It bounced the scythe hard once against the ground and raised it up to repeat the motion a second time.

"Wait," Gad sputtered, gathering his wits before fear robbed him of speech or consciousness. He peered up into the blackness of the half-faced corpse looming over him, rain pelting his face. He wasn't sure, but it looked as though there were a point of light within its one eyehole. He looked into it, pleading. "I need to ask you something."

The reaper stood motionless before him, giving neither consent nor denial.

"You know I will die soon, don't you?"

The edges of the reaper's form shifted and swirled like tendrils of black smoke.

Yes. The reaper's massive head nodded slowly.

"How do I stop it?"

No. The form swayed back and forth.

Gad's stomach dropped. "Why not? Why can't I change it...wait!"

The reaper drifted backward.

"Wait!" Gad shouted.

But the reaper would not wait. It disappeared into the shadows beyond the light pole, leaving Gad alone to pick up the broken pieces of yet another passing.

WHILE HE WASN'T able to get the answer he was looking for, Gad rationalized that he had gotten a reaper's attention and lived to tell the tale. For now. That was a win. He had also helped escort a soul to a better place, saving the neighborhood and the young woman herself from an eternity of haunting. Another win.

He had to take the conversation with the reapers further. Should he show a reaper his watch and ask why it shows him the date and time of his death? Or ask why he had been allowed to save other souls from reapings, but why not his own?

Tonight the sky was clearer than the last few nights with no clouds and a full moon to help light the way. Gad decided to explore the town closer to his usual rounds, but would only follow the death alarms that led him to a less populated space. Tonight, the watch buzzed in several places on Fremont Street and the strip, but revelers crowded the sidewalks and the casinos bustled. He did not want the attention of a crowd while intervening in mortal coils. He was nearly ready to pack it in for the night when the watch lit up as he passed a hotel set for demolition. He parked, exited Mercy, and followed the watch's directions on foot and into the hotel.

The hotel had long since closed, not having a theme fun enough to compete with pirates, tigers, or fake European countries. The watch's light led him up a darkened service staircase, winding ever upward through flickering fluorescent lighting. Deathly quiet, Gad felt as though he crept through the skeleton of a place once full of life.

The watch's buzzing grew stronger. Gad carefully opened the stairwell door and slipped through into a dark hallway. He stepped softly on the worn and faded carpeting past the closed doors. Everything was m

usty, moldy, dirty.

Gad stopped outside room 20024, his pocket watch growing warmer by the second in his sweaty palm.

The stale air stirred.

The door stood cracked open. Voices spoke softly from the shadows. Gad put his ear to the crack.

"Thank you for coming all this way to see me."

"Of course, (muffled). I almost asked you how you've been, but-"

"Oh no, you did not, silly." The female's laugh was pleasant and southern, like little bells tinkling.

"Well, I've been plugging along, you know. The girls, they're grown and almost through college. Old Blue passed onto the great dog house in the sky."

The pocket watch, hot in his hand, vibrated in occasional bursts in his clenched fist. Gad couldn't wrap his mind around how, but the pocket watch insisted somebody's death was imminent. In ten minutes or so.

"Oh, I've missed you so much, Wayne."

It seemed to be only two people in the room. The woman's voice was clear.

All moisture had left his mouth, now parched, while every crease of his body was getting uncomfortably moist with flop sweat. He pushed the door open with his fingertip. It opened smoothly, soundlessly. Gad slipped into the dark entryway inside the room and pushed the door almost closed again. Now the male voice was clear.

"Gale, I just don't know how to say this. Well, you know."

"No, I don't know. Spill it."

It took a moment for Gad's eyes to adjust to the dark. A double bed with a paisley coverlet sat beneath a nondescript art deco picture against the wall. Before the parted window curtains was a round breakfast table with two chairs. In them, an older man in his fifties and a woman in her twenties faced one another. They held hands in the inch of pale moonlight passing through the parted curtains and gazed into each other's eyes.

"You have always been the love of my life, you know that."

The woman, Gale, smiled and stroked his hand. "And you've always been my one and only, Wayne."

He smiled, wistfully.

Utterly stumped, Gad sensed that the man was sad about something he had to do. The conversation seemed pleasant, even though oddly clandestine in a decaying hotel. Was this an affair?

An awful thought struck. *Was he going to murder her?*

"And now we can finally be together," she reached across the table to smooth a piece of wayward peppery hair away from his neatly groomed beard. From his light sports coat to his pointed cowboy boots over blue jeans, he looked every bit as though he'd stepped off the ranch to come to this hotel room.

Something wasn't right.

"You know, about that," he breathed in and stopped, considering.

"Together, Wayne. Together! We've waited so long for this."

The woman's honey-blond hair tumbled over pale shoulders and a sexy champagne silk nightgown. She was easily half his age.

He sighed and stood, opening the curtains a few more inches. A larger strip of moonlight and colorful blinking neon poured in through the elevated window and across the table to a glint of metal. A snub-nosed pistol lay on the table between them.

The man heaved a deep breath of resignation, his gaze falling on the pistol.

"I don't know that this is the answer right now for us. For me. Can't we just take it slow, let nature take its course?"

"Your kids are grown, Wayne. Your wife moved on. You're free now." Her finger rested atop the gun, and it skittered an inch toward Wayne. "Take back what we lost so long ago."

Wayne crossed his arms over his chest.

"I don't know, Gale."

"You said you loved me."

"But-"

"You'd do it if you really loved me."

He looked out the window again.

In Gad's hand, the pocket watch vibrated endlessly, painfully hot. He dropped it silently into the oven-glove in the leg pocket of his uniform.

"But I...I'm afraid." He sat in the chair and clasped her hands in his again. "Will it hurt? Will I feel it?"

"Not if your aim is steady." Gale leaned forward to kiss his fingertips. She was so much younger than him. Or rather, she would have been if she were actually alive. Her perfect figure and beautiful features shimmered translucent, moonlight passing through her to the pile carpet. Only the gash in her chest dripping dark onto her silk gown marred her beauty.

"Will you do it, then?" He winced and looked from her to the pistol.

"You know I can't, hon. But it's such an easy thing. Just aim and pull the trigger."

Wayne slowly picked up the pistol, his hand shaking.

"Do it," she urged. "And be with me." She moved soundlessly from her chair to stand behind him, her arms around him, her hands over his. He turned it toward his chest and put the muzzle to his heart. "Together forever," she whispered in his ear, her lips stretching up into a wide grin.

Gad pulled his iron shears from their pocket. This guy would not spend eternity with his beloved, no matter how hard she wanted it to be true. He was about to commit suicide, the unforgivable sin that would open a reaper's maw to hell.

Frigid cold blanketed Gad's skin as the super-heated metal in the oven-glove of his pocket vibrated endlessly. It was too dark to see the shadows coalesce around Wayne's feet, the hisses and whispers of perdition carried from the unseen reaper taking form. Gad's arm hair stood at attention, and a moving tower of shadow swept in between Gad and the couple, obscuring the moonlight with void. The reaper was here.

"Stop!" Gad's voice cracked, his throat tight. "Put the gun down."

In a blink, Wayne's pistol pivoted from his chest to Gad. Gale's beauty disintegrated instantly to bruised sagging skin.

She fixed her dead glassy eyes on Gad, her cracked lips forming an angry circle around broken yellowed teeth.

Gad's blood ran cold, the momentary thought flickered that his death might be sooner than Halloween based on his next move.

"Who are you? What do you want?" The gun trembled in Wayne's hands. He got to his feet, partially obscured by the form of death that towered over Wayne, waiting for his final moment to arrive. Obsidian smoke leaked upward from the bottom of its shin and the top of its head, the reaper's form having taken on the various gunshots of its reaped souls.

"Who I am doesn't matter. What does is that, if you shoot yourself, you have a reaper standing right there, ready to take you to hell."

Gale drifted around the reaper toward Gad, bloated and rotten, her fingers outstretched like claws toward his throat. "Lies," she gurgled.

Gad's nostrils filled with the stench of decay. He brandished the points of his iron shears at the menacing ghost.

"Nope, truth. By the looks of it, someone murdered you in your prime and Wayne here is your unfinished business. But Wayne," he pointed the shears to Wayne. "If you kill yourself, you're committing the unforgivable sin. And the hair standing up straight on the back of your neck? That's your reaper, waiting for you to pull that trigger. So don't do it."

"I see nothing," Wayne said faintly, waving the gun as he searched the vacant area around him. "But I can't exactly call you crazy, can I? Not while we're walking and talking with my long since passed fiancee."

"Exactly right, Wayne. But trust me when I say that you are in danger. I can see death when it comes for people. And your reaper, well, it's getting impatient, looking at its-"

POCKET WATCH.

The words screamed through Gad's head, his eyes smarting with the feeling of popping from their sockets.

Yellow-white finger bones protruded from draping ebony that drifted about the reaper's arm like falling tendrils of smoke. In the center of its bony hand sat an open pocket-watch, just like Gad's, with a point of light beaming directly at Wayne. It shimmered and shook, wavering as though it existed in multiple planes of existence simultaneously. The fingers snapped the watch shut with a clack.

"Looking at its what?" Wayne's voice drifted faintly into Gad's ears.

The reaper's massive form shifted in a blink, having moved its attention from its intended soul collection to Gad.

"Unload the gun now, Wayne. And put it down." Gad did his best to keep his voice even as he issued the command.

Gale turned back to Wayne. "Wayne, no!" And for the first time, Wayne saw Gale's true rotting form and shrieked. He wheeled back up against the window and dropped the pistol to the floor, where it landed with a heavy thunk.

The reaper's elongated arm lifted and drew forth a single bony finger to point into Gad's face.

In the dark of the shadows, Gad could make out some of the reaper's details. Exposed bone. Angry hollow eye sockets, drawn downward in the center, shining crimson. A misshapen cavity above two rows of unnaturally long clenched teeth, all drawn downward into a scowl within gray mottled flesh. Gad's empathic soul absorbed the reaper's mood like a sponge. Death was not just angry. It was livid.

Its long, yellowed finger bones curled into a fist. It lifted its arm and, with a powerful downward motion, moved as though pounding an unseen staff solidly against the floor twice. A pole as tall as the reaper sprang from its skeletal hand.

A voice in Gad's brain screamed at him to run, get the hell out of there now.

Wayne stood flat against the window, the color drained from his face as Gale, her rotting flesh swinging from her arms, scooped fruitlessly at the gun on the floor. "Do it now, Wayne," she growled through half-rotted vocal chords. "We can be together, forever." She stood and grinned at him, her remaining teeth broken and mottled.

"Balanccccceee," the reaper said to Gad, its voice like shed snake skin scraping against desert sand. This reaper could speak. Or would.

At the top of its pole, the familiar wicked reaper's blade sprung forth with a sound like sharp metal pulling along metal.

Gad swallowed at the lump in his throat. This was it for him, he was sure of it.

The reaper lifted its scythe back and whirled. Gad squeezed his eyes shut.

Gale's screech halted.

Gad opened his eyes. The scythe stuck in Gale's back. Her ghostly hands thrown outward with surprise, she stood frozen in midair, her dry and patchy hair on end. The reaper tugged the blade through ethereal matter and, in the next moment, Gale's form sped toward the flickering red light in the reaper's chest. Whispers and cries of delight, oohs and aahs emanated from the crimson glow. The reaper's chest closed around the soul, silencing the sounds of perdition.

"Where did she go? What was that? In the name of God." Wayne gibbered, every inch of his body shaking against the window. "Sh-she, Gale, cut in half-"

"She was just taken by the reaper. You've just gotten a second chance, Wayne." Each word from Gad was loud with articulation. "You better run."

Gad's own feet were two unmovable concrete blocks, his heart hammering in his chest.

Wayne streaked past Gad and out the door, the movement whipping up a slight swirling of the reaper's vaporous outline.

The reaper turned back to Gad and pounded the blade once, twice, against the floor. The scythe collapsed into thin air.

Its eyes had changed, now regarding Gad with a pair of white-blue points of light from within the void of the cowl. Its price paid, the reaper prepared to leave.

"Wait." The words flew from Gad's lips in a rush as he did the unthinkable. He grabbed at the reaper's arm.

Cold like he had never known flooded his fingers, his hand, his arm. A great nothingness shot through his torso, up through his shoulders and down through his waist, hips, thighs, legs, feet, toes. He was no longer a speck in the universe. The void filled him, pushing out everything and emptying him completely. His body, his organs, his lungs squeezed from three-dimensions into two, everything flattening, and then from two dimensions into...he couldn't even think. He was emptying into nothing, nothingness. No pain, no joy, no life or death.

Pop!

The next thing Gad knew, the reaper stood feet away from him. It had stepped away, pulling its arm from Gad's touch. Gad gasped, a long rasping intake of sweet air into his, once again, three-dimensional lungs.

The reaper's finger, pointed to the ceiling, drifted slowly back and forth. He knew was being admonished, but it was overkill having almost wiped himself from universal existence of his own accord. Never touch a reaper. Yup, got it.

Gad swallowed air into his re-expanding lungs as quickly as he could before he lost another chance. "I will die...soon."

"Sssooooooooon," the deep ethereal voice concurred all around him.

"Can I stop it? Can I change my fate?"

The reaper leaked black vapor fluid from the new wound on its chest where Gale's death wound had been. Its massive head towered frighteningly far above him and shook back and forth. *No.*

His stomach clenched. He wouldn't take no for an answer this time. "But I've changed so many other lives. Other souls' fates. Kept people from an early death."

The blue-white gaze shifted to red.

"Balanncccce." The last syllable was akin to a hiss, making Gad wonder whether this was the reaper's anger or just how it communicated when choosing to do so.

A bony finger protruded from its ragged clothing, and the skeletal yellowed tip leveled at Gad's nose.

"Sephhhhhh," the rasping word filled his being.

Seth? Who or what is Seth?

But Gad would get nothing more. The reaper glided backward into the dark corner of the room, and as it did, its darkness melded with the shadows until it was gone.

21

"It's way past my bedtime, so spill. What happened?" Pete slid the second glass of bourbon over to Gad. "Spare no details."

Gad drew in a shaky breath and took a deep swallow from the glass. It tasted of wood, leather, earth...all the manliest things. He wondered if he wasn't becoming too familiar with the flavor lately.

Gad pulled the silver pocket watch from the oven mitt in his pocket and held it out. "It's a reaper's watch, Pete."

Pete peered unblinking at the relic in Gad's hand, trying to digest that new hunk of information. "Say again?"

"This," Gad tapped the watch. "This watch belonged to a reaper. And I don't know how, but Dad ended up with it."

"Sweet Jesus." Pete took another swallow of his drink and set the glass down with a thunk. "I mean, I've always figured that thing to be rare magic, but that's...holy shit."

Gad offered it to him and Pete nearly rocked backward off his seat. "I'm not touching it, Gideon."

Gad pulled his hand back, realizing the consequences of touching the watch. "Oh yeah, sorry."

"Yeah, let's let my death date remain a mystery. Next week or next century, it'll be too soon for me. So, go on, what happened with the reapers? Did the suckers talk or what?"

"First ones I talked to didn't say a word, but the last one did. Tonight."

Gad went into great detail with each encounter, especially the part where he made the mistake of trying to grab the reaper's robe. The memory raised gooseflesh all over his body. "It was like someone pulled my power plug while what made up 'me' was being replaced by a vacuum."

Pete mulled it around for a minute, swirling the rich amber alcohol around the walls of the glass. Gad had described the reapers to Pete before, including what their job was and how they should be avoided at all costs, but he'd never pissed one off before. Pete guffawed at that. Now he could say the reapers themselves were no-nonsense entities mostly with the occasional twist of anger.

"And whenever I asked about changing fate, saving people from dying, their eyes always turned red. Like it was a bad thing." Gad frowned at the thought.

"The one that spoke after you pissed it off, what did it say?"

"It said 'balance'. And weirdest of all, when I told Wayne to get out of there, it reaped the ghost of the woman. Wayne was the idiot ready to put a bullet through his heart."

"Huh. So it took a ghost instead. To the light?"

Gad shook his head.

"To hell? You kidding me?" Wide-eyed, Pete set his drink down.

"Yup. A ghost that could've moved on to the light got taken down instead."

"Well, there you go. That's what it meant. Balance."

Gad scowled. "It had to take a soul in place of Wayne's, so it took hers?"

"Be glad it wasn't yours, kid."

"But, that just doesn't sound right. I mean, a soul meant to go upward has two choices: go to the light or stay here as a ghost with unfinished business. And a soul damned to go down never has the luxury of getting to stay but gets sent down that slippery slide."

"What the reaper did sounds fair to me. A soul paid for a soul due."

Gad tapped his fingers on the polished bar surface. "But that's not fair. Nobody died, so things should just continue on the way the way they are."

Pete chuckled into his drink, downing the last swallow. "You know it's not that simple, Gad. You and I just learned something about the reapers. We know angels want you to do good, demons want you to do bad, and the reapers, well, sounds like they just need you to stick to the grand plan. And you, Gideon Goodwin, keep messing with the plan whenever you save lives. Bet that's why they went all red-eye on you."

"Were reapers a part of the Catholic stuff you learned?"

"Nah. Just heaven and hell in their eternal struggle for souls." Pete signaled the bartender for another round.

Gad sighed. "You ever see one up close?"

"See what?"

"An angel. Or a demon."

Pete's expression became weary, as though thinking back to those memories aged him. "Before I answer that, I will give you a choice. One, I tell you everything I have learned in my long years on this planet about good and evil. Two, I don't tell you and you remain as naïve and carefree as you are right now."

Gad twisted around to face him. "Are you kidding me?"

"Nope. Dead serious. There's a reason I left the church, Gad. I've never talked to you about it before because, well, there's no call to burden you with it. But once you know what's really going on in the world underneath it all? Let's just say that when I'm lying awake scared shitless at three in the morning I sometimes wish I'd chosen a different path. Ignorance is bliss, as they say."

"Seeing ghosts and reapers is no bed of roses, you know," Gad grumbled and threw back the dregs of his glass just in time for the bartender to slide the next round in front of them on the bar.

Pete threw back his head with a hearty laugh.

Gad didn't know whether the jovial dismissal offended him or not.

"Forgive me, Gad. I've never seen spirits so I can't throw stones. But death is only the transition to the much bigger picture. I need to clue you in that, once you've come into contact with something hellborn...we're talking true evil now, it changes you. Forever."

Gad was silent for a moment, considering Pete's words. "You mean, like Bob?"

"Oh, Bob is a friggin' delight, my boy." Pete slapped the bar top. "No, worse. Much worse." His gaze drifted to the mirrored wall with a haunted grimace.

The way Pete glared at the mirror, not at his reflection, gave Gad the creeps. "Pete, you promised you'd tell me what that mirror in the cellar was for."

Pete sighed, almost resolutely. "So, I'm hearing a vote for option one. Truth over blissful ignorance. That about right?"

Gad scowled into his glass, the contents of which were making his mind fuzzy around the edges. "Might as well tell me Pete. How much worse can it be than seeing reapers take souls?"

Pete locked eyes with him. "It's much worse. And you can never un-know it."

Gad swallowed.

"Like, did you know that, once you know a demon's true name, and that name is in your head, you've got an open channel to that...thing...every time you conjure the name in your brain, even by accident? It hears you. It can talk to you in your head. And it does. It'll drive you bat shit crazy." Pete took another swig of his drink and shuddered.

"Why? To what end?"

Pete looked at him as if he had two heads. "Boy, what have I been talking to you about since we got here? What do you think it would be after trying to drive you to insane?"

Gad shrugged, starting to feel defensive.

"Your soul, Gad. Your soul." Pete shook his head. "Demon drives you loopy as a squirrel that's lost its nuts and boom, you blow your brains out. Score one for the bad guys."

"One soul is worth that?"

"One soul is everything. It's what heaven and hell are in a fight over for every single day. And you live smack in the middle of sin city."

"So? Aren't there good and bad people everywhere in the world?"

Pete's eyebrow arched. "C'mon, Gideon. We both know you're smarter than that."

Gad's eyes dropped to the bar top, one side of his mouth curled up. It was true; he was being deliberately obstinate. "I do. Just don't want to hear about how shitty this place is. I see it every day."

"You of all people know what goes on behind closed doors in this town."

"Doors aren't even closed sometimes," Gad snorted.

"People come here to get messed up. They cheat in the worst ways possible, with drugs, with drink, on each other. This is the big show for demons. It's why I moved here after they ordained me. In fact, they sent me here."

"The church?"

Pete nodded. "Moved here. Got to know what was what. And

boy did I ever get the shock of my life. Like I said, if I knew then what I know now, I'd have had another think coming when the church handed me the plane ticket. There are plenty of small towns across this great nation where a priest can join a parish and settle down, aim for becoming a deacon. But I had a special knack, a certain set of skills that apparently set me out from the rest."

Gad waited expectantly. He could see Pete chewing the scenery, a smile playing at his lips.

Gad sighed. "Okay what, basket-weaving?"

"Exorcisms."

Gad chuffed. "You mean people with mental health problems that want attention."

Pete's jaw dropped. "Are you shitting me? Are you, Gideon Goodwin, sitting right there on that bar stool and telling me, Peter Owens, about invisible twenty-foot death-dudes and, in the same breath, telling me demons don't possess people?"

Gad shrugged. "I'm not saying there aren't demons. I've seen scary shit pop up when hell opens for someone. I just think after seeing twenty-foot death-dudes, ghosts and Mr. Green-jeans on your chapel roof, that those 'possessed' people are super fakers. In fact, that's why I say they're full of shit. Attention seekers."

Pete blinked rapidly, the jaw-drop frozen on his face. "They're around us all the time, Gad, just waiting for the chance to come through. You just invite one in, that's all it takes for a possession."

"Really," Gad continued, swallowing a quick shot of bourbon. "Shouldn't someone who's possessed have like, their heads spinning or getting all green and bubbly? Spewing pea soup? I've seen the exorcism videos, Pete. All they ever do is bark and throw out mildly witty repartee."

Pete set his glass down hard. "Can I have a pen?" He

motioned to the bartender. "And another round, come to think of it. He's gonna need more after this."

Gad shook his buzzing head. He didn't know what Pete thought he would do to prove his point.

Pete snatched up a red cocktail napkin over and wrote out a word in black pen. He slid the napkin over under Gad's nose. "Look in the mirror and say...that." He stabbed the napkin with his index finger.

Gad peered at the shaky letters. "Bart? Sable?"

Pete just slapped his arm and pointed at the mirror. "Say it."

Gad snorted. "Fine, whatever." He looked into his tipsy reflection above the row of shot glasses. "Bartzebel."

"Again."

"Bart-ze-bel." Gad over annunciated each syllable loudly for Pete and smirked back at his sallow-eyed and skeptical reflection.

GAD'S REFLECTION CHANGED. He watched his own eyes turn to obsidian with red slits. His image in the mirror winked and grinned back at him, wider and wider. The edges of his mouth touched each earlobe.

"What the fuck?" Gad jumped up off his barstool. It fell backward into the path of a server with a tray who then tumbled over the stool, sending the tray full of food flying, coincidentally, all over Gad.

Pete grabbed his stomach, his laughter carrying above the cacophony.

As staff and patrons alike came to the aid of the fallen server, Gad swung back to his reflection. Now it was only a red-faced asshole covered in the beef wellington glaring back at him. He shook his head, baffled.

It took a few minutes for Gad to help the server up and pick up the broken dishes. With the dishwasher mopping up the last of the mess, Gad parked again on the bar stool.

"I hate to say I told you so, but...no, wait. Actually, I love it. Probably why I'm not a priest anymore." Pete used the cocktail napkin to smear away some gravy on Gad's chest.

"Har, har," Gad glowered. "What was that thing? What did I just summon?"

"Lesser chaos demon. Very minor. But see? He did his job. And all it would have taken was an invitation into your skin suit and he'd be driving you around like a Cadillac through Graceland." Pete shoved a fresh bourbon at him.

Gad pushed it back. "Thanks, but I've had enough. Why didn't Beezlebutt come through the mirror at me?"

"It can't. Only way it can cross to this plane is by possessing something."

"But I've seen them here before whenever I couldn't save someone and hell opened up to take them."

"Those would have to be half-demons."

"Half? As in, half human?"

"There's half-human demons and half-human angels. Never heard of cambion or nephilim?"

Gad blinked. "Ok, yeah. Nephilim I know."

"It's in the bible, in Ezekiel. But true demons, like Beezlebutt in the mirror, use reflective surfaces to see into this plane. But if they want to cross over, they need a vessel to ride in. And since a human body won't house another soul, it degrades after a while. Not with face bubbling and pea soup, but with wasting. So that was my job in the church, save the afflicted. Turns out, I'm fantastic with casting out demons. It's how I met your dad."

"How?" Gad leaned forward.

"He needed an exorcism."

"You're shitting me," Gad said, and meant it. His dad knew

things about the occult and how to solve problems, not become a problem.

"Not your dad himself, ya' idjit. Someone who came to him for help. They had a possessed teenage son. James was known for being able to clear spaces of bad spirits, that sort of stuff. He tried to do it, but he failed. You have to be ordained and know what you're doing. So, he found me."

"You two were a crime-fighting duo after that, huh?"

"Best friends after that. But your dad, he was the sidekick," Pete said, with a wink.

"I shudder to imagine the tights."

"So, don't. What's important is that the more we did to help people, the more we got to know about Vegas. This place, what it really is, who runs it, all of that. It's bigger than you know."

Pete brought a fresh bourbon to his lips, but Gad touched his wrist and held back the glass. "You've got to tell me, Pete. Tell me everything."

Pete took a deep breath and exhaled slowly. "Sure. How do I put this?" He rubbed his eyebrows. "Got it. Okay, here it is. Gideon," he turned on his stool and faced Gad. "Arch demons run Vegas. You know the big ones from the Seven Deadly Sins, right? Lust, Gluttony, Pride, yadda yadda?"

Gad nodded.

"Yeah, those. The seven arch demons sit under Big Red himself. They own the casinos chains here. Each chain caters to the arch demon's temptation specialty. If your weakness is great food, there's that casino on the strip that has ten stories dedicated to the best restaurants in the world, celebrity chefs and all that. Or if gambling and money is more your speed, the five-star casino with the sports cars and VIP suites caters completely to your ego at every turn. And the arch demons have this competition going, it seems. Each one wants to be the one with the most customers."

Pete's words floored Gad. "You mean the most souls going down."

"Yes, that's' right."

"How did you two figure this out?"

Pete waved a hand. "We don't have the hours it would take for me to tell you all the stories. But that mirror in the cellar? It looks in on the main floor of lust-central, Asmodeus' domain. We kept tabs on everything that went down there, your dad even got a job as a handyman so we could keep our collective ear to the ground."

Gad's eyebrows shot up. "I barely remember that. I had a babysitter at nights and she'd microwave me TV dinners."

"Sorry he wasn't home for you when you were so young, kiddo. Your dad was fighting crime."

"It's okay. I like Salisbury steak and brownies. But go on. What kinds of things did you guys do?"

"Oh hell, saved a lot of ladies from damnation, that's for sure. And some troubled dudes, too. It's difficult to pull people safely out of a cult, because as you know, cults don't like quitters. But we saved quite a few and got them to not only move out of Vegas but move out of state. Some of them stay in contact. One of them is with my old church even to this day."

"Is Dahlia one of them?"

Pete laughed. "Oh no, not her. She's something entirely else. But I tell you what. If you're ever in trouble and I'm not answering the phone, you call her."

"Why? Why her?" Gad softened, thinking back on her golden wavy hair and blue eyes.

"You know that song, 'Everything you can do, I can do better'? That's Dahlia."

"Is she from the church, too?"

"In a way," Pete threw back the last of his drink. "A lot of experience helping people. You should talk with her some time. She hates Vegas, though. You have to go to her side of Nevada."

Gad shrugged. "No problem. After what you just told me, I totally get it. Why'd you two quit helping people?"

"For you."

"Huh? Me?"

"Your father's heart attack was no accident. We had pulled multiple people out of that casino, and we recruited others to help. Our group had grown. We called ourselves The Watchers. But to our detriment, Asmodeus caught on. And those arch demons may compete with each other, but they will work together to stamp out holy opposition. The day your dad died was the day the man in black found us."

Gad was stunned. "A man in black..." he repeated, not knowing what else to say.

"He belonged to one of the casinos. He and his thugs found our meeting place, found out where we worked, where we lived. Realized we had infiltrated the casinos." Pete took a deep swallow of amber liquid and shut his eyes. "He was a higher up, that's all we know. But a few of us were in a meeting with your dad at his dad's cabin."

"In the basement," Gad added.

"Yeah, in the basement. This man came through that fucking mirror. He took one look at your dad and..."

"And heart attack," Gad breathed. "You guys always told me he died on the job."

"Technically, that's true. Just not the job you thought. So we had to stop what we were doing. We covered the mirror, threw charms and wards around the cabin, I left the church, hid out. Your dad, well, he stayed with you. And you know the rest."

"Yeah. Which is apparently that Vegas is hell on earth."

"Ain't that the truth."

"Hey, wait a minute." Gad watched the bartender mixing cocktails. "You know Drake, right?"

"Course I do. Lived with you a while. Kind of a punk, but he meant well."

"That's fair. Yeah. But anyway, Drake moved out. He got a job at a new casino called Inferno, he's been there for weeks."

Pete winced. "Mm. That's bad news, then. Guessing you can't talk him into a different job at this point."

"Why do you say that? The arch demon thing?"

"It's no joke, Gad. I don't think my arch diocese would have the testicular fortitude to stay in a casino for more than a couple weeks and withstand the evil pouring in. Have you seen him lately?"

Gad shook his head. "In fact, last time I saw him, he was packing to move out. Didn't tell me he was leaving or anything, just came home and he was almost ready to leave. He was so...cold. Indifferent. Not like himself at all."

Pete grimaced. "Sorry to hear it, Gideon. Likely they already got to him. We went through it with the people from Asmodeus's over and over. It all starts when you sign a contract with them. Next thing you know, you feel like something important is missing. It's because it is. Always read the fine print, Gad."

"What? What did they take from Drake, Pete?"

Pete's jaw set, the muscles flexing as he ground his teeth. "God's gift to all his children. They took his free will."

22

"Drake! Bossman X needs you."

Kiera's announcement from the office door followed by her come-hither finger gesture was part of Drake's daily routine. And even though it hadn't been very long, Drake felt so at home at Inferno, the new job didn't feel new anymore. It was more than a job. Hell, it was his life.

He never had to leave, nor did he want to. His suite on the fourth floor was insane. The TV on the wall was practically the whole wall. The view of the strip from his window was incredible with neon and twinkling lights for miles. When he was hungry, he could order anything from room service or he could walk down to the twenty-four-hour buffet where every imaginable dish was there for the taking. His work clothes and casuals were dry cleaned when he hung them in the plastic bags in his walk-in closet. Next day, boom, they appeared clean, pressed and back in the closet again.

And with work being one floor down from his suite, getting there early and pulling double-shifts was not even a consideration. His paychecks were growing faster than a politician's promises before election day.

Drake used the on-site gym at least four times a week, taking advantage of the "supplements" Xavier slipped him. His body and his confidence were now rock hard. The spa offered him free tanning, massages, and haircuts, and the tailor at the men's clothing store ordered his clothes custom fit. His new convertible sat unused and shiny in the valet parking of the garage.

The job itself never felt like work. They simply paid Drake to be Drake. As Floor Manager, he kept his eyes on the casino guests. If anyone threatened to become a problem, Drake solutioned it. He even had a former linebacker named Red at his beck and call to enforce whatever needed enforcing. Drake had started on the Third Level where any shmoe off the street could play card and table games or get tickets to the nightly magic show. But Drake had upped his game, so they promoted him to the Fourth Level. The Fourth Level was the place where they offered influential clients a higher level of service for casino membership.

This was where Drake really shined. If years of bartending had taught him anything, it was who had money and who could be influenced. He could spot a lonely mid-life crisis a mile away and, inside of ten minutes, have his signature on a new Inferno Lifetime Membership. It made him happy, because, each time he secured a new membership, everybody won. Drake got another pat on the back, Inferno got a new big spender with annual membership fees, and mid-life crisis got to be less lonely with a lap-dance from Cleopatra at the *Storm* club on the Second Level. Speaking of which, Drake had recently discovered Inferno offered employee perks on that point, too. The *Storm* girls loved the view of the strip from his hot tub and obligingly made room calls anytime.

All the while, Drake's focus was on pleasing Xavier. If the Fourth Level was a fool's paradise, who knew what awaited on the Fifth Level? And the Sixth? Xavier had promised that

Drake's black keycard would get more and more access as he worked his way up and earned their trust. With enough hard work and loyalty, someday he'd get a suite up on the Ninth Level, too. Sure, it was pretty damned cold up there, but he was certain the admission was worth the price.

Drake still didn't know what was in the packages and boxes that he delivered to Xavier's door. Not that they limited it to package delivery. He also delivered important people. He was on a first-name basis with several members of the Luciano family. Last week, he had escorted the Academy's Actor of the Year and his entourage to Xavier's door. It had bothered him a little at first that they never asked him to escort anyone back out. He reasoned that the wild benders going on behind that chrome door must cause incognito walks of shame or something. Xavier had stressed that the Ninth Level was for maintaining the privacy of the exclusive, after all.

Whenever he found himself tempted to ask who, what or why something was, he remembered Kiera's words, "I've learned not to ask."

His watch read 12:03 a.m. when Drake got a call to make the next delivery to Xavier's room. Without further explanation needed, Drake hustled to the Fourth Level office door.

Red stood at the door and gestured for Drake to step in. "Boss is havin' a fancy private party for some Japanese clients." He jerked his thumb toward a long serving cart with a nude woman. Drake's jaw dropped.

Sushi and sashimi covered the woman's "pink parts," as Drake thought of them. A black cloth covered her face and neck.

"Can she breathe?"

"Dunno. Better get her up there before you find out she can't."

"Sure thing." Drake grabbed the handle to the cart and, struggling with the cart's weight, got it slowly rolling to the private elevator. He read the note card propped next to her feet.

NYOTAIMORI, the perfect gift to celebrate a victorious battle. Congratulations! - INFERNO

"Must be some bachelor party thing," Drake muttered, frowning at the red flowers and baby's breath surrounding the nude form. The woman wore diamonds at her throat and equally glittering high heels on her delicate feet. Her skin was nearly as pale as the white fish resting on the banana leaves over her breasts and thighs.

He rolled the cart off the elevator. The black cloth over her face moved.

Drake stopped. "Hey, can you breathe okay under there?"

She didn't answer. Carefully, he pulled the cloth back from her face.

Her platinum hair pinned up with diamond combs, Kiera's red and swollen tear-filled eyes opened wide upon seeing Drake. The black tape over her mouth muffled her words. "MMMM! MMM MMEE MMMOW MMMM MEEER!"

Her chest heaved with the effort to breathe through a runny nose. A piece of tuna rolled off her navel to the cart.

"Kiera, what's going on?" Drake peeled back the tape enough for her to gasp for air like a fish out of water.

"Help me," she whispered, water flowing from her eyes and nose. "Cut the restraints." She looked from the table next to her face down to her wrists. Next to her head on either side were Japanese chef sushi knives, the longest blades Drake had ever seen. Drake pushed aside the diamond bracelet on her wrist and another on her ankle to see her wrists and ankles bound to the cart by white nylon zip-tie bands. One large band secured her waist and two more secured her thighs beneath banana leaves filled with delicacies.

"Cut me out of here," she insisted. "Before they come looking for me."

Drake reached for a blade, his fingers coming to rest on the wooden handle. "Wait a sec. Who did this to you?"

"Xavier!" Kira's eyes were wild.

"X? Because?"

Kiera sucked in air and held it, her chest poised. She bit her lip. "Because...I...I... he... I said no. I wouldn't do it. And then I told-"

That was all Drake needed. Before she could finish, he secured the black tape back over her mouth and pushed the cart forward, arcing carefully to the left.

"MMMM!! MMMM!" Kiera struggled against the tight restraints, the pale skin around her wrists turning beet red with straining. He dropped the black cloth back over her face and both fish-gutting knives.

The door opened to the sounds of drunken cheering. "Why hello, my loyal Drake. I see you've brought me a dirty little geisha filled with treats." Xavier's grin was sinister as he pulled the cart backward into his room.

Muffled by tape, the sounds of betrayal were still understandable. "Whhhyyyy? Whhhhyyyyyy?"

As the cart crossed the threshold, Drake replied. "You know, I've learned not to ask."

The door shut with a click.

rabbed us both some coffee. Meet me at a table on the patio.

Gad typed his reply methodically into his phone's text window.

OK, be right there.

He peered into his rear-view mirror at the unruly dark hair hanging over his eyes and smoothed it back behind his ear. It stayed in place for almost three seconds before flopping forward again. He sighed, his aspirations of looking sharp for Dahlia dwindling. Gad tugged the bottom of his oatmeal-toned Henley shirt neatly into place. It looked good with his "newest" pair of dark wash jeans, but he realized with dismay it had been quite a while since he last bought a pair of jeans. The knees were already fading. Hopefully she wouldn't notice.

"It is what it is," he mumbled to himself. He threw the driver door soundly shut and strolled to the cafe patio.

As promised in her text, Dahlia sat at the far side of the patio perched over an open book on the iron-wrought cafe table. Morning sunlight poured over her champagne hair, golden waves almost glittering down to her earlobes. Even her silky white blouse seemed to reflect sunlight radiantly all around her.

"So, you weren't kidding when you said 'outside of Vegas'," Gad said, as he settled into the chair opposite her with a grin.

Dahlia's pale pink lips spread into a wide smile. As before, she wore no make-up. She was as God had made her, and to Gad it was as though Michaelangelo himself had sculpted her aquiline features from marble.

"It is a bit remote for townies like you, I suppose. You made it, though, so well done." She nudged a cup and a saucer filled to nearly the brim with steaming black coffee. "I quite literally just sat down. Coffee is hot. Cream and sugar?" She gestured to a china sugar bowl and matching small pitcher on the table in front of her.

"No thanks. I like it black, like my soul." Gad pulled the coffee closer, grateful for the boost it would deliver. Had Dahlia not called early to take him up on his offer for "a coffee some-time", he'd likely still be snoring in the comfort of bed. He was still feeling the foggy haze of the previous night's bourbon-fest with Pete.

Gad watched with fascination as she loaded her coffee with several heaping spoonfuls of sugar.

"I can feel you judging me, Gideon."

"Oh, no. No judgment here. If you've got a sweet tooth, I say, indulge."

Her lips curled up, watching the coffee swirl around her spoon. "You can never have too much sugar, it's quite a wonderful thing. And wherever it's too dark, you must let in the light." She poured a splash of cream into the cup. The cloud of cream erupted throughout the swirling dark liquid, trans-forming it under the guidance of her stirring to a warm caramel color.

"And your soul is not black, my dear." Dahlia glanced to him with a smirk, her crystal blue eyes twinkling.

"How do you know?"

Dahlia brought the cup to her lips. "I suppose the best way to explain it is to say that I can see auras."

"Auras? What's that? Like when you've got a bad migraine?"

She laughed. It was pleasant, like bird song. "I've never had one, so I don't know. But what I can tell you is that it's like seeing colors around a person. Some people emit the most beautiful colors, like a rainbow. Red, green, blue, purple, you name it. Sometimes it's only a few colors at a time. Sometimes there's only one."

"So, what do you see when you look at me?"

Her smile was sly. "You have a few colors going on. A bit of royal blue here, a bit of light green there. Primarily, there's a lemon-yellow thing happening. But definitely no black."

"So? What does that mean? Do I have a pleasant lemon-lime flavor?"

She set her coffee down on its plate. "Really Gideon, you didn't come all this way for a clairvoyant reading, did you?"

"I can't say that I'm didn't," he shrugged. "Things have been tougher than usual lately. And none of it has been...normal stuff."

"The spirits, you mean?"

"No. Don't get me wrong, they're no picnic either. But it's just been, not normal stuff. Weird stuff. Weird for even me."

"Love, you're talking in circles."

He felt his face warm despite knowing that British conversation commonly included calling each other "love" or "mate". He took a deep breath. "Normally I'd keep this sort of stuff to myself because-"

"It sounds crazy." She sipped at her coffee, her eyes locked on his.

"Yeah."

"You can tell me anything, Gideon. Supernaturally speaking, I've quite literally seen it all. I guarantee there is nothing you can tell me that would shock me in the least."

Gad inhaled the breath that was ready to fuel the words about the alastor, but the words stopped. As kind as her offer to hear the strangeness was, he really liked her. Like, really. He couldn't remember how long it had been since he'd asked anyone out.

"Oh c'mon, Gad. Truly, I've seen things that would turn the bravest's hair white. My calling has always been to help those lost in shadow."

"You mean banishing ghosts?" He leaned forward on his elbows, his curiosity fully captured.

"No. And while lost spirits can be quite troublesome, my work focuses on the struggle between above and below. I've come face to face with forms of darkness rarely seen."

Gad hung on every word. And as much as he wanted to prod her again, he waited.

She took another drink from her cup and set it down with a clink on the saucer. "Every hour of every day, the fallen of perdition seek every possibility to damn the souls of humanity."

"The fallen of perdition. You mean demons." He rubbed at the back of his hand. This topic was both what he didn't want to hear and what he needed to know more about.

Dahlia nodded. "Every soul added to Lucifer's realm gains him power. With power, he creates more demons. With more demons, his army grows. With a bigger army, his influence to sway souls to darkness increases. While one soul damned here or one lost soul there might seem trivial, they're not. Not at all."

"So let me dumb this way down for a minute. You're saying every soul added to hell is like a Satan battery. He gets stronger with more people going down?"

Her steady gaze unnerved Gad. "That's it exactly. And my work is to save every soul that I can, steering them to grace. Sometimes, that involves a battle with the demons themselves. I specialize in exorcisms."

"Is that how you met Pete?"

"Yes. He was called to this place to save souls for the church. And Gad, truth be told, Peter is truly the most gifted in that skill that I've ever met."

Gad chuckled. "It's hard to imagine Uncle Pete like that."

"Then you need to know him better." Her words cleanly cut away his mirth. "I've fought at Peter's side more times than I could count. When put to the task, he is relentless. Together, we have won more than we've lost. Sometimes I wonder if he knows the difference he's made here."

"Here. Las Vegas?"

"Yes. This place is the capitol of bad decisions." She looked around her with a scowl. "It's rife with demonic influence, pushing people toward committing acts that ensure their place in the inferno. Those little voices you hear on your shoulder when faced with a decision? One is an angel and the other, a devil. You may not see them, but their influence is most definitely there. And here, where there are more demons than angels, the house tends to win."

In his mind's eye, he again saw his eyes in the mirror turn to obsidian with red slits. It made the hair on the back of his neck stand on end.

"You've seen some things with Pete." Gad's voice belayed his sinking feeling.

"Oh, quite. This place is a battleground for souls, and some will go all in with forces they can't comprehend. Laughably, when asked if they want to put their existential selves on the table with everything else, some don't even believe in their eternal souls as being real." She rolled her eyes. "Pete and I have gone toe to toe with some of hell's heaviest hitters, as you might say. And sadly, when Pete left the church, we lost one of our own. I would do almost anything to bring him back to the fold."

Gad frowned. "Why did he leave? When I ask him, he doesn't want to talk about it."

She smiled wistfully. "It was a boy, Dean, nearly a man by a year. Afflicted by not one, but a host of demons. The effects of one demon on a body are devastating, but many are rapid and deadly. And if the body dies while possessed..."

"The soul is damned, too," Gad finished.

"Sadly, yes. This was a case your father brought to Pete and me. For three days and nights, we fought with the legion. It was one of the most horrific battles I've ever endured. We freed Dean from weaker demons, but the entire host was too strong." Dahlia's stern gaze drifted from Gad's. "Darkness prevailed in the room. Hellborn used the boy as a portal to enter our domain. Blood rained within the chamber. Peter's body was nearly taken, twice. They broke your father's arm and ribs pitching him into the ceiling and walls. We couldn't keep Dean restrained, he...he tore out his own eyes."

Gad suddenly felt as though he were falling. He wrapped his fingers around the edge of the table, reminding himself through touch that his body sat safely and solidly in a chair. "What happened to Dean?" he asked quietly.

"He died." Her lips pressed tightly together, her face hard.

"His soul was lost, then," Gad said, voice tight.

"And Pete left the church. We had faced too many losses by that point. Dean was his final straw." Her arms crossed over her chest. "Dean's soul was important, Gad. Some souls burn more brightly, more colorfully. His was-" She chewed the corner of her bottom lip. "I failed. And I can never forgive myself."

"And neither can Pete." And just like that, everything about Pete finally clicked. This is why Pete taught him everything he knew about faith, Catholicism and protection against the dead, but had never spoke of his past with the church, or what was really happening under the surface of Vegas, until the night before.

Gad realized something with a start as he stared at his wavering reflection in his lukewarm coffee. "Dahlia, I have a friend named Drake who recently went to work for that new casino, Inferno."

"How long has he been there? A few days?"

"A couple months, I think."

Dahlia's face fell. "Go on."

"Well, after everything you and Pete have told me about the casinos and who, or rather what's, running them...I mean, is Drake ok?"

"Have you talked to him lately?"

"No, and that's the thing. We were the best of friends. He was my roommate. He was even there every step of the way when I got my emergency transport business running. And then one night, I come from work, and he's packing. Said the hotel offered him a place to live, a new job. And he must've gotten a fat stack of cash somehow because he went from living paycheck to paycheck and splitting rent with me to paying or rent ahead. And he was so different, so totally the opposite of the guy I've hung out with for years. So-"

"Cold."

"Yeah! Exactly. Pete said they took Drake's free will, and it changed him."

Dahlia sighed. "I know this will sound just awful Gad but take it for what it's worth. Hang onto the memories you had of Drake and leave it at that. He's not Drake anymore."

"But why? I don't understand. Isn't free will just choosing right from wrong?"

"Yes. Yes, it is. And that was taken from your friend.

Remember that I said just minutes ago that everyone has an angel and a demon on each shoulder. I don't mean that there are literally little entities telling you what to do. But there is always a temptation and grace in your every decision. Except now for your friend."

"But how is that possible?"

"The casinos make deals with those who make the choice to work for them. They offer a contract. If your friend signed it, he likely didn't read it or understand what he was agreeing to. The casino took his moral voice and left him incomplete. His is now voiceless in matters of the heart. Imagine that you worked in a place where people are bought and sold, they disappear, or worse yet, they're murdered before your very eyes."

Gad was aghast. "Never. Everything I do is about saving people."

"But if your ability to choose the righteous path was stolen? Your free will removed?"

Gad opened his mouth and shut it, flabbergasted.

"He may have even agreed to have the mark of his tribe inked somewhere into his skin. But one day, sooner or later, he'll come to know that it's the mark of the demon he works for."

"What can I do to save him?"

Dahlia chewed her lip again. After a moment, she spoke. "Gideon, I will never lie to you. So trust me when I tell you, in all of my research, I have never found a way to restore a soul's free will. It's a gift from God, you see. When it is willingly given up, well." She shrugged. "This is why I say you should just try to move on and remember him for the friend he was."

"But you're talking about him like he's dead and gone."

Dahlia said nothing.

This bothered Gad most of all. Drake was a lost cause? Like a match striking a flame deep within Gad, he needed to see Drake. He needed to save him. Gad was actually angry. "That just can't be. There has to be a way. I need to talk to him." Gad pushed his chair back and stood.

"You're not going to Inferno?" The alarm in Dahlia's voice drew the attention of patrons entering the cafe. She stood, her eyes wide. At her full height and taller than Gad, Dahlia was unintentionally intimidating.

"I have to. I can't just do nothing."

Dahlia grabbed his wrist. "Gideon, he made his choice."

"Not according to you, he didn't. Sounds to me like they tricked him into giving away his soul. He's damned to hell, right? Am I understanding the situation?"

The air left Dahlia's nose with a huff of resignation. She dropped his wrist. "Yes."

"Then I need to talk to him. I need to tell him what's happened, what he's up against. I mean, what if he went to church, and he asked forgiveness? What then?"

She shook her head and leaned back in her chair. "He won't do it, Gad. I understand your pain, but this is not how to deal with it."

"But Dahlia-"

She pulled a black leather cord out from under the collar of her white blouse. Pulling it quickly over her head, she held it out to Gad. "If you need to go try, then go talk to him. Just know you're putting yourself in great danger over a fool's errand. And wear this."

He reached out and took the pendant she extended to him. "What is it?" The rectangular pendant appeared to be made of metal covered with arcane inscriptions etched in black. "Is this a Hebrew tablet or something?"

"Something like that, yes. It's a seal. The magical law of Moses."

Gad looked up from the pendant. "Split the Red Sea Moses?"

"The very same. Wear that and the ghosts and the demons

won't notice you anymore. Now I'm not saying they can't see you, they will, but this seal hides your abilities and makes you just like anyone else."

"I can't take yours," Gad began and held it toward her.

"Take it, I can make another." She took it from him and stood, placing it over his head. "Now, it does more than you think. Say these words." She held out one side of the seal to his eyes. "Loudly. Three times. You'll summon help to your side. Just don't look their way if you can help it."

Gad twisted his lips at her.

"Just trust me. No need to look at them. Just let them help you out of the situation you're in. Now, on the other side," she flipped it over. "If you're lost and looking for a way out, concentrate on these symbols and speak to me."

"Out loud?"

"Or in your mind."

"Like a psychic call?"

"Yes."

"Nope, that's not weird at all. Tell me again why I shouldn't just text you?"

The hard look on Dahlia's face told Gad that he wouldn't get away with very much more.

"Because texting with a lit phone in the darkness is more obvious than a psychic ping if you've demons hunting you on their grounds."

Gad swallowed. He hadn't imagined in his wildest dreams that a visit to Inferno could go that terrifying route.

"Please, Gideon. Please think about this first. Don't do anything rash." She wrapped her hands around his. Her touch was instantly comforting, an attribute of her skills as a healer and medium. Feeling as though they were being watched, Gad looked around the patio. Other patrons were now staring at Dahlia with respectful admiration.

"I need to go now." She dropped his hands abruptly and talked as she gathered her things. "Like I said, don't just go into the viper pit unprepared. Think about it first. Bring Pete with you if you must go."

"Would you come with me?"

Dahlia stood, her bag over one shoulder. "I simply can't, I'm sorry. The influence is too heavy there and I can't keep my wits about me. But, again, should you need me, hold the seal in your hand, concentrate, and speak to me." She turned to walk to the parking lot.

"Dahlia, wait."

"I need to go, Gad." Despite her insisted urgency, she waited. The eyes of the patrons were glued to her, their murmurs and whispers growing in number.

"Can we...could I maybe take you out for dinner?"

Dahlia smiled, but her expression was already apologetic. Gad's heart fell.

"I can't but thank you for extending the invitation."

"Is it, I mean, are you-"

"With someone? No, it's not that. I just can't be with anyone right now. But, if I could," Dahlia leaned toward his face and brushed her lips across his cheek. "I would love to have dinner with you. Just know that it's me, not you."

Gad's face burned with the heat of ten thousand suns. "Okay then, until the next coffee, I guess. Or psychic ping."

"Until then," she dipped her head slightly to him, turned and made her way to the sidewalk with a long and purposeful gait.

Gad pushed his chair in and looked about the patio where all had returned to their own conversations. She was stunning, he couldn't blame them for staring. He dropped the pendant inside his shirt with a sigh, letting the combo of awkward vulnerability and rejection settle in his chest. The feeling would fade if he concentrated on anything else, like pouring himself to the evening shift ahead.

Gad walked toward Mercy in the parking lot and looked over his shoulder, allowing himself to steal one last glance of the beautiful woman who had turned him down flat. The sidewalk was empty.

~

AT THE END of his ten-hour shift, Gad dragged himself upstairs for a hot shower and a tumbler of bourbon.

The night itself had been, by Gad's barometer, a fairly normal evening. No reaper calls. And the radioed calls for busses had been fairly innocuous, all things considered. No death, only par for the course drunken injuries and a supposed heart attack that ended up being heartburn. There were also ghosts of course, but unlike every other day in his life, tonight they had gloriously looked right past him as though he was anyone else.

The shower in the master bath had been a good deal nicer than he had imagined it would be. The shower water temperature went from cool to steaming in less than a minute. His twin bed looked small in the spacious room that had once been Drake's. He fell on the mattress and turned on the TV.

The full tumbler of bourbon sat on the nightstand next to him. Normally by now, it would be half empty. But for whatever reason, tonight he didn't feel compelled to drink it.

He pulled the pendant and black cord off over his head and laid it on the nightstand. With a luxurious stretch, he settled into his mattress and let his head sink into his pillow. A welcome wave of oncoming unconsciousness washed over him. He was ready to succumb to it, let the snoring begin.

A nagging feeling tugged at him. Someone was in the room

watching him. A whooshing sound followed.

As if to answer his worry with affirmation, an ice-cold drop of water splashed across his forehead. Tentatively, he opened one eye a crack.

Cold dead eyes stared at him, blueish gray and cloudy, from just above him. A woman in a translucent and deteriorating nightdress floated above him, her long and black hair flowing about her head and body like an entity unto itself. Her arms floated outstretched from her torso. A gaping hole where one breast should have been exposed her ribs while the remaining breast floated up to the side like a gray leather pouch. Her white bloated skin drifted about her, her body eternally trapped below some water's surface. She opened her plump lips and a muffled scream poured forth through unseen water, bubbles flowing forth with sound trapped in fragments.

"Fuck!" Gad jumped from bed, his heart hammering in his chest. He strode angrily to the doorway and marched toward his old room, not daring to look behind him. He knew the obstinate spirit would float rapidly after him.

He looked here and there across the floor of his former bedroom, street light pouring through the crack in the curtains to fall upon the familiar blue cardboard cylinder. Gad snatched it up and turned to the ghost stuck waiting at his old bedroom doorway. It could not cross his old room's original salt barrier and its fury came audibly through the doorway in muffled rapid bubbles rising to the loft ceiling.

"Oh, shut up," he growled and tossed a handful of table salt at the ghost. The woman melted, her screech suddenly snipped from existence as her form broke apart and drifted away at contact with the cleansing salt.

Grumbling, Gad chewed himself out for not having laid down the mandatory lines of salt in his eagerness to move into the bigger bedroom.

24

G ad stood before the black and faux-gold accented structure. From the ground floor and up he followed it, level by level, finding it nearly impossible to take the vast tower in fully. It reared over everything else, a dark form stretching impossibly high with jagged penthouse suites like horns piercing the night sky, eclipsing the moon and its pure light.

His head spun, suddenly dizzy as though he were falling. He reached out to steady himself, his slick palm cooling against the chilled fake marble surface of the column beside him. He gasped and took a deep breath, filling his lungs with cool air.

It was half-past eight. Drake would be inside, likely working the night-shift. It was now or never. "Never" was the louder voice in his ear. This time, it wasn't just a handful of spiteful shades that might get in his way and be easily dispatched by a variety of household items. No, through those golden doors was a whole other level of frightening the likes of which he had never had to face. But with the seal hanging from the cord around his neck and the sheer determination to save his best friend, Gad forced one foot after the other until he stood at the threshold. He laid his hand on the door handle. The door swung open.

The furniture, the curtains, the floor, the vivid colors, the disturbingly hellish artwork on glass and lit from within, everything was overdone. And what was that sickeningly sweet smell? It was like frosting-scented candles had been lit to mask the underlying and heady scent of rotting meat. It was almost too much. Gad blinked, frozen in the vestibule.

The clear ramp beneath his feet stretched out ahead and to either side over flowing water. The water's unnatural blue tone repulsed him. It was yet another example of fakery, water pretending to be crystal blue and fresh. The casino's design intended to give the impression of opulence and riches, but in truth, it was all just an elaborate facade hiding something else, something awful waiting just beneath the surface. The whole place made his skin crawl.

Pallid bodies in jewel-toned finery stood on walnut veneer, drinks in hand, dreary and uninterested in each other's company. The placard over their heads read "The Vestibule, Surrender your desires within." Wasn't that just a fancier way of saying "abandon all hope ye who enter here"? The whole place was vast, chilling, and oddly dead.

"Gad? What're you doing here?"

The sound of a familiar voice broke Gad from his statue-like trance. Drake approached from the Greek atrium and over the glass bridge. Or at least, a form of Drake approached. This wasn't the guy he had shared an apartment with for five years. That guy was imposing and somewhat beefy. The tan over-muscled hulk coming at him with swift strides was tall and menacing, a powerhouse, a one-man wrecking crew in a tailored suit and dress shoes.

"Drake!" Gad swallowed his shock and, stepping toward him,

threw an arm around his former roommate. It was like throwing his arm around granite; cold, hard and immovable. Dahlia was right. The person he thought he knew had transformed into someone else entirely. Flabbergasted, he didn't know what else to say. "What happened to you?"

"Dude, let go," Drake hissed, his icy blue eyes shifting left and right.

Embarrassed, Gad opted to slap Drake's bicep like a coach giving his player a pep talk. "Oh, sorry. It's been a while so, uh, yeah."

Drake subtly motioned for Gad to follow him, and they crossed the bridge back to the atrium. "So, how's business, Gad? What're you up to these days?"

"Oh, y'know, same old same old." Life had been miles from both "same" and "old", but Gad had no time to waste. "How about you? How's the new, well, everything?"

"Demanding, but well worth it. Long hours, big responsibility. But hey, they keep moving me up the food chain, so I must be doing something right."

They passed by a row of blinking slot machines, at the end of which sat a bickering elderly couple.

"No, I said this is a vacation, Margaret. You going to ruin that for me, too, with your constant nagging?"

"It's our fiftieth, Nicholas. You can at least do that much for me?" The white-haired woman in a fine sequined turquoise dress and a white fur about her shoulders pleaded with her husband.

"How're you both doing, Mr. and Mrs. Peterson? Having a good time?" Drake stopped to address the couple.

Margaret glanced up to Drake with a star-struck grin. "Oh yes, thank you." She patted her husband's hand, and their wedding rings clinked. "Nicholas, tell the young man you're having fun, too." Nicholas, also dressed to the nines with a matching turquoise bow tie and white wingtip shoes, blinked with a scowl from behind thick glasses. He motioned for Drake, who bent his ear down next to the man's face. He whispered to Drake. Drake nodded, "Tonight, Mr. Peterson, absolutely. Give us a few minutes, won't you?"

The old man nodded, eying Gad with an air of distaste.

Drake put a firm hand on Gad's shoulder. "Gad, it's great to see you, but I've got a lot going on right now."

Before he could make his case, Gad was already being dismissed. "I can come back later. Buy you a drink?"

Drake paused, a muscle in his jaw twitching. He seemed to consider Gad's offer. But something about the way Drake's gaze slid over Gad like oil made him uneasy.

"Wanna see some real magic?" Drake reached into his tailored jacket and, with the flourish of a magician, produced a white ticket and extended it between two fingers to Gad. "Front and center. Check it out. After the show, play some games, grab a bite. On my shift break tonight, we'll catch up over bourbon."

Gad took the ticket with a sinking feeling. "Sure, sounds fun," he lied. This wasn't at all how he'd planned it would go. He hadn't wanted to stay one minute longer than necessary. Now he had agreed to stay many minutes or hours longer than necessary.

"Meet me here at midnight." Drake was already backing away though the open office door, pointing to the spot where Gad's feet felt existentially glued to the floor.

"Your break is at midnight?" But his retort went unheard as the office door clicked shut, Drake long since having left Gad to get to whatever Mr. Peterson had asked him to do. He rubbed the edge of the ticket with his fingertip, perturbed.

"Yowch," he sucked in his breath. The white ticket now had a red smear over its formerly pristine border, the sharp edge having sliced into his skin. A fine line of flesh parted, red drops beading in the fresh paper cut.

Gad took in his surroundings with a growing sense of unease. People at the slot machines surrounded him, but he'd never felt more alone. Outside of the Petersons, no one sat with anyone else. The many individuals in all shapes, colors and sizes sat at their slot machine and pulled their lever with mechanical repetitiveness, eyes blank, and the blue-white glow of the slots pulling all color from their faces. They had no expression, no emotion. Zombies, all of them. They moved, but for all intents and purposes, they were dead.

Gad turned away, unable to bear the sight.

THE THEATER WAS LITERALLY BREATHTAKING. Gad realized he had stopped breathing as he entered the sweeping hall whose sumptuous burgundy velvet seats appeared filled. Polished wooden walls stretched stories high into the finely designed carvings and Renaissance-inspired murals on the ceiling. They had painted all nearly black in the sloping theater's dim lighting.

There was not one other person in the establishment wearing street clothes, instead wearing cocktail dresses and high fashion. He couldn't have felt more out of place if he'd been in a swimsuit and flippers. Mostly out of shame, Gad's eyes remained locked on his simple sneakers as they dared to tread on the rich carpet weaving intricate Victorian patterns of gold, purples and red.

Row AA, Seat 15

To his ever-growing dismay, Gad passed row after row, drawing closer to the stage with every step. The ticket must truly be for the most front and center seat in the hall. He could feel the glares and hear the whispers of the finely dressed around him not-so-silently judging him as he passed by.

"Excuse me, pardon me," he muttered to the already-seated denizens of Row AA, turning and contorting to squeeze past knees, legs, and shoes to the only open seat left in an otherwise packed venue. "Sorry." He pulled a glittering rhinestone purse from his seat cushion and handed to the woman in the matching rhinestone outfit in the next seat.

"Shhhh," she admonished, one finger with a long pink-painted nail pressed to her injected glittering pink lips. The finger pointed to the stage where a crate on wheels sat in front of all between two lovely assistants. The showgirls in sparkling red slowly spun the box around for all to see that the crate was obviously empty with its open panel in the front and empty space beneath. The ladies smiled, dropped a panel into the front of the crate to close it, and waved goodbye to the audience before walking offstage in opposite directions. The lights dimmed.

Gad fell into his seat.

"Ladies and Gentlemen," the announcer's voice boomed over the speaker system throughout the darkened theater. "Welcome to the Seventh Level. Tonight, the illusions performed on this stage will seem very real. These performances have been tested by our Illusionist, and are designed to influence, to inspire, and to ignite each of your senses. With this in mind, there will be moments of sudden and dramatic action, loud sound, flashing light and highly theatrical performances. For your safety and the safety of those around you, please stay seated throughout the entire performance and do not attempt anything you are about to see. Thank you. Now, sit back, relax, and focus your full attention...to the stage!"

A pinpoint of a spotlight burst to a wide beam of light on the crate. The crate's front panel lifted, and out stepped a man in a tuxedo. He pulled a flat black disk from within his jacket and tapped it with a wand. The disk transformed into a top hat, which he placed at a jaunty angle on his head. Dark ethereal trance music with a thrumming bass beat pounded rhythmically over the sound of the audience's thunderous applause.

A chill ran down Gad's spine upon seeing that the magician wore white gloves and an expressionless white mask. Even the eye holes were too dark to provide the relief of seeing human eyes within.

The illusionist pulled at his red pocket square, and it instantly unfurled into a sizable diaphanous cloth that seemed to float on air. With the wave of his hand, a sea of gasps erupted from the audience as the red square of fabric floated along next to him, mimicking his movements. With every step from the magician, the fabric followed, and they danced together to the beat of the music.

Even Gad started to smile, slipping into the lull of the rhythmic music, the sway of the magician's elegant gestures, and the mesmerizing falling and floating of the gossamer red fabric. It rose higher and higher above the magician until it floated out above the audience, to which came more gasps of sheer amazement. Then, with the flick of his hand and a gesture to return, the square shot back to his hand. With a deep bow from both the magician and the fabric, it retreated to his pocket.

The music switched gears, its cadence slowing for the next bit. "Watch. Watch. Watch," a voice whispered to the rhythm, and then, "believe."

He swayed back and forth, this time producing playing cards from thin air. He plucked card after card from the air with empty hands, throwing each new card out into the audience with perfect spinning motions. Soon, cascades of cards fell from his left hand to his right, then formed a fan he threw end over end above his head and caught again, like a geisha in an elaborate dance. It was anybody's guess how the cards kept their fan shape once released to the air, yet they did.

Next he removed his eerie white mask and held it out to the audience for all to see. Yet he had not revealed his face, for another white mask with a frown covered his visage. He tossed the mask offstage and pulled away the frowning mask. Beneath was a smiling mask. With a flourish, he abandoned the smiling mask to reveal a mask with a frightened expression, its eye holes curling inward like a squint, and its mouth hanging open in a grotesque frozen scream. The magician walked to the edge of the stage and pointed to the woman in rhinestones next to Gad.

"Me?" She placed her fingertips over her heart, a mixture of both excitement and trepidation on her face.

The magician pointed at her insistently, nodding largely and dramatically. He lifted his palms to the audience and put a cupped hand to his ear. The audience roared their capitulation, calling for the woman to accept the invitation to the stage. She nodded and followed the magician-extended hand to the short stairs at the side of the stage as the music grew even louder, the beat deeper, the tempo increasing.

He pulled the grinning woman to his side and faced the audience. In a flash, the fright mask was in his hand and revealed his new cruel red mask, its expression sneering at her. He silently held the mask of fright out to her and gestured for her to place it over her face. Her grin melted away, replaced by confusion. Again, he motioned to the audience to encourage her.

"Put it on, put it on," they chanted to the beat.

With trembling fingers, she slid the mask over her face. Behind them, the curtains rose.

A much larger portion of the stage with the curtains lifted

and, in the darkness, lights grew brighter. A table with a giant saw blade moved forward, as if by magic, to the center stage.

The woman visibly jumped, her fingers at her sides splayed. The audience laughed.

The magician took her hands and playfully danced with her, gently spinning her around in a waltz-like fashion ever closer to the table, his tux tails flying out behind him. He pulled her to the table's edge and pressed her rigid form gently against it.

To Gad's surprise, she lifted the mask and shook her head, wide-eyed. Every inch of her body radiated "no" to the Illusionist.

Without a word, he lifted his fingers to her eyes and brought his masked face within inches of hers. The music dropped away, replaced by the sound of a drum-roll. He stared intently into her face, his fingers poised before her. For a moment, time stood still.

The magician moved to the right, and so did she. He moved to the left, and so did she. Somehow, she became his reflection. He mimicked pulling the mask down over his face, and she pulled the mask of fright over hers. He took a step back and gestured to the table. She compliantly laid down.

The drum-roll completed with the tap of a high-hat cymbal, and the audience cheered. Dramatically, he retrieved his sentient red cloth from his pocket and used it to bind her wrists beneath the table.

In a flash, the magician crossed the stage and stopped before Gad, his white fingered glove pointed directly at Gad's forehead.

Gad's heart almost stopped. "Oh, uh, no thanks," he tried to say over the noise of the surrounding crowd catcalling and goading him to get onstage.

Again, the magician held out his white gloved palm to the audience, and the goading grew louder. Gad's blood pumped through his veins. Someone's fingers delved into the muscles below his neck, pushing him upward against his will. He felt himself rise to his feet, the whole time hearing the voice on his shoulder screaming for him to get away. One of the sparkling assistants motioned for him to come to the stairs at the side of the stage, her red smile stretched from ear to ear with rows of white teeth glistening in the spotlight.

He made his way stiffly onstage to thunderous applause as the beat kicked back in. The lights surrounding the theater dimmed, focusing the spotlight solely on the magician and Gad.

The magician pointed to the Saw Table. A new spotlight appeared and shone on a big red button.

"Oooooooooooooooo," the audience intoned.

The white gloved finger tapped Gad's chest and slowly moved to point again to the button. The sound of hand-played drums increased, the music becoming drums beating with tribal commandment.

Gad moved toward the red button and the lighting over the Saw table came fully on. He surveyed the table, the woman tied to the table compliantly just in front of the blade. He wanted to push the button, somehow he knew he was meant to.

THUMP, THUMP, THUMP, THUMP.

The drum beat pounded in his head, in his chest. He couldn't think clearly. He raised his hand to the red button, seeing himself press it. *It will only be a magic trick, just press the button.*

"Do it, do it, do it," the audience began to chant again.

Gad's pocket vibrated. Not intermittently, but one long solid vibration that grew immediately hot against the skin of his hand in his sweat jacket pocket. Someone was about to die.

Gad snapped to, squeezing his eyes shut. He saw his own hand poised before the red button and pulled it back, as though burned. The realization of what he was about to do struck him with horror.

Gad looked to the woman on the table and the area around her. Crimson stains across the stage floor caught his attention. Huge swaths of dark red that had seeped into the polished floor beneath the table...and around a missing panel in the floor. A hole at least three feet long and two feet wide lay directly beneath the woman's body. And in the bright light on the saw table, red masked figures in black robes under the stage waited. All of their masks were the scowls of evil intent, just like the magician's. The murderous masked faces turned upward to him expectantly. Waiting.

People had died here before, been murdered here before, he realized.

THUMP, THUMP, THUMP, THUMP.

White-gloved fingers touched Gad's cheek and roughly pushed his face back toward the button.

Defiantly, Gad swung his face away from the magician's hand and caught movement. The woman had awoken from whatever trance he had put her under and she struggled to free her face from the mask. It had slipped to the side, revealing her wide and pleading eyes. Somehow, a gag bound her mouth. Red, thick, between her clenched teeth.

THUMP, THUMP, THUMP, THUMP.

How?

Gad stepped back from the magician, the full impact of fight or flight flooding his senses. His legs and fists tensed, his heart hammering in his chest. He put one foot behind him and stepped back. The shadows beneath the saw table began to gather, running together. Gad could see his breath in the sudden cold and knew what was coming.

The magician turned and, with a swift upward sweeping motion reminiscent of a Caesar demanding the coliseum's thirst for blood, lifted his arms to the crowd.

"Push the button," they cried in unison.

At the opposite side of the stage and behind the curtain, several security guards gathered, fingers to their ear to receive instructions. They didn't look like they were there to escort him back to his seat.

With one last step backward, he turned and shot offstage. In his peripheral vision, the magician reached for the button. The sound of the saw spinning up and buzzing filled the area as Gad tripped blindly down backstage stairs.

BZZZZZZZZZZZZZZZZzzzzzzzzz...ZZZZZZZZZ.

The woman's scream rent the air amidst the sounds of a spinning blade cutting and slowing against solid matter. Gad glanced back over his shoulder. His stomach clenched, the sour hint of bile rose to the back of his throat.

There are things in life that, at the first experience, are traumatizing and leave a scar in the psyche. But after a while of encountering it again and again, shock fades and the thing itself becomes an accepted albeit disappointing reality. Reapers were something Gad could never and would never get used to. They reminded him of vampires draining life from the living, soul leeches that left nothing but an empty husk.

A reaper stood next the saw table, hunched over the woman's body, its form withered and dripping viscera from gaping holes around its body. Its chest had opened toward her, the gray decaying fingers of its rib cage unfurling. He refused to watch any longer to see which way her soul would go, and he was pretty sure he knew, anyway.

The security guards turned and disappeared into the darkness of the other side of the stage. Onstage, a spray of crimson had flown out from the spinning blade to splatter the back half of the stage. Her torso hung almost cut through, her organs dropping under the table and through the open panel that no one else could see into the darkness below. The audience reeled with mostly mixed reactions of groaning horror, squeals of titillation and gasping shock. Yet not one person stood to see if perhaps the trick had gone wrong.

Gad's head swam again, pounding with the beat of the tribal drums, all reason and logic gone. He turned and bolted through the backstage door without a clue where it led. His only purpose was to find a way out.

25

D rake whistled his favorite devil may care tune the whole way up to Mr. and Mrs. Peterson's room in the first rounded hall of the Seventh Level. Under normal circumstances, Drake or another employee would have called their room to check in on any needs, but this was a married couple who had been together for fifty years. He needed to watch their rare story unfold in person.

Drake knocked at the door. "Mr. Peterson? It's ten o'clock and I'm here, as you requested.".

Heavy footsteps stopped at the door. It cracked open a few inches.

"Mr. Peterson? Everything all right?"

The man's eyes darted back and forth to the hall behind Drake. "Quick, come in." He pulled Drake abruptly inside, then slammed the door shut and locked it. Dried blood covered the old man's shaking hands.

"You were right, Drake. You said I'd feel free. Well, I do. I'm finally free, after all these years." He clasped his bloodied hands together with glee.

"That's great, Mr. Peterson. I'm happy to hear that. And don't trouble yourself with the mess, we'll take care of everything."

"Do I have time to get changed, maybe clean up a little?"

"Oh of course, sir." Drake glanced to the silver tray and upended cloche with all the unused weapons that Mr. Peterson could have used, including Drake's new favorite, garroting wire.

"Don't get married, son, no matter how hard your family pushes you to. Stay free, live life to the fullest. I'm going to start tonight." He tossed his red-stained jacket over his wife's body on the bed, as though she was a crumpled sheet.

"I've brought you a change of clothes, sir." Drake hung the fresh white suit in the open wardrobe. "When you're ready, we have two gorgeous hosts just outside the door, ready to escort you wherever your heart desires."

"Really?" His thick white eyebrows lifted high on his creased forehead.

"Yes. Oh wait, let me just, um." He picked up a fallen napkin from a discarded room service tray in the room. "May I, Mr. Peterson?" Drake gestured toward his right eyebrow with the tip of the napkin.

"Call me Nicholas," the old man shrugged and stuck his face out toward Drake.

Drake used the corner of the napkin to scrub away a spot of dried blood from a thick white eyebrow. "There. Now you go get ready, you don't want to keep our lovely ladies waiting."

Nicholas grinned and wiggled his eyebrows. "Tell them I'll be out in ten minutes."

Drake gave him a subtle nod. "Enjoy your stay with us, Nicholas. Now that we've got you, we'll see to every need."

∾

GAD RAN BLINDLY up cement stairwells and through winding, shadowed halls desperate for a door that didn't require badge access. He had to have climbed at least five or six flights with no luck. His chest burned with each breath, his lungs squeezed by the vice of his exertion.

He skidded to a halt at the steel door on the next landing. It opened with a click and a room service runner stepped through with a tray of dirty dishes. Gad smiled in as friendly a manner as he could manage before shooting through the closing door.

He found himself in a mostly dark hall where the only illumination came from light panels lining the marble walkway. A sea of closed chrome doors stretched out before him without an obvious way out. His panic rising, he turned and nearly smacked into a little old man.

"Hey, slow down, kid. Enjoy the scenery."

Gad glanced sideways at the old man with statuesque beauties on either arm. The ladies towered over Gad in sparkling red showgirl outfits and matching high heels. Together, they brushed past Gad, who realized this was the bitter old man hunched over slot machines earlier. Yet now he walked straight and spry with a spring in his step. Where was his wife?

Gad glanced back at the man, his attention falling to the bright red drops of blood on the man's otherwise white shoes. Gad's stomach knotted. Whatever had happened, it was because this place made it so.

To Gad's right was a bank of elevators, but he didn't have the time to press buttons and wait. Instead, he darted through the elevator bay and into a new, shifting the scene from endless quiet hotel rooms to noisy public spaces.

COVERED in black leather with brass buttons, one door stood out with promise as a place to escape through. The sign above it read "Garden of Earthly Delights". It had no window or any way to know what lay on the other side, but clattering footfalls echoed toward him from down the hall. He had no other choice if he wanted to get out of sight.

The leather door swung open under his fingertips almost too easily. He slipped through and into total darkness, the dim light from the hall snuffed out as the door closed.

Ambient club music thrummed all around. Instinctively, he stretched his arms out before him, fingers feelings for anything tangible.

A triangle of light sliced through the dark. After several blinks, the silhouette of a man became clear. He held back a thick fold of curtain. "Membership please."

"Oh, I'm here to try it out, first time. Drake sent me."

It was too dark to see the man's face. Gad's heart thumped double-time to the rhythmic beat that bumped above all. The man had a finger to his ear, his lips moved but Gad couldn't make out what he was saying. Gad's legs tensed, almost cramped, with the need to push past and run.

The man nodded and pulled the curtain open to the world beyond. "Welcome. Enjoy."

Gad stepped in through a muggy wall of humidity scented with musky perfumes and colognes.

The club stretched out before him on two levels. He stood on the upper balcony with tables lining the balustrade, while below, a dance floor pulsated with red and purple beams of light piercing billowing jets of fog. Through the haze, he could see scantily clad club-goers moving together on the dance floor, hips swinging and hands freely roaming wherever on whoever. Bodies gyrated, bare skin glittered in the pulsing lasers. Writhing bodies packed the place, wall to wall.

Time to blend in and find a way out of here.

Gad hurried downstairs to the dance floor, glancing over his shoulder as he did so, affirming that security guards hadn't followed him inside.

The lower level had a lot more light than upstairs. Gad could better make out that he wasn't the only one in street clothes. Some danced in cocktail dresses and designer wear while others were shirtless and in jeans with ripped knees. Some wore a lot less, doing the bump and grind in little more than G-strings and sparkling sequined pasties. It was the strangest dichotomy of people Gad had ever witnessed, which was odd for a Vegas EMT to admit.

He maneuvered through the throng, hopeful that he'd find an exit on the other side of the dance floor. Or Drake.

Hands encircled his waist and brought him to a jarring halt. Feminine hands with long, pointed black nails locked around his stomach and pulled him back, shockingly strong for their size. He turned to address his captor, both alarmed and intrigued by the raven-haired beauty that held him fast. Her eyes were blue or green, hard to tell in the dark. Her outfit comprised solely of crisscrossing black electric tape compressing her ample breasts and flat pelvis in just the right way.

Gad shook his head, smiling, and gently tried to extricate himself, but her muscled and oiled male dance partner sandwiched Gad between them. With his own arms pinned by the herculean sparkling arms coming from behind him, Gad could only watch helplessly as the male fingers deftly undid all of Gad's shirt buttons. The woman's full black-painted lips spread into an enticing grin. The pointed tip of her index fingernail scratched deliciously down Gad's chest, over his stomach, and stopped to tease the dark hair above his waistband. The rock-hard body holding him in place pressed into him, aroused. For one shining moment, Gad's fears melted away. He didn't need to leave so fast, did he? The long, black nails played with the metal button on his jeans. Her enticing lips curled upward as she gazed at him, her long black eyelashes curved upward above...solidly black eyes with red slits.

Gad jumped, scrambling to twist out of the arms that pinned him. His panicked flailing shoved a series of people on the floor aside and he stumbled away without a backward glance. Her eyes had been just like the eyes of the demon Pete had shown him in the mirror. He re-buttoned his shirt with fumbling fingers, his heart beating a mile a minute. He looked back, and the dancers had closed the gap in the throng and reformed their undulating pattern.

He had to get out of here!

Gad spun away from the dance floor in search of a door. To his chagrin, there were many doors. Too many. The doors lined the wall across from the dance floor as well as either side of the lengthy hall stretching straight ahead in a t-shape. Some doors had round windows that, apparently, were okay to use for peeping at whatever was happening on the other side.

With trepidation, Gad sauntered past the nearest door. He rocked up onto his toes and glimpsed the scene inside. A doctor in green scrubs and a surgical mask held a scalpel over his patient's bared chest. The patient herself was a frail young woman with mouse brown hair and glasses, wearing a front-opening paper-gown. She sat upright at an angle, her bare legs propped open in stirrups. The scalpel arced and disappeared below the window and a high-pitched scream broke out over the musical din.

Gad rushed to the window, his hand frozen on the door handle, shock coursing through him when he saw the rest. The doctor was pulling the scalpel along through her flesh, making a thin red line along her inner-thigh above many, many oozing red cuts on her legs and across her pelvis. The look on her face was one of pure desire. The scream he took for terror had actually been ecstasy. Gad backed away from the door.

Through the next window, several females dressed as Nazis in full regalia held a naked and bound man on the floor. One had pulled her nearly finished cigar from her lips and crushed it out on the man's back. The man shuddered, his skin immediately angry white and red within the ring of cigar ash. *Second-degree burn. Cold water. Sterile bandages.* The steps to help the man echoed in his mind as Gad watched the next Nazi deliver a smart thwack to the crouching man's back with a pig whip.

The man, with a rag tied through his teeth and knotted behind his head, nodded, and the next wicked lash delivered smartly between his puffy and streaked shoulder blades split the skin.

"You going in or what?" A voice whispered hotly in Gad's ear. Gad scowled and turned away, not wanting to address the speaker. The door opened and swung shut behind him.

Gad swept around the corner to the hallway, passing several windowless doors. Across the hall, the next door with a window was dark with promise. A darkened room held the possibility for an easy escape if there was another door within. He passed between two red-satin covered tables in the middle of the hallway, each containing a myriad of adult toys, oils, feathers, sharp objects, flails, animal masks, and lingerie. Gad's body hair stood on end at the next table with cuffs, lighters, polished guns, gags, rope, tazers and sizable wicked blades glinting in the light.

"Help yourself, buddy." A bubbly cigarette girl offered Gad her party tray. Shots of alcohol were probably the least dangerous items amongst the neat stacks of hypodermic needles, and piles of pills and powders in every size and color. "Whatcha into?"

"Is there an exit?" Gad said loudly in a carefully casual tone. "I think my wife might look for me here."

"Oh hon, you need to bring her along for the fun," the girl cackled and flounced to the line of people gawking at another window. They gleefully pawed through the party tray, helping one another to the delights within.

Gad moved over to a windowless door and pulled his phone from his pocket. He frantically swiped through his contacts, stopping on the listing for Drake Reiner. He dialed, but it wouldn't ring.

A liver-spotted hand gripped his wrist painfully tight.

"You know the rules. Put it away." Gad looked up into the narrowed eyes of a balding man in an expensive suit. He dropped Gad's wrist with an air of disgust and walked away.

"He's the CEO for that family network, the one that makes all the kid cartoons." The cigarette girl explained to him as though Gad had asked. "He's high on the food chain here, y'know. Don't wanna piss him off."

"Thanks," Gad replied loudly with no sincerity and stepped through the nearest door.

Light in this larger room flickered. The black-and-white checkered floor was barely discernible beneath layers of filth. A roach scuttled to the kitchen counter and sink shadows. An old-fashioned fridge whirred in the corner. Its freezer hung open, dark liquid dripping across the floor to the cheap plastic kitchen table with green chairs.

A young man sat at the table, passed out. Tentatively, Gad approached. "Hey. You okay? Hey, man." The blond youth lay prone on the table, his head resting in his arms.

"Uhhhnnnnn," he moaned. For all intents and purposes, he needed help. Gad inched closer and pulled his wrist out to get a pulse.

The wrist left an arc of cold sticky red on the plastic surface.

Gad swallowed at the lump in his throat. The youth's pulse was weak.

"Hey. Hey. Can you open your eyes? Can you sit up?" Gad

asked. The overhead light continued to flicker, giving Gad flashes of slow movement.

"Uhhhhhhhh," came the unintelligible reply.

Gad had to try. This guy could have been trying to find a way out when something found him first. Gad gently lifted his shoulders and pushed him upright.

A gush of red spilled from the hole in the side of his head. His eyes pointed in opposite directions. His arms flopped from the table to reveal a drill and a square can of hydrochloric acid. The acrid rotting smell hit him full-force and Gad spun for the kitchen sink, retching.

"Hey, this room's mine. Get out. Now." The threatening voice emerged from the open door.

Gad didn't need to be told twice. Stomach convulsing, Gad shoved past the scowling blond man with the cleft chin, whose pants hung unbuckled and unzipped.

Desperate to escape at any cost, Gad opened every door.

In the next room, elegant guests in fine dress lined a long dining table. A host carved a length of meat too large to be anything ordinary. At the head of the table, her fine china red with the juices of her half-eaten slice, a beautiful woman with perfectly pinned red hair held aloft her wineglass to toast the host, her ears and neck dripping with jewels, her leg, missing and recently bandaged. The host inclined his head gratefully.

Gad pulled away, his head spinning. He dove through the next door without a thought, all reason and logic now gone. This room seemed to be a nice office, perhaps the respite of an average manager's workroom tucked away amidst hellish everything else and he stifled a laugh of relief at the sight. Behind the oak desk covered in paperwork was another door marked "Staff Only". This had to be the way out.

He crossed the room with haste and tried the doorknob. It

turned with a click and the door opened. He stepped through and shut it behind him.

The lights flickered on automatically, probably by movement. And then, Gad saw it.

The form on the bed. It was a naked torso with perfect creamy white breasts. It lay upright, propped up by pillows.

Once, it had arms and legs, but only angry red scars in the shape of folded and stitched skin remained. Maybe once, it had hair. Ears. Eyes. A nose. But no more.

The only feature left was its lips. Perfectly lined with a red lip pencil, perfectly moisturized and painted by a perfect brush with cherry red. Its chest rose and fell, its cherry red lips parted. It gasped.

All that this thing had left was its perfect red lips. And its other lips.

Gad felt for the door handle behind him, his feet rooted to the spot. The thing's head moved, turning ever so slightly. It moaned.

Shakily, he forced one foot over the other, slipped from the room and stumbled for the office door. It seemed to stretch away from him, farther and farther, his hand reaching for the brass doorknob.

Out into the hallway, thick and humid, sweat and sweet.

Thump, thump, thump, the music drove the dancers on the floor to grind and slide against one another. Clothes not already discarded were being stripped or torn away. The dance floor had progressed far from just dancing.

Gad left the center hall and crept through the shadows to the last hall toward the bar and beyond. *Behind the bar, that's where the exit had to be. Staff had to come in and out from behind the bar.* This was Gad's mantra as he moved toward the last door on the left, next to the bar.

Sweat coated Gad's back and chest and he stood rigid with fear. He pushed the big door open and stepped through.

"Stop."

A large hand against Gad's chest brought him to an abrupt halt, knocking the wind out of him.

"You can't come in here." The large man sat on a stool before a thick black velvet curtain. His voice was so deep, the bass music nearly drowned it out.

"I'm, I'm looking for a friend," Gad stuttered.

"Not in here, you're not." The sounds coming from behind the man and his curtain were like chains clanking. And moaning. Sexual.

"I'm supposed to meet him." Gad clutched at the pendant at the base of his neck, desperation building to a fever pitch again.

The large man pushed Gad back through the door. Something beyond the black curtain chittered. Something else clacked and clanked. Something tore and wept. And something gasped with delight.

"How do I get out of here?" Gad tried his best to keep an even tone, but fear gripped his throat, making every word tightly strung.

The man stood to his full height. "You want to leave?" He filled the doorway with his frame.

"Yes, leave," Gad nodded emphatically, the mere sound of the word bringing him a modicum of hope. He squeezed the seal tight in his sweaty palm and looked up at the man, imploring.

The man stared back at Gad unblinkingly with black eyes with red slits. "You're not supposed to be here, little man." The threat was clear. Now he'd done it.

Gad swiveled to run, run with everything he had back through the orgy on the dance floor and up the stairs to the only door he knew would take him out of this place. But the massive hand gripped the back of his shirt and the skin around his neck, burning with pain that rose until it was fire. He was being lifted up in the man's one hand. Somewhere in the back of Gad's mind, his body told him that the skin on the back his neck was about to tear free. He was being raised off the floor; his toes dangled, and he kicked and punched in a fruitless effort to get free. He jammed his hand into his pocket and pulled the watch out on its chain to swing it at the hulk holding him up high. Shaking his fist, he swung it this way and that.

And in a flash, a weapon appeared in his hand. Lengthy, sizable and strangely familiar.

SHINK

A scythe. Its carved ebony handle was cool in his hand as the wicked arced metal blade sprang out to its full length. With all of his strength, Gad pulled it straight down through the arm that held him aloft. It cut without hardly any effort, like a hot knife through butter. Blood pumped outward in spurts from freshly exposed muscle and severed veins, and an unearthly screech erupted from the possessed man, something between rage and pain. The arm fell to the floor with Gad, its fingers still twitching.

Gad sprang to his feet, so full of adrenaline he couldn't feel the burning at the back of his neck anymore. The man howled, his head tipped back and mouth open wider than any human could physically manage. The hideous sound was like a thousand swine shrieking in unison, the worst sort of alarm imaginable. Every creature in the place turned to find the source. And every creature could now see that Gad was the reason.

He swung the scythe blade around and into the large man's left shoulder, cutting through it and into his chest where it stuck. The man's eyes were so very black and wide as Gad pulled once, twice, and somehow freed black smoky tendrils from the man with the third tug of the scythe handle. His deafening caterwaul ceased, and he collapsed to the floor, the black color draining from the man's eyes like ink from water. Gad had pulled something from the man with the scythe; a dark misty trail stuck on the end of the blade for a moment before it melted away.

The demon-alarm was working. Security sprung up throughout the crowds, all pushing through to get to Gad.

Gad slammed the handle of the scythe on the ground as he had seen reapers do countless times. It shrank obediently into its watch form, which he dropped back into his pocket. Shouts of "he's here," "wants him alive," and "get him," came from all around him above the din. He'd never make it to the dance floor, let alone up the stairs to the only exit.

And then his stomach caved inward under the knuckles of a security guard's fist with an explosion of pain that rippled into instant nausea. Gad dropped like a bag of wet cement to the shiny black floor. Shoes came at him from all directions. More shoes than there had been people around him before he fell. More demon-possessed humans had come. They came at his face, connecting with his head, his cheek. He tried to look up his attackers between blows. More black eyes above him, angry. So very angry. Stars and flashes of light danced before his eyes. Something wet tickled his ear, red plopped to the shiny black floor. A shoe battered his lower back, while another, his legs. Gad tried to breathe in, but a shoe knocked the wind from his stomach and prevented it. Without air, he couldn't even groan. A possessed human appeared over him with one of the wicked blades from the tables of kink. She looked gleeful with her black eyes, a grin from ear to ear as the demon that puppeted her licked the blade tip.

This was it. He would die here on the floor of this evil place.

In this surreal moment just before his death, Gad caught sight of Drake passing by only a few feet away. "Help me," he pleaded as loud as he could manage. Drake, his best friend, would save him from imminent death.

Drake looked down at Gad, unmoving. He almost seemed to study Gad's pain and predicament. And with a shrug and a cruel smile, Drake moved on somewhere else.

The metal from the seal dug into his palm as he gripped it with all he had left. And he remembered Dahlia.

Goodbye Dahlia, you tried to warn me.

The sparkles in front of him grew, his chest hurt too badly to draw air. He was suffocating. The watch buzzed hot in his pocket. How strange, it was probably a call for his own reaper. He was in so much pain from the repeated blows that death would be a sweet release. He didn't have the strength to squeeze the seal anymore, his hand dropped to the floor.

Goodbye Pete, goodbye Harriet. Goodbye.

A flash of golden light exploded somewhere in the club. Screams surrounded him. Squelching sounds. Was his reaper here, pulling his soul from his body?

The light grew brighter. This must be the "moving on" part of the ride. He opened his eyes to see his reaper and gasped.

There were no reapers. But there were two entities as big as reapers, if not bigger. They towered over all, emitting the most powerful pure light Gad had ever seen. He squinted in their direction, but it was like trying to stare into the sun. Here and there, he could tell that they brandished two-handed sword-like weapons and, as they swung and stabbed, they cleared out huge swaths of possessed. Bodies and body parts flew back from the golden-lighted pair.

Everything was chaos. Several possessed humans had taken up the unearthly alarm screech for backup, their heads tipped back to the ceiling and jaws preternaturally wide.

Gad mustered every ounce of strength to pull himself up, but the stabbing agony in his head, arms and torso was too great to take a deep breath, let alone move. He couldn't sit up to see how, but he could tell that more and more possessed had joined the fray, pouring in from somewhere. Swarms of feet and legs leapt over him or, worse yet, used him as a stepping stone to get to the golden entities ahead; they had reduced him to a bleeding speed bump.

A keening wail cracked through the general pandemonium and a boisterous cheer erupted, punctuated by snorts, growls, hisses and cackles. The golden light dimmed by half, crowds parted for something. It was too far away to make out, but Gad thought he saw the tips of massive wings dragging along the floor, larger than he had ever seen on any statue, feathers falling from the wings and getting trampled in the chaos.

Cries of victory erupted all around. A group of humans dragged a sword after the thing with wings, its tip cutting along the floor and sending up sparks like flint on steel. It was so large it made a claymore look like a toothpick.

In a rush, the remaining golden light burst through the crowds like a lightning bolt straight at Gad. Gad squinted again into the blinding light, this time able to make out a face. It was as though Michelangelo's David looked back at him with perfect colorless marble features, its massive fingers outstretched to him as it flew up fast. Gad would have mustered a scream of terror if he'd had the strength or time to. The fingertip as big as his fist touched his forehead.

In a flash of light, Gad's vision pinpointed to blackness.

26

"I'm telling you, gank this asshole right now, before he wakes up."

The voice came from a face that seemed to hover just about two feet above Gad's. It was the only clear thing in the center of his blurred vision. Spiky ginger hair punctuated the scruffy pale face with a beak-like nose, sallow baggy eyes and thin lips twisted into an appraising scowl.

"Sorry, Dax, you know I have a strict 'no ganking in my shop' rule," a gruff voice replied from the shadows.

Gad shot up with a start, the images of incoming fists and shiny leather shoes still fresh in his mind's eye. He pulled his shirt out before him to find dark scuffs and drips or smears of blood covered it. Tears in his pants showcased the punches, kicks and grabs he had endured. Strange, he didn't feel any of the abuse. He yanked his shirt up above his ribs; there was no bruising or abrasion to match the damage to his clothes. He was, for all intents and purposes, unharmed outside of a minor headache.

"Stupid rules are meant to be broken." Dax, the guy who had

dubbed Gad an asshole, stuffed his hands in the pockets of his black cargo pants and shuffled away.

"Where am I?" Gad glanced around to assess his danger level. He sat upright on a worn oriental rug on the ground floor of a two-story-tall room. Above him, an old-fashioned oil-rubbed bronze ceiling fan spun just above bookshelves with rows and rows of books. Through the top of the shop's windows, he could see that it was dark out, still probably the middle of the night. The room smelled of must and beeswax polish, like his grandma's old attic.

"You're in my shop," said the owner of the gruff voice as he stepped forward from shadow into the pool of light on the rug. Gad shuddered, the man's physique being nearly identical to the hulk that had just held him dangling above the floor single handedly. With a shaved head and deep creases between his brows, he looked to be middle-aged, but it was hard to pin down whether he was in his forties or fifties. His body was more physically fit than anyone in the room could ever hope to be; his right bicep alone being bigger than Gad's head. "What's the last thing you remember?"

Gad struggled to recall anything through the three-foot-thick haze in his head. "I was in this club in Inferno. I pissed off security. Got lost trying to get out."

"Table games? You counting cards or something?" The shop owner scrutinized him, giving Gad the distinct feeling that he wasn't any safer with this new crowd than he was with the demons. He shook his head.

"No, I don't gamble. I went there to hang out with my friend at his new job. Hadn't seen him in a while."

"What's your name?" Dax fell into an armchair with his laptop, kicking his leg over a chair arm.

"What's yours?" Gad drew his knees up to his chest. If he had to, he'd be able to get to his feet quickly.

"I'm Levi," the gruff voice interjected where a sardonic reply was likely. "And the creeper lurking behind you is Jim," Levi gestured for Gad to look over his shoulder.

Gad twisted around, alarmed to find a man in his forties with a receding hairline silently brooding with his back to a post behind Gad, one foot crossed casually over the other. He tipped his head to Gad and brought a silver lighter's flame to the cigarette pinched between his lips.

"You said you'd quit, Jim." Levi's words were calm but authoritative.

One side of Jim's mouth curled up, revealing a dimple. "Yeah, I will. Didn't say today was the day." Jim's vibe was very east-coast.

Levi raised one eyebrow and folded his arms across his massive chest.

Jim sighed, flipped the lighter shut, and tucked the cigarette behind one ear. "Starting now, yeah, gotcha."

"And that's Dax," Jim said, motioning to the dick with ridiculous hair spikes. "Try to ignore him, for the most part."

"Charmed, I'm sure." Dax flipped Gad the bird and used the same middle finger to swipe through something on his laptop screen.

"Now it's your turn to tell us who are," Jim pretend-whispered behind his hand.

"My name is Gideon but call me Gad."

"Or just 'asshole'," Dax murmured as he ticked-tacked on his keyboard.

"What the hell is your problem?" Gad stood to his full height, his fists clenched at his sides. He was beginning to not give a shit who this dick was.

Jim swiftly inserted himself between Gad standing rigidly and Dax casually reclining in the armchair. "Something you should know about Dax here is that, well, we try to give him some leeway with his douchiness because his 'unique expertise' rubs off on him a lot. A lot," Jim emphasized with a glare in Dax's direction.

"What expertise? Stupid haircuts?" Gad fumed, staring over Jim's shoulder.

"Touche," Dax replied, focused on his screen. "Black hat hack master, software and social."

"But Jim meant his demonology expertise," Levi added.

"Yeah, that too," Dax muttered. His eyes grew wide. He jumped to his feet, laptop in hand. "I knew it, I told you! We need to gank this motherfucker." He pointed at his screen with a rigid index finger. "He's buddies with a Level Seven!"

Levi and Jim leaned in to peer at the screen that Gad couldn't see.

"Wait, how could you know anything about me?" Gad's adrenaline pumped through his veins, the need to run rushing through him again. He had no idea what Dax's words meant, but he was certain it was bad.

Dax held up Gad's wallet, delivering Gad a cocky smirk.

Gad stepped toward Dax, fist cocked and ready to swing, but Levi put an uncomfortably firm hand on Gad's shoulder. "Was Drake Reiner the guy you were meeting with?"

Running from this man would not be an option. Gad glared at Levi, ready for the giant man's inevitable fist-to-Gad's-face impact. "Yes. He was my roommate for five years before he got the job at Inferno."

The impact didn't come. Levi studied him intently. After a few moments, he released Gad's shoulder. "Gad here's telling the truth. Drake would be a recent corruption."

"That's right," Gad added forcefully. "I think."

Dax snorted.

Gad tried to ignore the elephant jackass in the room and

crossed his arms over his chest. "So, you guys know about the demons?"

Levi and Jim glanced to one another, and Levi nodded.

"Uh, yeah, Captain Obvi." Dax added, with an exaggerated eye-roll. Levi put his finger to Dax's chest and pushed him back down into the armchair.

"Sorry, but outside of the heartfelt death threats, I still know nothing about you guys or why I'm even here. Just what the hell is going on?"

"You're right," Levi nodded. "Let me elucidate. Are you aware of what's going on in Vegas? The big picture?"

"If you mean the demons running the casinos, I just sort of stumbled on that factoid, yeah."

"Oh, it goes much further than that, buddy," Jim said, leaning back on a bookshelf, his expression almost pleasant with amusement. "You don't know the half of it."

"Why do people come to Vegas, Gad?" Levi continued. "Surely not for the family fun and squeaky-clean entertainment?"

"People come here to do the stuff they wouldn't normally do. Bad stuff. It's even in the city's lame-ass tagline," Jim said.

"Temptation," Dax added, finally snapping his laptop shut. "Demons. It's their bread and butter."

"I saw it firsthand tonight at the club I stumbled into at Inferno. The club's name was 'Garden of Earthly Delights', but the stuff that was going on in there, it was like the people were..."

"Uninhibited?" Jim offered.

Gad shook his head. "More like pushed into doing... things."

"Yes. The demons used to just influence or tempt humanity into doing bad, whispering in their ears and hopefully getting the soul to damn itself to hell. But here in Vegas, where people save up vacation money to come and pay for the privilege of following their baser instincts, the demons rack up much bigger numbers of souls by using corrupted humans to do their dirty work."

"I don't understand," Gad said. "What's the difference between tempting someone and using a human to tempt a human?"

"Big difference, kid," Jim replied. "First off, demons can't physically exist in our plane. They can only tempt you through suggestion. It's part of God's promise to humanity, free will. We all have the choice to make good or bad decisions."

The image of the beautiful woman with black eyes and red slits sent an involuntary shudder through Gad. "So that's why there were so many people in the club, possessed."

"Yes. In a human body, or by controlling a corrupted human, they have a whole new set of weapons to force people into committing soul-damning sin. Why tempt someone to take drugs or drink, hope they choose to, and then try to influence them to commit murder? It's a lot easier to just drug them and put them in a room with their victim and a knife."

Another image flitted to Gad's eye of the old man's blood-tainted white shoe.

"Or sign away a soul for a club membership with all of its unspoken privilege, and not read the fine print," Levi finished.

"Are you saying that's what happened to Drake?"

Dax frowned. "Without a doubt. The casinos look for the people who have like the finer things in life or people who feel entitled. Anyone who's willing to look the other way to get over."

"Drake wasn't like that. At least not before."

But even as the words came from Gad's mouth, they slowed. Drake had been a good person. Mostly. Except sometimes when he felt like he hadn't gotten what he felt he deserved. He had admitted to Gad on more than a few occasions that he took "the lion's share" from the tip jar because he had worked hardest for it, unknown to the wait staff. And he had been good at his used car sales job, selling known lemons to unsuspecting customers to make his monthly quotas. The more Gad thought about it, the more he realized that Drake had been a fairly gray person overall.

"They lured him to Inferno with a ton of free things like clothes, a nicer place to stay, a car. Even I thought it was weird. I'm guessing the more he did for them, the more they gave him."

"The more he pushes people to do bad things, the more they give him," Dax said.

"So what's a Level Seven?"

"Pretty fucking far up there. It means your buddy works for a demon and gave up his soul. Oh, and he loves his job," Dax scowled.

"And his job is to push humans into doing stuff so bad, they're hell-bound." Gad grimaced.

"Ding! One thousand points to the new guy," Dax said and stood from the chair. "That's it exactly. But how far is bad enough to be hell-bound, would you say?"

The night's horrors flitted through Gad's brain again. The orgy on the dance floor. Lust. The surgical table. The skin-splitting whips. Torture. The disturbing feast. Cannibalism. Gluttony. The guy with a hole drilled into his head. Mr. Peterson's red-stained shoes. Murder. And of all the things he'd witnessed, the most disturbing of all, his former friend who saw him being beaten to death on the floor. The worst of it had been Drake's cold smile. Because-

"They take souls," Gad murmured, feeling sick. Everything Pete had told him just nights before all fell into place now. And Inferno, this was just one newer casino in a town built to be a play-land of sin, a web of downfall.

"Yes," Dax said. "And we're here, because we've all lost someone. My older brother. He went missing when I was in college."

"My partner," Jim added. "I was a cop. My partner and I

worked together almost seven years undercover in Jersey with the biggest mob families. They sent him here to infiltrate the Luciano family and, well, I've been looking for him ever since. Quit the force and picked up PI work to pay the bills. I still have a few leads, and I'm hoping he's still alive."

"But what if he's alive, but he's," Gad trailed off.

"Without a soul? Believe it or not, you can come back. It's rare, but it's not impossible." Jim glanced briefly toward Levi, who said nothing.

"So, Gad, this leaves us with the little pickle of how you got here," Levi said, gesturing for Gad to take a seat in an antique velvet recliner.

"I don't want to hear about his little pickle." Dax's full-frontal sarcasm returned in the wake of finally having shown empathy.

Gad sighed.

"What happened to you at Inferno?" Jim leaned on the bookshelf, his eyes narrow.

Gad lowered himself into the recliner and related everything he had endured in excruciating detail, from the magician's ghastly act onstage to the nightmare rooms in the club. The only details spared were those related to his ability to see reapers. Having only just met these people, that secret would remain his. It was when he reached the part about the two golden lights that everyone in the room perked up noticeably, their expressions transforming from mild interest and empathy to a piqued preoccupation.

"Did you see wings?" Jim's arms uncrossed from his chest, his green eyes round.

"Yeah, the one that was being dragged across the floor was losing these giant feathers."

Levi's expression was akin to spitting nails. "And they had the angel's sword, too."

Angel. Someone had said it out loud. Gad shivered and

shook off the feeling. "Yes. It took a few of them to carry it, but they were pulling the...angel's...sword after it."

Levi breathed out slowly, staring so hard at the wall that Gad expected a burn mark to appear with smoke.

"Holy fuck," Dax breathed.

"They have an angel," Jim said, with a shaky voice.

"What does that mean?" Gad was sure he three steps behind everyone else in the room.

Dax did not mince words. "It means they've got a fucking powerful weapon. If they figure out how to tap into that power, we're all royally screwed."

"What are they? Giant batteries?" Gad laughed.

"So to speak." Jim rubbed at his cheek stubble. "There's a balance of power between heaven and hell. When heaven fell, Lucifer took one-third of the fallen angels and demons' powers diminished. One angel is vastly more powerful than several demons. But all things being considered, I'd like to think that angel wakes up from whatever they did to it and kicks their demon asses all over. Hey, can I see that seal you were holding?"

Gad pulled the cord and pendant out from his shirt for Jim.

"Yeah, that's Saint Christopher's medallion, all right. Ok, you sent out a call for holy help. And not one, but two angels came to the heart of evil to save you." He leaned back to look Gad up and down. "You must be something special, my friend. There something about you we should know?"

"Like what?"

Dax had already dug into something on his laptop. "He's an emergency transport dude, saves a shit-ton of lives. They call him the Angel of Death. Wait, huh?"

"Yeah, it pisses me off. Other EMTs spread a rumor that I know when someone will die before anyone else, so they call me Angel of Death. They're just sore they don't know the roads of Vegas like I do. You've got to take zig-zags through the city, you see." Gad held his hand up sideways and mimicked driving up one street, turning, and then going straight again.

Levi stood and leaned on a beam. "Heavenly host healed and delivered Gad to us for a reason. We need to figure out what the reason is. Could be, he'll help save the lost angel."

"Um, what?" Dax stood, snapping his laptop shut again. "This guy just shows up out of nowhere saying an angel dropped him off and you're ready to throw down with him in the heart of darkness? For all we know, Xavier sent him here and the horde followed."

"Who?" Gad rubbed his throbbing temples.

"Don't worry, demons can't get in here," Jim said, behind his hand to Gad. "It's technically sacred ground. And a corrupted couldn't get in either." Jim addressed the last part directly to Dax.

"So maybe Goodwin here hasn't signed the paperwork yet," Dax shot Jim a dirty look. "But I, for one, don't want to throw down in evil central with a dude who claims to have beamed in somehow. It's a trap, nerds." The tone of his voice dripped with the idiocy of their blind faith. "Kick him out and let's call it a day."

"Yes, by all means, please kick me out! At least I've leveled up from being ganked." Gad stood and strode toward the front door. He didn't ask for any of this and he definitely would not plead his case to join a group of strangers in a quest he didn't want any part of. He was quite done with the shittiest night of his life, no longer caring whether he had arrived by angel or a British nanny's umbrella.

Levi stepped deftly between Gad and the curtained glass door. "Stop, Gideon."

Gad looked up into the stern face crossly. "What're you now, my grandma?"

"No. But I'll haunt you relentlessly if you try to walk out that door without talking this through."

"Hm. If you only knew why that isn't a real threat to me. Have a nice life."

"Let him go, Levi," Jim said, rubbing his eyebrows. "Dax is right. We don't know what really happened or why he's here. If he's meant to be here, he'll be back."

Gad nodded and shrugged, then motioned for Levi to unblock the door.

Instead, Levi placed his hand on Gad's chest. Suddenly, Gad puffed out a lungful of air, as though all the anxiety that had welled in his chest was trying to get out. In that moment, Gad calmed almost completely. Emotion and exhaustion drained from his tightened chest, his shoulders dropped and relaxed.

"I will ask this only the one time. Is everything you told us about being at Inferno the truth?" Levi's gaze was hypnotic.

Without hesitation, Gad replied. "Yes."

Levi removed his hand. "Then you are supposed to be here. Welcome to the team. Sit down."

No longer feeling the need to rush out, suddenly feeling accepted, Gad heaved a sigh. "Well. Shit."

27

Drake stood in front of the chrome door on the eighth level as he had countless times before. But this time was different. This time, Xavier had included instructions to meet him inside his suite. Drake had never crossed Xavier's threshold before. Only people of great importance went inside. If they weren't of great importance, well, they likely weren't coming back out.

Because he considered himself of only mild importance working his way up the food chain, Drake's mouth had gone as dry as the Vegas desert. He tapped his fingers arrhythmically against his thigh.

For a moment, the thought flitted through his mind that he could still make a break for it. This was his last chance to go back down the hall, take the service stairs and get the fuck out of Dodge. But really, was he that guy? No, he was a risk-taker. So if this was it, this was it. Face the music, or the glory, or the whatever, *que sera sera*. Drake rapped sharply three times on the door.

The door swung open. There was no one at the door, but this was not the time to question it.

"Drake, come in. I have some urgent matters to discuss."

Xavier's voice from the office ahead was, per usual, unreadable. He might want to discuss casino concerns or, conversely, the details of how Drake's murder would play out momentarily. Drake's palms were growing moist. He wiped them hastily on his trousers and crossed the plush oriental rug, his wingtip shoes stepping on an antique that was likely worth more than his annual salary. Xavier enjoyed obtaining the unobtainable and squeezing every drop of joy from it.

Drake opened the polished dark wood double doors to the office. Xavier sat behind a matching and intricately carved antique desk, every brass or glass item on its immaculate surface polished to perfection. Xavier himself sat rigid in his tailored pinstripe suit, his manicured hands folded neatly before him.

"Take a seat," he said, gesturing to the two empty chairs opposite his desk. "How's that shoulder feeling?"

"Oh," Drake, too focused on his potential imminent demise, hadn't acknowledged the distant ache of his left shoulder. "It's almost gone, finally. Laid off the lats in the gym for the time being."

"Glad to hear it. Well then, let's just jump right to it, shall we?" He leaned over the desk, his eyes intent on Drake. "The events of the Garden Club."

Drake's heart kicked into high gear, slamming hard and fast against his chest. "I've already addressed updating our security protocols with the staff, sir. I don't know how that weapon made it through the casino let alone the club door, but I've got orders in with purchasing for-"

"We lost two-thirds of the Elites on that floor, Drake. Those security teams are the best of the best, not easily replaced."

Drake scratched the back of his head. The voice in his ear was telling him not to ask what he was certain he wanted to ask, anyway. "About that, sir."

"What?"

"The Elite team. They're only used on the more restricted levels and, they um, well..."

"Yes, what of it?"

"What are they?"

Xavier paused.

"What are they?" Drake repeated. Having received a rare Level Seven security clearance, he had been brought up to speed on certain highly confidential and bizarre facts about Inferno and its practices, such as their use of dark magic to influence the guests who craved depravity. He had seen the Elite Security team with their black eyes and red pupils and had witnessed their superhuman strength. His assumption was that they, like the invisible hounds and unseen creatures supposedly sent out into the world to do Xavier's bidding, were part of the dark magic.

Drake was not an idiot. He knew the key to Inferno was deeper and more powerful than "dark magic." He did not know what exactly what went on behind the last curtain in the club he helped manage, but the things he heard through that curtain...

Drake reworded the question. "Why are Elites so hard to replace?" It was a verbal dance around the answer they both knew, yet neither could speak it.

"Drake, I don't need to remind you that there are intricacies of the business you can't know unless you're a Level Eight." Drake opened his mouth to speak, but Xavier stood abruptly and came around the desk, leaning almost over Drake. "And you are not here to ask me questions. You are here to answer to me for what happened in the Garden Club under your watch."

Drake's mouth snapped shut, his heart continuing to hammer away at his sternum.

"So," Xavier sat on the desk corner, uncomfortably close. "I have interviewed a majority of the remaining club staff and already have the picture of how the events unfolded, so we'll skip the play by plays. What I really want to know is this." Xavier leaned in, his dark eyes peering into Drake's. "How are you acquainted with the trespasser?"

That question struck Drake like a small bolt of lightning to his brain. "Sir?"

"The perpetrator who first took Dominic's arm and then his life. With a scythe." Xavier pronounced the last words as though they were offensive to say aloud. "How do you know him and who is he?"

Drake blinked. He didn't mind throwing Gad under the bus, but he didn't want to cop to his part in Gad's access to the club and its disastrous results. "He's just an old roommate."

"Ah, an associate of yours. Name, first and last?"

"Gideon Goodwin. But I didn't know he was coming to Inferno." Better to not over-inform. That had actually been the truth, because he kept the answer so short.

"You didn't invite him in?" Xavier's gaze was piercing, as though directly reading Drake's thoughts.

Drake shook his head. "No." *Truth.*

"Didn't escort him anywhere?"

"No, I was working, sir. I was on my shift." *Still truth.*

"I see." Xavier stood. "So, this Goodwin fellow made his way of his own accord to the most front and center seat of the magic theater?"

Fuck.

"I gave him a ticket to see the show. Figured that would loosen him up, maybe get him to play the table games." He could feel Xavier's stare boring into his skull. "He must've explored his way up to the Garden."

Xavier grinned with perfect white teeth. It was more than disconcerting. "Why no, that's not what occurred. As it happens, your friend destroyed the magic show. Security rushed to the stage to eject him from the casino. He gave chase. And then, do you know what happened?"

"He found the club." Drake's tone belayed his utter resignation to his impending doom.

"He found the club, indeed. And he was certain to drop your name as a key to belonging there. It worked, too. He got as far as The Gate before Dominic discovered him."

Drake's lips pressed together so tight, they tingled. "Sir, I'm a no bullshit guy."

"And that is what I have always liked about you, Drake. Straight to the point." Xavier returned to his chair, folding his hands on the desk again.

"Is there anything I can say or do to make it right?"

Drake felt Xavier lean toward him over the desk. "Bring me Gideon Goodwin."

He looked from the floor back up to his boss, having to ensure there was no shit-eating grin on his face. And there wasn't.

"Bring him to me."

"Alive?"

"Yes. That is quite non-negotiable. Alive and compliant."

"Unharmed?"

"Compliant."

He would live. For now. Drake stood and gratefully moved toward the door. "How long do I have?"

"Sooner than later. But Drake..."

Drake stopped in the office doorway.

"You bring him to me, and we'll discuss opportunities in the Eighth level. Oh, and as with Vinny Luciano's recent and unfortunate demise, club rules apply."

"Collateral damage is fine if I cover tracks."

"That's right. And take Red with you."

Drake gave a nod of acknowledgment and shut the office

door behind him. He had no choice now. If it came down to him or Gad, it would be Gad. Funny, he used to care about that guy. Drake stepped into the elevator and rubbed at the ache in his left shoulder as the black doors slid shut.

GAD'S EYES opened to an unfamiliar gray-spattered duct work ceiling high overhead. Panic washed over him and he twisted to see the worn couch he lay stretched across. Moving on the squashy discolored cushions released the well-absorbed funk of body odor and old soup. *Where was he? Oh, yeah.* The memory of a few hours ago came flooding back. The owner of the occult bookstore and the ex-cop convinced Gad to stay at the asshole hacker's place because demons. Because, just before that, Gad tripped into a little slice of hell, hacked off a demony-thing's arm and buried his scythe in its chest as the whole place exploded into chaos because angels. He rubbed his aching eyes.

"Oh good, you're up," Dax said, with as much contempt as he could humanly muster. He shuffled past with a steaming brown "Coffee Makes Me Poop" mug. "We're meeting for breakfast in thirty. Be ready."

Gad looked over his wrinkled and blood-spattered clothes. "Can I borrow something a little less conspicuous? Either that or I go home."

"Negatory on the home-going. The horde'll be waiting for you there. Lucky for you, you're in the safe-house. Shower, then lockers. Go." He shuffled onward, pointing half-heartedly toward an industrial door in the corner with a blue gender sign featuring Cthulhu's silhouette and the word "Whatever".

"Wait, what? What's the horde?" But Dax had moved over to what appeared to be command central, a desk before a wall of computer monitors. It had the look of being able to launch something into space single-handedly.

A stairway over the bathroom led up to a smaller second floor with an office meant for a floor manager to oversee work on the massive floor below. One office area had curtained windows, and the other, a solid cement wall. Judging by the tacky window curtains, this was Dax's bedroom.

Gad made his way into the industrial bathroom and found the gray lockers against yellow and ivory-tiled everything. The shower had new soap, shampoo, and fresh rough white towels hanging over the shower's half-wall. It was a relief to step into hot water with bubbling soap and cleanse away the horrors of the night before.

True to Dax's word, Gad found a stack of dental "cleaning visit" pouches, each with a new toothbrush, toothpaste, mouthwash, and floss. One locker had a stack of cheap new black sweatpants in various sizes, and another had t-shirts, new white sports socks and boxer shorts in small, medium and large. The t-shirt choices were grim. On the first was an ugly cat making a face beneath, "I hate Mondays". He skipped "OBNOXIOUS", an old Siegfried and Roy shirt, and the t-shirt with the Nirvana logo under a picture of the Hansen brothers. Instead, he chose the least lame of the bunch and pulled a black faded t-shirt with the word "L33T" over his head.

Dax heard the bathroom door open and spun away from his monitors, eying Gad's t-shirt selection from his throne-like computer chair. "Huh. No," he snorted.

"But I love Mondays, so here we are."

"'Obnoxious' was right on top."

"Oh no, no, Dax. I could never fill your shoes like that."

"I've got two more," Dax shrugged and returned to the scrolling code on one of the many monitors.

"So why is everything new in there except the t-shirts?" Gad rubbed the towel over his still wet hair.

"It's our ongoing competition to find the worst t-shirt. If we see one, we add it to the locker." Dax wore a faded yellow t-shirt with "FREE KEVIN" in black print and old jeans full of rips and holes.

"So which one is the current winner?"

"It's Lilith's. You haven't seen it yet." Dax took a swig of steaming coffee which, outside the threat of the worst t-shirt ever still looming, caught Gad off-guard. Either Dax had a high tolerance for pain or no taste buds left to burn.

Someone knocked at the door with "shave and a haircut, two bits". Dax swiveled to a camera feed on the highest monitor. "Speak of the witch."

"Wow, do you have a problem with literally everyone?"

"No, dude. Just you. Lilith is actually a witch." Dax pressed a button under the desk and a buzzer sounded, followed by the ka-chunking sound of a heavy electric bar releasing the front door.

"C'mon kids. The boys are getting our table at Carson's. I'm your escort." The female voice at the door was raspy, like someone who had smoked early in life.

"That's not a phrase to use lightly this side of town," Dax said and grabbed his keys.

"Or just, 'this town'," she replied.

Having slipped his shoes on, Gad got to his feet and turned the corner. The raspy voice belonged to a woman in her twenties; he'd expected someone much older. She leaned on the wall under an explosion of kinked ebony hair spilling over her shoulders, her arms folded neatly over her black t-shirt over black skirt over black fishnet stockings over black thigh-high socks in black military boots. "Name's Lilith, nice to meet you." She stuck her hand out to Gad.

"Gad," he said with a smile and shook her hand.

"You're the guy saved by providence, I hear." Lilith's eyebrows lifted high, impressed.

"Or so I'm told. I'm not exactly sure what happened, still trying to work through it all."

"Guess it's still too fresh, huh? Just last night and all. Well, welcome to the team." She slugged the side of his bicep and opened the door. "Let's grub."

"Team, shmeem," Dax ushered Gad through the door with a shove and grumbled something about wearing the wrong shirt.

Outside with the door shut, Dax locked an exceedingly paranoid number of deadbolts and electronic devices on the heavy factory door. Gad recognized the industrial area as being just off Fremont Street, the original, old, and somewhat dying area of Vegas. Fate had called him and Mercy here more times than he could count. The area was thick with gang fights, shootings, stabbings, drug overdoses and everything that goes wrong with prostitution.

"Yeah, it can be a kind of shithole, huh? But there're bright spots if you look for them. There's the art park up the road. And look, great donuts. They actually have beer pairing nights," Lilith pointed to a barely noticeable glass door in an otherwise blank slate of white brick wall across the street. "Next to amazing food. That's where we're headed. It's a hidden oasis. C'mon."

Gad followed her and Dax across the street, questioning why on earth he was allowing himself to be ordered around as "part of a team" he'd only just met hours before. He especially couldn't wrap his head around Dax, who even now was loudly voicing his opinion on the matter as they entered the glass double-doors ahead of him into the restaurant. "I know! I wanted to kill him. But they were all like 'oh no, no. He might be important and stuff', blah, blah."

Lilith looked over her shoulder to Gad, rolled her eyes and mouthed, "Ignore him." That alone gave Gad a chuckle. Maybe it wasn't as bad a group as it could be. He'd give it until after breakfast to judge.

The brick theme continued on the inside with lots of glass, exposed wood and modern decor. Gad inhaled the scent of roasting pork belly, his stomach growling audibly in response. How long had it been since he had eaten anything?

Lilith led the way through the dining room to another glass door. This opened out to a plastic-grass patio under the breezy blue sky.

"Okay, I'll give you that. But this guy is for sure, a good guy," said a familiarish voice that abruptly dropped off.

Levi and Jim sat at a bar-height table in the corner with a new face. Both Jim and the new guy already had pints in hand. But new guy's vaguely familiar face made Gad search his memory banks to pin down his name. Longish dark brown hair hanging limp above black glasses, the patchy five o'clock shadow on pale doughy skin. New guy raised his beer to Gad with a quizzical yet pleasant smile.

"Sam?" Gad walked toward him.

"No one calls him Sam," Lilith pulled a tall stool up to the table and flopped down, her large black satchel pooling onto the table. "He's Bean."

"Beany or Sammy. Yup, it's me again, Gad." Sam stood and came around the table to throw an arm around Gad in bro-hug greeting, as though they were longtime friends that hadn't seen one another in a while.

"You part of this group, too?"

"I am. I know I don't look it, but yes, I fight crime in my spare time. Demon crime." Sam pushed his glasses up the bridge of his nose over a sheepish grin.

"And he's saved our butts on more than one occasion." Jim

lifted his bottle of lager to Sam sitting next to him. A toothpick took the place of a cigarette at the corner of his lips as he dealt long thick paper menus out sliding across the table like a dealer in Vegas.

"Wow bro, mad skills," Sam said with appreciation.

"Years of poker-night training," Jim said with a wink.

"So how did Sam save your butts? I mean, I get that you guys fight demons, but how do you do that, exactly?"

"Well, Dax works for them, for one," Sam said and took a gulp of beer.

Dax must have expected Gad's mixture of shock and disbelief because he jumped in to clarify. "I'm a net admin over a big casino at the end of the strip. I keep my head down and my ear to the ground."

"He's intel, basically," Levi added. "And oh, the intel he has picked up for us. We've been a few steps ahead of some downright evil. We've put a wrench into it a few times."

"The casinos are well-connected," Dax added, not without a note of pride. "Owned by the same seven major syndicates. What one does, the other six have info about it. And that's what we're here to talk about today, the latest and greatest." Dax's gaze shifted to Levi. "There's buzz that Inferno just picked up a major asset, but they're not giving any specifics. It's like they want to brag like they've got a WMD but won't give any details."

"Asset, huh? That could be anything, mean anything." Lilith grabbed Sam's lager and took a swig.

"But we know it has to be the angel. That is a WMD." Jim's brows knit. "We need a plan to get the angel back."

"What about the other angel? Can't he rescue his buddy?" Gad knew he was out of his depth. This conversation felt to him like debating whether the Loch Ness Monster lived in fresh or saltwater.

"The short answer is no." Levi leaned on the table, his large arms taking up some of Sam's table space. Sam didn't seem to mind, leaning back and looking to Levi for further explanation. "The angels stay out of demon central because they aren't powerful enough to stay in it. It would be like sending two American soldiers over the border into Nazi territory; they'd get immediately overwhelmed. They only come in for short missions, or, if they're called upon for help, like you did."

The server came through the glass door behind them with help to deliver drinks and dishes of seared pork belly, truffled mac and cheese and bacon tomato jam with seared baguette. Gad wasted no time in smearing a piece of toast with the pungent sweet and sour mixture and crunching into it. It was only after he swallowed, grateful for delicious food filling the void in his stomach, that he realized all eyes around the table had fallen on Gad, their expressions quizzical.

"Like I did what?" Gad said, his voice muffled through a second huge bite of tomato-bacon jam toast.

"You called the angels with the seal of St. Christopher." Jim said. "In a time of great need, if you fixate on the need, the help will come. If you're worthy. And not one, but two came to save you. Save you and heal you."

Dax heaved a big sigh. "Spill, Goodwin. There's more to the Angel of Death thing than you're letting on. Are you a priest EMT or something? Saving the unworthy with last second rites?"

"Okay, so you're a demonologist network admin." Gad ignored answering Dax's question.

"Surprisingly, not as unique a combo as you'd expect." Dax shrugged and dug into his pork belly.

Gad pointed to Lilith. "And you're a witch."

"It sounds so bad when you say it like that," she winced.

"Sorry, you're a wiccan, rather. So how did you find these guys, Lilith?"

"I lost my best friend Hale a year ago. He's wiccan, too, you see. We used to go together to shop at Levi's store. But then Hale went into Inferno looking for someone in his family who went missing. But Hale never came out." Lilith's green eyes glittered. "I know he's still there, stuck somehow. It's only been a few times, but he's reached out to me." Her hand drifted up to a crystal pendant at her throat.

"He's alive?" Gad paused his voracious chewing.

"Well, I don't have any proof, but I sure feel like he is. When he reaches out, I only get one of two messages every freakin' time. I get 'help' and, and this still makes no sense to me, 'psycho'. I mean, Jim here is a PI and we've combed through all the connections. We keep coming back to either the Hitchcock movie or, literally, 'he's stuck with a psycho'. Anyway, I needed to figure it out, find Hale and save him. When I ran out of ideas, I came to Levi's store looking for ways to bump up my wicca vibes. Turns out Levi could help way more than my reading books could, he knows a lot of occult stuff."

"I do know a lot of occult stuff," Levi agreed.

"And now I work figuratively with this team and literally at the bookstore."

Gad sighed. Hale could easily be an angry ghost, otherwise known as a "ghast". And from extensive experience in the afterlife arena, he knew all too well that ghasts could project words on psychic radio. He wasn't as certain as Lilith that Hale was alive.

"And Jim, you said last night that you lost your partner on the force to Inferno?"

Jim nodded and swigged his beer. "That's right. Fuckin' Lucianos. And it was their blood money that built that damned casino."

"Did you get into the occult stuff, too?" Gad asked, scraping at the last of his mac and cheese, finally sated.

"Nope, born and raised Catholic. Fact is, I almost was a priest, until I wasn't. Ran into some faith issues along the way and dropped out of seminary." He held up a hand to the server for another beer, his last glass empty of all but foam. "But trust me, I got my faith back when I got up to my eyeballs in it around here. Turns out demons are real. So all that learning about faith, God, exorcisms, angels? My faith is my superpower in this war."

"And he's a badass." Lilith stuck her fist out and Jim returned the fist bump.

"Jim, if your partner is with the Lucianos somewhere, are you worried he might be," Gad paused, searching for a way to say it without total bluntness, "like Drake?"

"Without a soul? Believe it or not, you can come back. It's rare, but it's possible." Jim's glance flitted briefly toward Levi, who said nothing.

And just then, Gad's pocket watch began to buzz. Not once or twice, but erratically.

"You uh, got a back-up phone in your pocket, Gad?" Sam gestured to Gad's phone on the table that had died hours ago without a charge.

Lilith frowned, staring intently at Gad's pocket. "That's no phone. I'm getting major power coming off of whatever you've got there, buddy."

Levi stood. "You got an artifact there, Gad?"

Gad took a deep breath. He'd only just met these people, but under incredible circumstances. Could he trust them?

"Yes, you can," Lilith replied to his unspoken thought.

"Excuse me?" Gad squinted at Lilith, his mind whirling. *Had she just-*

"Yes, you can trust us," she insisted. "Please overlook the irony in my reading your thoughts and then saying you can trust us, but, just believe me. We're the good guys." She pointed to his pocket. "You a good guy?"

"Yes. I am. I always have been, I think, anyway. At least, I've always tried to help people whenever I can." He pulled the pocket watch out and flipped it open. The little voice inside was being very clear. *Trust them.* "Yes, it's an artifact. My father uncovered it and gave it to me before he passed away. It's a pocket watch that reveals when someone nearby is about to die."

"I knew it! Tanti Zelda told me she could see you saving souls," Sam exclaimed.

"Who?"

"Great-Aunt Z. I can see ghosts, Gad. I talk to my dead great-aunt every day. I mean, I think she's here now," he swiveled around, checking behind him. "Huh. Nope, she's not here right now, but she'll usually around."

Aunt Z's whereabouts was not the important thing at the moment. "You see ghosts, too?" Gad exclaimed.

"You know when someone will die *and* you see ghosts." Jim stared at the pocket watch, scanning the blinking light on the dial and etched numbers.

"Yeah. And," he paused and checked to make sure no one else was on the patio to hear him. It was time to say it. "And I see the reapers. The ones who take souls when they die."

Lilith's mouth fell open.

Jim grimaced. "You mean angels, right?"

"No, I mean the reapers. They're not good or bad. They're just sort of like the doorway to...whatever is next. They only show up when someone dies. It's hard to explain. But right now, somewhere not far away, a reaper is coming to collect someone's soul."

"Wait, you see them?" Levi put his hand to his temple, fascinated.

"Yeah. It's never been fun. But I've tried to make it my super-power and help the people who can be helped. It's why I became an EMT. And, I'm sorry guys, I need to go." Gad tossed the ever-warming watch to his other hand and jumped to his feet.

"No, totally. We'll catch up with you... after, I guess," Lilith said.

"Yeah, I'll be back," Gad said and stopped in the doorway. Dax had tilted his head and stared at him, as though seeing Gad from a different point of view. "You give the dying who can be saved a second chance."

Jim nodded. "Then that must be why the angels came to save you."

"And that is why we need to save the angel," Levi added, and set his empty beer glass down with a clank. "So, let's work the problem, people. We need a plan."

"Catch me up later," Gad nodded and raced out of the restaurant to Mercy.

28

I t was late, at least for most people. But in Vegas, the town that never rests, pleasure pursuit begins at sunset. Drake's shift had just begun. His mission was clear; Xavier wanted Drake to bring back Gad alive. Mostly alive, at least.

It made the most sense to start the search at their old townhouse. Drake got in easily enough, thanks to the spare key still hidden in the planter's fake rock, and settled in to wait.

The minutes ticked slowly by, marked by the movement of the moonlight across the living room carpet. By the time the hour in which Gad normally wandered home had come and gone, Drake's impatience was starting to get the better of him. Considering the amount of mail littering the hallway, he guessed that Gad might not have been home for at least two or three days. Had he finally nutted up and asked that nurse out? Maybe was staying at her place for a few days? He winced, hoping for the girl's sake that Drake wouldn't have to kill her. He really hated the inevitable mess and clean-up.

At last, he couldn't wait any longer.

Drake exited the townhouse as carefully as he had entered, replaced the key, and headed to the van around the corner where Red waited. Before he reached it, however, a voice called out behind him.

"Drake! Where ya' been, buddy?"

Drake recognized the chipper voice of Luis, the property manager for all the rental units on the block. He turned and flashed the other man his trademark greeting grin. "Hi Luis. Got a new job on the strip, so I moved."

"The strip? Five minutes away not close enough for you?" Luis laughed.

Drake let the time-wasting remark pass. "Say, Gad wanted me to pick him up for drinks. You haven't seen him, have you?"

"Huh, nope. But last time I saw him, his Elvis buddy was here on the porch saying 'see you Wednesday night.' Couldn't help overhearing it; he's just one of those people whose voice carries. You know that guy, right?"

"Matter of fact, I do," Drake replied, with a smug sense of satisfaction.

THE ELVIS CHAPEL'S cheesy southern-inspired charm made it stick out like a sore thumb amongst the dirty strip malls and pawn shops surrounding it. Red parked the van along the sidewalk across the street from the chapel.

"So where is this invisible monster? The uh, alastor?" Drake searched the roof and spire silhouetted against the moon.

Red pointed wordlessly to the smaller sloped roof over the chapel's porch.

"You can see it? What's it look like?" Drake stared hard at the roof and empty porch that wrapped from the front to the side of the building.

As a Level Eight and an Elite, Red could not only see the creatures allegedly summoned by dark magic but was aware of all of Inferno's inner workings. Red knew what happened behind closed doors. Red had achieved what Drake wanted.

Red nodded, his gaze fixed on what Drake perceived as empty air. "Looks like death. For the old woman."

Drake scowled. Not only did Red have what he, Drake, coveted, but Red was also infuriatingly inhuman. He only spoke when necessary or in anger, and typically in as few words as possible. His only saving grace as a partner was his frightening efficiency.

"All right, I'll go check it out." Drake slipped out of the van. An alarming thought struck, and he stuck his face back in. "The alastor thing. I can't piss it off, right? Step on its big toe or something and get my face ripped off?"

"It's only there for her. Don't give two shits about you or your pretty face." Red's blue eyes were cold and empty.

"Great. I'll signal if I need you." Drake stepped out of the van and made his way to the chapel, eyes peeled for anything out of the ordinary coming from the side porch.

Blinds covered the dimly lit windows. Even though the office was closed, he heard voices inside. Gad's wasn't one of them. Drake knocked at the chapel door.

"Sorry, we're closed," an old lady called through the door.

He knocked again with insistence.

"Probably a happy pair too hammered to see the damned closed sign." Her muffled words came through the door heavy with annoyance. Blinds over the door's window lifted abruptly and the porch light clicked on, bathing zdrake in incandescent light. She peeked through the blinds, the wrinkles surrounding her narrowed eyes deepening as she peered from his face to the area behind him.

"Good evening, ma'am. How're you doing?"

The blinds dropped back into place and the door swung partially open.

The woman's silver hair hung sloppily from a rubber band, the stray hairs standing on end around her face making her look somewhat crazed. Her leopard print leisure pants and a Vegas sweatshirt suggested she was ready for an evening in front of the TV. She scanned him over, from the top of his trim black sports jacket down to his leather shoes. Although he stood with his hands folded neatly before him, innocent and unassuming, she was clearly uneasy.

"It's a bit late, matter of fact. Chapel's past closing."

His smile continued unabated. "Oh, I'm not a customer. I'm a friend of Gad's. He said he wanted to hang out, but he wasn't home. Thought I might find him here with Mr. Owens."

The van door shut softly behind him. Drake knew without looking that Red waited nearby, ready for his signal. She squinted through the door gap at the van.

"Well, sorry to disappoint. Gad's not here right now. I'll let him know you stopped by." She paused, probably waiting for him to volunteer his name. He didn't. She shrugged and began to shut the door.

He gripped the door edge firmly and flashed her his most winning smile. "Are you expecting him tonight, um, Mrs.?" Drake left his question open for her to fill in her name.

"It's Harriet. And no, I'm not. But like I said, I'll tell him you stopped by." Her face flushed red.

"I really need to see him, Harriet. I have something he needs." Drake was getting the strong sense that she knew more than she was letting on. Either she knew where Gad was or, at the very least, how to reach him.

She eyed him warily. "Did you try calling him? He's very good about returning calls."

"Mm, I'd love to, but my phone died. How about I come in and use yours?" This situation was getting old, fast. His impatience from the townhouse amplified with this new time-suck.

He took a step into the door frame, forming a barrier that both prevented potential escape or shutting the door. He towered over her, making obvious her frail and diminutive size compared to his own.

Harriet took a step back, her eyes round. "Hang on a minute. Pete," she called over her shoulder, her voice pinched. "Pete, someone is here for Gad." She whirled back to him. "What'd you say your name was?"

"I didn't." He snapped his fingers. Red approached.

"Pete," she called over her shoulder. "C'mere please. Now!"

THUD. Thump, thump, thump, thump.

Drake couldn't see it, but he could hear the monster. It had responded to Harriet's tense voice. The thud of its descent from the roof to the porch meant it was coming. It would be around the corner any moment.

Harriet heard it; her hand began to shake on the door handle.

Drake watched her closely, fascinated by her heightened fear. She knew the alastor hunted her. He wondered if she could see it.

Drake addressed Red, just feet from him. "Where is it now? There?" He gestured to the porch corner where the last thump had emanated from. Red bowed his head with solid affirmation.

"Drake." The man Gad called 'Uncle Pete' strode in behind Harriet from the back room, his white rhinestone jumpsuit sparkling in the track lighting. He pulled his reading glasses from his face. "Drake, is that you?"

"Yes, Mr. Owens. I'm here for Gad." Again, he plastered his most pleasant smile across his face.

"Sorry Drake, he's not here yet. He said he'd be by after-"

Harriet reached out and put her hand on Pete's arm. Pete's eyebrows furrowed.

"After a week or two," he said, his story facts adjusting per

Harriet's not-so-subtle guidance. "Said he was skipping game night tonight."

"Taking a trip, maybe?" Harriet added. She turned back to Drake and nodded emphatically.

Drake could see Red's familiar square buzz-cut reflected in the window, and his hulking frame wrapped in a suit just like Drake's. Harriet could finally see Red, too. A gasp escaped her lips and her hand flew to cover her mouth.

She knew Red, and she was afraid. Good.

"What is he doing here?" She pointed, her finger shaking, to the man behind Drake standing motionless with squared shoulders, his hands folded. Her finger targeted Drake next. "Are you from Inferno, too?"

"Oh, you know Red here? Well, isn't that a coincidence? You must've done something bad, Harriet, if you're already acquainted with Red." Drake's cool gaze shifted from Harriet to Red, then back. "Look, now. I don't have all night. If you know where Gad is, tell me where to find him. Otherwise..." He glanced to the ominous porch corner emitting gurgling chortles and then back to Harriet with mock concern.

Harriet clutched Pete's arm. "Pete, that red-haired man... he slit... Gary's throat."

Well, shit. So that's how she knew good ol' Red. Was the execution of Harriet's husband how Red made Level Eight?

Pete's eyes widened. The old man reached behind the door and, with a long step backward, aimed a pump-action shotgun barrel squarely at Drake. "Get the hell out of here, both of you, right now."

"Oh, for Pete's sake," Drake said with an eye roll. He hadn't wanted collateral damage. They were forcing him into this; he had no choice.

Before she could react, he reached through the doorway, locked his hand tightly around her wrist and yanked hard.

Harriet yelped, stumbling helplessly over the threshold to him on the porch. He pinned her back roughly against his chest, his thick arm locked solidly over her torso. "It's still right there?" Drake asked Red.

Red nodded.

Drake roughly faced her toward the porch corner.

"Let her go, now!" Pete pulled the shotgun bolt forward and leveled the barrel at Red. Red grinned, unflinching.

SLURRRRRRP

Drake couldn't see the thing, but there was no doubt it was there. The sound of its hunger was unmistakable, and the humid stink wafting toward Harriet was akin to roadkill on a hot summer afternoon.

Harriet's body quaked against his. She could see the alastor. And it could see her, helpless, trapped outside the safety of the chapel.

"Haaarrrrriiiiiieetttttttt..." Its voice was something other-worldly trying to imitate human sound. The monster's clicks and slurps raised the hair on Drake's arms and neck.

This was Harriet's last chance to spill her guts and tell him where Gad was. Or she would, literally, have her guts spilled.

"Let me go!" Thrashing and pulling, Harriet struggled to wrestle free from his iron grip. They both knew it was a futile effort.

"Tell me where Gad is!" Drake boomed in her ear. He wanted answers and only fright flowing through every fiber of her being would get them.

Harriet froze, her gaze set on the corner of the porch. "Its teeth, its claws. It's coming, it's coming, it's coming..." Harriet had slipped into fear beyond reason, her whispered mantra on infinite loop.

"I said, let her go!" Pete yelled.

Drake looked to Red for guidance on the alastor's whereabouts. Red's stare locked with Drake's and he smiled, his eyes black as coal with red cat-eye slits. He pointed to the space directly before Drake.

"Like the man says," Drake said and shoved Harriet, sending the old woman skittering to that space on the floor. She screamed. A shotgun blast boomed. Red flew backward.

Before Pete could get off a second shot, Drake dove through the doorway at the old man and knocked him down. They struggled for control over the shotgun, Pete's strength nearly matching Drake's own. But Pete's eyes widened in disbelief to see Red standing again casually in the doorway, a red blotch blossoming on his white shirt around the shotgun blast. Next to Red in the window, something smeared Harriet's decapitated head back and forth on the glass with glee. It was obviously too much of a shock to the system, and Pete's grip loosened.

Drake wrenched the weapon from Pete's hands, pressed the barrel to Pete's chest, and pulled the trigger.

Ugh. Clean-up would be a bitch.

29

The weather had taken a definitive turn that Vegas rarely encountered in October. Blue skies had given way to dark clouds too thick to determine the time of day. A chill wind gusted through the dry, smog-coated trees along the strip and the trees littered filthy sidewalks with the brown, brittle skeletons of dead leaves.

Gad pulled his sweat jacket tight around his torso as he walked between his new ragtag group of friends into their bookstore. They were busy chattering about supplies, weapons, spells, defenses, et cetera. It was stuff he should probably listen to because it concerned him putting his life on the line to do it. Yet all he could do was stare at the pocket watch. It sat silent and cool in his palm, displaying the date and time of his death just a couple days from now. Halloween, at just the stroke of midnight.

With his demise imminent and the clock counting down his remaining hours, Gad had transitioned through several of the seven stages of grief. "Shock" was distant in the rear-view mirror, and he had long since moved through "anger" and "denial". Maybe he was in the "bargaining" stage? If only he could find who he needed to bargain with. With "depression" and "testing" left to go, he was fairly certain he didn't have enough time to make it to "acceptance" before kicking off. What would his reaper look like when it came for him?

"Yo, Goodwin. You heard that, right?" Jim hunched over to get into Gad's line of sight while, around the long wooden table at which he sat, each of the gang looked at him expectantly.

Gad snapped back into the present to find himself in the bookstore's reading room, the rebels all seated around the table save for Levi, who flipped the store's closed sign around and dead-bolted the door. Gad didn't recall walking through the bookstore, let alone being seated.

"Sorry, no. What?"

Perched on the stool next to him, Lilith put her hand over his. "What's going on in that head?"

"Oh, leave him be, Lil. I'm sure he's feeling like the rest of us. I mean, this whole 'saving an angel' from a demon horde has my boxers in a twist," Sam said with a frown.

"It's that too, but there's something else," Lilith said, her gaze fixed on Gad. It was as if she used his eyes as peepholes to see into what he was really thinking. Gad leaned back, suddenly feeling vulnerable.

"It's the watch, isn't it?" She scanned his face, as though the words "It's the watch," had appeared on his forehead.

"Yes, and stop that," Gad muttered and wiped at the prickly hot feeling above his eyebrows.

"What about it?" Sam leaned in.

Gad's chest ached from a continual tightness, the stress of his impending doom wrapped inflexible around his torso, squeezing each time he drew breath. He sighed. He supposed it didn't matter if he told them or not. If they thought he was crazy, he wouldn't be around to care. So he told them about his death date.

"Two days? In two days, at midnight?" Jim scoffed.

"Yeah, kind of messes with the rescue plan, I know," Gad said with a sigh and slumped in his seat, defeated.

"Levi, got anything we could research on this artifact?" Jim said.

Levi rubbed his chin and began to pace, slow and deliberate.

"I could go check the," Sam began.

"Shh!" Jim and Lilith admonished. To Gad's mild surprise, even Dax, perched on a barstool seat, remained respectfully tight-lipped. He pulled open his laptop and began ticking and tapping, the glow of his monitor lighting his features from below.

Levi stopped. "I have a few ideas. One less conventional than the rest."

"And I have someone I'm reaching out to right now," Dax muttered to his screen. "Also unconventional. But if she doesn't have any info on reapers, she'll know where to point me."

"See? We'll get it figured out some how." Lilith's hand squeezed Gad's. In this moment at the rock bottom, it was nice.

"You better. Or I'll haunt your asses in this bookstore for all eternity." Gad forced the joke out. Deflection by humor was the only way he knew how to draw uncomfortable attention away from himself.

Something smashed through the bookstore window. Levi, who had been on a path to the table, swiveled around. "What the hell was that?"

High-pitched laughter accompanied tinkling glass. Everyone got to their feet and rushed to the bookstore's main floor in time to see a gang of teens scattering, their hoodies drawn up over their heads, their sneakers slapping the pavement as they dispersed, laughing.

"They got the Crowley books I had on display in the window," Levi sighed.

"Not first editions?" Lilith rushed to the window dressing covered in chunks of shattered glass.

"No, I keep those in the back. Stay back, I'll clean it up."

Dax touched his hand to his head. "Yow. Something's not right. Anyone else feel weird?"

"Weird? As in?" Jim unlocked the door and stuck his head out to look up and down the street.

"As in, light-headed. Warm, tingly. Kinda... like I'm a few beers in right now or something. I need um, I need to... go..." Dax stood, closed his laptop and set it on a shelf. His expression was a mixture of confusion and worry. He pulled out his wallet and thumbed through his cash.

"No, he's right." Lilith's fingers twitched as she raised her hands out, palms toward the open door. "There's some kind of heavy juju happening out there. What is that? It's like it's familiar, but, I've never felt this heavy before. It's like a spiritual blanket over everything."

"I need a cigarette. Bad." The determination on Jim's face was plain. "Who's got one?"

Levi lifted one eyebrow. "And I need fried chicken. A bucket of fried chicken, right now. Two buckets, even."

"But you swore off fried chicken, we're not allowed to let you have any." Sam made a half-hearted move to stand in the open doorway.

"I know." Levi looked just as surprised as Sam. "But if I don't get some fried chicken damned quick, there's gonna' be trouble." Levi's right eye twitched.

"No one's got a cig? I-I gotta go," Jim stammered and strode out to the sidewalk.

Lilith grabbed his arm. "Wait Jim, something is really not right here."

"I don't care, Lilith. If I don't get a cigarette right now-" Jim didn't finish his sentence. His skin beaded with sweat. "I'm gonna smoke a whole damned pack or two in one sitting." He yanked his wrist from Lilith's grip and walked speedily away.

"Ow, Jim! Wait," she pleaded, rubbing her hand. Her face reddened. "Jim, stop, I said!"

Jim waved his hand over his shoulder dismissively and continued his manic pace. "Sorry, gotta go."

Lilith's hands moved fluidly with an elaborate set of precise motions, her lips moving with words Gad could not hear. Abruptly, Jim's arms flew straight up and he tripped, sprawling across the sidewalk. His lighter flew from his hand and skittered to the gutter, falling down an open grate.

"Fuck!" He scrambled to the sidewalk's edge and hung his head above the open grate, searching for the lost silver flip lighter. It was Levi who jogged to Jim and pulled him back from the grate. "C'mon Jim, back to the bookstore."

"No, man, I need my lighter for cigs." Levi hoisted Jim to his feet. "Fine, I'll buy another one." Jim turned to go, but Levi's hand grasped Jim's should firmly. "Ow! Hey man." Jim was the picture of anger.

"C'mon Jim." Levi had Jim by the upper-arm and walked with purpose back to the bookstore. Jim had to follow or lose his arm. "Hey, ow! Let go!"

"You need cancer like I need a heart attack," Levi replied without breaking stride. "Everybody, back inside."

"Sam," Levi gestured to Dax who slunk away and flipped through something as he crossed the street. Sam rushed out and snatched the back of his windbreaker in his fist.

"Hey, let go!" Dax twisted and swung his fists, sending the cards he was holding fluttering in the wind to the surrounding pavement. A car driving way too fast held the horn down as it swerved around them both.

"C'mon Dax, inside." Sam might not have been Levi, but he was significantly taller and much stronger. The visual was not unlike a school teacher dragging a mischievous student to the principal's office by the scruff of the neck. The cards on the street flipped and fluttered in the wind. On each card, topless hookers posed salaciously beneath their all-caps contact info.

Gad stepped out onto the sidewalk to hold the door open for the incoming, when suddenly, his depression washed over him like a crashing wave. The need to get out, to go, filled him. These people didn't need him. He was useless. He was doomed anyway. Images of the ghosts on the Hoover Dam bridge filled his mind, playing back in a blissful loop of escape. They were all so lucky. The sweet release of this painful existence. His eyes stung with sudden moisture, his chest heavy.

"Not you, too? Inside, now."

Gad vaguely heard Lilith's unimportant words and felt a rough shove that propelled him through the bookstore doorway.

"So why aren't you two freaking out?" Levi slammed the door and pinched the bridge of his nose, his eyes squeezed shut.

"Me?" Sam looked himself over quizzically.

"For me, it's probably my ring of wards." Lilith pulled the arm of her black t-shirt up to show the ring of colorful hieroglyphs around her upper arm. One symbol was a black-outlined Egyptian eye.

"Ah, the Eye of Horus," Levi folded his arms across his chest.

"Yeah. Wisdom, prosperity, good health, protection from darkness. All the good stuff."

"Oh, sweet! I've always wanted tats. Mine's just my gram's necklace." Sam pulled the silver chain from his neck and held up the dangling Star of David.

"You're Jewish?" Jim said.

"Nah, not exactly. My family is, I mean. But when I was little and bad ghosts used to harass me, she gave me this. It protects you from bad spirits and their influence."

Levi pointed to the star. "It's much older than you think. Druids used that symbol to ward off evil spirits."

"You got any others? Of the eye or the star, that is," Sam said, dropping his necklace back inside his shirt.

Levi snapped his fingers. "As a matter of fact, I do. Guys, this way." Sam stayed by the front door with a watchful eye on the others who followed Levi up creaking stairs to his storage room. After some box shuffling and digging, he passed a small plastic jewelry bag to Gad, Dax, and Jim. Each withdrew a small gold pendant of the Eye of Horus.

"Made in Taiwan? You sure this is gonna do it?" Jim smirked, dropping the chain over his head and onto his neck.

"You tell us. How do you feel?" Levi's necklace was nearly a choker across his wide neck. He leaned on the wall and watched Jim.

Jim's smirk faded, replaced by surprised approval. "I mean, I still want a cancer stick, but now you can reason with me."

"Says you," Lilith winked.

A squealing screech sounded, followed immediately by a thunderous crash and shattering. The building shook as though the briefest of earthquakes had hit the bookstore.

"Seriously, what the fuck?" Dax exclaimed.

They raced down the stairs and threw open the door. In the middle of the street, one smashed car had spun sideways into a fire hydrant which shot a fountain of water stories-high into the air. The other vehicle, an old white gardening truck, had run up onto the sidewalk and into the side of their building. The building only had a few loose bricks and cracks, but the truck's front had smashed in. The driver, a man with peppery hair under a worn cap, lay bleeding and unconscious over the steering wheel. In the street, the impact had thrown the woman from her car to lie in the street, blood trickling from her face.

A couple who had seen the accident had rushed to her. A

young woman in a leather jacket knelt at the car crash victim's side, waving her hand back and forth before her the victim's eyes. Meanwhile, her male partner leaned into the car, rummaged for a moment, and withdrew with the victim's purse and keys. He handed the purse to his girlfriend, who then pulled out her wallet and opened it.

"I'll check this guy, you go help the woman," Sam said to Gad and pulled at the dented truck door's handle.

"Holy shit. 9-1-1 is just a busy signal right now." Lilith pulled her cell phone from her and dialed again.

Gad got to the bleeding woman and knelt next to her. "You got her ID?" Gad said to the woman in the leather jacket.

"I got her cash and her credit cards. I don't give a fuck who she is." Her grin turned Gad's stomach. She pocketed the victim's wallet and tore down the street with her boyfriend.

Gad put his fingers to the victim's throat and felt for a pulse. It was weak, but it was there.

"She's alive, Sam," Gad yelled.

"This man is also," Sam called back.

"I'll get Mercy, let's get them boarded and on the bus."

Levi's pounding feet stopped at Gad's back. "Anything we can do?"

"Yeah, stay with her. I'll get my ambulance and these two to the ER. And Levi, be careful." Gad stood, looking up and down the street. "People are... not right."

"I noticed. Go on," Levi said and cast a stern eye around the street.

The man in the truck could sit up when he came to, which made getting them both safely strapped in on Mercy that much faster. Sam called in the info to the nearest ER while Gad drove as fast as possible, sirens blaring.

"Lookout!" Sam pointed to a Porsche running a red light. Gad swerved, standing on the brakes. A yellow Lamborghini blew past at record speed just inches from the front bumper. Gad took in a shaky breath just as several police cars tore past, their lights flashing and sirens blaring.

Gad pulled out into the intersection and turned onto the strip.

"Dude." Sam gawked out the passenger window at pure chaos. The famous Bellagio fountains were rampant with people. Half clothed or outright nude, they partied in the water as though it were a massive Roman bath. Jets of water danced around them as they played, fell backward and mock swam in the water display.

"Gang fight!" Gad wrenched Sam's arm down, pulling him into a hunch as something sounded sharply against the ambulance wall behind Gad. Two groups of men faced off on the corner between shopping malls, guns drawn and firing. Gad hit the gas.

The radio was nonstop calls for help and chatter. Sam pulled at his face. "What do we do? What is this?"

Even his favorite hot dog hangout was a mess, packed by people in line for dogs and crowded by patrons. At the table he liked to enjoy a late dinner at and reflect, a man and his family sat with a tray loaded with hot dogs, probably more than a dozen. Gad slowed the bus, mesmerized. The man was eating voraciously, as though in the middle of the last meal of his life. He didn't even appear to be chewing. Like a snake, he wrapped his lips further and further over the foot-long hot dog and continued to shove it in his mouth and down his throat. Behind him, someone vomited over the railing and, in a heartbeat, started wolfing down the next foot long.

They passed the homeless guys standing atop their paint buckets with their "The End is Nigh" sign. For once, their message didn't feel like a stretch.

"It's like everyone has gone crazy. It's that heavy thing Lilith was talking about. Making people want to just do whatever they feel." Sam turned away, squeamish at catching the obvious sex act happening in the alleyway as they drove past.

"Yeah, I felt compelled to be destructive. And the couple on the street stole this woman's money."

"It's like morals got switched off. Or-" Sam stopped.

"Or what?"

Sam's face blanched. "The demon network was bragging they had a WMD, and we guessed it was the angel. Gad, what if it is? Could the angel be doing this somehow?"

"Sam, that makes no sense. How and why would an angel help the demons make people go crazy?"

"I don't know the how, but that has to be the why."

Gad pulled Mercy around the corner to the hospital entrance. It was already full, not only with ambulances but with cars and mobs of the injured and hurting, all trying to get into the ER. Nurses and security flanked the sliding glass doors, holding and pushing people back.

Sam's mouth hung agape. "I've never, I mean... What do we do?"

"I don't know." Gad shook his head. "The way the radio's blowing up. Sounds like all the hospitals in the area will have the same issues. We can try to triage them on the bus and wait our turn?"

With the chapel just down the street, he wondered if he could treat them and bring them there for a while. Gad pulled out his mobile phone and dialed the chapel.

No one answered.

"No one's answering at the chapel. Pete's not answering his cell phone. I mean, they live there. That's never happened. I need to check in on them." Gad had absentmindedly twisted a napkin so tight between his fingers, what remained resembled rope.

"I'm telling you, Gad, this is not a good idea. Inferno goons will come looking for you wherever you usually hang out, and this is a hang-outty place for you, right?" Sam shut off the headlights and glided his dented old four-seater Corolla to a spot against the sidewalk behind the chapel's darkened parking lot.

"That's what I'm afraid of." Gad tugged at the mangled brown fibers tight in his hands.

"Couldn't they just be out seeing a movie?" Sam asked. He peered under his visor to the chapel.

A keening wail tore through the sounds of nighttime Vegas, sending a chill down Gad's spine. Sam looked to Gad, worried, but Gad said nothing. They were both all too familiar with that sound. For the first time in a long while, he searched the chapel roof for the alastor, but couldn't see it. His heart began to thump.

"Wait here." Gad quietly opened the door and stepped out, every nerve on alert.

"Hell no," Sam whispered. He slipped from the driver's seat with his messenger bag, shut his door with a soft click, and crept after Gad.

Gad's hand slipped just inside his shirt collar and drew out the pendant of St. Christopher, squeezing it tight between his fingertips. Knowing the powerful level of protection it offered gave him some comfort.

They crossed the parking lot to the back door. *So far, so good.* He pressed the door code, and the bolt released with a click. One gentle tug at the door and it opened. Gad's hopes plummeted. Pete would have had both deadbolts engaged and the wooden brace across the door at this time of night. Pete would expect Gad at the front door.

Pete's laptop computer was open to his business spreadsheet, the cursor still blinking in the Daily Total cell. A half-empty glass of bourbon sat in the pool of light from the desk lamp. The black and white security camera screens showed the angles of the porch, around the chapel and the parking lot, all empty.

Gad moved carefully to the office door and listened. It was deathly quiet. Gad took a deep breath and held it. Holding his shoulder to the door frame, he checked down the hall. It was too dark to see. Beyond Pete's office door, all lights were off. Gad's anxiety ratcheted higher. Pete never shut off the entryway lights. They were always either on during business hours or dimmed when the chapel was closed.

Gad moved to the security camera monitors and pressed a key on the laptop. The view switched from the front stoop to the scene in the entryway where the lights should have been dim.

Despite the entryway's lack of light, the security camera's enhanced low lighting imaging showed the room to be empty. Until someone, or something, rushed past.

Sam rummaged briefly in his bag and produced an iron railroad spike knife in one hand and a sawed-off shotgun in the other. Sam mouthed "rock salt" and offered the shotgun to Gad. Gad shook his head and opened his hand to show Sam the silver pocket watch on his palm. Sam's eyebrow lifted, as if to say, "And?"

Gad made a fist over the watch and made the slamming motion twice. The scythe burst from his hand with supernatural force, the shining blade sprang forth, silver like the watch itself and arced to a wicked point above Gad's head.

Sam took an inadvertent step back, his eyes wide. He inclined his head to Gad with admiration.

Gad used the same motion to retract the blade to its pocket watch form. The scythe was too large and unwieldy to walk with stealth through the chapels' corridors. Instead, he held it tight in his fist, ready at a moment's notice, and stepped out into the corridor.

Through the back hall and along the chapel walls, Gad and Sam moved noiselessly, gazes darting left and right to discern movement from shadow. The only thing Gad knew for certain was that this wasn't normal, any of it. The chapel had never felt more empty than it did now; he could feel it in his gut.

They reached the double doors that led from the chapel to the entryway. They were wide open. Streetlight filtered through the slats of the closed blinds behind the desk. The air was bitingly cold, like stepping into a meat locker.

Carefully, step by step, Gad made his way to the desk and found nothing behind or in front of it.

Sam lifted his shotgun and pointed it to the door, his body tensed.

Something rushed from the closed front door to the chapel, too fast for Gad to discern anything. He quickly produced the scythe, and it sprung to life. He grasped it in both hands, readying the blade to strike. Sam broke the silence and slid the shotgun bolt forward and back, loading the shell into the chamber. The breath from his nostrils formed clouds of vapor.

The thing flew past again, blindingly fast, this time throwing itself down on hands and feet at the chapel's entrance. It looked human. It hunched over something on the floor and... it was crying. Its back convulsed several times, and the sound of weeping filled the chapel. A wave of emotion broke over Gad, he nearly lost his footing with the sudden overwhelming pain washing over him. Sam must have felt it, too, he stumbled back against the wall and laid the shotgun flat to his chest, gasping for air.

Gad fought through the imperceptible weight to move through the dark to the light switch. He flipped it on. Light erased every shadow in the room, including the hunched figure.

The entry rug was missing and, where it normally lay, was a faint stain on the floor. Scrubbed nearly away, it was still discernable on the hardwood floor, a large misshapen tint.

Sam bent to the floor and touched it. His eyes rolled up. He spoke, his voice hollow. "Pete is gone, Gad. There's nothing we can do. But she is still here."

The thing appeared again, this time in the chapel, shaking, vibrating and shooting from one place to the next in an erratic blur.

"Still here?" Gad repeated, his mind suddenly stuck. "Who?"

"Harriet."

The crying ceased abruptly. The blur in the chapel stopped, its vibrating shape coming into focus as though someone turned dials to sharpen the picture.

It was Harriet. She was dead.

Her eyes, once bright and wise, were a clouded blue-white. Her head misshapen, her clothing had neatly lined gashes as though five knives had sliced at her repeatedly. Black smoke trailed in thick wisps from the wounds. Before he could react, she rushed at him and stopped just inches from his face, her eyes filled with pooling light.

"Leave, now," Harriet said, her ethereal voice hollow. "They're coming for you."

"Where's Pete, Harriet? What happened?"

"Get out," she said, louder this time. Her hair whipped around her head as through blown in a gale force wind. Light shone from her dead eyes, red like fire.

"But Harriet-" Gad needed to know what had happened, who did this, what was this-

The ghost threw back her head and screeched with the power of a band of banshees, a sound so terrible that Sam dropped to the floor with his hands over his ears, shaking. She threw her arms wide and rushed at Gad, wild and furious. The impact of her force pushed every ounce of air from his body. He flew backward as she passed through him; the scream reverberated in every molecule of his being. Cold, empty, heavy, he fell like a stone to clatter on the floor as her soul pushed through his. In this moment, he saw it all through her eyes, how it had happened.

The vision poured forth, exchanging his sight for hers from hours before. The man stood at the front door, coldly polite and threatening. The security guard from Inferno stood behind. He wouldn't tell. Pete! Pete, wait. NO! The alastor came around the corner, coming for him. *BANG.* The scream, the agonizing scream. Pete on the floor, bleeding out. The alastor's claws wrapping over his head, squeezing, squeezing, until...

Gad's stomach rolled and heaved, sending him crawling for the trashcan by the desk. Everything that had been in his stomach came out. It was Drake. Drake had done this.

Pete was gone, Pete was gone, and Harriett, Harriet's ghost, this, Harriet is dead, too, all my fault, all my fault.

He couldn't breathe; his chest was too tight. Gad's vision shrank to a pinpoint, oxygen and consciousness slipping from him.

"Gad, breathe." Sam had somehow found a brown paper bag and now held it to Gad's mouth. His head swimming, he did as Sam instructed. The semi-sweet smell of recycled paper filled his nose and mouth. He breathed in and out, his hands shaking.

"Harriet, you need to go to the light," Sam called to the room. Harriet had disappeared, but they both knew it didn't mean she had left. Sam pushed his glasses back into place with a trembling finger.

"I will not, I will not, I will not..." The angry voice resounded around the room in a rushing wind. Papers flew in a tumult, and pictures jumped from the wall to smash on the floor. "They will pay, they must all pay. "They took my husband. They took Peter."

Sam covered his eyes with his arms against the chaos, but his wrists flew outward as though suddenly grasped and yanked from his face. Harriet reappeared and floated before him, her eyes now holes of dark peering into Sam's. Black smoke tendrils spread from her wounds, poured out from her gashes, transforming the chapel entryway into a nimbus cloud of spiritual darkness. "They took me." Sam shrank from her, flattening against the wall.

"And they will come to take Gideon."

"Gad," Sam yelled, his wrists in her ethereal grasp.

"Harriet!" Gad stood and shouted over the pandemonium. His iron knife was ready in his left hand. "Alright, I'm leaving now."

It worked. She released Sam's wrists and turned to Gad.

"Please, rest now. I'm leaving so I can be safe. Rest." He reached up to her and touched her drifting hand. Or at least, he left his fingers lingering where hers floated.

Harriet's face softened. The harsh black holes that were her eyes, faded. She dissipated, her form drifting apart into wisps of black smoke.

"Let's go, Sam." Gad dropped the iron knife back into its holster on his belt.

"Don't gotta ask me twice," Sam muttered and sprang to his feet, shaking.

30

D rake checked his reflection in the mirrored elevator several times, smoothed back his already flawless hair, straightened his tie, and ensured his dress shirt and pants were lint-free and impeccable. The elevator shot upward, the digital display for floor numbers changed too fast to read.

It was finally happening.

"Eighth Level." The elevator's feminine voice broke the silence. The elevator doors slid open.

The shadowed chrome and tile hallway he had traversed countless times before now seemed to stretch onward into infinite. Each step toward Xavier's door echoed through the empty and otherwise silent expanse of polished, sleek decor. Of the few details there were, each was immaculate and cold.

Drake stopped in front of Xavier's door and raised his knuckles to its surface to knock. The door swung open.

"Punctual, as usual." Xavier's voice carried out to the hall almost musically. "Please come in. Take a seat."

Drake stepped inside, every nerve of his being electric. Would he have a new role? A raise? New perks? A new apartment on the next level? He could see himself seated in a black leather office chair with his feet kicked up on a chrome desk, admiring the nighttime spectacle of the Las Vegas strip through floor-to-ceiling windows.

For the first time, Xavier stood at his office door and held it open. His Cheshire Cat smile extended from ear to ear with perfect white teeth. "Congratulations, Drake. You've made great strides recently."

"Well, while I lent an assist on another case, I am still one hundred percent dedicated to tracking down Goodwin, sir."

"Oh, of that there is no doubt. We have utmost faith in you. Which brings me to why we've asked you here today."

"'We', sir?" That was a new term. Until this moment, anything from Xavier had always been "I need this" or "this is my highest priority".

Xavier smiled again. "The managerial 'we'."

Management. Everyone knew they existed, but few had ever seen them. Any attempts from Drake to wheedle details from Red had resulted in nothing more than a silent smirk or total disregard.

"You've done well. The alastor has returned to us, his debt finally repaid. In your assistance with the closure of that long-open project, we've decided to grant you what you so richly deserve. The status and knowledge you seek here is behind that door." Xavier held out a stiff hand to the intricately engraved door to the left of his desk, its hand-carved symbols weaving in and out. It had always remained shut and locked.

Drake shot to his feet, more eager than he had ever been.

"I appreciate your enthusiasm, but there's just one small detail before we can proceed." Xavier gestured to the chair Drake had shot up from, and Drake begrudgingly returned to sitting in it. "Just some paperwork."

"Of course, sir." He readily agreed even though having to

sign more paperwork struck him as odd; he had been an Inferno employee for months already.

In whisked Xavier's beautiful executive admin, Jessica, her a-line dress hugging every curve tighter than a Ferrari on the speedway. Drake followed the seam up the back of her stockings, from the back of her red pumps and up her shapely calves to edge of her skirt at her thighs and then-

Xavier cleared his throat, snatching Drake's attention back. "Now the next step will require a little sample."

She set a silver tray on the desk containing a sheaf of paper, a red fountain pen, an elastic tourniquet, an antiseptic wipe, and a syringe.

"Like a drug test?" Drake examined the needle with trepidation.

Xavier snorted. "You think we'd give a shit if you had drugs in your system?"

Jessica exchanged a look of shared amusement with Xavier and held the tourniquet at both ends above his arm. "Roll up your sleeve, please."

Drake did as instructed and watched wordlessly as Jessica tied the tourniquet uncomfortably tight above his elbow. She swabbed his inner-arm with the antiseptic wipe and the sharp scent of isopropyl alcohol permeated his sinuses. He held his breath for a moment to let it clear.

"Now make a fist." Jessica held his wrist in one hand and, after a moment of scanning his flesh, jabbed the needle deftly into the skin over a thick green vein.

Drake kept his expression stony despite the sting of the blood being sucked from the vein into the clear cylinder. Jessica caught his eye and gave him a sly smile. She must really like this part of the job.

The slender silver needle withdrew from his skin. Jessica held the syringe aloft and twisted the needle free from the thin cylinder now filled crimson. She held it out to Xavier between her thumb and forefinger.

"Thank you, my dear." Xavier waved his free hand to the door to excuse Jessica from his service. She left with a wink and red-painted smile for Drake. Xavier popped the thin cylinder inside the fountain pen, screwing the red marbled casing back on. "There we are." With a flourish, he swept the stack of papers up and dropped them on the desk before Drake, then set the pen before Drake's fingertips. "Sign away."

Drake was almost embarrassed by the elegance of the paperwork and the pen, each thick sheet of paperwork like parchment and covered in fine script. There were a lot of legal phrases like "henceforth" and "in perpetuity". It was difficult to comprehend.

"It's really more of a confidentiality agreement, Drake," Xavier said casually with a wave of his hand. "We are enhancing your role and authority within Inferno and, in exchange, you will receive the benefits commensurate with a Level Eight employee."

Drake swallowed. "Does that mean I'm getting a raise?"

Xavier flashed another pearly grin. "Oh, that and so much more. A raise with a guaranteed annual bonus, all benefits included. Your apartment? Upgraded to an Eighth Level suite. Unrestricted access within all eight levels. And authorization to access the most restricted information within our organization. You, Drake, are about to become an Elite. A whole other world awaits you with your signature on the last page." Xavier thumbed though the multitude of papers to the last sheet and moved it to the top. "Just sign away, right there." He stabbed the signatory line with his finger.

Drake scanned the words just above the signature line.

The Employee, Drake Reinier certifies to the Company, Inferno, in perpetuity that the Company is the legal and rightful owner of the Employee and has full right and authority to convey the same. The undersigned Employee declares under penalty that the statements herein contained are true and correct to the best of his knowledge, information and belief. The Employee will be subject to the decisions and declarations of the Company, including but not limited to security enterprise which includes jeopardous or risk-based efforts which require the possession and retention of superior force. The undersigned accepts receipt of the agreement described herein.

Drake read the sentences over a few times. Everything seemed fairly straight-forward. As a member of the Elite security team, he was acknowledging the danger involved by Inferno directing him to take charge in hairy situations.

"We've had to increase the awareness of high-risk factors in our terms for security team openings, ever since your associate breached the club, you see."

"Yeah, that Elite lost his arm and his life. I totally get it. Inferno needs indemnification if I get hurt." Drake picked up the fountain pen and pressed the golden nib to the signature line. A drop of his own blood beaded on the page. Drake scowled at the odd choice of ink.

"We have a flare for the dramatic at Inferno," Xavier said with a twinkle in his eye. "Don't let it stop you from receiving everything you've worked toward, Drake. And just think of how much more there is to come here at Inferno." His voice was like silk, so smooth and so very right.

Drake signed the page.

"And mine." Xavier leaned over the desk and signed under "The Company", the ink flowing from his black fountain pen a disturbingly dark tone. "Wonderful!" He whisked the stack out from under Drake's nose and the papers disappeared somewhere behind the great desk. "Now then." He clapped his hands together and rubbed them as though with great anticipation. "Your time has come."

The engraved door clicked.

Drake stood and moved to the door, his hand out before him toward the polished brass handle. He couldn't pinpoint why he suddenly felt so anxious. This was the very thing he had been working toward since his first day on the job. He touched the brass handle, his ability to move somehow halted in a wave of insecurity and trepidation. What was beyond this door?

Xavier's hand on his back was too warm, almost hot. "Drake, beyond this door is the answer to all the questions you've asked about Inferno. You've signed an agreement to work for Inferno and only Inferno from here on out, and to be privy to Inferno's most confidential works."

"Am I meeting management or something?"

"Yes, and they're eager to meet you, of course. But first, they want to offer you your first perk. When you step inside, you'll find three perks to choose from. You can choose any of the three, but you may only choose one. The one you choose is yours to keep without question."

The vision of his own office swam over everything for a moment, his feet up on the shining chrome desk before night-time Vegas. He hits a button on his office phone to invoke his executive admin. "Jessica, I need you in my office right now."

"Go on, Drake. Your future is waiting." Xavier's voice sounded in his ear, the temptation on his right shoulder.

Drake pulled the heavy door open. Whatever lay beyond was total darkness. He put a foot through the threshold. Cold. It was freezing in the next room. He turned to Xavier. "Are you coming too?"

"No, Drake. This is for you alone. They're waiting for you."

Drake knew that whatever lay ahead would be surreal and beyond basic understanding, just like managing the club. He would soon know what type of things lay beyond the black curtains. And he knew better than anyone to never ask questions. Soon, he wouldn't need to.

Drake stepped through the threshold, and in doing so, felt an inexorable chill rush over him, as though stepping through a sheet of ice. His breath exited his lungs with shock, wanting to take a deep breath of air but was unable. After a few moments, he gasped, finally able to take in air again. It was bitingly cold. He wondered if this was some kind of walk-in freezer.

He opened his eyes wide to the darkness, hoping against hope that his sight could adjust enough to pick up shapes or movement. Each step forward clicked on some kind of hard surface, his shoe leather squeaking as it bent. To his great relief, a dim light came into view ahead.

A high-back chair with engraving similar to Xavier's door sat at the end of a richly decorated matching table. Three thick candles provided dim light to the tabletop's contents. Before a yellow candle was a silver tray bearing a yellow cloth with an elaborate sigil. Upon the sigil lay a deadbolt key.

Drake touched the key and instantly, the room filled with a bold, loud clanging music. He jumped back, startled. The room fell silent. Curious, he extended his fingertips to the key again. The moment his skin touched the cool metal, the brass and drum music burst forth again. This time, he let his touch linger on the key. This was a key to a new place to live and better than an Eighth Level suite. This image of a penthouse at the top of the massive building filled his mind's eye. He stood adjacent a spa on the patio that overlooked Vegas, behind him a penthouse of windows allowing him to see inside to the expensive furnishings and sumptuous materials within. With a snap of his fingers, servers appeared with trays of cocktails, caviar, whatever he desired. Drake was a king. He let go, stunned. Silence reigned once more.

The fat red candle cast light upon a silver tray with a red cloth and sigil. This held an obviously rare antique bejeweled bottle, something one would expect to find on Queen Victoria's dressing table. He touched its surface. A wave of intoxicating scent filled the room. It was neither cologne nor perfume, and it was by far the most amazing scent he had ever encountered. Freshly baked bread, jasmine on a summer's day, the scent of a lover on the bed pillow... The vision filled his senses of men and women of all walks of life, all drawn to him. And Drake knew, he could have any of them, wholly and completely. He had the power to control love and desire. He looked from one man to a woman adjacent and wished them together. They complied whole heartedly, falling into each other's arms to kiss, their souls on fire. Hands touched and caressed him, whispers of devotion, yearning and lust surrounded him. Drake's fingers lifted from the bottle's surface. The vision and its intoxicating scent ceased.

The last candle dribbled blue wax and cast a flickering light upon the blue cloth and its twisting sigil. This tray held a series of plastic cards and car keys. Wait, those weren't just any car keys. His hand shot out to the keys and, instantly, a blue ocean filled his mind's eye. He flew far above the Mediterranean in a private jet. Men and women in fine clothes casually reclined in swiveling chairs and pillowed couches, champagne flutes and cocktails held aloft as they chatted. A gorgeous woman with a decollete dress that allowed her rose tattoo to be peek out, asked in Greek if he had a cigarette. He handed her the cigarette case from his inner jacket pocket. The man to his left told him in Italian that the coffee needed to be stronger, like his women. Drake replied that this coffee was the finest, and the man replied that it was indeed. The Japanese couple on the couch read aloud the stock market numbers from their electronic tablet. Drake read the hiragana report over their shoulders and added his own thoughts on rising tech trade in fluent Japanese. They immediately purchased his suggested stocks. With this perk from Inferno, he could travel anywhere, understand anyone, and convince them of anything. He pulled away from the car keys, now seeing that each plastic card was from a different country, and each bearing his name.

This was not a tough choice. He snatched up the cards and the keys.

The flames of the red and yellow candles snuffed out. Only the chair remained visible in the dim light.

Brimming with anticipation, Drake settled into the chair, his grip on the keys to the Bugatti and his credit cards tight. How would he gain this arcane knowledge? Would he just know it suddenly?

The light dimmed further. Drake's excitement waned as did his ability to see his surroundings.

Whispers. He couldn't understand the words. Whispers surrounded him from the pitch black. He strained to understand them, but the sounds were harsh, consonants with no vowels. Angry? Excited? Growing louder by the second.

A breeze stirred his hair, tickled the hairs on the back of his neck. He gasped, the pace of his heart picking up like a drum beating faster and faster. Drake's rational mind fought with the rising panic. *Don't you get up, you can't get up.*

Whispering became chittering. High pitched cackling. Deep throated guttural chortles. Laughter, as if played in reverse.

The breeze picked up, growing stronger and stronger, wind whipping and buffeting him.

Panic reached a fever pitch, his heart slamming against his chest. Drake gripped the arms of the chair, his mouth dry as sand. He looked to the surrounding floor to get his bearings. His chair sat within a chalk triangle. Around that, the sigil in blue from the tray he had chosen, and around all of that, a circle.

The blue candle's flame sputtered, sparked, and turned color. It now burned black, sending the room into near total darkness.

A noxious smell hit Drake like a punch to the face. It was

rotting refuse. It was diseased blood and leaking pus. It was shit. It was rotting dead animals on the roadside in the middle of a heatwave. Drake gagged and wretched.

Something hissed from the dark before him. Something clicked, like hooves on cement. Something slithered. A flapping sound preceded a breath of hot wind over Drake, blowing the stink over him two-fold.

Scuttling and buzzing surrounded him, the sounds closed in. Drake couldn't breathe, he didn't want to, but he couldn't even if he tried. His eyes bulged straining to see the source of the sounds at his feet. Cockroaches, centipedes, praying mantis, scorpions, spiders, wasps, and locusts... all swarmed over his shoes and up his pant legs. Buzzing insects bounced against his face, smacked into his skin, tangled in his hair, crawled into his ears and up his nose. He couldn't scream, he couldn't open his mouth, he couldn't breathe.

And that's when he saw-

The eyes.

Glowing impossibly red, black slits in the center like a cat's. Eyes larger than softballs. They blinked, coming closer.

Drake spit at the imposing crawling creatures, crunching on carapaces to open his mouth. He screamed, anguish and fear from the center of his being propelling his voice.

The chittering and laughter in reverse grew louder as though at Drake's expense. They found his fear funny, whoever they were. Management?

And the massive thing that slithered and clicked its way across the floor toward him, its eyes were at the same level as his own eyes, the edges of its form providing glimpses of stretching arms crawling, and hands pulling, fingers with claws scratching along the floor.

"NO!" Drake shouted through the bugs in his mouth, garbled.

Below the massive eyes, something lighter appeared. It was two rows of perfectly large and deadly sharp teeth, white and perfect in the darkness below its predator eyes. The thing was grinning as it crept into the chalk circle, crawled over the triangle, and stopped before him.

Drake could see it all now. Its skin was perfect and inky, like leather stretched over hardened muscle and sinew. Black marble, carved from the substrate of a nether realm. Its face was flawless, almost beautiful in its perfection.

The tip of its pointed nose pressed to his, its grin spreading wider. Drake's nose burned with cold. His muscles, his skin, his body, everything was paralyzed.

It turned its head, amused, the tip of its giant nose grinding Drake's flat. Drake's scalp prickled with the insects crawling over every part of him except his face, where the creature's cold form held them at bay.

"P-p-please..." Drake tried to spit out, saliva dripping from his lower lip. He gulped for air, unable to move, his chest heaving.

The glowing eyes closed slowly and reopened wide. The grin spread unnaturally wide, the rows of pointed bone so close and wide Drake couldn't see the edges of the smile.

Just as Drake felt his consciousness slipping from his control, its lips closed over its teeth, coming together in a purse. Its glowing red eyes closed. All light in the room snuffed out.

Cold like Drake had never known pressed to his lips, his chin, his face. It was a kiss.

He couldn't breathe, couldn't breathe.

The air from his lungs left in an involuntary gasp. All air pulled forth to the creature's kiss. And then, as Drake felt he would implode, a rush of iciness poured into his nose, into his mouth, his ears, his every orifice. It was filling him, pushing out everything that had once been Drake and it filled him until his skin stretched and the agony was unbearable. He wanted to burst, to be finished and the pain to be over. He was too small for this power, this thing, this...

Demon.

The pain subsided. The insects flowed down and away from them both, receding back into the dark. Drake's head throbbed, but the pain that had pressed from behind his eyes numbed and froze.

He blinked. Or rather, they blinked.

Stand.

The command in his mind forced his legs to action. He wobbled for a moment.

On his feet, the power surged through him. Unstoppable strength filled every muscle fiber. Drake flexed his fingers, the demon within flexing with him. Its power surged through his veins.

And now, the promise.

The words in his mind were the sound of rock effacing down a mountainside.

Lightning struck Drake's brain. Electric and on fire, his head fell limply back, his arms went rigid. His body shook violently.

The knowledge of thousands of years flowed into Drake's mind. Languages, tongues, communication, connection, control, connivance, convincing, coercion. Within seconds, Drake understood the art of global elocution and the mastery of manipulation. From a remote tribesman in the outback to the head of Russia, Drake knew the nature and motivations of every type of human throughout the world. And better yet, he would never be denied. Ever.

Drake filled his lungs with air, finally in control of his own movement. He opened his new eyes, the darkness now easy to see the way in. The stairs leading upward lay fifty feet ahead. The new Drake strode forward, perfect with the knowledge of his demon host, the Marquis Forneus. Without effort, he crossed the distance in no time at all, climbed the stairs, and pulled the door handle. The door clicked and opened.

Steeped with pride, the combined being that was Drake and a Marquis of Hell stepped through the threshold for the last step in the Drakes ascension, which was a meeting with The Council.

Drake would finally meet Management.

31

"So everyone is crystal clear now on what they're doing?" Jim over annunciated the words "crystal" and "clear".

Gad slipped his finger under his nose like an impromptu mustache, subtly attempting to filter the air he drew into his nostrils. Five people crammed into the back of Mercy combined with the sun blazing on the mobile metal box did not make for optimal air quality. Not designed for over two or three people in the back at once, Mercy's AC unit was not the greatest. Gad tried to feign the finger under his nose as being a "lost in thought" pose.

"Crystal," Dax said deadpan, not bothering to turn or make eye contact with anyone as he typed into the laptop keyboard. He was too busy putting the Inferno network worm he had written the night before on thumbsticks, not that he would have turned around, anyway.

"Glamor Gad and I are going in with Dax to find the nearest network terminal. Easy peasy." Lilith shrugged as though this was something they did every day.

"Uh, can you not call me that?" Gad made a face.

"What? You'll be under a glamor spell. Not only will no one recognize you, but you'll be glamorous." Lilith rolled her eyes.

"No. Just plain Gad, please."

"Ok, just plain Gad. Wow, sheltered much?"

"Hey!" Jim stepped between them, his irritation forcing his eyebrows to the top of his hairline. "This is serious shit here, people. You're about to go behind enemy lines. Who do you think has the advantage? You or them?"

Lilith's face fell. "Sorry, Jim, you're right. But honestly, I'm better off not trying to focus on the fact that we're walking into demon-central."

Jim nodded, chewing on the tip of his toothpick. He paced back to his place next to Levi at the head of the ambulance.

"Glasses, D?" Lilith held out her hand.

Dax reached into a messenger bag and withdrew pairs of black glasses. He put a pair in Lilith's hand and handed another to Gad.

"Sweet, now we all match," Sam said from the wall bench, watching Dax, Lilith and Gad don the standard-issue plain black glasses.

"Except yours don't have a camera," Levi muttered, peering into his laptop screen. "There, feeds are live." He swiveled the laptop around and four windows on his screen displayed the point of view of each of the pair of glasses.

"That's cause my glasses help me see, so my camera is on my hat." Sam stood and pointed to his black baseball hat. The view in Levi's lower-left window changed to the gear stowage rack above Lilith and Dax.

"So that's what it's like to be tall," Lilith mused.

"And here's the worm. Whoever gets it into a USB port first wins." Dax handed a thumbstick to Gad and another to Lilith. "Any Inferno computer terminal or cash register with a port. Plug it in and it'll autorun the batch file."

"I want one," Sam said with a note of melancholy.

"You're the diversion. You don't get one." Levi replied. "And on that note, weapons check. Holy water?"

"Check." Lilith patted the water bottle hanging from her fanny pack belt.

Gad pointed to his, also on a fanny pack belt, and Sam pulled a flask from his back pocket.

"Blessed salt and iron?"

"Check," Gad and Sam said simultaneously.

"Tazer? Check." Lilith patted the front of her runner's belt.

"Plastic shiv disguised as a comb? Check." Sam grinned.

"Are you serious?" Gad turned to him.

"Yeah, dude." Sam pulled the comb from his pocket and pulled the comb cover from the small blade. "Goes right through a metal detector, no problem."

"Guys, it should never come to violence. This is a simple get in, get out job. Shouldn't take more than a few minutes." Levi lifted one eyebrow, looking each person in the eye to drive home his point. "I'll be in here watching the feeds. Anyone even suspects things could go sideways, get the hell out of Dodge and into this bus. I don't want anyone using shivs, for God's sake." He aimed his last words at Sam. "We get the worm installed, it adds Dax's temp cloud server as a place to dump the angel's info." After a pointed reminder glare to Sam, Levi slipped a headset on and spoke into the microphone. "Now, can everyone hear me?"

Lilith cringed. "Too well, yeah."

"Good. Dax? Gad?"

They nodded, Levi's voice crisp in their hidden ear pieces.

"One, two. One, two." Dax whispered toward the top button of his shirt.

"Ditto and stuff," Sam said to the top of his shirt.

"Yup, me three," Gad replied.

"I can hear you all," Lilith confirmed.

"Perfect." Levi gave everyone a thumbs up. "And what's the code word for hauling ass to the bus?"

"Code orange," Lilith, Gad and Dax said in unison as Sam said, "Banana."

Sam's cheeks flushed. "I thought we were going with banana. Code orange, got it."

"So that's everything, right?" Lilith put her hands on her hips.

"Except this." Gad pointed to himself, circling his face.

"Ah, right! Almost forgot." Lilith pulled a small vial from her fanny pack, poured out a viscous liquid onto her thumb and wiped it across Gad's forehead.

"Ugh, what was that? Why do I smell like pizza?"

"It's basil oil. I ran out of lavender and rose. Now shush." She took out three tea lights and set them on a shelf, lighting each with a plastic lighter. "Here watch your reflection and focus on wanting your appearance to change." She handed him an open make-up compact.

Gad glanced from the well-used capsules of purple and sparkling cream eye shadows to his beady eyes in the small mirror.

Her lips moved with a quietly uttered incantation, her hands and fingers mirroring each other with a series of intricate movements.

To Gad's amazement, his reflection's eyes and face began to shift. The bridge of his nose slid back and widened. His eyelashes grew longer and blonder. His cheek bones stretched upward. He shifted the small mirror down to his chin in time to see it stretching.

"Wow," Sam said and shoved his eyeglasses up closer.

Gad appeared to be a tanned, blond, surfing college kid. "Cool," he said to his new reflection, impressed.

"Shaka," Levi said, with a delighted smile and mimicked a hang-ten waggle of his fingers.

"Fine work, if I do say so myself." Lilith crossed her arms proudly over her chest. "But we've got to get in and get out. The glamour only lasts as long as the candle flames do."

"We only need fifteen minutes or so, it'll be fine." Dax slapped his laptop shut and stood.

"Let's do this," Jim said, pulling the brim of a panama hat down over his eyes. Jim seemed very un-Jim-like in a flower-festooned Hawaiian shirt and cargo shorts.

Checking both ways, each member of the team waited for passersby to look the other way before exiting from different doors of Mercy. Normally, it would have been difficult to avoid detection, but with the Vegas population under heavy demonic influence, they focused their attention mainly on their favorite vices. The streets themselves were chaotic with people drinking, dancing or chasing one another with weapons. The strip had become one giant, out-of-control, frat party.

Dax, surfer Gad, and Lilith breezed through Inferno's golden doors. Jim went in separately and found a slot machine near the front. Sam hung back in the bus, waiting for his cue. It didn't take long.

"Hey, hey, hey. What gives?" Jim stood and slapped the glass of his slot machine. "I put in a twenty spot and it didn't gimme no credits!"

Gad, Dax and Lilith walked through shadow with stealth toward a door labeled "Staff Only", their heads down and the brims of their caps low over their eyes.

"Hey, this thing ate my money," Jim yelled, pointing with both hands to his slot machine. "What kind of bullshit scam you guys runnin' here?"

Like clockwork, a man sporting a stern expression and a beige suit put his finger to his ear and approached Jim. Within seconds, the Staff Only door swung open wide and two burly security guards strode out. The pressurized slow-close door began to shut, and Gad, Lilith and Dax slipped around the door and through.

"We're in," Lilith whispered into her microphone and everyone's ears.

"Copy that." Levi's reply came through each of their earpieces.

"Which way, Dax?" Gad said under his breath to the microphone.

"Just follow me. Turns out the Server Room is on the ground floor, two lefts from here. If we play our cards right, it's easier to get to than trying to get behind a register in the gift shop."

The brightly lit staff hallways were the opposite of the glitz and elegance on the other side of the wall. Fluorescent lights illuminated gray painted concrete brick. They walked at a marathon pace with Dax in the lead. Every nerve in Gad's body was tense, despite knowing he looked nothing like his normal self. He had seen firsthand the horrors that this place kept secret, and he had no desire to be part of it.

"There it is." Dax strode toward a dark gray metal door with a badge access panel. A small window in the door revealed the racks of servers within, their lights flashing with mind-boggling data activity.

"How do we get in?" Gad peered through the window into the room that seemed to stretch on forever in the dark.

Dax nodded to the phone on the wall. "There's a cube in there." He cupped his hands around his eyes and peered through the window. "Nameplate says Bryan and his extension is 51286." Dax got to the phone and punched in numbers. "Bryan Campbell, please. Oh, is this Bryan? Yeah, I think the wifi is down on the eighth floor. E-mail has pulled nothing new. I just sent a test e-mail, and it just sits on the same screen and says it's sending. Yeah. Sure. One of the higher-ups on the eighth level, Drake Rain-something. He told me heads would roll if it didn't get fixed like, now."

Dax grinned and hung the receiver up quickly. He waved Lilith and Gad back around the corner, then struck a casual pose leaning against the wall near the gray door. A moment later, Bryan presumably threw open the door and caught a glance of Dax leaning there casually, highly invested in watching something on his phone. With a frown, Bryan waited for the slowly closing door to shut with a click behind him and for the lock to engage before striding down the hall with purpose.

Dax stuck his tongue out at Bryan's retreating backside and rejoined Gad and Lilith. "I can't believe today is the day I run into a Net Admin actually following security protocols. C'mon, let's get back out to the lobby."

"Gift Shop?" Lilith asked.

"Gift Shop," Dax confirmed. "Operation 'distract the cashier' is in effect. Let's move."

SECURITY WAS DOING their best to lead Jim toward the Staff Only door.

"Now you owe me more than twenty, bucko," Jim had cranked both his volume and his obnoxious meter to full blast. "I have rights, you know."

"And we will discuss your compensation. We just have a form to fill out first." The Floor Manager smoothed his beige suit down and opened the Staff Only door for the security guards actively pushing Jim's heels-dug in feet across the carpet. They were about to take him behind closed doors. It was time for the evasive maneuver.

"My heart! My heart! Someone call 9-1-1. Oh!" He flailed and went boneless, falling to the floor like a jellyfish. Both security guards stumbled at the sudden lack of resistance and struggled to scoop some part of Jim up. He stubbornly flopped this way and that. "Don't worry, ow! I... pressed my... my medic alert. They'll find me here and... take me to... the ER." Jim gasped and flopped.

"You mean to say you have a medical tracking device?" The Floor Manager's cool demeanor disappeared.

"Oh yeah, they always know... where to find... me. See?" He held up a flashing red LED on a white plastic square on the cord from his neck. "They're getting... my location... for an ambu... lance."

The Floor Manager quickly shook his head at the Security Guards and let the door fall closed again.

"Mr. Smith? Mr. Smith?" Sam called from the golden doors at the front of the lobby. Jim had to suppress a smile. Everyone on the first floor had stopped chattering and turned to see how this drama would play out. By the trundling sound, Sam was pushing a wheeled gurney thunderously over every step, bump and obstacle he could find. Everyone was getting a great show.

"That was remarkably fast," the Floor Manager remarked with unmistakable skepticism.

"I pay top-dollar baby," Jim winked and clutched his chest before yelling again. "Over here! Help!"

Sam jogged to an exaggerated halt, panting. "Mr. Smith, there you are." He fell to his knees, dramatically ripped open Jim's Hawaiian shirt, and put his stethoscope on Jim's chest. Buttons popped off and tinkled as they bounced over tile.

GAD, Lilith, and Dax exited into the lobby through a staff door adjacent to the Gift Shop.

The shop was of considerable size and carried everything from chocolate poker chips in gold foil to gold-painted cocktail glasses in the shape of flame. Lilith loaded her arms with every tacky knick-knack she could find, including a t-shirt that read "Winning makes me horny at Inferno" with an image of golden horns springing from flame. Dax nodded his approval.

"I'd like all of this, please." Lilith dumped the armload of items on the counter.

The cashier's pleasant smile melted into something between plastered on and disbelief. "Wow, um. All of that?"

Lilith grinned and nodded enthusiastically.

"That's like, a lot. You must be having a good time here."

"Hell to the yes. And, I'm gonna need to wrap each breakable up because, y'know, packing. You know what assholes the airlines can be with your luggage."

The cashier smiled the most wooden smile Gad had ever seen. It was obvious he hated this woman with every fiber of his being.

"Oh! Do you have this in XXL? My boyfriend is like a giraffe. This medium would be a sports bra on him."

The cashier stared daggers at her. "All of our available sizes are out on the rack."

Dax, who had been pretending to be fascinated by a golden shot glass, set it down and rolled along the counter to the area behind the cashier. He leaned on the display and sized up the register.

"Oh really? Cause I didn't see XXL out there. He's also enormous and buff. He's a wrestler, y'know, and such a temper on that guy."

"How about I go check?"

"Peachy!" Lilith exclaimed with a clap of her hands.

The cashier entered numbers into his register keyboard and the screen went from "Scan Items" to "Closed Terminal". Gad shot Dax a questioning look, but Dax shrugged. As the cashier turned his back to the register to follow Lilith to the t-shirts, Dax slipped the thumbstick into a USB port on the back of the register.

~

ANOTHER BEAD of sweat dripped down Levi's temple. The AC in this ambulance was bogus. The back of his t-shirt was damp and he desperately needed fresh air. He left his post at the laptop for a mere moment to cross to the back and open a small window meant to provide a bit of cross breeze or release pressure.

A puff of fresh air passed over his damp skin. Satisfied, he returned to his post.

"Worm is deployed." Dax's words through the headset sent a bolt of exhilaration flowing through Levi.

"Good work people. Now find a way out. Walk casual. Don't draw any attention."

We're almost home. And God-willing, we'll have the angel's location within the hour.

The clattering of the gurney being wheeled across pavement came through the open window in the back.

"We're back," Sam announced, throwing open both big doors. Jim grinned from his prone position on the gurney.

The suction of the doors opening pulled the outdoor breeze through the back doors and out the little window above the candles. All three flames went out.

"Oh, shit," Levi said.

~

"OH, SHIT?" Dax repeated, pulling the thumbstick from the register and dropping it back into his pocket.

"The candles went out." Levi's voice was grim.

"Oh, shit." Dax looked at Gad, his face pale.

Gad swiveled to the gift shop full-length mirror. "Oh, shit." There he was, back to normal as the Gideon Goodwin that Inferno was looking for.

"Is something the matter?" The cashier turned to see Gad's reflection in the mirror. They looked at one another, Gad hopeful the cashier would see absolutely nothing remarkable about the man in the mirror.

The cashier's expression of indifference changed instantly to recognition. In a flash, he slipped behind the counter and reached for something under the register. Dax flew to the same spot, diving between the cashier and the thing he reached for. "No alarms!"

Gad was too far away to stop him. The cashier's middle finger pressed something immediately under the register.

"Go, go, go!" Lilith pulled Dax to his feet, and the trio dashed from the gift shop.

Unfortunately, there were two stocky security guards shuffling around near the front door. They had their fingers to their earpieces, listening.

"This way," Dax led them into a raucous bunch of middle-aged revelers, all drunk, swaying and hooting. They moved as a loud unit against the flow of people making their way to the card tables. Gad, Lilith, and Dax hunched over and moved between the bodies out of sight. Their herd shuffled right past a Floor Manager in beige speaking into his hand. Their group was too loud to hear what was being said, but Gad knew by the way the manager looked over the heads of all to the back wall that reinforcements were on the way. They had to get out of the building fast.

Dax tugged Gad's sleeve and motioned toward a short set of stairs behind a red velvet rope. With no one looking, they crept up the edge of the stairs to a landing with an empty hallway and a restaurant closed for refurbishment.

"Code Orange," Lilith said into her mike. "Gad's made. They hit the alarm."

"Are you near any exits?" Levi's voice was full of tension.

"We were, but then guards showed up at the front," Gad answered.

"Look around, describe where you're at."

"Uh, we're at a closed restaurant called Temptation," Gad whispered.

"Perfect. Go down the hall with red curtains and gold benches. Hang a left. Look for a door marked 'Maintenance'."

The sound of footsteps and voices at the stairs sent them down the only hallway with sloping red curtains and gold-cushioned chaise lounges. True to Levi's word, they hooked a left and found the door with a brass plate embossed with "Maintenance". Gad grabbed the handle and twisted, his heart in his throat for fear it was locked. It wasn't. The door opened; they slipped inside and locked it.

"We're in," Dax muttered into his mike. "Now what?

"Look for the mirror."

"Mirror?" Dax said, scowling. "Is it small or large?"

Gad and Lilith both nudged Dax's ribs and pointed to a shoulder-height oval piece of furniture under a white cover. Dax lifted back the dust cover. Underneath was a full-length ornate mirror with gold filigree around an aged looking-glass.

"Levi, we found your fancy mirror. Guessing you want us to step through," Dax said into his microphone.

Gad took Dax's offhand remark as wry sarcasm, per usual. He didn't actually expect Dax's foot, leg and body to pass through the mirror the way they did.

"Where does this lead, Levi?" Lilith's face was pale.

The door handle jiggled. "Somebody in there?"

"It's a shortcut. Trust me, Lil."

How?

Lilith took a deep breath, crouched and stepped through the mirror, the surface of the glass rippling around her as she passed through.

"Who has the key?"

"Just kick it in!" Voices came from just outside the door.

Gad blinked, his panic and bewilderment over the mirror causing brain lock.

Lilith's disembodied arm reached out from the looking glass, grabbed Gad's wrist, and pulled him stumbling through the mirror's surface.

32

Waves of penetrating cold ripped through Gad's body, like breaking through a sheet of ice into the frigid water below with the total saturation of excruciating cold. He felt suspended in it, frozen and unable to move. But after a few moments, his muscles responded. He found himself on solid ground in the dark. He blinked and waited with trepidation for his eyes to adjust to the dim surroundings. Behind him, a full-length oval mirror stood on the gray ground, out of place and singular amongst the rest of the plain gray nothingness that surrounded them.

Static filled the earpiece, punctuated by Levi's distant voice. "Need you to... other mirror... safe."

"Say again," Dax whispered from somewhere ahead.

"You're breaking up," Lilith added.

Now Gad could see Lilith just ahead of him to the left, and the shape of Dax a few steps beyond her. Wherever they were, it was shadowed and gloomy. A cool mist drifted through, its thick gray vapor covering the little visibility they had.

"Follow the rock wall... for a crevice... in and follow it to...

room... red mirror." Levi sounded as though he were speaking through a radio inside a can on the other side of the world.

"So a rock wall, then a crevice, and follow it to a room with a red mirror." Dax repeated what Levi had most likely tried to tell them.

"Yes. And listen to m... don't talk to... one. Just go, fast."

"Don't talk to who?" Lilith asked.

"Anyone... not help..." Levi's voice came through loud and clear. "Just go."

Gad's head ached with tension. He had held his jaw tight for too long with ever-building anxiety. Whoever had been outside the Maintenance closet would probably follow them here any minute, despite the dust cover having dropped back over the mirror. It wouldn't take long to figure out what exit they had used. The fact that the path ahead was a complete blank didn't help with its near total a lack of light blanketed by a rolling mist.

Above them, the same dark and gray nothingness continued endlessly. If he had to guess where they were, he could hazard a guess they were "outside". The dirt beneath their feet was color-less and filled with flat pebbles. Tall shapes further out might be trees, but shapes or suggestions of form were all he could make out between the patches of mist, even with his eyes fully adjusted to the darkness.

"C'mon, we have to keep moving and find the crevice." Dax disappeared into a body of mist drifting past.

"Let's stick together, huh?" Lilith reached into the mist and grabbed Dax's arm while, with her other hand, reached back for Gad. He gladly took the offered hand and followed.

Someone moaned, low and mournful, very near. Gad stopped in his tracks. This sound, haunting and familiar, had always been synonymous with an angry or lost soul. If he didn't keep still, it would latch onto his presence almost immediately and terrorize him.

"Levi, where are we?" Lilith whispered in a rush. Her grip on Gad's hand tightened.

"Shhhh," Gad held still and gave her fingers a quick warning squeeze.

"Just do... say, keep mov..." Levi's reply popped and crackled.

A wail echoed across the expanse from behind them, the resonance long and forlorn. It was almost inhuman. Gooseflesh prickled along Gad's arms and legs, like thousands of small spiders running over his skin. A second and then third wail joined from somewhere to the left, and somewhere to the right. Whatever was out there, they weren't far and they were all around.

"Go Dax, go!" Lilith's whisper was harsh with fright.

Dax pulled them along faster, yanking Lilith forward who, in turn, pulled Gad from his motionless stance. Dax moved with his hand out before him to the shadows, his fingertips ready to encounter anything solid.

Something moaned, this time, very close. It was directly ahead of them in the mist.

Someone sobbed softly. The sounds were muffled, as though a woman covered her face with cloth as she wept.

"I... her. Don't stop.... a trick," Levi said with an edge in his voice.

Dax took a step, his shoe kicking a pebble forward in the dust.

The weeping abruptly ceased. The woman began to whimper, her voice breaking. "Mi aiuti per favore. Aiutami..."

"Go, get...of there," Levi's voice urged through static.

Lilith shoved Dax diagonally away from the sound, her grip on Gad's wrist like steel. But she didn't have to pull; Gad was right on her heels. He didn't speak other languages, yet he empathetically felt she was asking for help. And shades that asked for help were often not looking for help at all.

The mist where the sound emanated from began to take shape, the shape of a woman's face. It was twisted, malformed and shifting, long strands of hair moving about and around her face.

"Aiutami. Aiutami!" The repeated word rose in pitch and volume, which invoked more moaning and a rising chorus of misery far and wide.

They broke into a run blindly forward into dark and mist, the woman behind them following, her plea more insistent with each repetition. Dread filled Gad's senses, recognizing that her words no longer came from ground level. He didn't know if it would work in this...wherever they were. He stuffed his hand into the pack around his waist, pulled out a fistful of salt and threw it in a showering arc up to the sky behind them as they ran.

A screech tore through the surrounding air, falling behind as they flew further ahead. And to his great relief, feelings of pain and disgust suddenly inundated Gad. She would no longer follow them.

Dax yanked them sharply away from the fading scream. The chilling mist fell across Gad's skin like a cold breath on his face and neck. He searched the dark ahead and, when the mist had passed, could make out a looming shadow with edges suggesting a wall. "Look, over there."

"That the wall?" Lilith said.

"I see it," Dax whispered and adjusted course. They reached a craggy wall which, in the dark and dim, might have stretched on infinitely for all they knew.

"I hear you," something said and giggled from within the mist. "I know where to get you, get you all."

Gad's stomach dropped, his whole being awash in the feeling of spiritual unrest. "Have to get away," he insisted, pointing to the wall, suddenly nauseous. The spiritual input was overpowering, his senses overwhelmed. They were all crazy, or miserable, or both. All with bad intent.

"Ven aca," a new voice cried, sending them scuttling along the wall in the opposite direction. "Necesito ayuda!"

"Did...find?" Levi broke through.

"There! It's just ahead." Dax sped up, pulling Lilith and Gad awkwardly along.

From somewhere not too far behind them, wailing burst forth, outrage at having lost track of the living souls. Gad shot forward, wrenching Lilith and pushing Dax into a pitch-black opening in the rock wall just wide enough for all three of them.

"Ugh, is this it?" Lilith pulled a flip lighter from her pocket. "Can't see a thing."

"Don't!" Gad put his hand over the lighter. "The light would draw every spirit in the vicinity down on us in a heartbeat."

"Gad's right," Dax pushed her hand back. "No way, not in this place. Pretty sure this is like, Limbo."

"Yes." Levi's voice said in their ears. "... found crevice? There are openings...rock...and they...lead...same place...crevice is safe."

"Got it," Lilith nodded.

"Got to k...moving. Almost th..."

"C'mon," Dax took Lilith's hand and stepped into the darkness.

They moved forward through the pitch black in a single file line, Lilith's hand on Dax's shoulder and Gad's hand on Lilith's. The passage was just wide enough for two to walk side-by-side and, at some point, allowed for only one person, requiring them to turn sideways to fit through. Together they moved through the passage with care and without sight, their other senses on high alert for unexpected sounds or movement. Gad heard Dax grumbling under his breath and it came through Gad's earpiece, something about "probably Shelob". Levi's line had gone to pure static.

Finally, an orange-red light at the end of the narrow passage revealed the way out. It was getting much warmer as they approached, even humid. The faint sounds of moaning and wailing gave Gad a start.

"I hear more of the shades ahead," Gad blurted.

"I don't think so." Dax replied quietly into their earpieces. "This is probably just a torture chamber."

"Are you kidding? I mean it, I can't tell," Lilith whispered.

"I'm serious. Casinos all have them. Never seen one in person, but I saw some confidential stuff in feeds. There's fire and cages and, well, torture."

"Wait, are there demons?" Gad said.

"I don't think Levi would lead us into a room with demons, Gad." Dax looked over his shoulder at Gad, and the flickering light was now bright enough to illuminate his incredulity.

"But how does Levi know? How does he even know where we should go?"

"He used to work here. Like your good buddy," Lilith replied.

"Wait, what? He worked here?"

"It's all right, Gad. Jim saved him," she said as though everyone already knew that.

"Saved him? How?" Gad's mind reeled. He couldn't process the flood of questions unleashed with the new and alarming information about their fearless leader.

"Not now, Gad." Dax warned and stopped at the passageway's end. "Yup. It's a torture chamber."

The end of the passageway through the rock opened into a vast cavern. Niches in the gray rock walls illuminated all with their flickering flame. Gad tugged his shirt collar from his skin beading with moisture and looked around the corner with Lilith.

"What the hell," Lilith said, her mouth falling open.

"Yes," Dax agreed.

Rusty iron cages lined one portion of the wall, stacked side by side and on top of one another five rows high. The cages were just large enough to fit a grown man. Many were filled with hunched bodies curled over, limbs wrapped around their own torsos or legs in the cramped spaces. Scattered about the dirt floor were all manner of horrors. A wheel at the top of a pole held a nearly naked man whose broken arms and legs twined within the wooden spokes. A chain suspended another, his elbows bound behind him and hooked on the chain to cause his weight to dislocate his arms and shoulders over time. A woman wearing an iron mask with a pig's ears and snout could not lift her head from above a trough of rotting swill with her hands shackled to the sides of the trough.

Lilith's face had gone white as a sheet and sweaty. She leaned on the wall for support. "Dax, we're in hell?"

"Yes, a minor level of it."

"So those people are souls, too? Like the shades we just left behind?

"This time it was Gad who shook his head, the truth dawning on him. He couldn't sense them the way he could sense spirits. "They're alive, like us."

"Right. These folks all pissed off the casino somehow."

"They're imprisoned," Gad said, bile at the back of his throat.

"It's not right." Lilith added, her hand over her stomach.

"No, it's not. And if we don't find the goddamn mirror right quick, we're next. C'mon, it's probably in torture central. Demons would want easy access there." Dax lead the way in the shadows along the farthest wall of medieval horrors.

They hurried past wooden and iron maidens crafted into the shapes of people with screaming faces, some shaking with movement and muffled weeping. Past men suspended horizontally from iron bars with shackles over beds of flame, past men and womae hanging from the wall with weights dangling from their ankles, their bodies positioned over thick metal spears. Past wooden thrones lined with nails, the living and naked bodies in each chair covered with myriads of points oozing red where nail points disappeared into flesh.

Have to help them. Have to set them free. Find the exit. Bring them home.

Each scene passed into Gad's mind, puncturing his spirit forever. Suddenly dizzy, nausea overwhelmed him. He fell to his knees and heaved, his stomach contracting against his will in painful knots.

"Hale!"

Lilith had nearly screamed this word. Gad looked up from his prone position on the dusty floor to see Lilith in the middle of the vast cavern, her fists balled at her sides. She stared to the rows of cages.

"Lilith? Is that you?" A wild-eyed young man hunched over in a cage on the floor, his long thin arms covered in oozing cuts and wrapped tight around his equally abused legs. His wavy dark hair, matted with filth, hung over gaunt cheekbones and stuck to the wounds on his forehead and face. He released his hold on his knees to grasp the rusted bars. "Lil!"

"Found it!" Dax announced from the far end of the cavern. He stood at the mouth of another thin passageway. "It's hanging right here. Let's go."

"Hale, oh my God," Lilith cried again and rushed to his cage.

Gad pulled himself to his feet and steadied himself on the wall, waiting for the world to stop rocking this way and that. "Dax, wait."

"For what, the big bad to come get us?" Dax retorted.

Lilith rattled the door of Hale's cage, desperate. "Gad, help! Help me open it."

"Just use an unlocking spell and let's get the fuck out of Dodge!" Dax threw his hands in the air.

"You can't in here, I've tried. They're warded." Hale tapped the iron padlock with a weak finger.

Gad's deep breaths returned not only his equilibrium, but also his resolve. He swept up a poker from its station at the beds of fire, marched to Hale's cage and jammed it into the padlock, pressing down to use it as a fulcrum and bust the lock apart. He pushed, straining until he thought his eyes might burst. The lock was too thick and strong.

"Leave him!" Dax yelled.

"No, you selfish prick!" Lilith screamed back. She was the picture of rage, her face red and tears streaming.

"Fine. You guys wanna stay and die? Be my guests." Dax swept around the corner and disappeared.

"Found them!"

"There they are, get them!"

Four big men in suits rushed in from the crevice in the rock wall. Even from where Gad stood in the cavern, he could easily see their red eyes glowing in the shadow.

Lilith took a wide stance posture and her hands moved in a pattern.

"Run, please! Just leave me," Hale pleaded.

But this time, Gad wasn't afraid. He knew he had something that vanquished the red-eyed security guards. He pulled his silver pocket watch from its silicone oven mitt in his pocket and, holding it out to his side, made the motion of a staff banging on the ground twice. The scythe burst forth in a shining arc over his head. He grasped the staff and held it in striking position, ready to swing.

The men sprinted at them full force, their eyes glowing like red hot coals.

"Conlido!" With a punching motion from Lilith, a guard flew backward with the force of an invisible giant fist to the chest.

Gad brought the scythe around in a perfect arc toward his

closest target charging straight at him. The shining blade met the guard's throat and passed through effortlessly, neatly removing his head from his body. It left a cloud of trailing black smoke on the blade. Gad wiped it off on the chest of the decapitated body bleeding out into the gray dust.

This brought the remaining two guards to an abrupt halt. Their red eyes blinked, looking from Gad to their former teammate on the ground.

"Its him. It's Goodwin." One of the two guards spoke into his wrist, where somewhere, a microphone must be hidden.

"That's right. Say hi to your Inferno friends for me." Gad lifted the scythe high and brought it whistling down into the guard's chest. The guard's red eyes faded with the blade's departure from his chest, pulling with it the black smoky soul.

Lilith's mouth hung agape, even as she held her hands ready to cast another power force attack.

The last guard took cautious steps back, looking from Lilith to Gad and his weapon.

"You're never getting out of here," he said. "There's more of us on the way."

"You mean you are not getting out of here." Gad lunged to the last guard and brought the scythe around for the killing blow. To his great shock, the guard's hand shot out and grabbed the staff.

"Conlido!" Lilith a punching motion and the guard flew backward, landing unconscious just past the first victim of her spell. "Can you use that thing on the lock?"

Of course. Gad felt like an idiot for not having tried it from the moment they arrived. He brought the scythe tip down, solidly striking the iron lock. It flew apart into two pieces in the dirt, smoke rising from the newly severed metal.

Lilith pulled the rusty gate open and Hale fell out, his limbs unable to support him.

Gad reduced the scythe back to pocket watch form and, dropping it back into his pocket, tried to lift Hale to his shoulder in a fireman's carry. Hale was very tall and lean, much taller than Gad himself.

"Why, why, why are you still here?" It was Dax, to Gad's not so great surprise. He marched to Gad's side and leaned down to grab both of Hale's ankles. Gad slipped his arms under Hale's armpits and lifted Hale's torso.

"Mirror's this way. Lil, go." Dax motioned with his head.

Hissing, scuttling and buzzing came from the crevice.

"Fuck! Go, go, go!" Dax pushed Hale's body and Gad toward the mirror, causing Gad to stumble and correct his stance to keep up.

Cockroaches, spiders, scorpions and centipedes, flowed over the floor toward them. A massive thud sounded, followed by another, and another. Gad looked over his Dax's shoulder to the source of the oncoming sound and quickly wished he hadn't.

It had to be thirteen feet tall. Its black horns swept straight back over its head like a goat's. The nostrils of its canine nose flared within its flat face, and its gray and black mottled snake scale skin glistened in the flickering light. It dragged its thick black claws along the rock wall and smiled to show off rows of perfectly sharpened canines in an ear to ear grin, except it had no ears.

It dropped to all fours and tensed to spring at them, a low and guttural growl rumbling in its throat like a motorcycle engine.

They rushed into the mirror's corridor. "Go, go, go!" Dax urged Gad on.

Gad needed no encouragement to spring backward through the mirror with Hale. The cold enveloped Gad's body, stopping his breath in his chest. Gad and Hale tumbled backward to safety as Dax's scream reverberated through the mirror. Gad's heart leapt into his throat. He found himself before a mirror in a stockroom with an open exit door leading outside. Lilith stood in the exit doorway, waiting.

"Let's go," she commanded.

"Be right back." Gad leapt back through the mirror, leaving Lilith to rush to Hale laying prone but safe on the stockroom floor.

The world rippled and filled Gad painfully with stinging cold, his nerves still not over the first trip through moments before.

Dax dangled from the demon's grip feet over the floor.

"Dax Keaton. We now know who you are." The pointed grin spread over the monstrous gray face. Its long black claws and gray scaled hand closed over Dax's head.

Without thinking, Gad produced the scythe and brought the blade clean through the demon's wrist. It fell to the ground was black viscous fluid spurted everywhere. The demon's scream rent the air. Gad slammed the scythe back to pocket watch form, grabbed Dax's shirt in his fist and, with all of his strength, pulled them both back through the mirror.

Dax screamed again, writhing in pain, stuck halfway between worlds and unable to move. "My foot! It's got my foot," his front half cried, twisting and turning in his shirt.

Lilith, who still knelt at Hale's side, made a sweeping motion into the mirror. "Relevo!"

Dax came flying backward into the room without his shoe or sock, and deep talon cuts welling with blood across his foot and leg. He scuttled back from the mirror enough to sit up and, with a determined swing, punched the glass with his fist.

"What the fuck-" Lilith started to say as Dax prepared to swing again with bloody knuckles.

Gad grabbed his wrist. "I got it. Get back." With the handy iron scissors from his upper thigh pocket, scissors that had saved countless accident victims from restrictive clothing and seatbelts and Gad from angry ghosts, he swung the heavy iron handle at the glass and smacked it hard, sending a spiderweb pattern of breaks through the mirror. With one more swing, it shattered. Mirror shards burst from the frame and sprayed across the stockroom floor.

Levi and Sam had hustled inside to get Hale and Dax loaded into Mercy inside of a minute. With Jim in the driver's seat, Mercy was peeling out as the bus doors slammed shut.

33

"You did what?" Lilith's hands were on her hips, her elbows jutting out at sharp angles.

"I called forth a lesser demon." Hale lay on a makeshift hospital bed, which was actually just a roll-away bed outfitted with extra medical gear from Mercy. Gad and Sam had cleaned, stitched as necessary and dressed Hale's wounds. He rested comfortably in Dax's hideout, sitting up against a fat stack of pillows. An IV slowly dripped fluids, vitamins and antibiotics into his veins. "It was little."

"Little demon, ha," an elderly woman with a thick East European accent remarked. "Not bright one, is he?"

"Well, that was uncalled for," Hale said with reproach.

Gad tore his gloomy thoughts from the pocket watch in his palm. Its dials and date showed his impending doom as tomorrow night at 11:59 pm.

The spirit of an elderly woman sat with one leg crossed over the other next to Sam, her arm propped on the back of the chair. She sat casually as though her semi-translucent presence wasn't odd at all.

"Aunty Zel in the room, Sammy?" Jim said from behind a thick leather-bound book, his feet kicked up on a desk.

"Yeah," Sam replied and jerked his thumb toward the chair. "She's right here."

"And she's a mean old bat," Hale looked to the chair with narrowed eyes.

The translucent woman's purple headscarf kept her long crazy white hair mostly in place over a flowing dress layered with a black lace shawl and necklace made of silver coins.

"Um, everyone who can see her, raise your hand?" Gad said, raising his own hand.

Sam and Hale both raised their hands, neither seeing anything of import in Gad's discovery. The old woman raised her hand, too.

"Huh. This is a first for me," he added, amused. It was surreal enough that he wondered if wasn't really napping on a couch, dreaming. "You have the Sight too, Hale?"

"I'm a necromancer," Hale said flatly.

"In training," Lilith corrected.

Aunt Zelda pulled an ornate pipe from her lips and pointed it at Gad. "You have special friends, Samuel." The way she annunciated "special" made Gad think she didn't really mean special at all.

"As I was saying, I called forth a lesser demon, whose name I shall not speak. I was just trying to get info on my cousin."

"Charles," Aunt Zelda added. "A gambler, yes?"

"Yeah, a gambler." Hale briefly addressed the chair. "And this demon, I made sure I had the circle and sigil down on the floor with chalk, lines solid. Or so I thought."

"With the salts around?" Aunt Zelda interrupted.

"Uh-huh, with all the salt around that, as backup. Thought it was safe. So I put all the offering goodies in a bone bowl, lit the black candles, read the summoning-"

"Of Latin or the Greek?" she said, returning the pipe stem to her lips.

"Tante, let him finish," Sam chided. "Go on, Hale."

"So it works and the bugger pops in all irritated and whatnot. Then per the ritual, I commanded him to tell me what happened to cousin Chuck. And he messes with me, like, 'I'll tell you what you want to know if you blah-blah, and whatever.'"

"So you gave him something in exchange, yes? Is the bargain?" Aunt Zelda seemed to be a more of an active listener than passive.

Hale continued. "So I was like, 'No way, demon.' And I splashed him with holy water. But I guess my circle was wrong or something, cause he just stood up, grabbed me, and next thing I knew we were in hell."

"Why, Hale? Why did you assault the supernatural creature with greater powers? Holy crap!" Lilith was visibly angry.

Aunt Zelda slapped her non-existent forehead, which Hale either didn't see or chose to ignore.

"I wanted to show him who was boss," Hale replied, his words small and dripping with regret. "I see now that was not the best choice on my part."

"Not showing the demon any respect, you mean?" Lilith said, her eyebrows furrowed.

Levi, who had been working silently on his laptop, looked over the top of his monitor. "They only respond to mutual respect, Hale."

"Listen, you need to rethink this whole necromancer path." Lilith paced the floor next to his bed.

"Look, I get it now, okay? You get to do a lot of thinking when you're stuck in a cage for I don't know how long." His face turned red, the impact of his imprisonment changing his demeanor instantly.

"A year!" Lilith grabbed a throw pillow from the couch and thwacked him upside the head.

"Hey! Ow!" Hale winced, lifting a bandaged arm up to protect his head from further blows. He paused, his eyes round. "Wait. Did you say 'a year'?"

"Time passes differently on the other side," Jim said, turning a gold-leafed page.

Hale's face fell. "It felt like weeks. But even then, there was no night or day to be sure."

"And you were going to die," Lilith's strong countenance broke, her face twisting with the onset of angry tears. "If we hadn't found you-"

Hale's face fell. He looked into Lilith's eyes with an expression of pure remorse. "Oh hon, I'm so sorry."

She fell onto his chest and threw her arms around his neck, hiccuping between sobs of anguish. For Lilith, this was the catharsis of months of emotion.

"I'm leaving!" Dax burst from his bedroom upstairs with a backpack and a small suitcase. "Arrivederci, sayonara and goodnight, Irene." He stomped down the stairs with his right foot and hobbled with the injured left. It achieved an alternating clunk, thud effect the whole way down.

Gad heaved a sigh. He knew now he wasn't napping and dreaming all of this. This was probably the norm when demons gained control over all influence. This must be the reacting human fallout just before the gates of hell opened, an overwhelming sense of dread and hopelessness. He glanced again to his death date on the watch face. Less than forty-eight hours to go and he'd been enjoying the torture room, too. Or maybe he'd end up with all the crazy lost ghosts in the Limbo place. It was all moot at this point.

"Where do you think you're going?" Levi shot to his feet. Jim also stood and shut his bible.

"I can't tell you, can I? You're all about to go back into the lion's den and, if they catch any of you and you know where I am, they'll know and I'm a dead man." Dax thrust his thumb into his own chest as he stood eye to eye with Levi. "The worm's info dump is loading to your account as we speak. Good luck on your angel mission. Peace out."

"Wait, Dax," Lilith grabbed his arm.

"Look Lilith, I don't have time for this. See?" He yanked his t-shirt collar over his right shoulder to expose dark red burn marks in the shape of a giant clawed hand. "Demon mark. That thing touched me. It knows who I am. It said my name. And yes, while demons may be slow on the uptake, I'm sure by now they figured out that the IT dude they caught breaking and entering somehow relates to the worm in their network."

"Dax, hold up." Jim stepped strategically between Dax and the door. "Stay. We're talking about demons ruling everything if we don't rescue the angel. We need you now more than ever."

"On the contrary, Jim, not only do I need to get the hell out of here, you guys should, too. It's only a matter of time before they link my name to this place, even with all the misdirects we put in place to hide it."

"You're our Overwatch, leading us safely around behind enemy lines. Who will be on comms to guide us to the angel?" Levi asked.

"We will." Hale sat with his legs over the side of the bed. He set his drip to closed and gingerly removed the IV needle from his arm. "Lil and I can track danger here with Wicca. We'll get you through. And you'll have help from the other side." Hale had meant his necromancer skills, but Aunt Zelda stood proudly.

"Tak," Aunt Zelda stepped forward, crossing her arms over her chest.

"Yes, Aunt Z says she'll be there to help." Sam said for her.

"Oh, okay. Ghost grandma's gonna' protect us from fifteen-foot hell beasts? Gee, um, no thanks." Dax rolled his eyes and pushed Jim out of the way.

"She's my great-great aunt, actually," Sam retorted quietly in Dax's general direction.

"I don't care if she's the ghost of fucking Hitler in a tank, Sam! She's a-"

And Dax flew backward into the wall, his head slamming against concrete. He slid to the floor and grabbed the back of his head, his face contorted with pain. Papers and debris fluttered down around him.

"You do NOT call me the Hitler, щоб ти пропав без сліду..."

"Oooo, bad call, dude. Nazis murdered Tante when she tried to escape Carpathia. She's saying you'll disappear without a trace if you say that again." Sam said, wincing.

Lilith ran to him and held out her hand to help Dax up, but Dax slapped it and got to his feet. "Fuck this, I'm out. I'll reach out when it's safe."

"But Dax-" Lilith started. Hale put his hand over hers and shook his head.

"Dax, there won't be a safe. There will be no future to reach out from. Not if we don't work together to stop this thing," Jim said.

"How are we gonna do that, Jim? We're just human."

"Yeah, but we've got this on our side." Jim held up an antique bronze and wood crucifix.

Dax stared at it, incredulous. "That's not a BFG, Jim."

"Yes, it is." Levi stood before everyone and pulled his t-shirt off. He pointed to a scar on the upper-left of his chest, just below his collar-bone. The skin of his scar was smooth and discolored against the rest of his chest. It was just the size and shape of the crucifix Jim held up. "When I signed my life over to Inferno, they took my soul and replaced it with a demon. And not a lesser demon or minion. It was a Marquis of Hell, Forneus."

"Don't say his name," Hale whispered, wincing.

"Inferno uses people as vessels to give their own army more power. Through using humans to be on this plane, demons directly influence humans into damning their own souls to hell. And why use humans? Because demons can't exist on earth. They can only be here if they possess humans. And at Inferno, when they inhabit a human, they remove your soul, your moral compass, your very being. They tell you you're being promoted, and step by step, they replace you with a powerful entity from their side. It's all lies. And the asshole demon wears you like a meat suit." He pulled his shirt back on. "Jim here not only kicked Forneus's ass out of my body with that crucifix, he also brought my soul back. Made me whole again. Most people in my shoes don't get that second chance."

"What makes that crucifix so special?" Gad asked.

"In its center is a splinter from Christ's crucifix." Jim laid it on a white silk cloth as he spoke. "This was a gift from my mentor at seminary before he passed away. At the time, I didn't understand how important the gift was as a weapon against evil. Its very touch is the sacrifice of Christ. No demon stands a chance against it. And this?" He held it up with a sly smile of admiration. "Touching it, feeling the purity and love as it saved Levi? This restored my faith."

Silence prevailed as all watched Jim wrap the crucifix.

Dax sighed. "Fine. I get it. But the fact is, I can't be on any computer without putting you all in danger. I can't do my job. They'll be looking for any kind of digital signature and they could trace it back to me. If I tried to help, it means killing us all." This time, he said his piece to Levi specifically. And the look that passed between them was one of understanding.

"Go, Dax. And when we've kicked evil's ass and things settle back down, you will send us word that you're coming back."

Dax nodded. With one final glance to each of them, he stepped out the door.

Levi clapped his hands together. "Everyone, listen up. This is the plan. Dax passed me all the intel he picked up from the worm's info dump. I've got the entire layout of the place and we can see where Inferno is keeping our angel. The bad news is, it's high level and on the other side."

"Through the mirror, you mean," Lilith added.

"Yes. So that's why Jim, Gad, Sam and I are going as a team, and team Wicca stays behind on comms. Lilith and Hale, we will need deception spells to get to the right floor. Luckily, I know a few shortcuts. We'll operate quickly and quietly to our destination."

Gad grimaced at the mention of Levi's shortcuts. The last one had been far from it. "Levi, I have to say something. You guys remember that I'm supposed to die tomorrow at midnight, right? My pocket watch, my scythe. It says I'm damned to hell, and the trip takes place at the stroke of midnight. I'm no good to you."

"You don't know for sure that that's what it means," Jim said, scowling.

"Yes, yes, I do. The pocket watch is never wrong. Its whole purpose is to indicate when the nearest death is taking place. And I'm holding this watch. When no one near me is dying sooner than me, this is my death date. Tomorrow. Midnight. Me. Hell." He touched the small hand pointing down.

"Now wait a minute. Who told you this?" Lilith grabbed her forehead.

Gad's frustration was mounting. "I explained all of this already. This is a reaper's tool. It calls the reaper to the nearest death to collect the dying soul. The scythe frees the soul from the body so the reaper can eat the soul, sending the soul onward. I'm telling you, it's not something that can be argued or reasoned with. It is what it is!" Gad wanted to scream.

Just end it all, end the waiting here and now, get it over with and get into the hellfire already.

This must be the Acceptance part of the Grieving Process. Ah, well, there was something at least. Progress.

"But you talked to the reapers, right? Isn't that what you said? That there was some message they gave you?" Jim squinted, trying to recall the details of Gad's story.

"Yeah. One said 'balance' and then 'Seth'." Gad sighed, running his fingers through his hair.

"Seph. Sephitis." Hale corrected him, his eyes wide. "Son of Thanatos, Greek god of Death. Sephitis is the keeper of universal balance, chief soul collector."

Everyone stared at Hale.

"What? I'm a necromancer, people. I have one job."

"Hale, can we summon him? Talk to him through something?" Lilith pulled a book from her bookbag and flipped through the pages.

"Well, I assume so. We'd just have to figure out what offerings to use and which telephone line to plug in."

"There's a telephone?" Sam said, awestruck.

"He means all the details the entity likes, like morning or evening, scented oils, cigars and brandy, all that kind of stuff," Lilith ran her finger down the page as she scanned.

In a blur, Aunt Zelda moved from one side of the room to directly before Hale on the other side. "I know this. You will not find in book. Write these things you will need," she said, looking down her nose at him.

Hale picked up a pen and grabbed a pizza advert from the end table. Writing in the white margins between veggie combos and large supremes, Hale wrote her every word.

"Got it. I think we can get most of this from the shop." Hale stood and showed the list and instructions to Lilith.

"Where did you? Oh." Lilith followed Hale's discreet head nods to the empty chair by Sam.

"Yeah, I agree. A few of these need some prep time though. Levi, we're going to your shop and we'll be right back."

"No way, not alone. I'm coming with you," Levi said and grabbed his keys.

"Fine. Sam, Jim, please clear the floor wherever you think the moonlight will come through at almost midnight," Hale pointed.

"You got it," Jim said.

"Gad, don't worry. We will figure this out." Lilith smiled, her hand warm on his arm. It was comforting to know that, even if the problem couldn't be fixed, he finally had friends who cared enough to try to fix them.

"Okay people, I have confirmation on the angel's location." Levi had his keys in one hand and his laptop in the other. He flipped it around to a live camera feed of a cage.

Gad's knees went weak and he fell into the chair behind him.

"She's in the Eighth Level on the other side. There's only one place with more concentrated evil than this, and trust me, we do not want to go to the Ninth Level, ever. They have her corporeal body trapped here."

"So angels are like demons? They have to catch a ride inside a physical body?" Lilith asked.

"Yes, exactly. And we sure as hell don't want her body damaged because if it dies, her true ethereal form would remain on the other side with the demons."

"She looks awful," Sam breathed. "Her face, her arms. They've been beating her!"

"No, Sam, she's possessed," Jim answered. "And by the look of it, it's not one or two demons. It's a lot of demons."

"That's the source of the imbalance with everyone outside. They're following their immoral side. The demons are using her power like a giant radio tower, broadcasting the strong desire to follow your worst impulses at full blast at the whole city."

"When do we leave? To save her?" Gad said, numb all over. The guilt was crushing. Suddenly, his own death didn't matter anymore. He had to fix this. The angel under demon thrall was his fault. All of this was his stupid fault.

"Tomorrow, once we got your stuff figured out. You feeling better about our chances now?" Levi asked.

Gad shook his head and pointed to the woman in the cage, her features swollen and misshapen, her eyes glowing red. "This is my fault and I have to fix it or die trying."

He gazed at the feed, watching her jerk violently and contort, her limbs completely out of her control. Somewhere in that body, the angel fought to come to the surface. And his death destined for tomorrow at the stroke of midnight was probably related to setting her free and dying. Well, so be it. Now that he saw her, saw the results of his own folly, he had no choice.

He had to save Dahlia.

34

"1 1:57 p.m." Lilith announced. Moonlight shone through the window directly on their small table of odd items.

"Let's cook," Hale said and snapped goggles over his eyes. He placed a small black candle on one side of an otherwise empty set of scales.

"Poppy seeds." Lilith patiently brushed the black seeds from half a dozen stale bagels into a steel bowl.

"Butterflies." Hale placed five dried butterfly chrysalises into the bowl.

"Lamb's wool." Lilith dropped in a piece of gray fluff.

Gad watched the process bleary-eyed and started to tune out. Without investment in changing his fate, he was convinced he would die saving Dahlia in less than twenty-four hours. And while he could opt to be cowardly and try to stay here in the hideout, he suspected he would likely just die in an embarrassing way. And no one knew better than an EMT that the list of ways to suffer an embarrassing death "at home" was long and varied. Somewhere ahead of him, Hale was setting something on fire and chanting.

"Keep it up, it's working." Lilith pointed to the bowl. As Hale repeated the mantra, the butterfly chrysalises wiggled. Gad should have been in awe, but wiggling things in a bowl paled in comparison to the recent trip to hell and back.

Hale and Lilith repeated the mantra in unison with joined hands over the bowl where the former dead chrysalises stretched and split open. Beautiful butterflies of iridescent blues, purples and yellows fluttered to the empty scale and landed, wings opening and closing slowly like breath, in and out. Impossibly, the scale beneath the butterflies tipped down. Then, a black flame sprang from the candle wick, causing the left scale to lower halfway and the butterfly scale to raise. The scales were in balance.

"Do you guys smell apple pie?" Hale mumbled, lifting his goggles up to his forehead.

"Not apple. It's...it's pumpkin," Gad replied, lost in the comforting scent. The freshly baked pumpkin pie aroma filled his senses. His next thought was even more odd.

The air conditioning is up way too high in this diner.

He pulled his sweat-jacket tight around him, zipping the front up to the top.

Diner?

Gad blinked. He sat on a stool at the counter of a diner. The spotless grill was only feet from the counter with a cook in all white and an old-fashioned mushroom-like chef's hat. He broke eggs onto the grill, then flipped sizzling strips of bacon over with a metal spatula.

Gad had a fat fresh slice of pumpkin pie before him, ready to eat with a fork stuck upright in the center of whipped cream. He poked at the fork handle. It gradually fell sideways through the pie and clinked on the plate.

"Everything okay, Chief? Need a cuppa joe with that?" The cook grinned.

Gad nodded, dazed.

"Comin' right up, pipin' hot."

Whatever Hale had set on fire in the bowl must've been righteous. This was the most vivid daydream he'd ever had. He touched the tip of the fork to the whipped cream and then to his tongue. Yup, it was real whipped cream all right, and not the fake stuff from a spray can. Usually dreams didn't have this level of detail.

The whole diner jolted and settled, bumping along. Gad looked to his left and right, realizing the diner itself was in a moving train car. It was narrow but neatly constructed for comfort and panache with polished oak tables, chairs, and matching paneling. Even his swiveling seat at the counter was luxurious red leather with brass fittings along the edge. A jukebox played Queen's "Another One Bites the Dust", although the few people on the train car had dressed for a business lunch in the late 1930s. A young woman perched on a chair in the corner in an all cream skirt and jacket with finger-waved black hair and ruby red lips. She looked as though she'd stepped straight off the cover of a WWII era magazine, when men yelled "Va-va-voom" and wolf whistled. She caught his eye and winked.

"Hello Gideon."

Gad startled. Sitting on the stool to his right was a distinguished man in his late fifties, handsome, svelte, and dressed impeccably in a perfect gray suit with a black pocket square.

"Cuppa joe for ya." The cook slid a cup and saucer before Gad of steaming dark sienna. He took a sip. "Black with two sugars, exactly how ya' like it." The scalding liquid burned for a moment before the taste of bitter and sweet settled on his tongue. The cook was right. It was just how he liked it.

"And for you, sir." He addressed the dapper man to Gad's right and placed a plate of raw oysters on ice on the counter. Next to that, he added a smaller plate with caviar and small toasts. Finally, a chilled glass of champagne clinked to the counter with strings of minuscule bubbles racing upward.

"Bon appétit," the man lifted an oyster toward Gad in a mock "cheers" and swallowed the shell's contents.

"Sure, why not," Gad lifted a forkful of the pumpkin pie toward his new neighbor and popped it into his mouth. It was heaven. *Wait, was this heaven?*

"No, it is not. We're somewhere between everything, actually." The man answered his inner thought.

"That's fantastic. I'm Gad, it's nice to meet you. And you are?" Gad thrust his hand out to the stranger, certain now that this was a dream.

"Sephitis. Pleased to meet you finally, Gad." He cordially shook his hand.

Gad swallowed hard before having chewed the bite of pie. It moved achingly slow and painfully down his esophagus. This was the son of death, the entity the reaper had named when Gad had asked how to change his fate. This wasn't a dream.

"Ah well, great. You know who I am, then." Gad stared into his pie. He suddenly couldn't take another bite. He was having coffee with one of the oldest entities of the universe.

"But, of course. I know you very well, Gideon Goodwin. Did you know your name means 'good friend'?"

"I did, yes. I mean, I do. Um, right. And you, you are?"

"The Arch reaper. Keeper of the Balance. But, back to your surname. Do you also know your family's motto?"

"Mm, no, can't say as I do."

Sephitis straightened in his seat, a finger in the air. "The Goodwin motto is 'Fide et virtute' which means 'By fidelity and valor'. You carry this motto in your heart, Gad. You've always acted as a good friend to your fellow humans with fidelity and valor."

Gad almost did a spit-take with his coffee. "So why am I being sent to hell?"

"Because," Sephitis threw back another oyster. "In your efforts to do what you perceive as right, you've greatly disrupted the balance."

"What do you mean 'what I perceive as right'? You're sending me to hell for helping people?"

"Oh, it's not me, Gad. I do not have any say in where you end up, nor am I privy to the universe's logic. I am only made to know what outcomes must be. My purpose, and the purpose of my reapers, is to follow the directives of the universe. We would never take sides between celestials and perdition."

"Really? You don't think being good is great and being evil sucks?"

"Well, of course I do. We aren't the judges on that, nor can we give answers as to what's right and wrong. Only one group in the universe was gifted with Free Will to choose."

"Humans," Gad said.

"Yes. And while many beings on earth can tempt or influence humanity, the choice to do good, bad or nothing has always been with humanity alone."

"Not you, too," Gad groaned.

"Oh yes, me, too. You most especially need to hear that message, over and over if need be." Sephitis's words grew sharper. "Did you ever stop to think your meddling with defined destinies might have consequences?" As he spoke, a ripple passed over his face, as though the facade laid over the truth of what Sephitis actually was threatened to break for a single moment.

"I've only ever saved people who could be saved," Gad said, bewildered.

"Yes, using something of mine. Stolen, by the way." He took a swig of champagne and set the glass down hard. "And in doing so, the souls meant to enter perdition never arrived. The scales tipped, Gad. And on the universal scales, every single soul makes a difference in the balance."

"So what?" Gad was getting angry, too. "The balance on some imaginary scale is more important than giving someone a second chance to be better?"

"Yes!" Sephitis's face contorted and rippled again. "The scales are the balance of power. When it tips too far to one side, the battle between heaven and hell becomes the final war!"

"Armageddon?"

"Ar-ma-ged-don?" Sephitis repeated with a mocking voice and sneer. "Yes, Armageddon. And mark my words, there's no stopping it. This world will end one day. It is written and so shall it be." He threw back the last of the champagne and tapped the top of the glass. "It just wasn't originally scheduled for tomorrow, thank you very much."

Gad felt suddenly small, like a naughty schoolboy in the principal's office. He silently watched the cook pour Sephitis another round.

"You've been causing trouble for years, my friend, but it wasn't anything we couldn't fix. But then oh, I must hand it to you. Using a soul blade to reap demons-"

"Hold on, back up a minute. I did what to the demons?"

"You reaped them. You took their celestial souls and ripped them from the universe."

"As in, gone, gone?"

"Poof. Gone from the fabric of existence. Scales shifted a bit. And then, you called upon divinity for help. Followed by," he continued, counting on his fingers with each grievance. "Leaving an angel in perdition as a weapon for darkness to further tip the scales in their favor. Do you know how many human souls have recently had to be reaped before their time? Sent below for having committed the most heinous of acts? An astounding number, Gad, all sent to hell when they were destined elsewhere. The scales are shifted heavily to the powers of darkness as we speak. It hasn't been this bad since World War II." He grimaced at his champagne glass, his eyes glazing over.

"Holy shit! I didn't even know they were demons in the first place. Funny red eyes, I mean, now I get it since I've seen been to hell and seen them up close. But how many souls went to hell? It's just Las Vegas under demon thrall, it can't be that many souls as compared to the entire world, right?" Gad swallowed, feeling queasy.

"Oh, their influence reaches far beyond the city of Las Vegas. It's been ever-growing, like a disease across the earth. Haven't you turned on the news recently? Souls are pouring into hell, Gad. In droves. Lucifer must be leading a conga line straight into the pit right now. So yes, that accounts for the end of existence by, oh," Sephitis pulled out a black pocket watch. "Friday, I expect. The seven seals will break, one right after the other."

The sickening taste of digesting pumpkin pie rose in the back of his throat. The jukebox song changed to Blondie's "One Way or Another".

"And so, I enjoy one of my last earthly extravagances before it all goes up in eternal flame. Would you like a bite?" He offered Gad a small toast with a healthy scoop of black caviar.

"No." Gad slumped in his seat, big fistfuls of his own hair in his hands. "So, what happens now? Can it be stopped?"

"You have until midnight tomorrow to take back the angel." Sephitis bit into his toast and chewed.

"Really? If we rescue her, if we get her out of hell, you can fix it?"

"If you can stop the demonic thrall causing the imbalance, we have a chance to right the scale. By Thursday, I should think. It won't be easy, mind you. The scales will remain tipped toward darkness for quite a while, but if we can stop the apocalypse, it gives us time to fix the balance."

Gad sat straight up. "I know I'm in the doghouse, but-"

"But is there anything I can offer to help you in your venture to save the world?" Sephitis bit into another piece of caviar-laden toast. He looked thoughtfully to the side, chewing while weighing options. "Frankly, Armageddon this week doesn't work for me. So I'm glad you thought to ask." He brushed the crumbs from his fingers. "This is what I can do. If you enter my employ, I can stop your otherwise inevitable demise tomorrow night."

"I thought you couldn't affect human outcomes?"

"Do I look like angel or a devil to you? I am the Keeper of Balance. As I was saying, if you agree to work for me, I can grant certain freedoms in your new role."

"New role as what?" Gad leaned forward on the counter.

"Mm, I was not prepared with a title. I will need to think on that. But let's just say, for now, you are an Operative of the Universe. You agree to, in cases similar to this, find the source of imbalance and right it, no questions asked. And in return, the date and time of your death will be, as you all like to say, put on 'pause'."

"I won't die tomorrow night?"

Sephitis shook his head. "Not as long as you are on earth. If you cross through a portal to the other side, I hold no sway. But whenever your feet are firmly planted on earth, and of course, you are in my employ, no reaper will take you."

"Wicked."

"Quite. Do you agree?"

"Do I get to keep the soul blade?"

"But of course. It is a tool of the trade. You knew it can do more than reap souls, yes?" He threw back another oyster.

"Well, yeah. I mean, I know it points the way to the nearest time and place of death, and where the soul will go."

Sephitis snorted into his champagne and took a healthy swallow. "You cut down demons, Gad. The soul blade is not just a formidable weapon in a fight. It is a tool meant to cleave celestial matter from solid. So not just human souls."

"You mean demons. I could destroy demons."

"Yes, anything celestial. Demons, angels, even reapers. But to do so affects the balance. That is why you would work for me because, unlike a true reaper, you do not have the innate knowledge of the universe. You would need guidance from reaper-kind."

"So why use me at all? Seems like I'd make a bad Operative."

Sephitis smiled and dabbed a napkin to his lips. "Because, dear Gad, you do not have to answer to the universe until the day of your death. Yet for Keepers of the Balance, our responsibility to the Universe is ever present. We cannot, as you say, 'fuck up'. For us, retribution is swift."

"If I work for you, death won't come for me."

Sephitis bowed. "Precisely."

Gad's mind raced. "Is there some other shoe that'll drop if I accept?"

"Sorry?" Sephitis cocked his head, confused.

"I mean, like, if I accept this job, will you turn it around on me and make me a soul-sucking ghoul or something?"

The gentleman stood, brushing crumbs from his suit with a chuckle. "No. How many times do I need to remind you I do not take sides? I would not make a Faustian deal. And anyway, you can consider this an 'At Will' agreement, meaning you or I can terminate your employment at any time for any reason."

"And no death?"

"No death."

"And I keep the soul blade?"

"To defend yourself and not to Reap unless enforcing the Balance. Do we have a deal?" Sephitis offered his hand.

"We do." Gad took it and firmly shook his hand.

Sephitis smiled. "And so it begins, as of now."

"But how do I get hold of you if I need to talk to you?"

"The pocket watch. I may not always be available, mind you."

Gad pulled the pocket watch out and checked its face. The watch hands spun in different directions, no longer showing tomorrow night as the nearest and next time of death.

"Pull out the crown, rotate it three times backward and speak to me. If I am not available at that moment, a reaper will come in my stead to assist."

Gad nodded, and Sephitis turned to go. "So, to clarify, my job is to make the changes you tell me to make to fix the balance, keep heaven and hell in check, and in doing all of that, I can't be hurt."

"Oh no, I didn't say that." Sephitis said over his shoulder at the train car's exit. "I only said you can't die. Now go save the angel and the world."

Gad sat up with a gasp. He was back with Hale and Lilith, sitting straight up in the chair before the table. They stared at him, wide-eyed.

"Did it work?"

Gad took a deep breath and let the herb-burnt pungent air leave his lungs slowly. "Yes. Either that or I just had the most realistic hallucination of my life." He opened his hand to see the pocket watch still in it. The hands on the pocket watch spun backward and forward.

"So spill, what did he say?" Lilith grabbed his hands in hers.

"My death is on hold and we have until tomorrow night to save the angel."

"Oh, well, that's great!" Hale's head bounced appreciatively. "But um, what if tomorrow's plan doesn't work out how we expect, y'know? What if we like, um, don't get her back?"

"Expect the end of the world by Friday." Gad said and bit his lip. "It was pretty straightforward."

"The apocalypse? Are you kidding?" The color drained from Lilith's face. "You're just making a bad joke, right?"

"I wish I was, Lilith." Gad related the experience in the train car with the pumpkin pie and Sephitis, the odd but on-the nose-choice in music, the details of the universal balance, and ended with his new mostly immortal job role.

"So you're safe while we're on this side of the mirror. But we have to go through, that's where they're keeping her. What happens to you if, you know, something happens to you in hell?" Lilith asked.

"I think we all know the answer to that. Let's not fail."

"Sure, no pressure," Hale muttered, glum.

KNOWING that he was safe from death when walking the earth was cold comfort to Gad. He curled into a ball on the couch and pulled the thin blanket tight over his shoulders. The room wasn't that chilly, but somehow, pulling the blanket tight over himself as a mock cocoon helped him feel a little more secure, even though it truly provided no safety whatsoever. The pressure of saving the angel weighed on him like a ten-ton anvil. This was all his fault. He was the Antichrist, as far as he was concerned. What had started out as good intentions to visit Drake had gone so drastically wrong, the world hung in the balance. The angel was stuck in a place no other angel could go for rescue. This was surely on his shoulders to fix. And even though he knew he needed sleep to be as sharp of mind and body as he could, the feed of Dahlia in the chair possessed by scores of demons played on a loop inside his eyelids. Her face, her mottled skin, bumpy and discolored as though diseased.

One eye swollen shut, darkened red, green, and purple. Demon souls filled her body and used her angelic influence to project their darkest wills outward to every human they could, using more demonic control than her human body could stand. Roiling pustules dotted the skin of her arms and, no doubt, the rest of her body beneath tattered and soiled clothing, once white and pure. The eye that was open and wide was red and without sight, her head tipped back and mouth hanging agape.

The head rolled to the side and stared toward Gad. "I wouldn't be here if it wasn't for your idiocy, Gideon Goodwin. I sit here suffering, in pain, and imprisoned in my body while Lucifer's minions use my powers to enslave thousands of inno-cent souls. And you, you lie there doing nothing. You are a disgusting, pathetic waste. And for that, everything in existence will burn. Hell's gates will open and the horsemen will ride. Your name will be heralded throughout perdition and across the burning earth as the one who brought the end. Gideon Good-win, with all of your good intentions, the true Son of Perdition, The Lawless One. Look what you have wrought."

The camera feed switched to the view outside of Inferno, on the streets under a black sky punctuated by a red moon. Hell beasts ran on all fours leaving trails of flame in their wake as they caught up fleeing people in maws of sharpened teeth, tearing flesh from their bones. Screaming, splattering, wailing, lamenting. Lilith, Hale, Jim, Levi and Sam sprinted across a street of chaos, narrowly avoiding a firetruck with blaring sirens as it crashed into an oncoming ambulance.

Lilith spun around, frantic. "Gad? Gad! Wake up. You're okay, just open your eyes. Wake up, hon." A two-story high demon with cloven hooves picked her up on one hand, wrapping its claws around her to squeeze her, and lift her into its open mouth full of razor-sharp-

"Gad!" Someone was shaking his shoulder, hard, and jostled

him away from the violent images. They faded from his vision as his eyes adjusted and reality sharpened.

Lilith knelt next to him, her hand warm on his shoulder. "Welcome back. That must've been a doozy of a nightmare. You were yelling so loud. I'm surprised you didn't wake yourself up."

"Me too," he muttered, rubbing the sleep from his eyes. "What time is it?"

"After four in the morning. But you've got plenty of time to rest. I gave everyone the lowdown. Levi and Jim already have the plan. They will get everything we need in the morning and we'll go over it all together."

"When do we go?" Gad started to sit up, but Lilith placed her palm on his chest and settled him back into place.

"Sunset. But like I said, we all need our rest. I will make you a mug of my special Go-Night-night brew. It'll help you sleep."

"Ugh, I don't want to dream like that anymore."

"Don't worry. This has a little of everything warm and sweet, and you'll be dreaming about puppies and rainbows before you know it."

"You putting heroin in it?" Gad asked suspiciously.

"Only the best," Lilith winked.

True to her word, the warm cup of milk had hints of cinnamon, lavender and honey, and something that made his ordinary couch cushion feel like a cloud of comfy fluff. Gad pulled his blanket up over his shoulders and, within no time at all, drifted off into something both pleasant and comforting that later on, he could not recall. Although he could remember one thing faintly, and that was Lilith being there with twinkling brown eyes and a black curl spilling over her shoulders, framing her beautiful smile.

35

"Everyone clear on where they are supposed to be?" Levi stood at the head of the ambulance by the steering wheel, his arms folded across his broad chest. A group of "yessirs" and "yups" answered Levi from the team crammed into an almost-circle in the back of Mercy.

Gad looked around at each member of the angel extraction team. This was not Strikeforce Delta, Green Berets, Navy Seals, or anything you'd expect to be a serious threat to the army of evil trying to take over the world just outside of his vehicle. This was two EMTs, two goth wiccans, a retired cop, and a man who could deadlift four hundred pounds. Oh, and a dead Ukrainian gypsy.

He wiped his hands over his face, trying hard to smother his rising dread.

Levi and Jim went over each step of the way in, the way through, and each backup plan to the backup plan before it. And having heard them all almost a hundred times today, Gad focused on each teammate again.

Sam. He wasn't just an EMT. He was a healer with a gift, like Gad, to see into the beyond and all that most cannot see.

Further, he had a wise spirit with the knowledge of hundreds of years of magic and lore as his guardian. Not to mention, the gypsy spirit had thrown a full-grown man into the wall with an angry thought. Sam watched Levi, his jaw set, his fists clenched. He was the very picture of determination and courage in the face of looming disaster, ready to go head to head with darkness, ready to bring the light.

Lilith and Hale sat side by side on the bench, holding hands, their fingers interlaced. Lilith's eyes were intent on Levi, she seemed to picture each step of the way, throwing a force spell here and opening a gateway there. Hale wore small round sunglasses, which made reading his emotional state nearly impossible. This was likely by design because, like a poker player at the table, if fear was coursing through his veins, it was better that no one could see it. Now free from his funk of depression, it dawned on Gad that they made a perfect yin and yang in magic. Lilith's life magic and strong force of will was the exact opposite of Hale's studies of death magic and the power of the beyond. Together, they were their own magical army with the ability to draw on whatever they needed. Gad smirked as he realized that Lilith and Hale were also a walking metaphor for his own life. His gaze drifted back to their interlocked fingers. Was that an act of friendship or something more? What he knew for sure was that, if they all lived past Friday, he would find out.

Levi and Jim were into the angel-rescue part of the plan, going over all the potential pitfalls of the Other Side. That info sure would have been handy before their last trip to hell, which felt rather like drinking from the demon-knowledge firehose. Today, that talk felt like a refresher course. Jim gesticulated with an unlit cigarette between his fingers. Levi likely would have said something about getting rid of the deathstick, but with what they were about to face, who cared? Gad studied James, his movements, his voice... all rock solid. He spoke about the plan as if they were about to fry an egg. Been there, done that, you know the drill, nothin' to it. Just listening to Jim talk made Gad confident. Jim had years of kicking ass, taking names and being behind a gun. Then add that he had years of existential training under a spiritual master and Jim also had kicking ass and taking names behind a bible on his resume. No human or demon stood a chance of getting one over on Jim. And Jim had the weapons of choice, a holy relic of, literally, biblical proportions on one hip and his trusty Beretta on the other. Not to mention that Gad wouldn't want to face Jim in a fist fight because, while he could guarantee Jim would get hurt, Gad knew he'd be on the losing side. Jim brought the brains, the brawn and the force of good.

And then there was Levi. He wasn't just a powerhouse of muscle that could put you in a headlock and pin you down. Which he could, in a heartbeat. Levi was also a powerhouse of knowledge and a former Marquis of Hell. Just the title was formidable, but what it meant was that the man had experienced a data dump from a leader in the ranks of the armies of Lucifer, hundreds of years of mystical and arcane knowledge. And while Levi admitted his human brain couldn't possibly keep all that Forneus had imparted, he remembered plenty enough to be dangerous. "Jackass of all trades, master of none" was how he had coined it. Yet Levi was the furthest from jackass that Gad could ever imagine. Whether the moment called for a Voodoo prayer to the Loa or an Egyptian chant to open the gates to the dead, Levi knew it. He was a master of mysticism and language, and he could twist your head right off your shoulders if you pissed him off enough.

It was finally a moment of clarity for Gad as he looked around the bus. In terms of role-playing, everyone that should be on the team was here. There was a paladin, two tanks, two wizards, a spirit and...what was Gad? Probably something stupid like the bard. But it didn't matter. He had been looking at everything all wrong. This was a team to be reckoned with.

"Earth to Gideon, are you ready?"

They were all staring at him expectantly.

He smiled. "You know what? I am. Let's go save an angel."

36

"Gideon will come to us." Forneus's words resonated in Drake's mind. He no longer felt like a passenger in Drake's body, but like a guiding force, ancient and powerful. When he spoke to Drake, it was the sound of a boulder splitting from a mountainside.

Drake felt Forneus was right, as always, but he wanted to know more, to understand what Forneus understood. The demon's worldly knowledge of mortals was light years beyond anything any human could have tried to achieve in multiple life-times. "But why? Why would he come to the very place we're waiting for him?"

They walked, this time with Forneus in control. There was never any warning when Forneus took over, and he pushed Drake's consciousness to the back of their mind where Drake could still see and hear what was happening. It had become such a standard way of living, Drake no longer questioned it when it happened.

"The mortal will come for the angel." Forneus replied and stepped through a long black mirror to the other side. "I know everything you know, and thus I can clearly see Gideon and the paths before him. Tell me, what do you think he would do when faced with the guilt of having aided the Fallen in capturing a Celestial?"

Forneus guided Drake's body through the darkened granite-lined pathways of perdition, the stinging cold leeching through their clothing to their skin. There had been a time when Drake hated to be that cold, but now he barely noticed it. Images of Gideon in the club flickered through his mind's eye. Gad flailed desperately like a worm on the floor as two angels stormed through the Elite guards swarming them, only one escaping with Gad. "Our angel was one of two that came to us to fight when Gad was in trouble. Gad called them forth. Gad is suffering. I understand."

Forneus approached the prison, a cavernous, shadowed chamber of granite and ice. In its center, a cold white-blue light illuminated its caged prisoner. She twisted and thrashed in her metal chair, rattling the many chains that crisscrossed over her torso and twined about her waist, pinning her in place. "Do as we say," she spat, her eyes brilliant red within the rusty bars of her cage. "Do as you feel, do what feels good!" Her voice was not one but many, and her grin to no one in particular stretched wide.

"Then with the angel is where I must wait." Drake's thoughts answered Forneus.

"This is where we must wait," Forneus corrected.

"Yes, we," Drake blurted. "We should bring more to wait with us. He won't be alone when he comes for her."

Forneus laughed, the uproarious sound thunderous in Drake's mind. "We do not need help. I am Forneus. A group of simple monkeys cannot overpower me. Let them come."

Forneus receded, leaving Drake alone in the prison with his thoughts. He watched the angel twist and bend as far as her chains would allow, speaking in multiple tongues, urging humanity to throw away morals in favor of earthly delight. Her message broadcast further and further across the earth. For a fleeting moment, he wondered what was next for him at Inferno with the world falling to pieces outside. Would the gates of hell open, allowing Forneus and the Fallen to walk the earth without human suits like him? Would they still need him? Best to not think on it and just go with the flow.

The angel threw back her head, her ranting reaching a fever pitch of random voices transmitting powerful compulsion. Drake waited for Gad, amused to find he easily understood every word she bellowed in every language.

37

"Entryway is free," Hale said, into their earpieces.

"Stand clear," Lilith added.

Gad, Sam, Levi and Jim stayed hidden behind the parked cars near the same warehouse door they had escaped from in their last adventure at the casino. Parked out of sight, Mercy sat around the corner where Lilith and Hale literally worked their magic. With Wiccan Overwatch chanting in their earpieces, the team watched the thick double doors click, and the door on the right swing open a few inches.

"Go, go," Lilith commanded. This meant there was no one in their path to interfere, and they moved quickly to the door and inside. Levi followed, carrying a large thin object wrapped in a sheet. He stepped in and shut the door. Aunt Zelda drifted through the door after them.

"There, Tante." Sam pointed to a black sphere in the middle of the ceiling. Aunt Zelda nodded and the camera on the ceiling imploded as though crushed by an invisible hand. Dark glass fell to the ground, followed by the mechanical pieces that used to make up its center.

Levi uncovered the awkward object he carried, dropping the

sheet to the floor. He set a full-length mirror on the ground on its stand next to the broken mirror Gad and Dax destroyed before exiting. While Inferno had since cleared the broken mirror shards from the floor, the nearly empty frame remained. "Well, this saves us a step." Carefully, he selected a three-inch fragment of mirror still in the broken frame and snapped it off. Touching it to the new mirror, he spoke in a language that baffled Gad. It sounded old, full of clicks and growling. After a moment, the mirror shard in Levi's fingers liquefied and melted into the new mirror seamlessly.

"Okay, this is it people. Weapons and gear check, then we go. Get ready," Jim said, and held his unlit cigarette in the corner of his mouth.

"Really?" Levi said, his nostrils flaring.

"Calms the nerves. Aunt Z, you're on portal watch."

"I know, Tante. I know. I'll be fine, promise." Sam addressed the small gypsy spirit, his hands out on shoulders with no substance. Gad knew Sam couldn't feel or touch his great-great aunt, but the gesture was important to her nonetheless. She kissed his cheek and nodded, speaking something softly in Ukrainian.

"Morph us, guys," Sam said into his microphone.

"Remember guys, this charm only works on this side of the mirror," Lilith said.

"By the power of two," Lilith and Hale's voices answered in chanting format. Jim, Levi and Sam began to waiver, and Gad felt the same tingling feeling pass over his face and arms. A moment later, his friends became Inferno employees in the recognizable black and red uniforms of each role. Gad jumped when he saw Levi, who looked alarmingly like the security guard he had ganked with his scythe, complete with red eyes with black slits.

"It's just me, Gad. Don't lose it now." Levi's familiar voice coming from the hulking demon-guy brought Gad's speedy heart-rate down a notch.

Jim and Sam had taken on the look of average male card dealers so generic, the only way to tell them apart was to note that the older balding card dealer was Jim, and the one with the full head of dark hair was Sam.

"Aunty Z, this portal is yours." Levi said to the room.

Knowing Levi couldn't hear her voice, Gad watched her nod and answer with the sound of a tinkling bell as she took her post next to the mirror. He had no doubts that this spirit would defend this portal with everything she had, which included deadly force.

"Let's go," Levi gestured to the mirror.

They each stepped through, and once again the feeling of falling into ice water enveloped Gad.

"Every...through?" Hale's words broke, one lost in the other world connection.

"We're through," Jim confirmed.

"Say again?" Lilith asked.

"Through," Levi replied.

"Copy that," Hale answered.

"This is where comms get spotty, I guess," Sam said and took his post at the corner of the crevice with the mirror, ready to guard their exit path. Here again, Gad waited for the hair on his arms to settle back down. It was just feet from this mirror that the cloven-hoofed demon had Dax fifteen feet in the air and threatened to crush his skull.

"Only for Hale and Lilith. We'll be in constant contact," Jim said in a calm and firm tone.

"This portal is under my watch. Go get her, guys. I'll see you in a few." Sam gave them a salute and readied his crossbow, loaded with iron bolts blessed by holy water.

"Coast is clear, move out," Levi said from the small walkway's opening.

They stepped silently through the Torture Chamber, past the wails and moans of those still able to breathe and move, strapped into the devices and cages.

"Help me!" A man cried weakly hanging over a bed of flame.

Gad made a mental note to, in the chaos that would ensue, use his scythe on every rusty lock he had time for once the angel was safe.

Jim moved up, his Beretta at the ready next to Levi and his shotgun, similarly locked and loaded with blessed iron filings. Jim held his cigarette briefly to one of the eternal hell flames in the wall. The tip burned bright red as he put the cigarette between his lips and inhaled.

Levi delivered his most disapproving scowl, but Jim shrugged. "Ah, c'mon Wolf. Smoke 'em if you got 'em."

"That's Levi Williams to you," Levi said with a one eyebrow arched. "This way."

They passed quickly and quietly along the wall, passing the crevice in the rock that led to Limbo. Further on and along the right side of the cavern, Levi checked the entrance to another passageway. "Clear," he said in a low voice and gestured to them to follow. The dark prevailed, but Gad had enough visibility to see Levi move forward and to the left. They followed, the cigarette a bouncing red beacon whenever Jim inhaled.

The passageway opened into a carpeted room lined with mirrors on each of the three rock walls, all dimly lit by a chandelier filled by fat lit candles. The decor as oddly combined, as though a Rockefeller had traveled back in time to a medieval cave and made it home.

Already, Hale and Lilith's charm had worn off this far into the other side. Their appearances were back to their usual ragtag selves, but it had lasted long enough to keep any of hell's denizen's from noticing them. Levi didn't seem at all concerned.

"It's this one, second from the left. This is it, folks." Levi stood next to the second to last mirror. Designed with a crystal-laden frame of silver and polished to perfection, it mimicked ice. "Eighth level, straight into demon territory. She'll be in a cage just on the other side here. Move fast. Jim, you know what to do. Gad, be ready."

To say Gad was not afraid to push his foot through the icy mirror surface would be an outright lie, but he was ready to do whatever it took to get Dahlia out of there. He needed to fix it, and he needed to fix it fast. He clutched his shotgun in sweaty palms.

"Let's go." His heart banging against his sternum, Gad pushed the tip of the gun through the mirror and stepped through.

38

I ce flowed through Gad, pain prickling his every nerve as he forced his body through the mirror portal. His foot planted on solid ground, or rather, plush carpet and the room came into sharp focus as he stepped completely through. Polished oak, brass lamp, leather-bound books on a built-in bookshelf. It reminded him of a CEO's office with its wall to wall finery. It didn't look at all like the room from the video feed where Dahlia was being kept.

"Hello Gideon."

Gad swiveled, the end of his shotgun immediately leveled at the familiar voice. It was Drake. *Fuck.* It was Drake, and yet it wasn't. This hulk in a black suit had his face and voice, but his body was like Levi's; he could crush Gad in a heartbeat. And his eyes... red with black slits. Drake stood with his feet apart, at ease, his hands folded behind his back. Behind him stood a set of closed double doors.

"Drake," Gad replied. He held the gun tight, prepared to blow demon heads off demon shoulders if need be. "What're you doing here?" He kept his voice even despite the tightness of his throat and hammering heart.

"Waiting for you," Drake said without expression. "We've been expecting you." Drake was the only one speaking, yet Gad heard two separate and distinct voices. One voice was Drake's. The other was deep, guttural and otherworldly.

"Forneus." Levi's tone was somewhere between hatred and revenge.

Drake's attention swiveled toward Levi, amused. "Ah, Wolf. We've missed you. Have you come back to us so soon?"

This wasn't Drake. He spoke with his voice, but they were someone else's thoughts. Gad looked to Jim questioningly. "Forneus?"

"That asshole talking, that's not your friend, Gad. It's the demon that used to infest Levi," Jim replied, sweat beading on his temples. He pressed his lips together, his blue eyes intense, and pulled the relic crucifix out with a deliberate slow step forward.

"Quite right, yes," Drake said with a chuckle. Or rather, Forneus said. "But no worry, I've adopted another monkey. Maybe not as smart as you, but he'll do." Drake's amused expression changed for just a moment to a scowl, then back to amused.

"That's right. Drake, was it? You know that's an arch demon controlling your body, right? Remember what demons are, Drake?"

"The angels who rebelled because God put humans above them in the pecking order," Levi answered, crossing one foot over the other toward the doors, shotgun at the ready.

"Demons call us monkeys, Drake. They don't like humans very much," Jim said and took another step toward him.

"We can help you, Drake, if you let us," Gad added. He took a slow step closer to Drake, their group closing in on his former friend.

"Can we please cut through the dull chitchat and just get straight to it? We all know why you are here."

"The angel," Levi said, his shotgun leveled at Drake's chest.

"The angel," Drake agreed with a note of sadness. "And my friend Gad is expected."

"Expected?" Gad scowled. This addition caught him off-guard.

"To a meeting. With Management."

"I'm not going anywhere with you," Gad said with another step toward his former best friend. Levi matched their movement to close the gap. They were nearly within striking distance.

"You know you're not leaving this place," Drake stated as a matter of fact. If he was at all worried about a melee, he didn't give any sign.

"But the odds are in our favor," Levi replied, now closest to Drake. "There's three of us and only one of you."

"Three little monkeys," the deep hellborn voice corrected with a pleased smile, Drake's natural voice gone. Only Forneus's deep voice now came from Drake's lips. "I am a Marquis of Hell, and you three are fleas. I will chew you up and consume you whole, souls and all." He grinned, dropping into a lowered stance with his hands held out before him. His eyes shown crimson, sending a chill down Gad's spine.

"Yeah yeah, you think you're so badass with the strength of ten men or some shit," Levi said with another step closer. "But remember, I learned as much from you as you did from me. We came prepared."

Forneus laughed. "You think your mortal toys scare me?"

Jim moved forward, his crucifix and Beretta aimed for Drake.

"Um, yeah, we load our mortal toys with blessed iron and salt." Levi shrugged and fired a round straight into Drake's left collarbone.

Two voices screamed as Drake reeled backward, clutching at puncture wounds caused by sizzling iron filings now embedded in his chest, arms and face. Drake's voice reverberated along with the deeper, ancient and otherworldly bellow.

Levi wasted no time. He slipped behind Drake and rolled his arm around Drake's neck and arms, pinning him in place.

Jim closed the gap, already speaking with his crucifix out, "In the Name and by the power of Our Lord, Forneus may you be snatched away and driven from the Church of God!"

Forneus struggled against Levi's hold with the brute strength of a small army as his muscles strained taut. Levi hung on doggedly to the demon that stomped and bucked, his eyes squeezed shut and teeth gritted with the effort of using every ounce of strength he had.

Desperate to help, Gad searched for any possible shot he could make. He had none, not without hitting his companions.

"Behold the Cross of the Lord," Jim continued, the crucifix steady in his hand before Forneus's livid face.

But the relic was having little effect and with a triumphant cry, Forneus freed his arms, sending Levi flying back to smash through the double doors. Forneus swung at Jim's arm with a powerful blow and sent the crucifix flying from Jim's grasp, then locked his hand around Jim's throat.

Jim's eyes bugged, his face red as a beet and veins bulging. He couldn't breathe; Forneus was squeezing the life out of him.

Gad had to do something! Thinking quickly, he pulled the iron shears from his upper pocket and drove them into the demon's forearm. Drake yelled out, this time in his own voice, but his grip didn't relinquish. Jim's eyes rolled upward. Gad wiggled the shears free from Drake's forearm and drove them deep again. This time, Drake scowled and his fingers released Jim, who staggered backward, nearly collapsing. With the shears in his arm, Drake reached for Jim again, but Gad was ready. With his shotgun aimed straight at Drake's chest, he fired.

Drake flew back through the open doors, Forneus's screech

emanating from Drake's angry face as he went. He tumbled backward into a dark chamber.

Jim snatched up the crucifix, and with Gad, they pushed through the shredded double-doors. There they found Levi on the ground with a thick iron chain wrestled around Forneus's throat and pulled tight, his heels dug into the dirt for leverage. Gad swallowed. For any normal human, this would be near strangulation. Demon-enhanced Drake fought on and clawed beet-faced at the chain around his throat, the iron against his skin making it sizzle.

"And from the souls made to the image and likeness of God and redeemed by the Precious Blood of the Divine Lamb!" Jim pressed the crucifix to Drake's chest, right above his heart. The sizzling that followed was like raw meat on a fiery grill, complete with black smoke curling upward. The stench of burning flesh that came with it nearly knocked Gad on his ass.

Forneus twisted and drove his right elbow backward full force into Levi's ribs. Levi recoiled with the blow, but would not relinquish his two-fisted grip and straining forearm hold on the chain. Gad deftly stepped around them.

"LET ME GO," Forneus's voice boomed, seemingly from everywhere.

"God the Father commands you. God the Son commands you. God the Holy Ghost commands you," Jim continued his chant at the top of his lungs. Tumultuous wind formed and whipped around them.

The bellow shook the room, emboldening Jim to move closer. He knelt and held the crucifix directly before the red eyes of the demon struggling against the chain.

Jim spoke with power and conviction, "In the Name of Jesus Christ, our God and Lord-"

Forneus's feet kicked out and caught Jim full in the chest, sending him flying backward to sprawl on the ground.

"Jim!" Gad turned toward him.

"No, help me finish it!" Levi said through gritted teeth. His arms shook pulling the chains tight, sweat pouring down his face and arms. "Say it with me."

Gad retrieved the crucifix and held it out toward Forneus from outside kicking range.

"God the Father commands you!" Levi yelled.

"God the Father commands you!" Gad repeated as forcefully as he could manage over the howling wind.

"God the Son commands you!" Levi now dug his heels into the ground to prevent Forneus's brute strength from ripping the chains from his fists.

"God the Son commands you!" Gad yelled. Forneus curled forward, all muscles straining with power. The force dragged Levi's heels forward through the dirt.

Gad knelt and pressed the crucifix to Drake's heart as Jim had done, right over the angry red cross mark left by the first attempt.

The scream tore through Gad, but this time, it was only Drake's. Drake threw back his head, his entire body convulsing.

"God the Holy... Ghost commands... you," Levi said through clenched teeth, every ounce of strength he had left pouring into keeping the chain tight around Drake's throat.

"God the Holy Ghost commands you!" Gad yelled, pressing the smoking crucifix hard against Drake's chest.

Drake's red eyes were open wide, his body shaking uncontrollably, his arms and legs rigid as boards.

Jim appeared once again at Gad's side, weakened yet ready to fight and win. "We drive you from us, Forneus," he said and splashed Drake vertically, then horizontally, with water from a small glass bottle wrapped with prayer beads.

Drake's red eyes rolled up into his head as he continued to convulse, foam and spittle building from his mouth.

"In the Name and by the power of Our Lord, be redeemed by the Precious Blood of the Divine Lamb," Jim and Levi said in unison.

"Get the fuck out, Forneus! You asshole!" Gad bellowed. His body shook entirely as he pressed the crucifix hard against Drake's convulsing chest.

Drake collapsed, his body suddenly slack. Trembling, Levi took a knee to catch his breath, the chain still in his grip. Black smoke poured from Drake's eyes, ears, nose, and mouth.

Something glittered above him. Gad recognized it, having seen it so many times in this life, but he had never seen the golden point of light without a reaper present, let alone floating down from above. It passed silently through the red cross mark on Drake's burned shirt and into his chest.

Drake's eyes popped open wide, and he gasped, drawing in air as fast and deep as he could manage. Gad sat back on his heels. Drake's eyes were green again.

Levi threatened to pull the chain tight again, but Jim shook his head and waved Levi off.

"Drake?" Gad knelt at his side.

Jim stood behind Gad, waiting.

Drake looked into Gad's face and, for the first time in a long time, he saw his friend again. "Gad. I think," he touched his hand to his chest, his eyes full of wonder. He took a deep breath and exhaled, a smile spreading into a grin. "I'm me again. I'm whole. How?"

Jim took his place beside Levi and smiled, crossing his arms slowly and carefully over his tender torso.

"Oh my God, buddy, you saved me." Drake grinned, tears spilling from his eyes. He threw his arms around Gad's shoulders and squeezed, slapping his back. "I mean, you really saved me."

"We're so glad you're back," Gad squeezed back in awe. The

moment was surreal. He didn't think he would ever see his friend again.

Levi looked on with pride and, finally, let the chain slip to the floor. His expression softened, and he exchanged a look with Jim. This was the second time Jim had saved a soul.

"Guys, let's save the catching up for later," Jim said.

"Yeah, we've got one more thing to do," Gad said, his hands on Drake's shoulders.

"The angel," Drake nodded. "There isn't much time. Follow me." Drake got to his feet a little worse for the wear. The cross had burned through his clothing and into his chest. Punctures peppered his body from the iron filings, and angry swelling skin was forming around the burns on his throat. Despite his wounds, Drake strode ahead into the darkness. "She's this way."

Drake led them further in, where shadows worked to snuff out any source of light. They left behind the polished world of wood and leather for a cold chamber of rock and earth ahead. The rock hallway twisted and turned, the way ahead nearly imperceivable until the last turn when Drake stepped into the dimly lit entrance to a vast rock chamber.

Chill penetrated Gad to the bone. He had expected perdition to be stereotypical fire and brimstone, especially after the Torture Chamber. This vast rock chamber felt more like the inside of a mountain in the frozen wilderness. It was bitingly cold and empty as they followed Drake.

Ahead, a rusty cage towered beneath a bright white-blue light. And from within the cage, a hellish cacophony poured forth in hundreds of voices. Despite the deep-freezer temperatures, sweat prickled at Gad's temples. The discord from the cage was unfathomable. It sounded as though a monster with a hundred heads waited inside for them, a hydra whose heads had been lopped off and regrown too many times to count. Yet as they drew near, he could see inside to a single metal chair.

Weighed down completely, length upon length of chain snaked around her torso and legs. The chair sat upon a sigil drawn in white and the sigil extended to the walls of her prison.

It was Dahlia. Beyond all the damage the demons caused her, the bubbling and bruised skin, the black circles beneath her crimson eyes, the mucus-like substance pouring from her ears, nose and mouth, it was still Dahlia.

Drake removed something from his pocket and, in a moment, the giant metal door swung open.

"Help me break the sigil," Levi pointed to the white lines on the ground forming intricate symbols and images and pushed his shoe through them. "This a trap, we need to destroy it. Jim, start the exorcism."

Drake and Gad used their hands and feet to shuffle through and break up the sigil along with Levi.

Jim held the crucifix out before Dahlia and, in his loudest voice, began to speak. "In the Name and by the power of Our Lord-"

Tremors shook beneath their feet with a low rumbling. Within moments, the ground shifted violently back and forth.

"What's happening?" Gad yelled, thrown down on his hands and feet.

"I don't know," Jim yelled back. The earth beneath him rolled so hard, he and Levi fell as well. A jagged split ripped through the dirt outside of the cage, a chasm opening like a maw across the floor as the earth tilted and dropped away. The shaking suddenly ceased.

Gad jumped and crab-walked backward from the familiar figure suddenly standing in the cage's doorway. Light could not escape his presence, his silhouette a void in the shape of a man. It was the man outside of the hospital room the night that Tom passed suddenly. The same figure had appeared just before Vinny Luciano nearly choked to death. He was faceless, all of him a blur in an out-of-focus picture. This man, this thing, who was it? What was it?

His voice was barely distinguishable. "What have you done?"

Levi jumped to his feet, pulled his shotgun from its holster and leveled it at the being shifting into existence. The being's head came into sharp focus followed by his tailored pinstripe suit. He entered the cage effortlessly, almost gliding to Drake. "Forneus?" He touched Drake's angry third-degree burn in the cross's shape. Drake recoiled.

Jim held the crucifix and Beretta toward the shadowed form.

"Get away from him, Xavier." Levi threatened, the shotgun aimed at the man's head.

Xavier didn't seem to care what anyone else had to say, his fingertips brushing Drake's cheek. "You were my finest acquisition, Drake."

Drake held his ground and didn't say a word, but the fear in his eyes was clear.

"You would've taken my place here when I moved up to the Master's table. Such a shame, too, that time being right around the corner from now."

"The Master?" Gad repeated. "Satan?" Was this thing a demon?

Xavier laughed. "Not quite. There are layers of authority here, just as above. No, my Master is Pride. And no primate before Drake has ever come so close to such a high rank, despite his humanity handicap."

"You stole my soul, you used my body," Drake said, his face red, his teeth bared.

"And mine," Levi added, his face dark with rage.

"Oh no, no, dear boys. You both signed those things away in exchange for the extravagance and material goods you enjoyed here. But alas, that time is past. Looks like Red will have to do."

Xavier pulled a black blade from an inner-jacket pocket and sunk it into Drake's chest.

"NO!" Gad shouted. Without thought, his finger squeezed the shotgun trigger and a round of blessed iron peppered the thing Levi called "Xavier". Its solid form vibrated, flickered, and shifted into shadow.

Drake dropped to his knees, his hand wrapped around the knife handle protruding from his heart. His eyes glazed over, and he toppled sideways.

"Jim, save the angel," Levi yelled and strode toward the shadow man, firing a round at its chest. "Don't stop, Jim, no matter what!"

Jim began his exorcism in earnest and at the top of his lungs. "In the Name and by the power of Our Lord..."

Despite two shotgun blasts, shadow Xavier remained unaffected. He reached down to Drake's chest and, with only one hand solid, yanked the knife from Drake's heart. He moved swiftly toward Gad with the knife gripped in solid flesh, ready to strike.

With the shotgun not working, Gad had only one other weapon to combat a demon. As fast as he could, he withdrew the silver watch from his pocket and motioned for the soul blade. Everything happened in an instant. The shadow man's ebony blade arced right for Gad's heart, but Levi leapt between them, his hand out to block the strike.

White-hot pain flooded the right side of Gad's chest as the blade sank through skin and muscle below his shoulder. Gad screamed, the watch falling from his hand as his fingers opened involuntarily. Thanks to Levi, the knife missed its target, Gad's heart. Levi, his hand over Xavier's, wrestled to extract the blade from Gad's chest. The knife had sunk in deep, it didn't want to release.

When the knife pulled from the fresh wound, Gad couldn't

scream. The agony was too much. Hot liquid leeched from the wound in his chest. Each new breath brought a searing torment. He staggered back from the pair as they fought for control over the blade's direction. The shadow man stood before Levi, his hand the only corporeal point for Levi to struggle against with both hands. He used his massive upper-body strength to force Xavier backward out of the cage, one step at a time.

Gad fought the pain and knelt to retrieve his watch. It was cold in his palm, almost comforting as he got back to his feet. Once, twice, he motioned and the blade sprang to life in his hand, cold and beautiful.

"God the Father commands you," Jim roared, throwing holy water in the sign of the cross over Dahlia. A thousand screams erupted from her open mouth. The ground quaked. The chasm outside the cage opened wider.

Xavier and his pinstripe suit flickered into being, and with his substance came the power to push Levi backward. With great effort and their arms shaking, Xavier raised the knife up and back to strike.

Gad knew he couldn't kill the demon, but he didn't have to kill it to save Levi. He raised the weapon and brought it down against Xavier's solid wrist. The blade cut cleanly through the arm, severing the hand. Xavier's resulting screech rent the air, its volume far beyond the cacophony. His dark form flickered and became solid, pinstripe suit to oiled hair, his wrist stump dripping black viscous liquid. It was all Levi needed.

"Save the angel!" he bellowed. Levi sprung at Xavier and caught his momentarily solid form up in his arms. With a warrior's cry, he wrenched Xavier's feet off the ground and dove for the chasm with the demon crushed to his chest.

"Levi!" Gad cried as both Levi and Xavier disappeared over the edge and into the black chasm.

Jim had not seen it happen. He continued the ritual against

all chaotic sounds, sights and taunts the demons speaking through Dahlia could throw at him. "God the Father commands you. God the Son commands you. God the Holy Ghost commands you."

"And you never should have fucked with me," a familiar voice resonated from the angel. It was Forneus.

"You little piss-ant." Her gray lips peeled back, and she bared her teeth at the former priest. "Where did you think I would go when you exorcised me? I'm already in hell, motherfucker." Uproarious laughter filled the chamber as the angel's head fell back with an insane grin, a thousand voices joining his in a chorus of maddening frivolity.

Jim slipped to his knees, exhaustion clear.

Gad knelt next to Jim. "Keep going, Jim."

"Can't." Jim took a deep breath. "There's too many. And with Forneus in the angel now, too? I could barely kick his ass when it was just him."

At this, the room filled with mocking laughter and squealing, jeering, cussing, garbled insults and caterwauling. Gad could barely think, his life slipping from the wound near his heart.

Jim stood and pulled Gad to his feet. He leaned in, his face close to Gad's ear.

"I don't know what to do. There's too many."

"This is it. Let's finish it." Gad said.

Yes, Jim nodded, his blue eyes locked on Gad's. Yes. It was the only way to save the world.

Jim turned and, with resolution, pressed the crucifix to Dahlia's forehead. Wailing and screeching filled the cavern, ear-piercing chaos.

"LET ME GO!" A thousand voices screamed. Jim flew backward with force, his head smacking into the rusty bars. He fell to the floor like a sack of rocks, unconscious.

Gad leaned on his soul blade, his strength ebbing. He could barely stand. He turned to Dahlia.

Her face. For one moment, it was Dahlia as he last saw her. Radiant, beautiful, golden.

"Kill me," she whispered, her voice audible above the din of hell.

Gad almost collapsed under the weight of her words, tears filling his eyes. Take away their only weapon. It was the only way.

He blinked. And just as fast as she had reached out to him, Dahlia the possessed was in the seat again, her head shaking as though a film clip played in reverse, her eyes red as blood.

With all the effort he could muster, he approached her. Her lips moved with words that meant nothing to Gad any longer.

"You filth, you creeping worm on a pile of vomitus shit, you killed your own precious father, you meat puppet sack of pus-"

He pulled the scythe blade up and back, metal glinting in the cold light.

All voices stopped. A gasp. Dahlia's mouth fell open. "Thank you." The whispered words meant only for him echoed through his being.

Gad swung the blade in a perfect arc and connected above the chains around her chest. She gasped again, her head tipping backward as golden light burst forth from her body in all directions. the cavern lit bright as though a light had been switched on in the void.

Wind burst forth and countless trails of black smoke poured forth from the cut, swarming in the cage, too thick to see.

Gad turned away, using the soul blade to steady his every step toward Jim. As the demons vacated the angel's dead vessel, he gently shook Jim to rouse him from his unconscious state. Jim's eyes opened and adjusted to the scene taking place around them.

"Gotta go. Gotta get out of here," Gad said weakly in Jim's ear.

"Levi?" He looked past Gad and then back to him with intense blue eyes.

Gad shook his head.

Jim staggered to his feet, hooked an arm around Gad and helped him move out of the cavern across the connecting patches of ground not cracked open by Xavier's anger. At the mirror, Jim stepped in first to pull Gad safely through.

The sounds of thudding reverberated through the Torture Chamber, telltale announcements that enormous demons were coming their way. Gad kept his soul blade in hand.

They crossed the Torture Chamber, and Gad swept the soul blade tip through each lock he could reach. Chains snapped, doors opened. Those who were freed worked to set free those still in cages.

Ahead lay the passage back to the living. And there stood the demon who had almost claimed Dax's life. It dropped to all fours, its black horns swept straight back over its head. They took a step toward it and it lifted its lips, its rows of perfectly pointed teeth set in an ear to ear grin.

Gad felt consciousness threatening to slip from his grasp. He let go of Jim to stand on his feet alone, his soul blade tight in his grip. Slowly, he brought it up and back.

The demon continued its maniacal grin. It was calling his bluff and it tensed to spring.

Gad swept toward the demon and swung the blade with an angry cry.

It yelped and sprang away, scuttling along the wall and out of the chamber, the blade never touching it.

"Let's go," he whispered and the world slipped out from his feet.

The rest was a bit of a blur. Jim must've caught him, and Sam appeared from somewhere. Ice filled his veins. Could've been death, could've been a mirror. At that point, Gad had slipped into a need for inevitable rest, so either would have been just fine.

A foreboding presence loomed above Gad. Could've been Hale in his usual black ensemble, could've been a reaper. Frankly, it was hard to tell the difference. It leaned over him and placed something cold, hard and spindly on his knife wound. His chest burned, like someone pressing a hot iron against his flesh. If he had had the energy to, he would have given the foreboding thing what for, but he slipped into sweet unconsciousness instead.

39

Lilith was in the room, in the middle of excited story-telling.

"And then there was this explosion of golden light. It expanded upward and outward from Las Vegas. It covered everything, flowed through everyone and everything. It was... beautiful."

Her voice cracked, and she blew her nose.

"Levi, do you copy?" Jim said from somewhere nearby. Static was his only answer.

"Jim, you've been at that for hours," Sam said. "Aunt Z says he can't answer you. He's not on this plane."

"Can't because he's alive or can't because he's dead?" Jim said, strained.

Gad struggled to open his eyes. His eyelids were heavy as though there were weights sitting on them. "Jim," he croaked. How long had he been out? His throat was drier than the Vegas desert. He blinked away the blurriness to make out an IV drip next to the gurney he was lying on.

"Gad, you awake?" Lilith said from somewhere. A moment later, she was at his side.

"Sort of," he answered, raspy.

"Hey kid," Jim sauntered over, hands in pockets and a tooth-pick poking out from the corner of his mouth. "How're you feeling?"

"Like they stabbed me in the chest," he grumbled.

Sam pulled up a stool at the foot of the gurney. "But lucky for you, there was an intervention. I watched you heal. Sponta-neously. Although it wasn't spontaneous at all. Aunt Z said a reaper healed you."

Gad snorted. "Well, I guess I made it back to Sephitis's turf in time."

"Dude, after what I saw happen to you, I'd take a reaper healing over surgery any day of the week."

A thought struck Gad. He struggled to sit up.

"Whoa there, chief. Where's the fire?" It was Hale, who must have been standing outside of his peripheral vision.

"Did we do it? Is everyone safe?"

Jim smiled and put his hand on Gad's arm. "We did. Outside, it's almost business as usual."

Lilith chimed in. "Yeah, maybe even better than usual. People are even being nicer to each other. It's... weird. But good."

"Just don't turn on the news," Hale muttered.

"Yeah, it's still all 'what bleeds, leads' or whatever," Lilith said. "Think they've got enough shit stories to last quite a while."

"Gad, I've got to know. What happened to Levi?" Jim asked, his eyebrows furrowed.

With a deep sigh, Gad explained the Dark Man that turned out to be Xavier. He wasn't a demon, nor was he human. Ulti-mately, Levi ensured that they could save the world by taking Xavier out of the equation.

Jim stared at the floor, unpacking Gad's words. "So, he's gone."

Gad didn't want to confirm that Levi was gone. So he didn't.

BACK IN HIS TOWNHOUSE, Gad had sunken into the deepest cushion on his couch to stare at the flickering TV screen as people said clever things in black and white. He held his bottle of bourbon loosely by the neck, taking a deep swig every once in a while. Ironically, it was a film about a pair of married ghosts trying to make someone else's life better so they could earn their way into heaven. Cary Grant was charming and devilishly handsome with his equally stunning wife. They carried on the fast-paced humorous patter of the time, until a dapper fellow at the next table over stood and stepped before the camera with a tip of the hat. Gad sat up.

"I say-" Cary interjected.

"Oh, I'll be out of the way in a moment." The familiar gentleman smiled and turned back to look at Gad through the TV screen. Gad leaned forward and blinked. It was Sephitis.

"I won't be too long, Gideon. Just wanted to drop in and give you a proverbial pat on the back. Job well done, you know. How are you?"

"Oh, uh, thanks? It really sucked and I'm drinking my way to a blackout, so I guess I'm not the greatest. In fact, this is probably a dream and I'm likely actually passed out on the couch."

"I'm sorry to hear it. But I assure you this is quite real. In fact, please put down the bottle. There are much better coping mechanisms than poisoning your liver."

"Sure," Gad set the bottle down hard on the coffee table. "You try putting out one of the lights in the universe and tell me how you cope. Or lose your godfather, and a friend or three. I mean, where is Levi? Is he dead, is he alive? Make it all your fault and, bonus!" He fell back into the seat cushion and belched.

Sephitis was non-plussed. "Try putting out the lives of

hundreds, and sometimes thousands, every day, Gad. This is how the universe works, and as much as humanity cries out for fairness and justice in all things life and death, it is just not possible. So while I'd like to be supportive of your self-thrown festivities of blame and self-loathing, there is work to be done. I will give you another few days to pull yourself together and then I will be back with your next assignment."

"A few days?"

"Just so, yes. We don't have a lot of time and the balance is still greatly in favor of perdition."

"Shit."

"Precisely. Please, and I mean this, please do feel better. For a number of reasons."

"And then I can get stuff done for you," Gad said glumly and picked the bottle back up.

The camera zoomed in on Sephitis's face. He looked at Gad with narrowed eyes, his expression stern. "Be careful, mortal. You do not have any inkling about me or what I truly am. Do not second guess my intentions nor my well wishes."

Gad snapped to, his pleasant fog dissipating in a flash. He got the distinct feeling that he had just unintentionally insulted the universal entity. "I'm sorry, Sephitis. Really, I didn't mean it."

The camera panned back out. "Yes, well, you're under the weather, as it were. It's time I should be going. I will see you in a few days, Gideon. Get some rest." He tipped his hat and turned to go.

Gad sat up, a thought suddenly occurring to him. "Wait!"

Sephitis turned back to the screen.

"Before you go, I've got to know. My father... the demons said it was my fault. His death, was it really my fault that he died?"

Sephitis exhaled. "You're responsible for his collection and we reaped him, but he should have been taken long ago. So thank you for that."

"Did he go to heaven or hell?"

Sephitis smiled and tipped his hat. "Neither."

Cary Grant and Constance Bennett picked right back up where they'd left off, leaving Gad to wonder at the retreating figure in the background.

40

E ven in having put a cork in the apocalypse, life was not easy-breezy. Gad thought about Levi constantly. Was he alive? Was he imprisoned? Could he somehow save Levi? Normally, this would be a question for the most supernaturally-savvy people he knew: Pete or Levi. And Levi knew everything because it had been imparted to him by a centuries-old entity. The gang had a bookstore to read through. Jim was pouring through books with Hale and Lillith, but they didn't know what they were looking for let alone how to find it. And no word from Dax had surfaced yet.

Pete's chapel would take a lot longer to organize than Gad realized, not only because Pete had not been the most organized individual but also because it pained Gad to go. Harriet's ghostly presence and inability to move on didn't make it any easier. Gad felt like the world's most selfish asshole if he didn't sit and talk with her at each visit. Sam being there with him had allowed him more time to focus on organizing and clean-up, because Sam could chat with her about almost anything and keep her company. In fact, Gad was truly grateful to have met Sam. In so many ways, Sam's kind and empathetic nature was helping save

Gad. Sam had officially joined the Mercy business and moved into Gad's old room in the townhouse. This was on the condition that Aunt Z respectfully knocked at the door and entered the house as any living guest would, with an audible greeting and equally audible exit.

The living room had slowly filled with boxes from Pete's chapel. Gad always had a reason to not part with each of Pete's fantastical Elvis get-ups. This one had white fringe, and that one had the iconic Blue Hawaii phase nailed.

Gad's head still pounded from his Bourbon-fest the night before. Even though having a conversation with his TV was a likely candidate for "drunk beyond the pale", he had a strong sense that the conversation had been real. He walked through the conversation in his head as he searched through the contents of today's Pete box. It had been a stack of notebooks of all shapes and sizes, some lined, some blank for sketching. He leafed through each, surprised to find notebooks filled cover to cover like wildlife journals. Except these were field guides to the supernatural. Anything and everything that Pete had studied (a lot of things with the help of Gad's father) was described in detail and with pictures penned by Pete.

The top-most lined notebook was his most recent, only half-filled with scribbling and theories. Gad flipped through the pages, scanning until his eye fell upon something very familiar. His hands froze, his eyes widened. On the page before him was a sketch of a box in his father's basement at the cabin. His heart began to thump.

On the page, inked in black, was a diagram of the pocket watch box. Lines pointed to each carefully reconstructed phrase.

"DRUIDIC - Holy EMP" was double underlined and pointed to hieroglyphs on the side of the box.

"SUMERIAN - Banishes ethereal entities!" A line pointed to

a corner on the box lid in a top-down view. Below all of it, in pencil, he had outlined his theories.

"In case someTHING tried to steal the box... but banishes them to?"

And then, written in all caps and underlined, "PURGATORY".

Gad shot up. Purgatory? Was that the same place he had been that Dax referred to as Limbo? Was it possible he could somehow find his father there?

"Sam!" he yelled up the stairs.

"What?" Sam's voice bounced off the walls.

"I need your help!"

"Sure, Gad. You need me to help move the bookshelf?"

"No. I need help getting back into the first ring of hell. Got a sec?"

∾

Gad's story continues in Reaper's Mark,
now available for preorder!

ABOUT CHRISTINE CONVERSE

 A gaming industry veteran with twenty+ years of production experience, Christine Converse has written strategy guides for some of the hottest genre properties available today, including Bladerunner, Resident Evil, Star Wars: Shadow of the Empire, and Aliens. She has also written comedy, action, adventure, sci-fi and horror for Dreamworks, Lucas Arts, Disney, Westwood Studios, Nintendo, Sega, Sony, Cartoon Network, and many more.

In conjunction with creator and director Pearry Teo, she's also the author of Bedlam Stories.

For more information
www.christineconverse.com

ABOUT JOSEPH NASSISE

Joseph Nassise is the New York Times and USA Today bestselling author of more than forty novels, including the TEMPLAR CHRONICLES series, the JEREMIAH HUNT trilogy, and the GREAT UNDEAD WAR series.

Joe is a multiple Bram Stoker Award and International Horror Guild Award nominee and served two terms as president of the Horror Writers Association, the world's largest organization of professional horror and dark fantasy writers.

If you want to stay up-to-date on the very latest news, you can follow Joe on Twitter @jnassise, hang out at his Facebook page, or visit his website at josephnassise.com.

For more information
www.josephnassise.com
author@josephnassise.com

COPYRIGHT INFORMATION